Born in [illegible] rge Mason University with a degree in art history. The author's résumé includes working as a museum guide, teaching English in Seoul, Korea and managing a bookshop. Twin interests in art and arcana inspired the author to write esoteric thrillers. C. M. Palov currently lives in West Virginia.

The Templar's Quest

C. M. PALOV

PENGUIN BOOKS

PENGUIN BOOKS

Published by the Penguin Group
Penguin Books Ltd, 80 Strand, London WC2R 0RL, England
Penguin Group (USA) Inc., 375 Hudson Street, New York, New York 10014, USA
Penguin Group (Canada), 90 Eglinton Avenue East, Suite 700, Toronto, Ontario, Canada M4P 2Y3 (a division of Pearson Penguin Canada Inc.)
Penguin Ireland, 25 St Stephen's Green, Dublin 2, Ireland (a division of Penguin Books Ltd)
Penguin Group (Australia), 250 Camberwell Road, Camberwell, Victoria 3124, Australia (a division of Pearson Australia Group Pty Ltd)
Penguin Books India Pvt Ltd, 11 Community Centre, Panchsheel Park, New Delhi – 110 017, India
Penguin Group (NZ), 67 Apollo Drive, Rosedale, Auckland 0632, New Zealand (a division of Pearson New Zealand Ltd)
Penguin Books (South Africa) (Pty) Ltd, 24 Sturdee Avenue, Rosebank, Johannesburg 2196, South Africa

Penguin Books Ltd, Registered Offices: 80 Strand, London WC2R 0RL, England

www.penguin.com

First published 2011
001

Set in 12.5/14.75 pt Garamond MT
Typeset by Jouve (UK), Milton Keynes
Printed in England by Clays Ltd, St Ives plc

IBSN: 978–1–405–93176–2

www.greenpenguin.co.uk

FSC www.fsc.org MIX Paper from responsible sources FSC™ C018179

Penguin Books is committed to a sustainable future for our business, our readers and our planet. This book is made from paper certified by the Forest Stewardship Council.

Paris, France

28 June, 1940

Death is the great equalizer, Friedrich Uhlemann silently mused.

As evidenced by the thousands of bones sandwiched between thick slabs of pitted limestone. Indeed, the catacombs of Paris morbidly flaunted the spirit of '*liberté, egalité, fraternité*', with no discernible difference between sinner and saint, prince and pauper, making him think that the French virtues of liberty, equality and brotherhood were only possible in the hereafter. One desiccated bone the same as the next.

Friedrich glanced at the bank of hollowed-out skulls. God alone knew the precise number of residents in the underground necropolis. And only God had known about the gold medallion hidden in these catacombs, safeguarded for centuries by an ossified Templar Knight.

Until the medallion had been uncovered by Friedrich and the six members of his academic team. 'The Seven' as some in the Ahnenerbe dismissively referred to them. Founded in 1935 by Heinrich Himmler, the Ahnenerbe was the academic research division for the Nazi SS.

Well aware that the Ahnenerbe did not cultivate or encourage creative vision, Friedrich and his six colleagues took the ridicule in their stride. The fact that they were the only interdisciplinary team in the Ahnenerbe was extraordinary. Even more extraordinary, they counted among their number three Germans, two Italians, a French atheist and a Sunni Muslim from Damascus. Although given the glacial expressions of the dignitaries who were now touring the dimly lit catacombs, the Seven had not yet proven their extraordinary worth.

Tempted to run a finger under his stiff neck collar, Friedrich refrained. They'd been issued new field-grey uniforms for the occasion, and the boiled wool was chafing his skin. In the background, somewhere in the shadows, he heard the steady *plop plop plop* of dripping water. Belatedly he realized that his heart beat in time with that incessant drip.

A stout fellow in the tour group raised steepled hands to his mouth and noisily blew a warm breath; the ambient air was at least thirty degrees cooler than the aboveground temperature.

Another member of the party, an Iron Cross medal prominently affixed to his uniform jacket, shuddered. 'My God, this place is macabre.' No doubt he referred to the twinkling candles inserted into disembodied skulls. This was Friedrich's doing, though even he agreed that it created a ghoulish effect.

Just then, a lone man broke away from the group and approached the limestone niche where the medallion had been placed. Polished Prussian boots gleamed in the candlelight. As the uniformed man neared, Friedrich took a deep breath, filling his lungs with musty air.

The man stopped in front of the niche, no more than

an arm's length from where Friedrich stood. At that close range, he could see that the other man had pale blue eyes. An unexpected surprise. While his visage was famous the world over, in all honesty, the photographs did not do him justice.

Long moments passed as the blue-eyed man gazed at the gold medallion.

Did he comprehend the importance of the symbols? Their connection to the movement of the great star Sirius? Or that they revealed an ancient and powerful technology?

'Have you translated the medallion?'

Nodding his head, Friedrich read aloud the engraved inscription. He didn't bother to mention that the inscription contained a combination of the Occitan language and medieval Latin, suspecting the blue-eyed man didn't care about the medallion's linguistic provenance.

'And you're certain that this inscription refers to the sacred relic?'

Again, Friedrich nodded, assuming he referred to the *Lapis Exillis*. 'We've ascertained that the inscription is encrypted and that the encoded message discloses the whereabouts of the sacred relic. Although –' he hesitated, fearful of the other man's reaction – 'we have not yet decoded the message.'

Hearing that, the blue-eyed man glowered. Which, in turn, caused Friedrich's stomach muscles to painfully cramp.

Like a hapless Christian in the Roman Colosseum, he nervously awaited his fate.

Thumbs up or thumbs down?

'Find the relic,' the blue-eyed man ordered brusquely. 'Its ancient power will decide the destiny of the Reich.'

Friedrich released a pent-up breath. *Yes! The blue-eyed man understood!*

Unable to contain his euphoria, Friedrich clicked his boot heels while he ardently raised and extended his right hand.

'Heil, mein Führer!'

Part I

'Better is little with the fear of the Lord, than great treasure, and trouble therewith' – Proverbs 15:16

I

Operation Ghost Warrior, Al-Qanawat, Syria

Present Day, 0342 hours

'What the . . . ?'

Stunned by what he'd just discovered hidden inside the thirteenth-century chapel, Master Sergeant Finn McGuire reached for the Maglite secured to the front of his battle cammies. Shining the flashlight, he examined the gold medallion nestled inside a velvet-lined box. It looked like something that might have been worn by an Arabian sultan. Or maybe an iced-out rapper. Unbelievably ornate, it was engraved with images of a sun, a moon and a big-ass star.

Finn carefully lifted the medallion out of the box. Three inches in diameter and attached to a heavy chain made of interlocking gold pieces, he estimated its weight at two pounds. *Two very valuable pounds, gold trading at a thousand dollars an ounce.*

Momentarily seduced, he tuned out the voice in his head urging him to put the medallion back in the box. Make like he never saw the damned thing and just continue with the mission.

Finn and his Delta Force troopers had infiltrated the Syrian village of Al-Qanawat to retrieve ten vials of contraband smallpox virus before they could be transported out of the country and weaponized. Having searched the chapel for the smallpox cache and come up empty-handed, it suddenly occurred to Finn that more than purloined bio-weapons were sold on the black market.

The thought triggered an uneasy feeling in the pit of his belly. General Robert Cavanaugh had personally classified the SpecOps as 'sensitive'. Loosely translated, that meant the mission was off the books.

Jesus H.

What did Cavanaugh think Finn's Delta squad was, his own private gang of tomb raiders? It didn't take a jeweller at Tiffany's to know the medallion was worth a small fortune. Seventeen years ago, when he first joined the US Army, he'd taken an oath to defend his country against all enemies, foreign and domestic. Commandeering biological weapons fell into that category. Stealing gold trinkets to pad a fat-cat general's bank account did not.

Angered that he'd been played for a fool, Finn glanced at the black Pathfinder watch strapped to his left wrist. *0343*. Two minutes to go before the scheduled helo pick-up. Certain there weren't any bio-weapons on the premises, he ripped open a Velcro flap and deposited the medallion in his cargo pocket.

Suddenly hearing a muffled footfall, Finn spun on his booted heel. In one smooth, practised motion, he reached for the HK Mark 23 pistol strapped to his right thigh. Ensnared in the beam of his flashlight was a robed Syrian carrying – of all things – a jewelled scimitar. While the other man's choice of weaponry was odd, the curved blade looked like it could easily cleave Finn in two.

Knowing a gunshot would awaken the somnolent village, Finn shoved the semi-automatic into his holster. He then lowered the flashlight beam from the other man's face, aiming it, instead, over his heart. The Syrian's eyes narrowed with suspicion as Finn reached for the sheath secured at the back of his waist.

A second later his fifteen-inch Bowie knife was airborne.

A second after that, the Syrian went down like a felled maple on a Berkshires' mountainside.

About to retrieve the ivory-handled Bowie knife, Finn stopped in mid-motion, hearing the familiar *rat-a-tat-tat* of automatic weapons fire. Instead, he whipped the Mark 23 out of his holster.

'We've got unfriendlies approaching from the west,' a disembodied voice announced in his earbud.

'Call in the team,' Finn ordered, speaking into the radio mouthpiece attached to the side of his helmet. 'We need to get to the landing zone on the double-quick.'

Leaving the knife embedded in the Syrian, Finn beat a hasty retreat from the chapel. No sooner did he exit the building than he came under intense fire, the Mark 23 blown clean from his hand.

'Crap!' he bellowed, rage and pain coursing through him in equal measure.

The five Delta troopers who made up Finn's squad – Deuce, Lou-Lou, Dixie, Johnny K and PJ – emerged from the shadows, automatic weapons blazing. Ghost warriors materializing out of thin air. A hundred metres away, the helo touched down in a cloud of dust. Insurgents neutralized, Finn and his men headed for the LZ at a fast trot.

A few moments later, safe onboard the bird, Finn sank to his haunches.

'Hey, boss, some Syrian sure had it out for – Shit!' Johnny K suddenly yelled. 'What happened to your hand? Medic!'

Feeling faint, Finn leaned his head against the hull. As the medic hovered over him, he belatedly realized there was blood everywhere. *His hand. His pant legs. The floor of the helo.* All of it spurting from the bloody mess that used to be his right index finger. 'Used to be' because Finn could see that half of his finger had been blown off, the severed digit gushing blood like a wildcat oil rig.

Jesus H! His trigger finger.

Angrily, he banged his head against the side of the helo.

While they'd let him stay in the army, Finn McGuire knew that he could kiss his Delta Force career goodbye.

And all because of some damned gold medallion.

2

The Pentagon

4 months later

'Master Sergeant Finnegan J. McGuire?'

Hand curled around a styrofoam cup, Finn peered over his shoulder. Seeing two strangers with 'Pentagon Visitor' badges pinned to the front of their jackets, he reached for the coffee jug. A few seconds later, steaming cup in hand, he turned to face the pair. 'Yeah, I'm McGuire. Who's asking?'

In tandem, the pair snapped open matching black leather wallets as they each thrust an arm in his direction. 'CID. I'm Warrant Officer Dennis Stackhouse and this is my partner, Special Agent Elizabeth Tonelli.'

The Criminal Investigation Division of the US Army . . . what did they want with him?

It was well known in the army ranks that CID investigators were a law unto themselves. In that way, they were a lot like the Delta Force. They didn't have to wear a military uniform, maintain a regulation haircut or follow the normal chain of command. They were cop and soldier rolled into one.

'Late yesterday evening, sometime between ten and eleven p.m., two murders were committed at Fort Bragg,' the Warrant Officer announced in a brusque, businesslike tone. 'We need to know your whereabouts during the time in question.'

Knowing the unspoken implication was that he had been somewhere yesterday that he wasn't supposed to be, Finn said, 'I spent last night at home. Alone, I might add. While sitting at home all by my lonesome, I ate leftover Kung Pao Chicken, caught the last half of *The Dirty Dozen* on a cable station, then turned in for the night.'

Even as he spoke, Finn had the uneasy feeling that this was one of those 'damned if he did/damned if he didn't' scenarios.

Special Agent Tonelli opened her mouth to speak.

'And before you ask, no, I do not have an alibi,' Finn volunteered. 'I also don't know anything about any murders. I haven't been to Fort Bragg in a couple of months.' Fort Bragg was home base to the Delta Force. Three months ago he'd cleared out of the Fayetteville apartment that he'd rented off base. He hadn't been back since.

Barely repressing a snicker, Finn gestured to the office bay adjacent to the break room. 'As you can see, I'm now working a desk job at the Pentagon.'

A mind-numbing desk job that was somehow connected to 'intelligence gathering' but had everything to do with spending eight hours a day staring at satellite photos. It was as far removed from combat duty as a soldier could get. Not a day passed that Finn didn't wish someone would take aim and put him out of his misery.

'I hope that answers all your questions. Now, if you'll excuse me, I need to get back to work.' He headed towards his cubbyhole of an office.

'Actually, we have a few more questions for you,' the Warrant Officer said to his backside, the twosome trailing behind him.

Finn snatched a chair from an unoccupied desk and rolled it into his office. With his free hand he motioned Agent Tonelli to seat herself on the chair. Finn sat himself behind his metal desk. As though it were a game of musical chairs, the Warrant Officer was left standing.

Agent Tonelli pointedly glanced at his right hand. 'How's your, um, finger doing?'

'Beats me . . . I left it somewhere in the Middle East.'

'I apologize. That didn't come out the way I intended. What I meant to ask is how is your recovery coming along?'

Pegging her for the 'good cop', Finn shrugged. 'I can't complain.'

What was the point? The army surgeon at Ramstein Airbase had had to amputate the mangled flesh of his right index finger, cutting it just below the second knuckle. Finn didn't know if it was on account of the original injury or the subsequent surgery, but he'd suffered nerve damage to the digitorum tendon, the connective tissue that flexed and extended the finger. Even though the digit healed faster than expected, the amputation ended his days as a Delta Force 'shooter'. While he could still fire a weapon, able to pull the trigger with his middle finger, he no longer had the speed and proficiency required of a Special Forces combat soldier.

'I don't know about the two of you, but I've got work to do,' Finn said brusquely. 'So, what do you say we get this interrogation over and done with?'

'Fine,' Warrant Officer Stackhouse replied. 'As we already stated, last night two Delta troopers stationed at Fort Bragg were found murdered.'

His spine instantly straightened. 'You didn't tell me that the victims were Delta troopers.'

'In fact, the two murdered troopers, Corporal Lamar Dixon and Corporal John Kelleher, were former comrades of yours.'

Finn felt like he'd just been sucker-punched, his gut cramping painfully. The two men had not just been comrades, they'd been friends.

Dixie and Johnny K. Dead. Both of them. *Christ.*

Finn looked the Warrant Officer straight in the eye. 'And you actually think that I drove down to Fort Bragg yesterday when I got off duty and killed Dixie and Johnny K?'

Openly smirking, Warrant Officer Stackhouse opened a leather portfolio that he'd carried in with him. From it he removed two 8 x 10 crime scene photos, placing them on top of the desk. 'These should jar your memory.'

Finn carefully examined the photos. What he saw sickened him. Other than the fact that one photo was of a black man and the other a Caucasian, the photos were nearly identical: The two men were naked and secured to O-bolts screwed into the floor, a strap of duct tape over their mouths, both bodies covered in blood. Someone didn't just murder Dixie and Johnny K; someone butchered them.

'Both of the victims were ritualistically tortured,' Stackhouse continued. 'Oh, and did I mention . . . the killer used *your* Bowie knife to commit the murders.'

Finn slapped the photos on to the desk. 'That's flat-out impossible.'

The Warrant Officer opened his portfolio and removed a third photo. Gleefully smiling, he dangled the glossy photo to-and-fro in front of Finn's face. 'Look familiar?'

Clearly annoyed with her partner's antics, Agent Tonelli snatched the photo from him and handed it to Finn. 'The knife hilt is made of fossilized ivory and etched in scrimshaw. Nowadays scrimshaw is a little practised art, but two hundred years ago, Boston whalers used scrimshaw to –'

'I know what scrimshaw is,' Finn interrupted, staring at the photo in complete disbelief.

'As you can see, the Gaelic phrase *Fé Mhóid Bheith Saor* is etched into the ivory,' she continued. Reaching across his desk, she pointed out the detail with her finger. 'We looked it up on the Internet: It means "Sworn to be free". Beneath the inscription are the initials FJM.'

'And don't deny that it's your knife,' Stackhouse cautioned. 'We've got proof to the contrary.'

'Look, I don't know how this happened, but –' Finn stopped in mid-sentence. The knife in the photo, the same Bowie knife that was used to kill Dixie and Johnny K, was the same Bowie knife he had used four months ago to take out a Syrian combatant on that fubar mission to retrieve the gold medallion. Had it not been for that damned pendant, his trigger finger would still be attached to his right hand.

But he'd left that knife in Al-Qanawat, embedded in the Syrian's chest.

How did it end up at Fort Bragg?

'You were about to say something, Sergeant?'

Finn shook his head. Simply put, there was nothing to say. Somehow, someone had managed to take out the last two members of his old Delta squad. Three months ago, Deuce, Lou-Lou and PJ had had their helo blown out of the Iraqi sky by a couple of insurgents.

That meant he was the only member of the Delta squad still drawing breath.

Reaching across the desk, Agent Elizabeth Tonelli took the photo from him. 'Losing your trigger finger, that *had* to have been a bitter pill to swallow. Moreover, it must have made you incredibly angry. Angry men have a propensity for violence. Combine that with your specialized training and . . . well, you get my drift.'

Loud and clear. Post-traumatic Stress Disorder. The ever-popular default motive for murder.

Agent Tonelli's sidekick slipped on a pair of reading glasses and re-opened his leather portfolio. Wearing a studious expression, the Warrant Officer examined a sheet of paper. Several seconds passed before he peered over the top of his metal frames. 'We did a little background check on you, Sergeant. Hope you don't mind.'

Ah, shit. Here it comes. The McGuire family laundry. Dirty sheets flapping in a gusty headwind.

'Seems that your brother Mychal has made quite a name for himself as a top lieutenant in Boston's Irish mob. According to our dossier, he spent six years in the Federal penitentiary in Lewisburg on an arms trafficking charge.' One side of the Warrant Officer's mouth twisted in a nasty sneer. 'Bet you couldn't be prouder.'

Finn made no comment. Every security clearance he'd ever been issued had been held up while the Department of Defense verified that Finn no longer had contact with his brother Mickey. Or any other member of the McGuire clan for that matter.

'Finnegan and Mychal McGuire. Blood brothers. *No. Wait.*' The bastard made a big to-do of glancing back at the dossier. '*Twin* brothers. Meaning that the two of you were cut from the very same bolt.'

'Let's get something straight – I'm not my brother's keeper,' Finn grated between clenched teeth. As he spoke, he noticed the pop-up box that had suddenly appeared on his computer monitor, alerting him to an incoming email. While the sender's name, FJ-58, meant nothing to him, the subject line caught his eye, the words 'UNJUSTLY ACCUSED' all in caps.

Casually moving his right hand to the mouse, he clicked on the email icon. As he read the missive, he schooled his features into a blank expression.

> What price freedom? Unless you wish to ponder the answer from the inside of a military prison, you will immediately leave the building and proceed to the reception at the French Embassy in Washington. Wait by the courtyard doors. You will receive further instructions. If you fail to arrive by 5.00 p.m., irrefutable DNA evidence linking you to the murders in question will be provided to the proper authorities. If you speak of this matter to anyone, they will be targeted for execution.

Finn clicked the delete button, the email instantly disappearing from the computer screen. *Leave the building?* Were they insane? He was on the verge of being arrested for murder. Not to mention the 'building' in question was the freaking Pentagon.

He stared at the blank computer screen. He didn't know anyone who worked at the French Embassy. Hell, he'd never even been to the French Embassy. But he suspected that someone at the embassy had ordered the hits on Dixie and Johnny K. That same somebody planted his Bowie knife at the murder scene. And they also knew *when* he'd be questioned by CID. Which meant that the enemy had eyes and ears inside the US military command.

And wasn't that a scary thought?

'Sergeant McGuire,' a voice suddenly boomed from the telephone intercom system. 'You were supposed to get me a copy of those updates ASAP. Where the hell are they?'

Finn knew the voice all too well. It was his commanding officer, Colonel Benjamin Duckworth, a spit-and-polish career officer who ran the Satellite Analysis Group, SAG, like it was his own private fiefdom.

Hitting the mute button, he glanced apologetically at the two CID agents. 'Sorry about that. I was supposed to get these satellite photos to the Colonel ten minutes ago. There's a commander in Kandahar who's currently on standby. He's waiting to get this intel downloaded before he sends out his security detail,' Finn told them, purposefully playing the 'patriot' card. 'Colonel Duckworth's office is just down the hall. It won't take but a second for me to deliver the file.'

The Warrant Officer's eyes narrowed as he glanced at the innocuous manila folder that Finn now held in his right hand. 'Can't you have someone else deliver the file?'

'Actually, I can't,' Finn lied. 'There's no one in the office with a high enough security clearance to open this file, let alone carry it down the hall to the Colonel.'

'All right,' the other man groused irritably. 'But make it snappy.'

Oh, I intend to.

3

Manila folder in hand, Finn walked down the corridor to the Colonel's office.

A quick glance over his shoulder proved what he already knew – the two CID agents were watching his every move.

'What took so long?' Colonel Duckworth bellowed as Finn stepped into his office. 'And who are those two suits?'

Finn knew that Duckworth didn't want the file so much as he wanted to know who had trespassed, unauthorized, into his domain.

'They're a couple of CID agents,' he replied. 'An incident happened down at Fort Bragg and they're checking on some background information.' He held the manila folder aloft as he strode over to the door on the other side of the Colonel's office. 'I need to make a quick copy for my files.'

When the Colonel nodded his consent, Finn opened the door and stepped into the administration bay. He'd cut a break. Not a big one, but enough to get him out of the SAG office suite before the two agents caught on to the ruse.

Quickly passing the copy machines, collators and a line of cubicles, he figured he had sixty, maybe seventy-five seconds before the alarm was sounded.

Exiting the admin bay, he hung a right and briskly strode down the hall towards an office wing currently under renovation, the area shrouded in clear plastic sheets. He wedged past a fifteen-foot stretch of linked trolleys piled high with office furniture and cardboard boxes.

Free and clear of the 'moving van', he threw open a door that led to a newly painted stairwell, 'WET PAINT' signs still tacked to the railing. A few seconds later, he emerged in the basement of the E-ring, the outermost ring of the Pentagon.

And that's when he took off at a fast trot, the manila folder still grasped in his hand. To the casual bystander, he looked like a man running late for a meeting.

As he charged past the Pentagon printing office, Finn tuned out the near-deafening roar of the printing presses that churned out documents, reports and manuals 24/7. At the end of the long hall, he sidestepped a forklift loaded with boxes of printed binders before entering another stairwell. Taking the steps three at a time, he climbed one flight, emerging on the first floor of the River Entrance wing of the Pentagon.

Five storeys high with five concentric rings and ten radial corridors, the Pentagon was a maze. A fact he intended to use to his advantage. Given that his Dodge Ram truck was parked in the South Lot, using that exit was not an option. He figured that'd be the first place they'd look for him. The second place would be the subway and bus exit. That's why he intended to take the road less travelled and leave the building via the River Entrance. All of the bigwigs – the Secretary of Defense, the Joint Chiefs – had their offices located in that wing of the

Pentagon. Not only was it the farthest removed from the SAG office, he figured it was the last place CID would look for him.

Slowing his pace, he caught sight of a burly staff sergeant leaving his rabbit warren. Finn quickly sized him up. *Six foot four. Two hundred and twenty pounds of ripped muscle*. A perfect match. Finn stepped into his empty office, lifting the sergeant's uniform jacket and beret from the hook on the back of the door. As he continued down the corridor, he donned the green service jacket and stuffed the beret under his arm. CID would be searching for a coatless NonCom. Wearing a jacket wouldn't save him, but it might buy him a few seconds.

As he approached the security checkpoint located at the River Entrance, he glanced at his Pathfinder watch. *1615*. If he didn't show up at the French Embassy in the next forty-five minutes, he would never find out who killed Dixie and Johnny K.

Suddenly catching sight of his military photo emblazoned on the guard station computer screen, Finn jammed the beret on his head. He then piggybacked on to a group of uniformed military personnel, shouldering his way into the middle of the pack.

Ten seconds later, Finn exited the Pentagon. Removing a pair of sunglasses from the jacket's breast pocket, he slipped them on.

The easy part was done. Now he had to get to the French Embassy.

He scanned the small parking lot on the other side of the covered concourse. Given that it was broad daylight, hotwiring a parked car was out of the question.

As he continued to search the lot, a Toyota Camry pulled up to the kerb. A man in a rumpled khaki suit emerged from the passenger door. Slamming the car door shut, the suit scurried up the steps towards the entrance. Finn glanced through the windscreen. *Scrawny build. Stick-straight black hair. Almond-shaped eyes and freckled cheeks.* The woman behind the wheel was a civilian contractor who worked in one of the cubicles down the hall from SAG.

What was her name?

Kathy? Karen?

Hell, her name didn't matter.

Needing an escape vehicle, Finn opened the passenger door and climbed inside the Toyota.

4

Barely stifling a scream, Kate Bauer recoiled from the large, unsmiling soldier who'd unceremoniously got into her Camry.

'I need your help,' the man announced abruptly, the request as unexpected as his sudden appearance.

Kate sat mute, her tongue tied in the proverbial knot.

It wasn't until the uninvited passenger reached up and removed his sunglasses that she belatedly realized she knew the man, although not very well – she and Sergeant McGuire were no more than passing acquaintances. If that. According to the rumour mill, he'd spent ten years on the vaunted Delta Force as a highly trained commando. Everyone in the office bay, herself included, gave him a wide berth when they passed him in the hallway.

'Sergeant McGuire, you scared the living daylights out of me,' she said tersely, annoyance trumping fear.

Unperturbed, he glanced at the commando-style watch strapped to his left wrist. 'Sorry. I didn't mean to scare you. It's just that my Dodge Ram is a dead dog and I've been waiting forty minutes for the tow truck.'

'I'm sorry to hear that you're having vehicle problems. But that doesn't explain why –'

'I was kinda hoping you could give me a lift into town,' he interjected, a beseeching look in his eyes. 'I need to be at the French Embassy no later than five p.m. You are on your way home, aren't you?'

'Um, yes . . . I just dropped off my boss. We had an off-site briefing at Bolling Air Force Base.' A private contractor, she worked for the Defense Department as a subject matter expert, her field of expertise cultural anthropology. She'd recently created an ethnic database that would be used by military personnel stationed abroad. While it didn't involve interaction with Sergeant McGuire, they did work in the same office suite.

Deciding there was no reason *not* to give the sergeant a ride, particularly since she lived a mile or so from the French Embassy, Kate pulled the Camry into the narrow lane. With a quick glance in the side-view mirror, she merged into the fast-moving rush-hour traffic.

'I appreciate the lift. Believe me, you pulled up in the nick of time.'

'Happy to assist.' She notched up the air conditioner, hoping to dispel the thick, muggy air. Washington in August was not for the weak-kneed. Even the towering oaks that lined either side of the G W Parkway had a limp noodle look about them.

Out of the corner of her eye, she noticed her passenger rubbing a mutilated right hand over his jaw. With his dark-brown hair cut military short, blade of a nose, and thin, well-shaped lips, Sergeant McGuire's Irish roots were clearly evident. Kate recalled the first time she had laid eyes on Sergeant McGuire. *Grim. Intimidating. Scary-looking.* Initial impressions that had not diminished in the passing weeks.

However, at the moment, he didn't appear all that scary. Maybe it was woman's intuition, but Kate sensed that something was deeply troubling him.

'Are you all right, Sergeant?'

A glimmer of surprise flashed across his face.

'I'm fine.' He attempted, but didn't quite muster, a light-hearted grin.

'You just seem . . . I don't know –' she shrugged, regretting that she'd asked the question in the first place – 'a bit upset.'

'Nope. Never felt better.'

'My mistake. I apologize.' Embarrassed, she made a big to-do of looking over her shoulder as she veered on to the Georgetown ramp.

Again, chalk it up to intuition, but not for one instant did she believe the sergeant's disclaimer. She knew the face of sorrow. Had stared at it in the bathroom mirror every morning for the last two years. Even now, people still tiptoed around Sammy's death, afraid of churning up the painful memories.

And it *had* been painful, as if someone had gutted her with a very sharp fillet knife.

The pain, however, came later. In the days immediately following her infant son's death, she'd been too numb to feel anything, having gone through the funeral in an almost catatonic state. To this day, she still couldn't recall a single detail from the ceremony. Only afterwards did she realize that the dazed fog had been a survival mechanism.

All too soon, that numbness gave way to an unbearable heartache.

At the time, she didn't think she could contain, let alone

exorcise, the pain. The best she could do was manage the grief – at least during the daylight hours – by binging on work. Gorging herself on an inhuman schedule. The constant white noise of office computers, printers, beepers and one-sided telephone conversations forced her to concentrate on the job at hand. The intense focus helped to keep the grief at bay.

In recent months, the pain had diminished somewhat. At least enough that she'd begun to think about resuming a 'normal' life. Whatever that meant.

Ten minutes into the mostly silent drive, Kate pulled up to the entrance of the French Embassy, tri-coloured flags waving jauntily in the humid breeze. A smartly dressed group walked past, the guard waving them through the open gate. Although Sergeant McGuire hadn't volunteered any specifics, she assumed he'd been invited to an embassy party.

'I see a space a little further down the street. How good are you at parallel parking?'

She shot her passenger a questioning glance. 'Why do I need to park?'

'I thought you might want to come in and, you know, mingle.'

'You want me to go with you to the party?'

'Yeah. You on board?'

Taken aback by the invitation, Kate stared at the uniformed man seated beside her. Under no circumstance would she describe him as handsome. Although she wouldn't go so far as to say that he was *un*-handsome. Rugged-looking best summed him up. And it had been nearly two years since the divorce.

Unfortunately . . .

'I'm afraid that I have to decline the, um, gracious invitation. As you can plainly see, Sergeant McGuire, I'm really not dressed for an embassy soiree.' Kate lamely gestured to her navy-blue linen skirt. Paired with a sleeveless cream-coloured blouse, it was the sort of nondescript office fare that rarely garnered a second glance from the opposite sex.

'Hey, I think you look great. By the way, my first name is Finn.' The sergeant stared expectantly at her.

'Oh, right . . . and I'm Kate.'

'Kate. I was damned close.'

'I beg your pardon?'

'Nothing. Listen, this is just my way of saying "Thank you". And, I promise, no strings attached. Come on. I bet there's free booze and a long buffet table. What do you say, Kate? You look like you've had a helluva day.'

While that was true, she barely knew Sergeant McGuire. A few weeks ago at an office birthday party, she'd accidentally bumped into him and spilled coffee on his uniform. She'd offered an awkward, bumbling apology. He, in turn, gruffly refused to let her pay for the dry cleaning. In the whole of that sixty-second exchange, there'd been no sparks. Not even a dim flicker.

Which might explain why she was tempted to accept Finn McGuire's offer. It was a 'no strings' opportunity to do something other than eat carryout and watch a DVD. 'No strings' was about all she could handle emotionally.

Giving the invitation serious consideration, Kate glanced at Finn's left hand. *He wasn't wearing a wedding band.* More importantly, there was no telltale tan line. Two years ago she swore that she'd never do to another woman what had been done to her.

Finn gave her a coaxing smile, managing to look *almost* handsome.

Okay, so what if he's not my type. A glass of wine and a little banter with a living, breathing member of the opposite sex might do her some good.

Mind made up, Kate steered the car towards the vacant parking space.

5

He was a bastard. No doubt about it.

But if the situation turned dicey, Finn figured he'd need the Camry to escape the premises. That's why he'd cajoled Kate into coming inside. And why he then lifted the key ring out of the leather bag hanging from her shoulder.

Having gone on red alert the moment they stepped inside the joint, he again scanned the well-heeled crowd.

'The smoked salmon canapé with caviar is to die for. You have to try one,' Kate said, wiping a crumb from her upper lip.

Not nearly so impressed, Finn glanced at the buffet table; a twenty-foot-long floral and candle-strewn extravaganza with enough food to feed an entire platoon. Although no red-blooded soldier of his acquaintance would willingly eat the crap that the French were serving at their fancy chow line.

'Thanks, but I'm more of a pigs-in-a-blanket kind of guy.'

Kate gave a good-natured chuckle. 'I'm afraid to ask.' As she spoke, a distinguished-looking African man dressed in a flowing yellow and brown *agbado* strolled between them, causing a brief separation.

'Jeez, we should have brought our own UN interpreter.'

'I'll have you know that I can say "Hello" in twenty different languages,' Kate informed him, a challenging cant to her chin. 'Although I'll spare you the litany.'

'Appreciate that.' Lightly placing his hand on the small of her back, Finn guided Kate through the crowded reception hall. With two hundred or so jibber-jabbering attendees, it was the perfect place for an assassin to lurk. *No wonder FJ-58 stipulated the embassy party.*

'The opulent *fête champêtre* and sumptuous *joie de vivre* put me in mind of a Watteau painting.'

'Sorry. Not registering. You lost me at French fries.' Flagging down a penguin-suited waiter, Finn snatched two glasses of champagne from a silver tray. 'Here you go. What's a party without a lil' bubbly?' Forcing his lips into a semblance of a smile, he handed Kate one of the glasses.

'What I was trying to say is that I feel out of my element.'

'I hear ya.' A few feet away, Finn observed two female guests bend and sway as they gave each other a well-practised air kiss.

'You know, Sergeant, er – I mean, Finn –' Kate took a measured sip of her champagne – 'I don't know anything about you. However, if I had to make an educated guess, I'd say that you hail from the Boston area.'

'Guilty as charged. I'm a Southie born and bred. The lady clearly knows her accents.' Mimicking his date, he took an obligatory swallow. *Christ. Talk about French pansy piss.*

'Given that you sound like Mark Wahlberg in *The Departed*, it wasn't so difficult. Good movie, by the way, although a bit on the violent side. It's all about all these Boston gangsters who –'

'Yeah, I saw it,' he lied.

'I grew up in Pasadena . . . in case you were wondering.'

He wasn't.

'Right. Pasadena. Rose Bowl parade.' He surreptitiously searched the tight clusters of champagne-swilling partygoers. *Come on, asshole. Come to daddy.*

'Don't they teach children to speak in full sentences in South Boston?'

'Nope. Can't recall that Sister Michael Patrick ever used a complete sentence. "Stand." "Sit." "Pray." "Open your books." '

Clearly amused, Kate laughed, champagne sloshing over the side of her glass. 'Which are complete sentences, albeit commands.'

Knowing it was time to cut her loose, Finn cleared his throat. 'Listen. Kate. I just caught sight of someone I know and I, um, need to talk shop for a few minutes. Would you mind if I –'

'Not to worry. I'm a big girl. Besides, the dessert table awaits me.' A good sport, she waved him on his way.

'Shouldn't be gone too long,' he said, the lies fast mounting.

Spying a double set of French doors that led to an outside courtyard, Finn headed in that direction. According to the email he'd received, he was to wait there until he received further instructions.

As he stood at the open doorway, Finn knew that he made an easy sniper target, although he figured that whoever lured him to the embassy wouldn't try to kill him until *after* they'd interrogated him. That was, after all, the point of the exercise. If they'd wanted him dead, he'd already be six feet under. Just like Dixie and Johnny K.

He still couldn't believe his two buddies had been murdered. *No, correction: tortured and then murdered.*

Once, in a drunken stupor, Lamar Dixon confessed that he liked the Dixie Chicks. Despite being one of the biggest, baddest, blackest men you'd ever want to meet, the inebriated admission instantly earned him a new nickname. When the team tried to stick John Kelleher with the handle 'Baby Huey' – on account of his shaved head and ruddy cheeks – the trooper went on a rampage and actually opened a bottle of Killian's Irish Red with his teeth. Thereafter he was known as Johnny K.

Corporals Dixon and Kelleher were not just personal friends, they were valiant soldiers. Dixie had joined the army two days after 9/11; Johnny K signed up soon thereafter. Both men were true patriots who put their lives on the line numerous times to protect and defend their country. They did not deserve to die like animals led to slaughter.

I swear that I will *get you guys the justice you deserve.* Or die trying.

Finn glanced at his watch. *1700.*

'Right on time,' he muttered under his breath as a tall, dark-haired man broke away from the crowd. *FJ-58. Coming round the mountain.*

'Monsieur McGuire, I am pleased that you managed to elude the two CID agents,' FJ-58 said by way of greeting, the words spoken with a cultivated French accent. 'But, then, we knew you would successfully escape your would-be captors. No doubt, it was child's play for a man with your training.' The Frenchman extended his right hand. 'Allow me to introduce myself. I am the Minister of Cultural Affairs, Fabius Jutier.'

Finn glared at the proffered hand, refusing to take it.

'How about we cut the crap and get down to business,' he growled, not in the mood for phony pleasantries.

'Ah, you Americans . . . such a colourful way with the language. Perhaps we should take this conversation to my office.'

'Lead the way.'

6

'May I offer you a cigar, Monsieur McGuire?'

Seated in a sleek white leather chair situated in front of Fabius Jutier's desk, Finn tersely shook his head. The Frenchman clearly thought that *he* was the one in control of this lil' shindig. They were, after all, on his turf – an ultra-modern office that gleamed with lots of shiny metal and shimmering glass. What the French dude didn't know was that Finn intended to yank the bright red carpet right out from under his leather-shod feet.

Jutier extended the inlaid walnut cigar box a few inches closer. 'Go ahead. It's perfectly legal. We French are not bound by the same trade restrictions with Cuba as you Americans.'

Again, Finn shook his head, determined to keep his cool.

'*D'accord*.' The Frenchman strolled to the humidor on the other side of the office. 'I imagine you've had a difficult time adjusting to your new job at the Pentagon,' he remarked casually as he placed the cigar box in the cedar-lined humidor. 'A pity, what happened to you in Al-Qanawat.'

'It's obvious you flipped someone in the command loop. There's no other way you could know about the Al-Qanawat mission in Syria. It was strictly black ops. Mind telling me who the turncoat is?'

'Was.' *Robusto* in hand, Jutier walked to the sideboard

where there was a miniature guillotine set on a black marble plinth. 'Given that General Cavanaugh died in a car accident yesterday morning, the question should be framed in the past tense.'

Finn sat up straighter in his chair, surprised the treachery went so high up the chain of command. General Robert 'Battling Bob' Cavanaugh had been a top planner at JSOC, the Joint Special Operations Command at Fort Bragg. He was also the same general who had put the Al-Qanawat mission into play.

'Dead men can't talk. Making me think the General's accident wasn't so accidental.'

'Alas, the General did not keep up his end of our bargain.' Smiling, Jutier slid his Cuban into the miniature guillotine and, staring directly at Finn's missing finger, let the blade drop.

A bolt of pain shot through Finn's phantom finger.

'Trust me when I say I derived no pleasure from the General's death,' the Frenchman glibly continued as he next removed a wooden match from an ebony container. 'However, we offered him a great sum of money and he failed to deliver as promised.'

'How about Dixie and Johnny K? Did you enjoy slicing them from stem to sternum?'

With a crisp snap of the wrist, Jutier struck the match against the side of the ebony container. In no apparent hurry to answer the question put to him, he held the match to the foot of the cigar, his cheeks moving like a bellows as he unhurriedly lit it. Finn assumed the theatrics were for his benefit and wondered if he should give the French jackal a round of applause.

Jutier blew a puff of smoke, filling the office with the tobacco's pungent scent. 'I am not the bloodthirsty fiend that you make me out to be. If you must know, I did not approve of how that particular matter was handled. But we took a vote and a majority of the Seven decided otherwise.'

'The Seven? What's that, some sort of crime syndicate?'

'Most certainly not. That implies we are little more than brigands and thieves.' He set his cigar on the rim of a huge sterling-silver ashtray.

'I was thinking more along the lines of *murderers* and thieves.'

'Again, you have jumped to an erroneous conclusion.' Jutier poured a healthy measure of fifty-year-old single malt whiskey into a cut-crystal tumbler and handed the glass to Finn. 'Given your last name, I assume that Irish whiskey is your drink of choice. If you like, I can have some ice sent up. Although personally I prefer my whiskey neat. It allows the underlying flavours of oak and peat to come through.'

Finn set the tumbler on the edge of the desk. 'I told you once already to cut the crap. I'm not here for the chitchat.'

'Very well.' Strolling over to his desk, Jutier reseated himself. 'The Seven is prepared to offer a most generous compensation package in exchange for the Montségur Medallion.'

The Montségur Medallion! Was this fucker actually saying that Dixie and Johnny K were killed because of that gold pendant that he'd found in Syria?

His gut tightened, every muscle in his body quivering with a barely repressed rage. Jutier's cronies *used* Dixie and Johnny K like cannon fodder. No, *worse than that.* Like something you'd tie up in a plastic bag and dump into the garbage.

Four months ago, during the Al-Qanawat mission, he'd taken the gold medallion to prevent some higher-up from using it to pad his retirement account. Royally pissed off, when he returned from Syria, he held on to it. In fact, during the mission debrief, Finn did something he'd never done before – he lied his ass off, claiming he didn't find *anything* inside the Al-Qanawat chapel.

For four months now, he'd been waiting for someone to dispute the claim so he could expose the rat bastard. Not only did the fraudulent mission put US military personnel needlessly into harm's way, but it had been funded with US tax dollars. He'd just never figured they'd resort to cold-blooded murder to get what they wanted.

'The Montségur Medallion?' One side of Finn's mouth turned down at the corner as he shook his head. 'Never heard of it.'

'Do not play me for the fool, monsieur. I speak of the thirteenth-century gold pendant that you recovered in Al-Qanawat.'

'What makes you think that I have it?'

'Because you are the only man on the Delta team who *could* have it.'

'Like I said –' folding his arms over his chest, Finn leaned back in his chair – 'I don't know what you're talking about.'

Jutier slapped the palm of his left hand against the glass table top. 'Do not lie to me, monsieur!' A blue vein throbbed at his temple. 'Before his death, General Cavanaugh was kind enough to provide us with a copy of the Al-Qanawat mission debrief. You were the *only* Delta trooper who entered the chapel where the Montségur Medallion was kept.'

'And so you naturally assume that I have your freakin' medallion.'

'*Mais, oui*,' he replied, lifting his shoulder in a Gallic shrug. 'In addition to the one million dollars that will be deposited into an offshore account, we will provide DNA evidence to prove your innocence. Not only will you be a free man, you will also be a very rich one.'

Even with the price of gold being sky high, the medallion couldn't be worth *that* much. Which meant it had some value other than a purely monetary one.

Just what the hell did I step into?

'You knew before you killed Dixie and Johnny K that you'd be offering me this deal, didn't you?' Finn shoved aside the untouched whiskey and leaned towards the desk. 'That's why you set me up for both their murders. With my back to the wall, you figured I'd be in no position to turn you down.'

'We even went to the trouble and expense of recovering your knife from Al-Qanawat. A clever plan, *n'est-ce pas*?'

'How about I take that plan and shove it up your skinny French ass!' Lurching to his feet, Finn strode behind the desk. Very deliberately, he placed his right hand on the back of Jutier's chair, imprisoning the Frenchman. 'I didn't come here for a "Get Out Of Jail Free" card. And I didn't show up to get my share of the blood money. I came here for one reason: to get the name of the bastard who killed Dixie and Johnny K.'

'I am not at liberty to say.'

Finn took a moment to ruminate on that. He already knew that Minister Fabius Jutier wasn't the killer. Men like Jutier never got their hands bloodied. They hired men like Finn – i.e. ex-commandos – to do their dirty work.

Finn leaned in close. Their faces separated by only a few inches, he could see the faint meandering of blood vessels splotched across the other man's cheekbones. 'Unless you want things to turn real ugly, real quick, you're going to give me that name.'

'Do not threaten me, monsieur.'

'Okay, fine.' Finn hauled Jutier out of the chair and bent him backwards over the glass-topped desk. 'Consider what I just said as a statement of intent.' He wrapped his hands around the Frenchman's neck, forcefully pressing his thumbs into Jutier's windpipe.

Eyes bulging, Jutier tried, unsuccessfully, to pull Finn's hands away from his neck.

'Please . . . let me go,' he gasped, his face starting to turn blue.

'I'm going to ask you again . . . who killed Dixie and Johnny K?' Knowing a show of mercy would get him nowhere, Finn tightened his hold. Strangulation wasn't an exact science, but he figured Jutier had another thirty seconds of life left in him. He also figured the Frenchman would surrender before those thirty seconds lapsed.

As if on cue, Jutier began to frantically beat his hands

against Finn's forearms. He eased his hold just enough for the other man to speak.

'The Dark Angel,' Jutier sputtered, his chest heaving as he noisily drew in a deep breath. 'The . . . Dark Angel . . . killed them.'

The Dark Angel? If there was an assassin operating under that name, Finn had never heard of him.

Granting a reprieve, Finn removed his hands from the Frenchman's throat. 'Next question: where can I find this Dark Angel?'

Gracelessly rolling on to his stomach, Jutier pushed himself upright. With a pained look on his face, he clutched the left side of his jacket. 'I'm having severe chest pains. In the lacquer box –' he jutted his chin at the cherry-red box on top of his desk – 'I keep my glyceryl trinitrate. Please permit me to –'

'Yeah, yeah.' Finn lifted the lid on the box, inspecting for hidden weapons. Not seeing anything suspicious, he shoved the box in Jutier's direction.

'Thank you, monsieur.' The Frenchman rummaged through the plastic prescription bottles before making his selection. He popped a capsule into his mouth, his hands shaking visibly.

'Okay, now that you've had your pharm candy, tell me where I can find the Dark Angel.'

'I've said too much already.'

Without warning, the Frenchman began to violently convulse. A second later, Finn caught the faint but distinct smell of almonds.

Potassium cyanide.

'Crap!'

Knowing he had to act fast, Finn roughly flipped Jutier over and wrapped his arms around him from behind. He then yanked violently upward to induce vomiting.

The Frenchman went limp as Finn lost the battle.

Furious that he'd been bested, Finn plunked the dead bastard into the black leather swivel chair. He searched methodically through Jutier's coat pockets and removed an engraved lighter, a set of keys and a gold Mont Blanc pen.

Hearing the hinges on the office door creak, Finn peered over his shoulder.

Jesus H! What was she doing here?

Face as pale as February snow, Kate Bauer stood in the doorway. Clearly stunned, she stared at the dead man sprawled in the chair . . . then shot Finn an accusing glare.

'My God . . . you killed him!'

7

'I know how bad this must look, but it's not what it seems,' Finn McGuire said as he closed the office door.

'Don't come near me!'

'Keep your voice down, will ya? I'm not going to hurt you.'

Refusing to trust a cold-blooded killer, Kate darted over to the sideboard and grabbed the first weapon she saw – an ornate letter opener.

'If you take one step in my direction, I will not hesitate to use this!' she exclaimed, grasping the letter opener like a dagger.

Instead of heeding the warning, Finn lunged in her direction, parrying her reflexive thrust with his left forearm. In a dizzyingly fast move, he gripped her right thumb and twisted. Like magic, the letter opener instantly slipped through Kate's fingers and bounced off the red carpet.

'You bastard!' Refusing to surrender, she used her nails like talons, slashing at his face with her free hand.

With a muttered expletive, Finn grabbed both her wrists and twirled her clockwise. With her arms now crossed over her breasts, he pinned her to his chest, the buttons of his uniform jacket pressing into her backside.

'Calm down!'

Instead of complying, she kicked him in the shins. He retaliated by lifting her several inches off the ground.

'If you promise not to do anything harebrained, I'll let go of you.'

Her heart painfully thumping in her chest cavity, Kate nodded.

'Good girl.' Finn lowered her, her feet once again making contact with the floor. 'Sorry for being so rough.'

Tottering unsteadily on her heels, Kate turned round to face the uniformed Goliath. 'What were you planning to do after you killed him? Rejoin me in the reception hall, drink a little champagne, then call it a night?'

'I'm only going to say this one time . . . I didn't kill him.'

'I've got two eyes. I can see what happened here.'

Finn McGuire's jaw tightened. 'Assuming you haven't lost your sense of smell, you can verify for yourself that I didn't kill anyone.' Seeing her quizzical frown, he elaborated. 'Walk over to the desk and take a whiff. You should be able to smell almonds. Although it wasn't almonds that killed him; it was a fatal dose of cyanide which emits the telltale scent of almonds.'

Wondering if he might actually be telling the truth, Kate walked over and peered at the dead man sprawled in the leather chair. With a frothy ribbon of spittle lodged at the corner of his open mouth, he bore little resemblance to the elegantly attired man she'd seen earlier in the reception hall.

'Well, what do you smell?'

'Almonds.' Shuddering, she stepped away from the desk. 'But that doesn't tell me what you're doing here or why this man committed suicide.'

'You wanna know what happened? Fine. Last night, two Delta troopers were brutally murdered and I'm next in line for execution,' Finn said matter-of-factly. 'Fabius Jutier was the mastermind behind the murders. As to why he killed himself . . . I have no idea.'

The explanation stunned her. 'Have you alerted the authorities?'

Rather than answer, Finn walked over to the computer work station on the other side of the office. Wordlessly, he picked up a notebook computer and tucked it under his arm.

'What are you doing?'

'Spoils of war.'

His answer was so coolly detached, it made Kate wonder what war she'd stumbled into.

'I am not going to stand idly by and watch you pilfer from a – Now what are you doing?' she demanded to know as he began to unbutton Jutier's shirt.

'It's called a costume change. This army uniform is like having an "Arrest Me" sign pinned to my back. I'll be less conspicuous in Jutier's black suit.'

'Meaning you have no intention of contacting the authorities.' She turned her head as he started to disrobe. Out of the corner of her eye she caught a flash of bronzed skin and a quick glimpse of a bunched bicep.

'Whoa!' Finn exclaimed. 'The bastard's got some ink. Check out the tat on his left pec.'

Kate glanced in Finn's direction. Confirming that he was decent, she walked over to the desk. A moment later, her breath caught in her throat. Transfixed, she stared at the strange tattoo centred above the Frenchman's heart.

'I think those are Norse runes and – my God!' Her eyes opened wide. 'I've seen this sun-wheel design before!

Unless I'm mistaken, it has something to do with Nazis and the occult.'

'Well, do me a favour and take a photo of it, will ya?' Still in the process of getting dressed, Finn handed his cell phone to her. 'The tat is too weird not to be significant.'

Kate snapped the shot.

'According to a documentary that I saw on TV last year, many of the high-ranking members of the Third Reich practised occult rituals. Not only that, but they were obsessed with the magical power of runes. Given the tattoo, I think it's safe to assume that Fabius Jutier was involved in an esoteric Nazi –'

'Later,' he interjected, snatching the cell phone and depositing it in his coat pocket. 'Right now, we need to get the hell out of here.'

Kate shook her head adamantly. 'I'm not going anywhere with you.'

'If you don't come with me, they'll kill you.'

'I don't believe –'

'You *have* to believe.' He cupped her cheek, the gesture curiously paternal. 'I'm sorry, Kate. I never intended to involve you in any of this. You weren't supposed to have walked through that door.'

'But I did.' Afraid of what might happen if she was left behind, she reluctantly acquiesced. 'All right, I'll go with you.'

Shoving his rolled-up uniform and Jutier's laptop under his arm, Finn walked over and opened the office door.

'The elevator is to the left,' she informed him.

'We're taking the stairs. You never know who'll greet you with a loaded gun when the elevator door slides open.'

8

Passing a trash receptacle, Finn nonchalantly shoved the wadded bundle into it. Uniform disposed of, he said, 'Scrunch down a few inches.'

Kate's eyes opened wide. '*What?*'

'Just like this.' Bending his knees, Finn instantly reduced his height to six feet. 'If we each shave a couple of inches, we stand a better chance of slinking out of here undetected.'

Like fishes and loaves, the crowd inside the ballroom had doubled during their absence. Navigating their way through the throng was slow going at best. Worried that he might lose Kate amidst all the schmoozing and networking, Finn took hold of her right hand. In his other hand was the pilfered notebook computer. It was probably a long shot, but he was hoping there might be something on the laptop that could help him track down Dixie and Johnny K's murderer.

'In case you haven't noticed, there are guards posted at all the exits,' Kate hissed out of the side of her mouth.

'Who are probably wearing bullet-proof vests under their dark-coloured jackets and have a loaded SIG Sauer in the shoulder holster.'

'*Oh, God.*' Her delicate features morphed into a panic-stricken expression.

'Stay calm. Don't give 'em a reason to notice you in the crowd.'

While they'd managed to return to the reception hall without incident, Finn didn't know how much longer their luck would hold. Despite the little meet-and-greet with Jutier, he still had no idea why the gold pendant was so valuable. The rat bastards in the Seven had proved that they'd stop at nothing to retrieve the Montségur Medallion.

The damned thing must have once belonged to some dead king. Why else would it be worth so much money?

Whatever the reason, the Seven had been willing to give him one million dollars for it. A paltry sum compared to the worth of two patriotic soldiers. Simply put, some things couldn't be measured in dollars and cents. Like valour and honour. *And retribution.* And as God was his witness, he'd personally make sure that the Dark Angel paid dearly for killing Dixie and Johnny K.

Still baffled by the Frenchman's suicide, Finn had no idea why Jutier had chomped down on the cyanide capsule. *It was like he'd been programmed to kill himself rather than be taken alive.* Which suggested that he had something to hide. Something he feared might be revealed during a gruelling interrogation.

Finn spared Kate a quick sideways glance. 'I've been meaning to ask: how did you wind up at Jutier's office?'

'When I saw you leave the reception hall, I found out your companion's name from an embassy employee. I then came across a directory in the main lobby. Using that, I managed to locate the Office of Cultural Affairs.'

'You're resourceful, I'll give you that.' Tugging on her hand, Finn pulled her towards a swinging door from which a steady stream of waiters went to and fro. On the other side of that swinging door there was a kitchen.

'Just follow my lead,' he said, pushing the door with his shoulder.

'I assume you've devised an exit strategy.'

Finn shook his head. 'Nope. I'm winging this all the way.'

'You do realize there's an eight-foot electric fence around the entire embassy compound and armed guards manning the front gate?'

'I never said getting out of here would be easy.'

On the other side of the swinging door, the kitchen was a veritable mob scene, with white-coated, white-capped staff scurrying pell-mell. Finn quickly surveyed the cavernous stainless-steel kitchen – there wasn't a red EXIT sign in sight. Undeterred, he pulled Kate down the central aisle. On his right flank, Finn spied a mustachioed man wearing a pleated chef's cap determinedly bearing down on them. While he wasn't wearing a badge, the guy had 'kitchen cop' written all over him.

'Do you happen to know the French word for vomit?' he hissed out of the corner of his mouth.

'Um, *vomir* . . . at least, I think that's the word.'

'Got it. Now hunch over and try to look nauseous.'

'What?'

'Just do it,' he ordered, putting an arm around her back as he loudly boomed, '*Vomir! Vomir!*'

Moses couldn't have done a better job parting the Red Sea, the kitchen staff hurriedly clearing the deck.

So far, so good.

'Now, how about giving me the French word for exit.'

Actually managing to look green around the gills, Kate looked up and croaked, '*Sortie.*'

'*Sortie! Sortie!*' he next hollered.

The mustachioed man rushed over and, in a flurry of unintelligible French, grabbed Kate's other arm, urging them to move at an even faster clip towards a set of double doors at the rear of the kitchen. Obviously he didn't want to mop up after a sick woman.

Their French escort shoved the doors wide open – just before he shoved Finn and Kate across the threshold and on to a concrete loading dock. The door slammed shut behind them.

Coming out from a climate-controlled environment, the humid night air hit both of them like a slap in the face.

Kate peered from side to side. 'Okay, now what?'

'I'm working on it.' Taking hold of her elbow, Finn ushered his companion down the flight of concrete steps that led to an asphalt parking area.

'I suggest that we walk around to the front gate. That is, after all, how we arrived at the embassy.'

Finn shook his head, putting the kibosh on her suggestion. 'We can't risk it. For all we know, Jutier's body has already been discovered. That makes the embassy a crime scene and everyone inside the embassy a potential suspect. Trust me, no one will be allowed to exit through the front gate until they've been cleared by the police.'

A crease appeared between Kate's brows. 'Bringing me right back to my original question . . . now what?'

He gestured to the three purple and gold catering trucks parked a few feet from the loading dock. 'Assuming one of these bad boys has a key in the ignition, we're going for a ride in a big purple truck.'

Kate baulked, coming to a complete standstill. 'Are you seriously suggesting that we *steal* a catering truck?'

'I prefer the word "borrow".'

'Beg, borrow or steal, it's all the same thing – we would be taking a vehicle that doesn't belong to us. And what about my car? We just can't leave it parked all night on Reservoir Road.'

'Sure we can. We'll pick up your Toyota first thing in the morning.'

Like most of the guests at the party, they'd had to park outside the embassy complex on the public street adjacent to the front gate.

Tuning out the barrage of dire scenarios that Kate proceeded to enumerate, Finn slid open the driver's-side door of the first truck. He leaned his upper body inside and peered at the dashboard.

No keys.

He slammed the door shut and jogged over to the next truck.

Catching sight of a silver key protruding from the ignition, he offered up a thankful prayer. 'Okay, this one's got a key. Hurry up and jump in.'

'I really don't think we should –'

'Just do it!' Regretting the harsh tone, he backtracked. 'Don't worry. We'll be out of here in a jiff.'

Her face scrunched in a leery frown, Kate scrambled into the passenger seat. Finn handed her the notebook computer for safekeeping. He then started the engine, flipped on the headlights and maneouvered the vehicle on to the nearby delivery access road that led to the entrance of the embassy compound.

Two hundred metres from the front gate, he glanced in the wing mirror. A dark-coloured Mercedes Benz SUV was riding their tail. When the vehicle gunned its engine menacingly, Finn knew it wasn't an impatient party guest. He figured it was either embassy security or an SUV full of gun-toting, tattooed Frenchmen.

'What's wrong?' Kate asked anxiously.

There being no time to reply – and besides, Finn knew she wouldn't much care for the answer – he pushed the accelerator to the floor.

At the main gate a uniformed guard motioned furiously for them to stop.

'Slow down!' Kate screamed. 'There's a guard up ahead!'

Finn tuned her out.

Seeing the uniformed guard pull a pistol from his holster and go into a crouched shooter's stance, Finn flipped on his high beams. Blinded by the glaring light, the armed guard dropped his weapon and dived to safety seconds before the catering truck crashed through the gate.

The ensuing scream from his co-pilot nearly pierced Finn's eardrum.

'Oh, my God! Have you lost your mind?'

'Hold on!' he yelled, yanking on the steering wheel, the catering truck going up on two wheels as they made the left-hand turn on to Reservoir Road.

In the back of the truck, pots and pans clanged together loudly.

Although they'd managed to exit the embassy compound, a quick glance in the mirror verified what Finn already suspected – the Mercedes was still dogging them. An easy enough feat since the truck's top speed was only fifty m.p.h. – a speed he wouldn't be able to maintain much longer. Up ahead were the congested streets of Georgetown.

'What's the first one-way cross street?' he hollered at Kate. Since she lived in the area, he hoped she might know.

One hand braced on the passenger door, the other clutching the notebook computer to her chest, she shook her head. 'I'm not sure. Maybe thirty-fourth street.'

'One-way going in which direction?'

'Um, south . . . I think.'

Finn eyeballed the passing street signs. *37th . . . 36th . . . 35th . . .*

34th Street.

About to risk everything on a 'maybe' and an 'I think', Finn made a sharp left-hand turn – putting the truck on a one-way street heading in the wrong direction. Overshooting the turn, the truck jumped the curve, careening through a neatly clipped hedge. Again, Finn yanked on the steering wheel, the truck wildly fishtailing from side to side.

As they mowed through the hedge, he heard Kate scream at the top of her lungs. 'Finn! Watch out for the –'

Fire hydrant.

Knowing it was a done deal, Finn threw out his right arm, pinning Kate to the passenger seat as the catering truck ploughed into the hydrant.

9

Sixth Arrondissement, Paris, France

The opening gambit had been played, a pawn sacrificed.

More resigned than shocked to learn that Fabius Jutier had died by his own hand, Ivo Uhlemann hung up the telephone. The latest turn of events could only mean one of two things – either Sergeant McGuire had got too close to the truth or Fabius feared that he might capitulate if the situation turned violent.

Dare il gambetto.

A Spanish priest in the sixteenth century coined the phrase to refer to an opening chess move. Roughly translated, it meant 'putting a leg forward to trip someone'. However, the American had proved himself surprisingly nimble, managing to sidestep their trap.

But to what end?

Lost in thought, Ivo walked over and closed the green velvet drapes; at night, Paris, annoyingly, became the city of headlights. That done, he seated himself at his desk, the Rococo furniture at odds with the modern lines of the laptop computer and wireless printer. The old and the new. The perennial clash as each battled the other for supremacy.

Ready to commence his weekly game of chess, Ivo signed on to the computer site using the tongue-in-cheek moniker 'German Knight'. His opponent, 'Java King', was already online. They played each Tuesday at twelve a.m., insomniacs, the both of them. Since there was nothing that he could personally do about the situation in Washington, other than issue new orders, he saw no reason to cancel the weekly bout.

Playing white, Ivo moved his pawn to E4. *The French Opening.* A fitting tribute to his friend and colleague, Fabius Jutier.

The Cultural Minister had been trained – *they had all been trained* – to swallow a cyanide tablet rather than surrender to the enemy. No different to what many SS officers had been forced to do at the close of the Second World War, the Reich in flames, the Allied army on a bloodthirsty manhunt.

Indeed, a brave man must always be prepared to make the ultimate sacrifice for the greater good.

Ivo glanced at the computer screen. It had taken but a few moments for Java King to position his pawn at E6; the first move of what he hoped would prove a ferocious battle. *Play. Counter-play. Attack.* The weekly match kept his 76-year-old brain sharp; a weak mind was endemic to the lacklustre horde. His father, the noted physicist Friedrich Uhlemann, had been convinced that the mass of men, possessed of middling intelligence, required a guiding hand. Only then could such men meaningfully contribute to society.

As with all of the Seven's founding members, Friedrich had been a brilliant scholar. Created in 1940 by the superintendent of the *Schutzstaffel*, Heinrich Himmler, the unit was envisioned as a seven-man think tank. Its members culled from the best universities in Göttingen, Vienna and Paris, the Seven bridged the divide between the humanities and the sciences. During the 1940s, interdisciplinary research had been a radical concept. In fact, the Ahnenerbe, the academic branch of the SS, had been subdivided into fifty different sections, each focused on a single narrow field of study.

With a click of the computer mouse, Ivo positioned his knight at C3, the diagonal now open.

As he waited for Java King to make the next move, he opened another tab on the computer, pleased to see that the two dossiers he'd ordered had been forwarded. He gave the photograph of Katsumi Rosamund Bauer a cursory glance before scanning the particulars of her life.

Hmm, a most interesting background.

Thirty-nine years of age, Katsumi Bauer had a doctorate in cultural anthropology and, until two years ago, had been a professor at Johns Hopkins University. According to the genealogy chart that a family member had obligingly posted online, the Bauer family emigrated to the American Colonies in 1710, part of a large contingent of Palatine German farmers who settled in New York. Her maternal line, which included several generations of samurai, arrived in California in the early twentieth century. Aiko, her mother, was a curator at the Pacific Asia Museum; father Alfred taught astrophysics at CalTech. As he read that, Ivo chuckled. *How ironic.*

He pulled up the second dossier.

'Hmm, it would seem that our commando hails from a less stellar background,' he murmured, again chuckling, amused by the pun. The parents, Patrick and Fiona

McGuire, moved to Boston in 1972 from Northern Ireland. Typical of working-class Irish Catholics, the mother had been a homemaker, the father a day labourer until his untimely death in 1988. Perhaps it was bred into them. Whatever the reason, the Irish had a long history of being a subjugated people, always serving one master or another.

Ivo quickly skimmed the next few paragraphs, eyes opening wide on reading that McGuire's twin brother, Mychal, was a member of Boston's notorious Irish mob.

Seventy years ago, the McGuire brothers would have been a prize catch; German researchers were particularly interested in studying twins. To advance the burgeoning field of eugenics, all test subjects were thoroughly photographed. Tissue biopsies were then performed. If male, semen samples were forcibly collected; if female, gynaecological exams were conducted. Once the tests were completed, the subjects were euthanized with a single injection of chloroform to the heart, the collected data used to winnow out society's undesirables.

As he finished reading the dossiers, Ivo clicked on the second computer tab. At a glance, he could see that his opponent had just moved his bishop to B4.

Well played, Java King. The move threatened Ivo's white knight. While his Tuesday-night opponent tended to be passive, overly concerned with losing a major piece, Ivo played a more brazen match.

Again, he wondered at the American's game, unable to determine if the commando was being passive or dangerously bold. What did Finn McGuire hope to gain in refusing the Seven's generous monetary offer? And the woman,

Katsumi Bauer – what role did she play in this recent turn of events?

Given her proud heritage and impressive education, Ivo suspected that he would have enjoyed the pleasure of her company.

A pity that Katsumi Bauer was not long for this world.

10

The serpent, the Cursed One, fouled the earth.
An orgy of blood, Paradise lost.
Kill the firstborn then burn in hell.
The serpent, the Cursed One, all covered in –

'Pathetic.'

The assassin known as the Dark Angel disabled the iPhone in mid-song, bored with the shrieking vocals and discordant rhythm of the Black Metal music. Nothing but a pack of alienated young white men, their primal screams evoking a violent fantasy world.

So much better to *live* the fantasy.

Hitching a leather-clad hip against the wrought-iron railing, the assassin scrutinized the little green brick house on the other side of the walkway. The cream-coloured shutters looked newly painted, the brass door knocker was shaped like a pineapple, and the window boxes on the first floor brimmed with pink pansies. *Too trite for words.* Overlooking a placid stretch of canal, the row of brightly painted residences was more reminiscent of Amsterdam than Washington.

Oh, to be in Amsterdam on a hot, muggy night. With the lurid fluorescent lights and writhing bodies behind plate-glass windows. A red-light district second to none. A true outpost of the erotic frontier. Raw, raunchy and real. *What's your pleasure, bébé?*

Annoyed to suddenly hear a tinny buzz, the assassin glanced down. It only took a few seconds for the intrepid mosquito to land on a patch of bare skin, oblivious to its fate. Unaware that the hand of God was two feet away, ready to strike.

How long should I let it live?

'Hmm . . . I think that's long enough.'

Intrigued by the sight of smeared blood and smashed wings, the assassin softly cackled. *Do give my regards to Fabius Jutier.* Who, no doubt, went to his grave snivelling and sobbing, the Frenchman having been an effeminate weakling.

Not like the two Delta Force commandoes. Fine specimens, the both of them. Real men, as the Americans are fond of saying. *All bunched muscles, tightened sinews, eyes burning bright with hatred.* Fighting against the restraints with every ounce of power in their big, muscular bodies. Right to the bittersweet end.

Such a shame that stolen pleasures never last long enough.

'But the night is still young.'

Smiling in anticipation, the assassin glanced at the address scrawled on a crumpled sheet of paper, verifying the house number.

Time to get to work.

11

'*Shit!*' Finn hollered as the front end of the catering truck smashed into the fire hydrant.

Folding his left arm over his face, he slammed against the steering wheel with a bruising intensity.

Beside him, Kate faired no better, the force of the collision propelling her against his outstretched right arm. Flung forward, a split-second later they boomeranged backward. Like a pair of crash dummies. Except they didn't have any airbags to cushion the impact.

His spine jangling, Finn turned towards Kate. 'You okay?'

'It's raining,' she murmured, a dazed look on her face. Then, an instant later, more lucid, she said, 'No, it's not raining. It's the hydrant.'

On the other side of the windscreen a fountain of water gushed skyward.

'The water main must have burst.'

Finn peered into the wing mirror; they'd had a lucky break. The Mercedes had overshot the turn. The bad guys would have to drive to the next block, turn left and come back around.

Meaning that he and Kate had thirty, maybe forty seconds to get the hell out of there.

'We've got to bolt on the double quick. Those goons will be coming round the corner any second.' As he spoke,

Finn searched the truck cab for a plastic bag. Finding one, he dumped the contents – a half-eaten sandwich and a half-drunk bottle of Coke – and handed the empty sack to Kate. 'Put the notebook computer inside that. We need to keep it dry.'

Blasted by spewing water when he exited the truck, Finn slogged around the back end and swung the passenger door wide open. Ignoring his co-pilot's panic-stricken expression, he grabbed the plastic-covered computer off her lap and stuffed it into the waistband of his trousers. That done, he cinched a hand around Kate's upper arm and yanked her out of the truck. She swayed unsteadily on her high-heel shoes, water trickling down her face.

Finn quickly sized up his teetering companion. *Five foot five, 115 pounds. Piece of cake.*

Knowing she wouldn't like what he was about to do, Finn decided to forego getting a signed permission slip. In a big-ass hurry, he shoved his left arm between Kate's legs, wrapped his right hand around her upper arm, and unceremoniously hefted her on to his shoulder. Turning towards the nearest house, he ran across the soggy front yard. There was no car in the driveway and he figured the happy homeowners were out for the night. *Good.*

No sooner did he make it to the driveway than Finn heard the roar of a powerful engine at the other end of the block.

The unfriendlies in the Mercedes.

Had to be.

Not planning to stick around long enough to find out, he sprinted down the driveway. A wooden privacy fence enclosed the back yard. Finn stopped at the gate and reached for the latch. If they could just get through the gate before –

Yes!

He noiselessly shut the gate. Peering through the wooden fence slats, he saw a black Mercedes G500 SUV pull up next to the demolished truck.

'Finn, what's hap–'

'Shhh!'

Two men with drawn weapons jumped out of the Mercedes.

Time to hustle.

Pivoting on his heel, Finn headed towards the back fence, sidestepping a kid's swing. He opened the rear gate and quickly made his way into the alley. Kate started to squirm. Not ready to unload his cargo, he put a hand on her wiggling ass. She instantly stilled.

Passenger subdued, he took off at a fast clip. The alley reeked of urine, rotting garbage and an unidentified dead *something.* It was a muggy night and the stench hung thickly in the air. As Finn continued down the alley, he heard the rumble of thunder. On the far horizon, like a broken neon sign, streaks of white lightning flickered on and off.

Please, God, no rain, he silently prayed. *We're wet enough as it is.*

Figuring they had enough of a lead, he came to a halt and set his passenger on her feet.

'How far away is Wisconsin Avenue?' he asked without preamble.

'Umm –' She glanced about. 'I'm guessing it's about a block and a half from here.' As she spoke, her lips trembled. 'We don't stand a chance, do we?'

Hearing the terrified hitch in Kate's voice, Finn mentally kicked himself. This was his mess, not hers. 'If you want to get out of this alive, we need to get a move on it. *Capiche?*'

She managed a shaky nod.

Thatta girl. Wisconsin Avenue on any given night was party town central, one of those streets where the beer flowed and the denizens flocked in drunken droves. The perfect place to fade into the crowd. He set a quick pace, keeping to the shadows as much as possible. As they neared the cross street, Finn heard the distinctive roar of a German-made V-8 engine.

Kate heard it as well. 'Oh, no!'

'Quick! Get behind that dumpster!' he hissed, placing a hand on Kate's shoulder as he shoved her towards a large metal receptacle. Right on her six, Finn crouched as close to Kate as humanly possible, wrapping his arms and legs around her backside. Attempting to make his six-foot-four frame as small as possible.

Twenty feet away, the Mercedes slowed, coming to a complete stop at the entrance of the alleyway. Finn heard the soft *whhrr* of an automatic window being lowered.

In front of him, Kate shook violently.

Tightening his arms around her torso, Finn silently urged her to keep calm. To stay motionless. His every sense directed towards the idling Mercedes, he listened to the steady purr of the vehicle's powerful engine.

Long seconds passed before the SUV continued down the street.

Doing a fair imitation of a deflated inner tube, Kate slumped against him. If not for the fact that he still had his arms wrapped around her, she would've toppled over.

'Come on. We need to get clear of the alley before the bad guys make the return trip.'

Grabbing Kate by the upper arm, Finn hauled her upright. Neither spoke as they rushed to the street corner.

A few moments later, they reached Wisconsin Avenue, the pavements teeming with pedestrians. Finn steered Kate towards a rowdy bunch of males, many of whom had Greek letters emblazoned on their T-shirts. Shouldering his way into the middle of the pack, he hoped the frat boys were too drunk to wonder how or why a soaking wet middle-aged couple had suddenly appeared in their midst.

Kate clutched her bag to her breasts, clearly unnerved by the crude language and loud-mouth jostling.

'Don't worry,' Finn whispered in her ear, his nose bumping against her cheek. 'These guys are harmless.' The real danger was the congested traffic on Wisconsin Avenue. The bastards in the Mercedes had only to lower a tinted window, take aim and fire. Target eliminated. Since the Seven had proved that they'd stop at nothing to retrieve the Montségur Medallion, Finn figured their henchmen would first take out Kate. Him, they'd keep alive. At least until they had their damned gold pendant.

Without warning, Finn yanked Kate away from the frat boys. 'Time to cross the street,' he said, jutting his chin at the nearby crossing.

To his surprise, Kate vehemently shook her head. 'The quickest route to my townhouse is down Wisconsin Avenue to the canal. It's only six blocks away.'

'Maybe so, but I'm starting to get a hinky feeling about all this.'

Like we're walking right into a trap.

12

'Quite frankly, I don't care how you feel. I *need* to go home.'

Determined to escape the terror of the last few minutes – *Those men in the Mercedes wanted to apprehend them. Or worse!* – Kate continued down Wisconsin Avenue. Ignoring Finn's muttered expletive, she limped gracelessly, hobbled by her four-inch-high heels. *Breathe deeply. Mind over matter. This, too, shall pass.*

Finn manacled her elbow in a powerful, one-handed grip. 'I don't think you comprehend the seriousness of our situation. The unfriendlies are still on the prowl.' In commando mode, he constantly surveyed the environs, his gaze ricocheting from person to street to passing vehicle.

'These being the same unfriendlies who incited the aforementioned hinkiness.'

'Can the sarcasm, will ya? The guys in the Mercedes have not called it quits. They *are* gunnin' for us.'

Taking exception to his rough tone, Kate pulled her elbow free from his grasp. 'Just because I gave you a ride earlier, it doesn't mean that I'm along for the ride. I'm through playing GI Jane.'

'News flash, Baby Jane: this isn't a game.'

'As I am well aware.'

The deeply etched lines on his face relaxed marginally. 'Okay. Just so we're on the same page.' Not breaking stride, Finn shrugged out of his ruined Savile Row jacket and draped it over her shoulders. 'Here. You need this more than I do. You're shaking like a leaf.'

The usual effect of terror, I believe. Although, for some inexplicable reason, she was as frightened of Finn McGuire as she was of the thugs in the Mercedes. Totally unpredictable, he'd transformed from Mr Nice Guy into a battle-ready war fighter with an intimidating take-no-prisoners mentality.

At the corner of Blues Alley, Kate gestured to the narrow passage tucked between a tight hedge of red-brick buildings. 'The alleyway is the quickest route to the canal towpath,' she informed him, sidestepping the queue of music aficionados waiting to get inside the famous jazz supper club.

Scowling, Finn scrutinized each and every patron. 'How far are we from your pad?'

'My house is two blocks away.'

While she routinely used Blues Alley as a short-cut and had trained herself to ignore the scurrying rats and occasional homeless huddle, Finn, his head methodically swivelling from side to side, scanned each and every shadow. Presumably making instantaneous threat assessments.

A few minutes later, they approached the towpath. Kate picked up the pace. Like a wooden lock on the historic canal, the floodgate of relief slowly creaked open inside her. *Almost there.*

'I'm the green brick house at the end of the row.'

'There's no paved street in front of these houses,' Finn muttered. 'Where the hell do you park?'

'There's a public garage on Wisconsin Avenue.'

Craning his neck, he peered back in that direction. 'But that's two blocks from here.'

Kate made no comment; she lived in one of the city's most charming neighbourhoods and considered the two blocks a paltry price to pay. Situated a few feet from the C&O Canal, the row of diminutive nineteenth-century townhouses was a far cry from the residence she'd shared with her ex-husband, a six-bedroom palatial mini-mansion in Chevy Chase, Maryland.

While modest, it was her sanctuary.

Immediately following her son's death and subsequent divorce, she moved into a drab, nondescript high-rise apartment building on Connecticut Avenue. Where, on several occasions, blindsided by grief, she barely got through her front door before she collapsed in the hallway, amidst the corrugated towers of unpacked cardboard boxes. One night she actually stayed there, curled on the parquet floor, until dawn.

The recent move to the little terraced house was her attempt to get on with her life; to move past the heartache of having lost a child. And having been betrayed by the man she once loved.

So far, she'd not had a whole lot of success 'moving on'. Truth be told, there was a decided sameness to her days. Every Monday and Thursday she went to Safeway for groceries. On Fridays she did her banking. And every Saturday she went to Georgetown Video to check out the new arrivals. Lately, she'd found herself fantasizing about leading a different sort of life.

Given what she'd just been through, sitting with a bowl of buttered popcorn on her lumpy sofa suddenly had a whole new appeal.

When they reached the black wrought-iron railing at

her front steps, Kate quickly turned to Finn and said, 'Thank you for escorting –'

'I need to perform a security check of the premises,' he rudely interjected, bulldozing right over her prepared speech.

'Under no circumstances are you coming inside my house.' That was an intrusion she couldn't tolerate, the thought of him roaming inside her house, *her sanctuary*, more than she could bear. '*This*, Sergeant McGuire, is where we part company and go our separate ways.'

For several drawn-out seconds, he stared intently at her. Caught in a silent battle of wills, Kate held her ground. No easy feat given the ferocity of Finn McGuire's brown-eyed stare.

To her surprise, Finn blinked. An instant later, he shook his head, surrendering the field.

'Look. Kate. I'm sorry.' The *mea culpa* was issued in short, choppy sentences. His signature speech pattern. 'I never meant to involve you in this mess.'

'Apology accepted,' she mumbled, too weary to hold a grudge. She was moments from retreating inside her house and slamming the door on this horrible night. Dead bolt and chain latch a given.

Extending a hand towards her face, Finn brushed the pad of his thumb against her lips. 'You got a clot of dried blood in the corner of your mouth.'

'Somewhere between the crash and the foot race, I must have bitten my lip,' she said when Finn showed her the blood on his thumb. 'I was scared as a ninny. Although I'm not exactly sure what a ninny is. I only know that when the Mercedes drove past the alley, I thought –' Kate self-consciously broke off in mid-babble, unnerved by the intimacy of his touch.

Earlier, at the Pentagon, when he had unexpectedly hopped into her Toyota, Kate had been convinced that there wasn't a hint of a spark between them. Now she wasn't so sure. Granted, it'd been a long time since she'd been with a man, but she definitely felt *something* when Finn touched her lip.

'Make sure you disinfect that cut with some rubbing alcohol.'

'Yes, I . . . I will.' She unzipped her handbag and rummaged for her keys. 'That's strange. I can't seem to find my –' She glanced up, surprised to see her key ring dangling from Finn's middle finger.

'I lifted them from your bag when we first arrived at the embassy.'

The confession, uttered without a trace of recrimination, stunned her. From the onset, he'd been using her.

'You mean that you stole them from me.' She snatched the key ring off his finger. Sexual spark be damned. 'Goodnight, Sergeant.'

'See you around, Kate.'

She gave him a tight parting smile before ascending the front steps. About to insert the key in the door lock, Kate belatedly realized that she still had Finn's suit jacket draped around her shoulders.

So much for a graceful exit.

'Finn! Wait!' She dashed down the steps, hurrying to catch up with him. 'I forgot to give you –'

A blinding flash of light accompanied by a sonic *boom!* was the only warning Kate had before being violently hurled several feet into the air, lifted off her feet by a powerful explosion.

In a peripheral blur, she glimpsed a huge fireball shoot heavenward, emanating from her house. The destructive force of the blast thrust a length of wrought iron over the towpath and pelted the canal with brick chunks and shards of glass. And heaved wooden trim at nearby trees.

Who? Why? My God, how?

Kate gasped. It took her breath away. *No* – breath knocked out of her. She'd seen it. Heard it. And painfully felt it. But still couldn't believe it. *A gas main blew. Or perhaps an unventilated propane tank exploded.* Something plausible, albeit shocking, just occurred. It couldn't have been something so improbable, so horrific, as a detonated bomb. But even as she tried to rationalize what had happened, coloured lights began to swirl nightmarishly and fuse in front of her eyes, only to expand into a dark void.

In that instant, she lost all sense of gravity. Suddenly weightless.

Oh, no . . . I think I'm dead.

13

Sixth Arrondissement, Paris, France

Ivo Uhlemann gleefully took his opponent's queen.

The field his, the battle won, he logged off the computer. Pushing the gilded Louis XV salon chair away from the desk, he rose to his feet. The sudden motion cost him, a bolt of pain bursting free and radiating to the back of his spine. Shuddering, Ivo placed a stabilizing hand on top of the desk, fighting the urge to gasp, well aware that a large intake of air would only intensify the agony.

Long moments passed, the pain finally ebbing to a tolerable level.

Ivo glanced at his right hand, palm still pressed against the smooth inlaid cherry desktop. Noticing the raised blue veins and splotchy, tissue-paper-like skin, he frowned. *If only the body kept pace with the mind.* Yet another battle he had to wage.

Chaos, destruction and death, the sum of each man's journey through life. Ivo first experienced the brutal trinity at a tender age. Even now, all these years later, he could still vividly recall that night in 1943 when British RAF pilots rained deadly bombs on Berlin's sleeping neighbourhoods. An act of callous savagery, thousands were immolated alive, with Ivo's own grandparents among the victims. But to the Allies utter disbelief, Berliners rose up from the ashes, Phoenix-like, the firebird heroically transformed into a *Reichsadler*, the proud eagle of the Reich.

Seized with patriotic fervour, his own spirit burnished in the flames, Ivo straight away joined the Hitler-Jugend. Eleven years and three days of age, he proudly wore the black shorts, long-sleeved brown shirt and peaked cap. And though he couldn't fully grasp the meaning of the slogan 'Blood and Honour', he nonetheless shouted it with great ferocity at war rallies. Assigned to an anti-aircraft crew, he was trained to use a flak gun. Bursting with pride, his mother Berthe showered him with adoring kisses. His father, stationed at the SS Headquarters in Wewelsburg, sent letters commending Ivo for his unparalleled bravery.

That bravery was put to a gruelling test seventeen months later when Ivo was issued a steel helmet, a Panzerfaust anti-tank weapon and a bolt-action rifle with one hundred rounds of ammunition. Marching in perfect unison, heel to toe as they'd been trained, Ivo and his regiment of Hitler-Jugend were ordered to take up a position on the Pichelsdorf Bridge. Part of the last German defence, the 'boy brigade' was to halt the Russian advance and prevent the enemy from entering Berlin.

For two gore-filled days, they held their ground. Of the five thousand boys sent to the bridge, only five hundred remained standing at the end of those horrific forty-eight hours. Just as the jubilant Red horde stormed across the bridge, Ivo was severely wounded in a mortar blast.

When he finally regained consciousness in an American field hospital, the Führer was dead, Germany a conquered nation. Bandaged from head to foot, immobilized in a traction device, Ivo was filled with shame.

If I'd only fought harder. Fired more bullets. Killed more Russians.

Six months would pass before he was discharged from the military hospital with a wooden cane, a Hershey's chocolate bar and a silver Reichspfennig coin. Oskar Baader, a grey-haired, bespectacled man who'd been his father's colleague in the physics department at Göttingen University, met him at the hospital gate. On the train ride to Göttingen, the professor informed Ivo that his mother had been killed during the Russian attack on Berlin and that his father, who'd risen within the SS to the rank of Oberführer, was a wanted fugitive. The shock more than he could bear, Ivo burst into tears.

As the months passed, Ivo settled into his new life in Göttingen with the elderly Baader couple, marching drills and combat practice replaced with violin lessons and science tutorials. Eventually the sorrow faded. In its stead was a wide-eyed curiosity as encoded letters from his father – postmarked from such far-flung places as Lisbon, Genoa and Cairo – began to arrive at the flat.

With each encoded letter, more and more of an incredible tale began to unfold. According to the missives, his father had been assigned to a highly-classified research project under the auspices of the Ahnenerbe. The project, which involved an ancient relic known as the *Lapis Exillis*, had been sanctioned by the Führer himself. Even more amazing, although the war had ended and the surviving members of the Ahnenerbe were either on the run or facing a military tribunal in Nuremberg, Friedrich Uhlemann still actively sought the relic. His father claimed that this relic contained unique properties that could be used to harness a heretofore untapped energy.

Hearing the ormolu clock on the mantel chime the new hour, Ivo turned his head. *One o'clock.* He assumed the Dark Angel had detonated the plastic explosive. With Katsumi Bauer removed from the equation, the American commando could be lured back to the bargaining table. Every man had his price. Too much was at stake. Encrypted clues to the whereabouts of the *Lapis Exillis* were engraved on the Montségur Medallion.

They had only five days to find it.

Five days until the Heliacal Rising of Sirius when the great star would appear on the eastern horizon just before sunrise. Five days until that powerful energy burst that could change the course of history.

Would change it, provided they located the *Lapis Exillis.*

Ivo again glanced at the clock, silently damning the reminder that each minute, each hour, each day lost could not be regained.

Only five days.

A trained physicist, Friedrich Uhlemann had gone to his grave convinced that the ancient technology contained within the *Lapis Exilis* could have saved the Reich from total annihilation.

Ivo, also a trained physicist, knew that it wasn't too late. If found, the *Lapis Exilis* could *still* save the Reich.

14

'Here. This should help.' Finn offered Kate a chipped Redskins mug filled with hot coffee and a slug of Jameson's whiskey. 'You're damned lucky to have landed in that barberry bush.'

Tersely shaking her head, Kate refused the pick-me-up. Instead, she continued to sit on the sofa with her arms wrapped around her chest, hands coiled around her elbows. Since the blast, the woman hadn't uttered a single word. They'd just entered the second hour of radio silence.

'Drink it, Kate. The booze will do you good. I don't want you fainting on me again.' He butted the mug against her chest, forcing her to accept the spiked coffee.

Her expression blank, Kate stared straight ahead as she obediently took a sip.

She must have had a sheltering angel standing sentry at the front door. Because, somehow, against all odds, she'd managed to survive the blast relatively unscathed. Scratches, bruises, minor abrasions and a swollen right knee; the kind of injuries that always hurt worse the morning after.

Immediately after the explosion, he'd thrown Kate over his shoulder and hauled ass to Wisconsin Avenue. Needing to find a hidey-hole on the double-quick, he'd flagged down a pizza delivery guy and paid him a hundred bucks to drive them to a houseboat docked at the Gangplank Marina. While he didn't personally know Major

James Bukowski, the owner of the houseboat, he'd once overheard the cocky officer bragging about his waterfront digs. Since Bukowski was currently deployed in Afghanistan, the trespass had been child's play. He'd even told the neighbour that 'Jimbo' gave him the key.

For the time being, they were safe.

Still nameless, still faceless, the enemy possessed the stealth of a well-trained Delta unit. If it wasn't for the freaking suit jacket, Kate would have been killed in the explosion.

'If you speak of this matter to anyone, they will be targeted for execution.'

Warning issued. Action taken. Clearly these rat bastards did not make idle threats.

Pricked by a guilty conscience, Finn turned away from Kate and walked over to the window. Pulling the drawn curtain aside, he watched silently as drops of rain plopped against the varnished deck before congealing into plump translucent beads. Scanning the marina, his gaze ricocheted between the dark waters of the Washington Channel and the wood-planked dock.

He let the curtain fall back into place.

'Listen, Kate, I need to know . . .' Finn hesitated, trying to think of a tactful way to phrase the question. Realizing there wasn't one, he got right to it. 'Is there anyone – a parent, a sibling, a close friend – that these murdering thugs can go after next?'

The question hung silently between them, Kate, no doubt, wrapping her dazed mind around this new, unforeseen danger.

'My parents are vacationing in Japan,' she said at last. 'I have no siblings. And I'm not altogether certain, but I believe that my ex-husband is conducting field research in Papua New Guinea. As for friends, well, let's just say that I've been something of a loner these last two years. After the divorce, Jeffrey retained custody of our social circle.'

Finn breathed a sigh of relief. *One less headache.*

'I just want you to know, Kate, that I'm truly sorry. I never meant to put you in harm's way.'

'I would prefer, Sergeant, that you not insult me with a phony apology. All along you've been using me. And now, because of *you*, all of my worldly possessions have been reduced to *this*.' Kate held her handbag aloft. Somehow, miraculously, she'd managed to keep it slung across her chest during the explosion.

About to inform her that with a death sentence hanging over her head, being homeless was the least of her worries, Finn thought better of it. Instead, he seated himself next to her on the sofa.

'You might find this hard to believe, but I know what you're going through,' he said without preamble, heartfelt confessions not his strong suit. 'No matter what, you've got to stay strong. Like a sapling. Bend. Don't break. Got it?'

The pep talk met with a derisive snort. 'Please spare me the sappy sentiments. I want you to tell me, *right now*, why someone tried to kill me. For God's sake! All I did was give you a ride to the embassy.'

'My guess? They think that I took you into my confidence.'

'About what?'

'Unfortunately, I'm not at liberty to –'

'Cut the crap, Finn! Either you tell me what's going on or I *will* pick up the phone and call the police.'

While Kate's fury was completely justified, Finn debated how much he should, or could, reveal. The mission in Al-Qanawat had been black ops and –

Ah, fuck it.

Whether she knew or didn't know, Jutier's henchmen would still be gunning for her. Better that she face the enemy with eyes wide open.

'You might find this hard to believe, but the men who set the explosive device at your house are after a thirteenth-century relic. And they'll stop at nothing to get it.'

Her expression said it all – Kate Bauer thought that he was a lying sack of shit. 'Hard to believe? Try flat-out impossible. And even if I did believe you, which I don't, what does that have to do with you? Or me, for that matter.'

'See, it's like this –' Leaning forward, Finn braced his elbows on top of his thighs. 'Four months ago, I led a black ops mission into Al-Qanawat, Syria. The mission was straightforward: grab contraband vials of smallpox and get out of Dodge with no one the wiser. But when we arrived at the coordinates, there was no contraband smallpox. There wasn't even a terrorist cell. There was just some relic hidden inside a chapel.'

Hearing that, her eyes narrowed suspiciously; the woman was a hard sell. 'You need to be more specific. For starters, what did this relic look like?'

'It was a gold disk about yea big –' he curved both his hands to give her an idea as to its size. 'At the time I was royally pissed that my team was being used; that we were sent into Al-Qanawat for the sole purpose of stealing a damned relic so a fat cat general could pad his retirement account. I'm a trained warrior, not Indiana Jones.'

'And what does the mission in Syria have to do with Fabius Jutier?'

'According to Jutier, he is – or *was* – a member of a group called the Seven. The group paid General Robert Cavanaugh to retrieve the Montségur Medallion for them. When Cavanaugh failed to deliver as promised, they arranged for him to have a fatal car accident.'

Kate made a T with her hands, signalling a time-out. 'Back up a moment. What's the Montségur Medallion?'

'That's the name of the Al-Qanawat relic. And the Seven is convinced that I have this Montségur Medallion. That's why they had an assassin called the Dark Angel murder two Delta troopers from my old outfit and make it look like I killed 'em. Earlier today, a couple of CID agents showed up at the Pentagon and accused me of doing just that.'

Closing his eyes, Finn massaged his sockets with his thumb and middle finger, envisioning the glossy 8 x 10 crime scene photos that the two CID agents had shown to him. He didn't particularly want those images floating around inside his head. It made him think about the horror, the sheer agony, that his two friends endured before the final coup de grâce.

He opened his eyes. Then shook his head to clear the gory images from his mind's eye.

To his surprise, Kate placed her hand on his forearm. 'I'm sorry about what happened to your comrades.'

'Yeah, me too. I loved them both like brothers,' he told her, man enough to own up to his feelings. Still grappling with the brutal slaying, he was grateful for the condolence.

Removing her hand, Kate said, 'I'm confused . . . why did the Seven frame you for murder?'

'They framed me for murder to force my hand. To get me to turn over the relic to them. According to the dead French dude, they've got DNA evidence that will prove my innocence. And to sweeten the deal, Jutier offered me a sign-up bonus of one million dollars.'

'But why, after offering you all that money, would Fabius Jutier turn around and kill himself?'

Finn shrugged. 'I have no friggin' idea.'

Snatching a plaid throw blanket from the arm of the sofa, Kate wrapped it around her shoulders. 'I'll be honest with you, Finn, it's an outrageous story. And, quite frankly, I'm having a hard time believing that these murders took place because some group erroneously thinks you have a gold relic in your –'

'I never said that I *didn't* have the Montségur Medallion.' As he spoke, Finn undid the top three buttons on his shirt. Slipping a finger under the ribbed collar of his undershirt, he pulled out the heavy-ass chain and medallion.

Eyes opening wide, Kate slumped against the sofa. '*Oh, my God.*'

15

'I suspect this is quite valuable,' Kate remarked, still stunned that Finn had been hiding the Montségur Medallion on his person.

'Worth a decent chunk, given the price of gold.' Holding the pendant by its heavy chain, Finn slowly swung it back and forth.

'That's not what I meant.' Kate blinked several times in rapid succession, breaking free of the relic's hypnotic allure. 'The value of the metal, in and of itself, wouldn't account for the Seven's deadly fanaticism. An educated guess? These engraved images that decorate the medallion are what they're really after.'

One side of Finn's mouth turned down dismissively. 'Bunch of old symbols. Big whup.'

A trained cultural anthropologist, Kate knew that symbols were an encoding system employed by all cultures. Depicted literally in art and expressed figuratively in myth, symbols communicated man's relationship to the world around him.

'May I?' She held out her hand. Finn obliged the request, passing the medallion to her.

One did not have to be a trained cultural anthropologist to know that there was a hidden meaning contained within the 'old symbols', as Finn had dismissively referred to them.

'Because an X divides the medallion into four different quadrants, I'm not sure if the symbols are meant to be read separately or as in integrated whole. What I do know is that these are symbols used in almost every culture of the world. The sun, as the eye of the world, symbolizes enlightenment. The moon refers to the dark side of nature.'

'Or the passage of time.' When she glanced at Finn, he shrugged. 'You know, moon tides and lunar calendars.'

'Or the passage of time,' Kate iterated, his observation very much on the mark. 'Stars usually designate the presence of some divinity.'

'Like the crown of stars on top of the Virgin Mary's head.'

She nodded, that being as good an example as any. 'As for the four strangely shaped "A"s, I haven't a clue. Perhaps they're a reference to the Four Ages of man or the four classical elements of air, water, earth and fire. Regardless, all of these symbols are prosaic to an extreme. As you said, big whup. Which leads me to the medallion's flipside –' she turned the pendant over and showed him the three lines of engraved text. 'I suspect that this inscription is what the Seven deems valuable.'

Finn's head jerked. 'The rat bastards killed my two buddies because of *that*?'

'Possibly,' she hedged.

'Okay, what the hell does it say?'

'I have no idea. However, I'm fairly certain that the last line is written in medieval Latin. I don't recognize the language used for the first two lines. Clearly, the message was crafted to withstand the ages.' She tapped the relic with her index finger for emphasis.

'No kidding. Someone would have to melt this sucker to erase the inscription. So how is it that you know so much about symbols?'

'My, um, PhD is in cultural anthropology.'

His brows noticeably lifted. 'You're a bona fide doctor? Are you shitting me?'

'"Yes" to the first question, "no" to the second. However, I rarely use the title.' Hard-earned though those three letters were, when she left the world of academia two years ago and ventured beyond the ivory tower, she discovered that her title was off-putting. 'I'm curious – why did you keep the medallion? Were you planning to sell it on the black market?' she asked, purposefully changing the subject.

Leaning against the tufted sofa, Finn crossed his arms over his chest. 'You don't think very highly of me, do you,

Doc? Actually, I kept it so no one else could sell the damned thing on the black market. My Delta team was sent into a very dangerous situation under false pretences. Put into harm's way to retrieve a gold trinket so some higher-up could have a nice payday. I held on to the medallion hoping it would force the crooked bastards out of the woodwork so they could be prosecuted.' Grim-faced, his chin dipped to his chest. But not before Kate glimpsed the stark grief that glimmered in his eyes. 'I just never thought they'd kill my buddies to get the damned medallion.'

All in all, an unexpected confession. One that bespoke a noble intent. A virtue Kate didn't necessarily associate with the foul-mouthed commando sitting across from her.

'All right, now what?' She carefully set the golden relic on the coffee table.

'Now I track down the assassin who executed Dixie and Johnny K.'

'Have you considered relinquishing the medallion to the Seven in order to clear –'

'Don't even go there,' Finn interjected, rudely cutting her off in mid-sentence. 'This medallion is the only leverage I have. As long as it's in my possession, I've got a chance of getting Dixie and Johnny K the justice they deserve. Just so you know, they were the bravest of the brave. The guys who went in under the cover of night to take out a dangerous threat so that you and everybody else in this country can sleep safely at night. They didn't deserve to die the way they did. Which is why I *will* find the sadistic shit who tortured them to death and I *will* make him pay.'

The vehemence in his voice sent a chill down Kate's spine. 'An eye for eye? Is that what you mean?'

Hearing that, Finn snorted derisively. 'I've killed enough men in the line of duty to know you don't gain a whole lot of satisfaction from pulling the trigger. I'm talking about hauling the Dark Angel into a court of law so that he can be tried and sentenced. More than anything else, I want him to be publicly held to account for slaying two American heroes.'

'What if you can't find him?' she countered, thinking it might prove a difficult, if not impossible, challenge. 'Other than his cryptic *nom de guerre*, you don't know anything about the killer.'

Getting up from the sofa, Finn snatched her coffee mug and walked over to the kitchenette that was located a few feet away. 'Actually, I do know one other thing about the killer,' he said over his shoulder. 'The fact that Jutier went to such lengths to protect his identity makes me think that the Dark Angel is one of 'em.'

'You mean a member of the Seven rather than a paid assassin?' When he nodded, Kate followed up by saying, 'Fabius Jutier's tattoo may provide a clue. Do you mind if I have a look at the digital photograph?'

Finn unhooked the cell phone from his waistband and scrolled through the log. Walking back to the sofa, he handed her the device. 'Any idea what it means?'

Trying to ignore the fact that she was staring at a photo of a corpse, she examined the disturbing tattoo. 'While I'm not a rune expert, I know that in the ancient Norse poems, runes were considered a magical talisman, capable of bringing the dead back to life. And during the

Third Reich, there were a number of occult groups that used runes in their rituals. That said, the runes suggest that Fabius Jutier was involved in some type of esoteric Nazism.'

'I take it that's different from the goose-stepping variety?'

'Different in that esoteric Nazism was, and still is, a pseudo-religious belief. While my knowledge of the Nazi movement is rudimentary, I do know that during the nineteen thirties and forties, esoteric Nazis were obsessed with finding sacred *objects d'art* such as the relics of the Bible, medieval icons and Egyptian artefacts. It's well documented that they sent archaeology teams all over Europe and the Middle East.'

'Yeah, I saw the movie,' Finn deadpanned. 'But instead of the Ark of the Covenant, our bad guys are looking for the Montségur Medallion.'

'So it would seem.'

Finn headed towards the dinette table situated on the other side of the living room. 'I'm gonna try to hack into Frenchie's computer. There might be something on it that I can use to track down the Seven.'

'Um, count me out,' she demurred.

Kate set the cell phone on the coffee table next to the medallion. The sudden motion cost her, the pain radiating up her spine and across her shoulders. Somewhat gingerly, she rose to her feet, only to teeter precariously to one side. Feeling like a shipwrecked woman washed ashore, she kicked off her shoes and limped over to the window.

Although she knew it was a pointless exercise, she pulled the dun-brown drapery to one side, needing to verify that the world still turned on its figurative axis. In the distance, the white spire of the Washington Monument gleamed theatrically, lit from below with giant floodlights. Directly across the river was the Pentagon.

God, what I wouldn't give to put back the clock. Since Finn McGuire had unexpectedly got into her car at the Pentagon, her life had become a surreal blur of events. Elegant embassy party. Dead man with bizarre tattoo. High-speed chase. Armed assailants. And the capstone, a bomb blast that destroyed her home.

And wasn't that a bitter irony?

After her infant son died, she lost the will to live, feeling as though someone had driven a railroad spike through her heart, pinning her to the tracks. Except the train never came to take her out of her misery. And then, one morning, she woke up and for the first time in nearly two years she could *hear* the birds chirping outside the window. Could *feel* the sun on her face. Could *taste* the sweetness of sugar in her coffee. Small everyday moments that most people take for granted. The fact that she experienced an instant's joy in them made her realize that she wanted to live. To make that clichéd fresh start.

And just when she'd decided to return to the land of the living, some group called the Seven decided that they wanted her dead.

Thank God she'd had the foresight to create a digital photo album with all of Sammy's pictures, the CD in her safe deposit box at the bank. She could bear losing the contents of her house, but not that. Those were the only memories that truly counted.

And I can only savour those cherished memories if I stay alive.

Pensively staring out of the window, Kate could feel the onslaught of emotion about to rear its ugly head. So many ugly heads. So many crashing fears and colliding thoughts. *Keep running. Don't stop.* If you do, they will hunt you down and kill you.

After the 1941 attack on Pearl Harbor, Japanese Americans were forcibly rounded up and interned in 'War Relocation Camps'. Refusing to be separated from her husband, Kate's grandmother accompanied her husband Yoshiro Tanaka when he was loaded on to the train bound for the Manzanar Camp. She was the only Caucasian in the internment facility other than the military police who guarded the compound. Like so many thousands of loyal Americans of Japanese descent, in the blink of an eye her grandparents lost their home, their livelihood and their community. She'd often wondered how they survived the shock of having their lives pulled out from under them. Now she knew.

You just put one foot in front of the other and keep on trudging.

Ready to trudge forward, Kate let the curtain fall back into place. Peering over her shoulder, she stared contemplatively at the man seated at the table.

Finn McGuire was the last person she ever thought she'd turn to for help. The fact that she had to turn to anyone made her acutely uncomfortable. After her husband's hideous betrayal, trust didn't come easy to her, although she sensed that Sergeant McGuire was loyal to a fault when it came to his brothers-in-arms.

Even though I don't know him, I can trust him to keep me alive.

That might be the only thing that she could trust him with. So be it. She needed a bodyguard, not a lifetime companion. And though nervous about spending an extended amount of time with a man she barely knew, the other option – going it alone – would be a death sentence.

16

'So, how are we coming along with computer hacking?'

'I was able to get on to Jutier's desktop, but I can't access any of his personal files without a password,' Finn muttered, surprised by Kate's sudden interest.

'Mind if I have a look?'

'Help yourself. Although I didn't peg you for the type who approved of computer hacking.' Particularly given the stink she raised when he snatched the laptop from Jutier's office.

Sitting down at a dinette chair, Kate swivelled the computer in her direction. 'Since you're locked out of Jutier's files, it's technically *not* hacking. I just want to take a quick peek at his desktop. You know. Curiosity. The cat.' As soon as she said it, she winced. 'How weird is that? We've been in each other's company for only a few hours and I'm already starting to sound like you.'

'Just as long as you don't start looking like me.'

'God forbid.' As she said it, Kate's gaze dropped to his right hand. An instant later, evidently realizing what she'd done, she glanced away.

'Luckily, the Syrian who pulled the trigger was a lousy shot. All he got was my finger,' Finn told her, trying to put a nonchalant spin on a potentially awkward moment.

'Does it ever hurt?' she asked.

Usually those kind of questions pissed the shit out of

him, but for some reason he found Kate's earnest expression oddly endearing.

'Nah, it doesn't hurt,' he lied. 'Although I can forecast when it's going to rain.' Because that's when it hurt like a mother.

From time to time, Finn still caught himself about to scratch his nose, rub an eye or press a keypad with his absentee index finger. As much as he wished the amputation hadn't happened, he tried to look on the bright side – he could still flip someone the bird. And, hell, it wasn't like he'd had his Johnson blown off. Luckily for him, that appendage worked just fine. Sometimes a little too fine.

He shot Kate an appraising glance.

High cheekbones, almond-shaped eyes, silky black hair and a wide nose gave her a slightly Asian look. *Kinda exotic, actually.* Which made the freckles that dotted those high cheekbones totally unexpected. Same with the eye colour; not quite grey, not quite blue. More like a muddy mix of the two.

As he continued to stare at the woman seated next to him, Finn wondered what would have happened if they'd gone on a 'regular date'. To the movies. Followed by a bite to eat. At that new Thai restaurant over in Rosslyn. Afterwards, they would have strolled along the canal before he took her home. It would have been a given that he'd kiss her goodnight at the front door. And, if the vibe was right, she might have invited him inside for a cup of coffee. If the vibe was *really* right, the coffee would've been served the next morning. *As perfect as a date can get.*

Nice daydream. Except they'd had a different kind of

date. Not to mention that it was hard to kiss a lady at the front door when she no longer had a front door. Or even a house, for that matter.

Jesus! She must think I'm a real bastard.

For some reason, that thought bothered him.

'Don't call retreat just yet,' Kate suddenly announced, tapping a fingertip against the laptop screen. 'Here's Jutier's Day Planner. Hopefully, we won't need a password to open it.'

'I can't imagine the French dude would have been stupid enough to schedule Dixie and Johnny K's murder, but yeah, go ahead, let's have a look-see.'

Kate's fingers deftly moved across the keyboard.

'I'm in.' She opened the calendar for the month of August. 'There's tonight's reception. Tomorrow morning, August third, he has a ten o'clock manicure scheduled. Later in the day, he's playing a round of golf at the Congressional Country Club.'

'I didn't know Frenchmen *could* play golf,' Finn snickered. 'And the thought that he was going to have his nails done ahead of time is more than this beer-swigging soldier can handle. Pass me the Freedom Fries on the double-quick.'

Ignoring him, Kate continued to read aloud from the calendar. 'The day after that, he's booked on Air France Flight 039. And, the following day, August fifth at eleven o'clock, he's scheduled to attend –' Kate grinned excitedly – '"*une réunion du sept*".'

'English would be nice.'

'A meeting of the Seven,' she translated, still grinning from ear to ear.

'Paydirt! Yeah, boy.' Although he didn't grin, Finn came damned close. 'Where's the meeting being held?'

Kate moved the cursor over the calendar date and clicked. 'The detail screen is blank.'

'No problem. Let's go out on the Internet and get the route information for Air France Flight 039.'

Minimizing the calendar, Kate quickly accessed the Air France webpage. 'It's a nonstop between Washington and Paris.'

'And Paris is a big, freaking city.' *Shit. A roadblock.* He got up and walked over to the kitchen, the bottle of Jameson's starting to look real good.

'I just found the Seven.'

'*What?*' Finn spun on his heel, wondering if he'd heard correctly. 'What do you mean, you just found the Seven?'

'I mean that I went to an online search engine and I typed the words "Paris", "Seven" and "Fabius Jutier". The Seven Research Foundation is a private endowment and Fabius Jutier is listed as one of the board members. A man by the name of Ivo Uhlemann is listed as the Director. Here. See for yourself.'

Bracing one hand on the back of Kate's chair and the other on the table, Finn leaned over her shoulder. Only to back away a split-second later. 'It's in French. As in no par-lay-voo.'

'According to their site, the Seven Research Foundation is a private institute that awards research grants to qualified scholars in the fields of astronomy, physics, geology, electrical engineering, linguistics, history and archaeology.' She peered at him, brows drawn together in a quizzical frown. 'That's a rather unusual mix, don't you think?

Particularly for a group that may be linked to esoteric Nazis.'

'Maybe the foundation is just a front. And what were you expecting? For them to put a bunch of Nazi symbols on the home page?'

Jesus. The Nazis. When he was a kid, their upstairs neighbour used to tell stories about the day his army unit liberated the Dachau concentration camp and how the black vultures were circling around stacked corpses left outside to rot. *Old man Garrett sure knew how to scare the shit out of a six-year-old.*

'According to the contact page, the Seven Research Foundation is headquartered in the Grande Arche office building just west of Paris,' Kate remarked.

'Then it's a do-able.'

Greyish-blue eyes opened wide. 'You're *actually* going to Paris?'

'You got a better plan?' Not waiting for her reply, he said, 'Something tells me that I want to have a little meet-and-greet with this Ivo Uhlemann dude. Best way to catch a lion is to track him to his lair.'

'And then what?'

Backing away from the table, Finn said, 'I'll figure that out once I get to Paris.'

'Then you better book two seats. I'm going with you.'

17

Paris, France

Alas, Paris is the key, Ivo Uhlemann ruminated. *A key that fitted a unique lock designed centuries ago by the Knights Templar.*

Not Berlin, or even Vienna, but Paris.

As his chauffer-driven Mercedes Benz cruised through the eighth arrondissement, the city lights passed in a blurred collage. Peering out of the window, Ivo contemplated the night sky, the cosmic sphere that taunted so many physicists.

And was so intimately conjoined to Paris and the *Lapis Exillis.*

Because Paris was the key, it had been spared from destruction in 1940. At the time, many feared the German Luftwaffe would reduce the city to rubble. But the Führer never gave the order. Not because he had a sentimental attachment to Baroque architecture or possessed a magnanimous heart. The order wasn't given because the Seven had briefed Adolf Hitler several months prior to the invasion of France. In that extraordinary meeting, they'd shown the Führer why *das Groß Versuch*, the Great Experiment, *had* to take place in Paris.

'For better or for worse,' Ivo muttered as he set his gaze on the Grande Arche, the massive white marble hypercube visible at the western terminus of the Avenue des Champs-Élysées.

'It's a warm night. Would you like me to turn on the air conditioner, Herr Doktor?'

Lost in thought, Ivo glanced at his driver. As usual, he thought the ridiculous chauffeur's cap accentuated Dolf Reinhardt's cauliflower ears and misshapen skull, the unsightly keepsakes of an ex-boxer who'd lost more bouts than he'd won. Like so many men of middling intelligence, Dolf had been forced to use his body to earn his keep. Although to his chauffeur's credit, he was loyal to a fault.

'I am comfortable. Thank you, Dolf.'

Having been apprised that Katsumi Bauer survived the explosion, Ivo now feared that they were dealing with a cunning enemy. Moreover, he worried that the American commando had somehow discovered that the Montségur Medallion contained a treasure map. One that had been devised nearly eight hundred years ago by a group of religious heretics known as the Cathars.

On the verge of total annihilation, the Pope having called a bloodthirsty crusade against them, the beleaguered Cathars sought the aid of the only Catholics who'd not turned against them, the Knights Templar. In exchange for their military support, the Cathars offered to give the Templars their most prized possession, the *Lapis Exillis*. Rightly concerned that the Templars might not hold up their end of the bargain, the Cathars crafted a magnificent gold medallion. Engraved on one side of the medallion was an encrypted map that indicated where the *Lapis Exillis* had been hidden. The Templars would not be given the encryption key until their battle-ready knights arrived at Montségur. Tragically, the besieged Cathar stronghold fell to papal forces before the military contingent arrived. To the Templars' great dismay, for without the encryption key, they could not decipher the ingeniously devised map.

Although that didn't stop them from spending the next sixty years searching for the *Lapis Exillis*. In 1307, their search came to an abrupt end when the French king, Philippe le Bel, issued a general arrest warrant for the Knights Templar, the entire order accused of committing religious heresy. To ensure that the covetous king didn't acquire the Montségur Medallion, the Templars hid it in the catacombs beneath their Paris preceptory.

Which is where the Seven discovered the medallion in the summer of 1940. Five years later, in the wake of the Reich's defeat, Friedrich Uhlemann managed to safely smuggle it out of Germany. Like the Templars before him, he spent years searching, in vain, for the *Lapis Exillis*.

In the hours before his death, Friedrich composed one last letter, imploring Ivo to continue the search for the *Lapis Exillis*. Considering it an honour, Ivo gladly accepted the passed torch.

In the hopes that, one day, he could shine a bright light upon a new Reich.

'*Gott in Himmel*,' his chauffeur angrily muttered. 'Do these people never sleep?'

Ivo wondered the same thing as he caught sight of a gypsy woman standing on the street corner, a passel of grubby-faced children huddled at her feet. *A repulsive display*, he thought, annoyed when the sloe-eyed slattern dared to raise her right hand, palm up, in his direction. The beggar's age-old appeal for alms.

'*Give me some of your hard-earned money because I am too stupid and lazy to earn my own keep.*'

An inbred race of conniving ingrates, the gypsies, or the Romani as they indignantly preferred; they were only skilled at one thing, sucking on society's teat. And they'd done so since their ragtag horde first emigrated to Europe from the Indian subcontinent during the Middle Ages. In all that time, they'd produced nothing of lasting value. No art. No science. No literature. No music worthy of the name. They merely reproduced. Fathers sleeping with daughters. Brothers sleeping with sisters. Uncles sleeping with anyone they could find. *Utterly disgusting.* Indeed, the marvel of the human brain was completely wasted on them. A spinal column alone would have sufficed.

Too busy rounding up Jews, the Reich's high command greatly erred when they didn't eradicate the Romani. Yes, many gypsies were killed, but like rodents, they spent the post-war years reproducing at a frantic pace. Six decades later, they littered the streets of every major city in Europe. Like so much trash.

Trash that would be picked up and put into a garbage bin once they located the *Lapis Exillis.*

But first they had to find the medallion. *And we only have five days to do so.*

Since his father had been afraid to ship the Montségur Medallion to Germany, lest it be confiscated by an inquisitive customs inspector, his last letter contained a drawing, front and back, of the pendant. Disastrously, by the time the missive arrived in Göttingen, the ink had smudged, the symbols and inscription illegible.

Although stymied by the setback, the seed of an idea

began to germinate: *what if the other members of the Seven had sent their children letters?* Perhaps there were others, like Ivo, who wanted to continue their fathers' research, but didn't know how to find the *Lapis Exillis.* Or, more importantly, what to do with the ancient relic should they manage to locate it.

Inspired, Ivo spent several months tracking down the second generation.

As fate would have it, those children, now grown adults, had also received letters from fathers who'd eluded arrest by stealing away to Buenos Aires, Cairo, New York. Contained within those dispatches was the cumulative research of the original Seven. Thrilled at the prospect of continuing the great work begun by their fathers, the second generation vowed to find the *Lapis Exillis.* To honour their fathers, they unanimously decided to call themselves 'The Seven Research Foundation'.

Naturally, the first order of business was to find the Montségur Medallion, Ivo's father making no mention in his last missive of its whereabouts. Since that letter had a Damascus postmark, they surmised that the medallion was in Syria. It took them more than twenty-five years to locate it, finally tracking the medallion to the remote village of Al-Qanawat. Not wishing to garner unwanted attention, they contracted a third party to retrieve the medallion.

A costly blunder. One that *must* be rectified as soon as possible.

Without the Montségur Medallion, they could not find the *Lapis Exillis*, the requisite component to perform *das Groß Versuch.* Once the Great Experiment was successfully executed, they would be able to awaken the sleeping soul of the Aryan people.

Then they could begin again. Bolder. Stronger. More resolute.

Just as their fathers had envisioned.

18

'Sorry, Kate. You can't come with me to Paris.'

'Since it's not safe for me to stay in Washington, what am I supposed to do?' Kate retorted, quick to bat the objection right back at Finn. 'I need you to protect me. There's no place in the city where I can hide. They know my name and address. No doubt, they've mined all my personal data off of a computer database. My place of employment and my –'

'This is strictly a one-man operation,' Finn said over the top of her. 'And just so you know, the matter is not open for debate.' Ultimatum issued, he walked over to the coffee table to retrieve his belongings.

Kate trailed after him. 'But I have an expertise that you'll need once you get to Paris.'

'Oh, really?' It was all he could do not to roll his eyes. 'Is this where you tell me that you took karate lessons at the local Y?'

'No. This is where I tell you that I speak passably good French. When I was an undergraduate in college, I had a three-month summer internship at the Musée de l'Homme.'

'Good for you.' Finn stuffed his cell phone into his pocket. 'But I was planning to buy one of those electronic translators.' He didn't enjoy being a hard ass, but he needed to end this discussion here and now. If he was going to get out of Washington without putting CID on the scent, he'd have to call in some old debts. Get the ball rolling. He already knew that if he went to an ATM or used a credit card, he'd be signing his death warrant.

Apocalypse now.

However, like any trained commando, he had a contingency plan. His involved a well-stocked storage locker in Arlington, Virginia. *Cash. Guns. KA-BAR knife. Night-vision goggles.* Everything he needed to take out the enemy.

'Okay, here's my second offer,' Kate said with a surprising measure of boldness. 'Not only does my friend Cædmon Aisquith live in Paris, but he's a walking encyclopedia when it comes to symbols and their meanings. If you want to decipher the tattoo and medallion, Cædmon is your man.'

Hearing that, his gaze narrowed suspiciously. 'I thought *you* were the symbol expert.'

'My field of expertise is the peoples and culture of Central Asia. Cædmon is a medieval scholar with a graduate degree from Oxford.'

'Loosely translated? He's one of those nut jobs who plays the lute at the Renaissance Festival.' This time, Finn did roll his eyes.

'I'll have you know that Cædmon is a serious scholar.'

'I don't need a scholar. All I need is a loaded weapon and a clear shot.'

'Did I mention that he owns a bookstore on the Left Bank?' Knowing full well that she hadn't, Kate kept pounding at a very dead horse. 'He has a zillion reference books at his fingertips.'

'And I've got Google at mine.'

'You said it yourself –' snatching the medallion off the

coffee table, Kate hefted it in the air – '*this* is your leverage with the Seven. So it might be a good idea to know what *this* means. As Cædmon is fond of saying, "Knowledge is power".'

'This is my fight, not yours. And it sure as hell ain't Lute Boy's battle.'

'Where do you get off claiming this isn't my fight? A few hours ago the Seven arranged to have me killed. Why? Because I chauffeured you to the embassy. And I only did that because you conned me into giving you a lift. You knew full well how dangerous these people are, yet that didn't stop you from dragging me into the viper's nest.' Having just laid the mother of all guilt trips on him, Kate, arms belligerently crossed over her chest, stared him down.

'Do I feel bad about what happened? Hell, yeah. But it doesn't change my mind.'

'Let me be blunt, Sergeant. Because you did drag me into this mess, I now require your protection. I'm scared to death. And, trust me, I didn't like saying that any more than you liked hearing it.'

Finn opened his mouth to lob the next salvo. Only to clamp it shut an instant later. Arguing with Kate Bauer was a lot like arguing with a computerized voicemail system. You could talk yourself blue in the face, but it wouldn't make a damned bit of difference.

He rubbed a hand over his jaw. Taking her to Paris would be a major pain in the ass. Hell, they'd be flying directly into the eye of the shit storm. *But what choice did he have?* She'd been targeted for execution. And he'd always been good at juggling more than one ball. So, yeah, he figured that he could protect her *and* hunt down the Dark Angel.

'You've got me pinned in a corner. You know that, don't you?'

'Does that mean you've changed your mind?' There was no mistaking the flicker of hope in those grey-blue eyes.

Finn nodded tersely, already regretting his decision. 'You might know a lot about symbols, *Doctor Bauer*, but when it comes to dealing with unfriendlies, you don't know your left from your right. My mission is to apprehend the Dark Angel and get my buddies the justice they deserve. And I don't want anything to distract me from that. Which is why you *will* obey all of my orders. Without question. Understood?'

She nodded eagerly. 'Understood. When do we leave?'

'As soon as we can pack it up. And, Kate –' he paused, making sure he had her full, undivided attention – 'once we leave this houseboat, the only safe day will be the day just passed.'

Part II

'I am convinced that there are universal currents of Divine Thought vibrating the ether everywhere and that any who can feel these vibrations is inspired' – Richard Wagner

19

Paris, France

4 August, 0848 hours

'Before we blow this joint, I need to lay down some ground rules. First of all, we're not on a French wine-tasting tour. This is a search and destroy mission. Period. The end. That said, you *will* stay close to me at all times; you *will* obey every order given to you; and you *will not* question my authority. Am I making myself clear?'

Topsails slack, Kate nodded silently. In that instant, it occurred to her, *yet again*, that Fate was not merely capricious, but threw a mean sucker punch.

She hitched the knapsack strap a bit higher on her shoulder and lengthened her stride. Several minutes ago they had disembarked from the high-speed Eurostar, Finn now in a 'big-ass hurry to put the mission op into play'. A one-man assault on the City of Love.

At this hour of the morning, the cavernous Gare du Nord train station brimmed with hundreds of travellers rushing pell-mell in every direction. Overhead, the departure board loudly *click-clacked*, yellow letters and numbers flipping past at a dizzying speed, like a slot machine run amuck. Kate averted her gaze, the rolling tabs inciting a nauseous churn. To add to the chaos, a strident female voice incessantly announced the arrivals and departures on the PA system.

Finn inclined his head in her direction. Although his lips moved, the ensuing remark was completely drowned out.

'You'll have to repeat that,' she told him, cupping a hand to her ear.

Coming to a halt, Finn leaned towards her, his cheek brushing against hers. 'Just outside the station, I see a line of cabs.'

Taken aback by the combination of warm breath, warm body and prickly stubble, Kate recoiled, hit with an unexpected jolt of sexual awareness. Something that had been happening with an unnerving frequency over the last few days. When they'd shared an office suite at the Pentagon, she'd been intimidated by Finn's sheer physicality, the man taller, broader, more muscular than most. Now, for some inexplicable reason, she found herself strangely attracted to those very qualities.

Baffled by her reaction, particularly since Finn McGuire wasn't her type, Kate wondered if she might be suffering from a variant form of Stockholm Syndrome. Like a hostage with her captor, was she attracted to Finn because she was so completely dependent on him to keep her safe?

'Hey, soldier, you okay?' A concerned look on his face, Finn gently squeezed her hand.

Even though Kate knew it was his way of bolstering the troops, it caused another spasm in the base of her spine. Wordlessly, she stared at him. At that close range, she could see each individual whisker that covered his lower face, the five o'clock shadow making him appear dangerously sexy.

'I'm fine,' she lied, fearing the frantic, non-stop pace was finally starting to catch up with her. 'Would it be possible to grab a cup of coffee? There's a café over by the –'

'Later,' Finn interjected, letting go of her hand. 'We need to hit the road.'

She suppressed a groan. For the last two days, they'd been pounding the pavement. *Hard.*

Travelling under the radar, they'd left the houseboat in Washington and headed straight to a storage facility in Arlington, Virginia. Much to her surprise, Finn maintained a rental unit well-stocked with guns, ammo, a metal box full of cash and a Harley Davidson 'Fat Boy'. Offering no explanation as to why a sane person would go to such extreme lengths, he'd packed what he called a 'Go Bag' – a heavy-duty canvas satchel with a leather strap reinforced with a stainless steel cable. He wore the Go Bag bandolier-style across his chest, having *yet* to take it off.

Leaving the storage unit, they'd travelled to Annapolis, Maryland, Kate clinging to Finn's waist, terrified she might jettison off the back-end of the twin-cam motorcycle. Again, giving no explanation for his actions, Finn stopped at a public photo booth where they each had their picture taken. From there, they went to a 24-hour FedEx office, the photos placed in an overnight envelope. The next stop was the Wal-Mart superstore. New clothing and a few basic toiletries were purchased, Finn insisting that she stick with neutral colours. '*The object is to blend into the scenery.*' Hoping a roadside hotel would be the final port-of-call, she was bewildered when they instead headed to Dover Air Force Base in Delaware.

Which is when the trip took a very strange and surreal turn.

Met at one of the gates by a uniformed airman named Barry DeSoto, an 'old buddy' who owed Finn an outstanding gambling debt, they were surreptitiously ushered on to a C-5 plane that was in the process of being loaded. Destination: Mildenhall Royal Air Force Base in England. Happy to discharge the three-thousand-dollar debt, Airman DeSoto arranged for her and Finn to stow away in the hull of the plane, wedged between stacked wooden crates and oversized metal containers.

No sooner did they touch down on English soil than another 'old buddy' met them on the tarmac. Finn gave the man a wad of cash and, in return, was handed two forged Dutch passports, a his and a hers, emblazoned with the photos that had been taken on the other side of the Atlantic. Newly dubbed 'Fons' and 'Katja', they'd crossed the Channel on the Eurostar.

Still mentally adjusting to the fact that she was actually in Paris, Kate followed Finn through the sliding glass doors as they exited the train station. Per his earlier instructions, she stayed directly on 'his six' as he headed towards the cab stand.

A few moments later, seated in the back of an idling taxi, Kate told the hirsute driver, '*Amenez-nous à rue de la Bûcherie, s'il vous plaît.*'

'*D'accord,*' the cabbie replied with a nod as he manoeuvred the Mercedes Benz cab out of the queue.

It had been decided ahead of time that their first stop

would be L'Equinoxe, the bookstore owned and operated by her friend Cædmon Aisquith.

'Any idea what time the bookstore opens?' Finn slid his dark sunglasses to the top of his head. Given their proximity, Kate could see the crow's feet radiating from the corners of his brown eyes. Obviously, the man had never heard of sun block. Although she had to admit that he wore his wrinkles well.

'I'm not certain. Most shops in Paris open for business at ten o'clock. Although it's my understanding that Cædmon maintains a flat in the back of the bookstore.'

'Wanna call what's-his-name and give him a head's up?'

'Um, I don't think that's necessary.' It'd been sixteen years since she'd last spoken to Cædmon. A fact that she'd purposefully refrained from mentioning to Finn. Several months ago, she'd bumped into an old Oxford chum who'd informed her that Cædmon currently owned the bookshop in Paris. Until that accidental meeting, she'd had no idea what had happened to 'what's-his-name' after he left Oxford.

Finn glanced at his commando watch. *Altimeter. Barometer. Thermometer. Digital compass.* The timepiece had more features than some cars.

'It's a few minutes shy of oh-nine-hundred,' he informed her. 'Your buddy Engelbert Humperdinck ought to be up and at 'em by now.'

'How many times do I have to tell you? His name is *Cædmon Aisquith.*'

'Whatever.'

On the verge of informing her travelling companion that she despised that dismissive expression, she instead gazed out of the window. It'd been nearly two decades since she'd last been in Paris, fabled city of wine, art, gargoyles and some of the best darned ice cream she'd ever eaten. Although she seriously doubted that a trip to the Berthillon ice-cream shop was on Finn McGuire's itinerary.

As their taxi made its way along the heavily trafficked Quai de la Tournelle, Finn craned his neck to peer out of the side window. His first sign of interest in the passing scenery.

'Is it just me? Or do those flying buttresses make the old dame look like a carcass that's been picked clean by the buzzards?'

'Are you always so irreverent?' Kate retorted, wondering if there was *anything* that Finn McGuire deemed sacred.

'I don't laugh at funerals, if that's what you're asking.'

It wasn't.

'I asked the question because you seem immune to the beauty of Paris,' she clarified. 'Most people are rendered awestruck at seeing Notre-Dame for the very first time.'

Clearly not one of those people, Finn shrugged. 'I boogie to my own tune. So why Japan?'

'I beg your pardon?' She shook her head, wondering if something had got lost in translation.

'You mentioned that your folks had taken a trip to Japan.'

'I mentioned that two days ago. You're only *now* getting around to asking the follow-up question?'

The retort elicited another shrug. 'What can I say? Been busy.'

'To answer your belated question, my parents are participating in the annual Shikoku *Hachijuhakkasho*.'

'What the hell is –'

'It's a Japanese pilgrimage,' she interjected, beating him to the punch. 'It's a two-month-long walking tour of eighty-eight different Shingon Buddhist temples. When I was a kid, we used to go every summer.'

His big shoulders noticeably shook, the man barely able to contain his mirth. 'So let me make sure I got this straight: you fly in an airplane more than five thousand miles so you can walk for sixty days. And I thought we had it bad at Catholic Teen Retreat.' Finn's umber-brown eyes twinkled merrily.

'I never said I enjoyed it. In fact, every summer I pleaded with my folks to go to Disneyland.' But she always ended up on Shikoku Island, attired in white cotton garments and a straw sedge hat, the traditional garb of a Shikoku pilgrim.

'I take it your folks are Japanese?'

'My mother is half-Japanese.' The product of an interracial marriage at a time in America's history when the Japanese were *persona non grata*.

'So, you're – *what?* – a Buddhist?'

'I used to be a Buddhist.'

Disinclined to answer any more 'follow-up' questions, Kate swung her knapsack on to her lap and busied herself with rummaging through its contents. As she did so, she quietly counted her breaths, focusing on each inhalation and exhalation. *Right concentration*. Refusing to let her mind wander to that horrific night when her Buddhist beliefs regarding 'acceptance' were utterly and irrevocably shattered, when she learned firsthand that there are some things that the heart can never accept.

'Hey, Kate. You okay?' Reaching across the seat, Finn lightly grasped her by the wrist. 'You look like you just chugged a glass of sour milk.'

'I'm fine.' Although it sounded like her voice, it was as if someone else was speaking the words for her.

'Well, you don't look fine.'

The cabbie peered over his shoulder. '*C'est rue de la Bûcherie. Quelle est l'addresse?*'

Grateful for the diversion, Kate said, '*Je ne sais pas. Arrêtez-vous ici.*' Turning towards Finn, she translated the exchange. 'Since I don't know the exact street address, I told him to let us out here.'

Fare paid, they got out of the taxi. Peering over the top of her blue-tinted granny glasses, she could see that the Left Bank neighbourhood was a medieval warren of tiny one-way streets.

Finn glanced up from the Paris street map that he'd earlier purchased at the train station. 'The rules for survival in the city are no different than those for the jungle, or the mountains, or the desert. Blend in with the environment. And no sudden moves. If you see a cop, hear a cop, or smell a cop, act natural. Don't give 'em a reason to question you.'

Her breath caught in her throat. 'Wh-why would the police want to question us?' she stammered. 'Do you think the authorities have tracked us to Paris?'

'No, I don't think that. But it's always good to be cautious, right?'

About to nod her head, she caught herself in mid-motion, uncertain if a nod constituted a 'sudden move'.

They'd gone approximately one block when Kate spotted a brightly painted shop sign with the name 'L'Equinoxe' in gold lettering. Beneath that was an image of the Fool, the first card in the Tarot deck. The age-old symbol for infinite possibilities.

'There's Cædmon's bookstore, just a few doors down.'

Several moments later, standing at the entryway, Kate frowned. A small white placard with the word 'Fermé' hung crookedly on the other side of the glass door. Behind that, a green curtain had been drawn, preventing her from seeing inside the shop. Turning the door knob, she verified that the shop was, indeed, closed.

'Do you wanna come back when the bookstore opens?'

Unsure, she glanced at her Seiko watch: *9.26*. Local time.

'Actually, I think it's best if we seize the bull –' she banged on the wooden door frame with a balled fist – 'by the proverbial horns.'

Several moments passed. Again, Kate banged on the door. A bit more forcibly this time.

'The bookshop is closed!' a distinctly English voice boomed from the other side of the locked door.

'It's important that we speak with you,' Kate said through the glass.

'*Je m'en fou! La librairie est fermé! Casse-toi maintenant!*'

Worriedly biting her lower lip, she glanced at Finn. 'He insists that the shop is closed.' She didn't bother to translate the profane preface and postscript that bracketed the announcement.

'Are you sure that's even Engelbert standing on the other side of the door?'

'Oh, yes, I'm sure.' She'd recognize that well-articulated

voice anywhere. Refusing to call retreat, Kate again rapped on the pane. 'Cædmon, please open the door. It's important that I speak with you.'

The entreaty worked, the deadbolt lock was released and the shop door swung open. A man, nearly as tall as Finn, with shoulder-length red hair, filled the entryway. Not only was his stained shirt completely unbuttoned, the tails limply hanging against a pair of corduroy trousers, but his feet were bare.

'*Kate?* Is that you?'

'Hello, Cædmon.' She pasted a cordial smile on to her lips. *A vision of grace under pressure.*

Blood-shot blue eyes narrowed. 'You have some bloody nerve, showing up on my doorstep.'

20

'May we please come inside, Cædmon?'

Mockingly sweeping his arm aside, the red-headed Brit gestured for Finn and Kate to enter the bookshop. 'By all means. *Mi casa, su casa.*'

As he stepped across the threshold, Finn sized up their 'host', instantly pegging the guy for a prick of the first order. *Cædmon Aisquith.* Hell, he could barely say it, let alone spell it. Standing approximately six foot three, Aisquith had the lean, rangy build of a long-distance runner. And the ashen, hollow-eyed look of an insomniac. That or the English dude was coming off one helluva bender.

Finn removed his Oakley sunglasses and hooked them on the collar of his T-shirt. Perusing the joint, he wondered how Aisquith made a living. Granted, he didn't know a lot about the book trade, but common sense told him that a dark, unkempt shop wasn't the kind of place that attracted a clientele. *Who the hell liked the smell of mildew?* Not only were the floor-to-ceiling bookcases covered in a visible layer of dust, there were unwieldy stacks of books haphazardly arranged on the floor, just waiting for an unsuspecting customer to plough into. To quote his great-uncle Seamus, the place was 'a slipshod shipwreck'.

Kate cleared her throat. Probably because, like Finn, she'd just swallowed a mouthful of dust motes. 'Gosh . . . it's been a long time. No doubt you're surprised to see me.'

Aisquith folded his arms over his chest. 'Baffled to say the least. In your *lettre de rupture* you succinctly stated that you never wanted to see me again.'

'I sent that letter sixteen years ago,' Kate retorted, an exasperated edge to her voice. 'In hindsight, conveying those sentiments in a letter was terribly unfair to you. However, I was young and inexperienced.'

'A poor excuse, given the nature of our relationship.'

Standing ringside, Finn quickly gathered that Kate had once shacked up with the dishevelled bookstore owner, and the prick was still royally pissed off that she'd given him the shaft. *You go, girl.*

'And including those lines of poetry from Yeats was unconscionable,' the prick continued. '"In courtesy I'd have her chiefly learned; Hearts are not had as a gift but hearts are earned."'

Finn sidled a few steps closer to Kate, a show of moral support. 'I don't know. Sounds like a classy "Dear John" letter to me.'

'And who might you be?'

'The name's Finn McGuire. I'm Kate's new BFF.' He didn't bother extending his hand.

The Brit gave him the once-over. 'A diminutive of Finnegan, I take it?'

Sorely tempted to tell Aisquith where he could shove it after he took it, Finn belligerently tilted his chin. 'What can I say? My mother had a wicked dark humour.'

'She must have, to have named you after a dead character in a James Joyce novel. But that's the Irish for you.'

'Irish-*American*,' he corrected.

'Mmmm . . . indeed.'

What the fuck did that *mean?*

'So, to what do I owe this unexpected visit?'

Kate hesitated, shifting her weight from one foot to the other. 'I, um, need your help, Cædmon. I've just made a long, arduous journey and –' Eyes bloodshot, cheeks flushed, she stared pleadingly at her old swain. By anyone's standard, she looked plenty pitiful. 'Please, Cædmon. I didn't know where else to go.'

Hearing that, the red-headed Brit instantly dropped the sarcastic attitude. Like he'd just had a deathbed conversion, he placed a solicitous hand on Kate's shoulder. 'Of course. Anything. Christ, I'm such a bastard. Arrow to the heart. Wounded to the quick. All that.'

And Kate complained about him *not speaking in full sentences.* This Aisquith guy had it down to an art form.

'I'm sorry. I probably should have called ahead or sent an email, but we've been on the run. Figuratively speaking, of course.' A red splotch instantly materialized on each freckled cheek. Two guilty bull's eyes.

Removing his hand from Kate's shoulder, Aisquith waved away the botched apology. 'Doesn't matter. For you, the door is always open.' As he spoke, he glanced down at his unbuttoned shirt. 'Forgive me. I've been under the weather.' He fumbled with one of the middle buttons. 'A touch of *la grippe,* as it were.' Calling it quits after just the one button, he clapped his hands together. 'Right. I'll get us some refreshments. A glass of sherry perhaps?' No sooner did he make the offer than Aisquith noticed the clock hanging on the adjacent wall. 'Oh, bloody hell! It's still morning.'

'Would it be too much to ask for a cup of tea? I'm in

dire need of a pick-me-up.' Visibly sagging, Kate lowered her knapsack to the floor.

'No doubt I have a canister somewhere. Please make yourselves comfortable.' Aisquith gestured distractedly to the two leather wingback chairs shoe-horned between a pair of towering bookcases. Hospitality dispensed, he ambled towards an open door in the back of the shop, disappearing from sight.

With a weary sigh, Kate seated herself in the nearest chair. A wilted flower in a dusty pot.

'I don't know how to break it to you, Katie, but your pal looks like one of those guys who lives under the bridge in a cardboard box.'

'You heard him, he just got over a bout of the flu.' Though quick to come to the Brit's defence, her brow furrowed. Like she wasn't entirely convinced of what she'd just said. 'While he may not look his best, I'm certain that Cædmon can help us to decipher Jutier's tattoo as well as the symbols on the Montségur –'

'Don't breathe a word about the medallion,' he interjected, cutting her off at the pass. Although Kate thought that if they deciphered the symbols on the medallion they'd gain some valuable insight, which would help him track down the Dark Angel, he wasn't entirely convinced. 'I can't put my finger on it, but I've got a hinky feeling about your ex-boyfriend.'

'Don't be so paranoid. Cædmon is utterly harmless. For goodness' sake, he owns a bookstore.'

'Speaking of which –' Craning his neck, Finn glanced at several of the hand-printed tags affixed to the front of the shelves. 'Let's see, we got *The Illuminati*, *The Knights*

Templar and something called *The Merovingian Bloodline*.' He turned towards a second bookcase. 'Ooh, here's a good section: *Extraterrestrials*, *Alien Abductions* and, not to be excluded, *The Faery People*.' Smirking, he glanced at his companion. 'We're talking conspiracy theorist of the first magnitude. What do you wanna bet Aisquith wears an aluminium foil shower cap?'

Kate shot him a chiding frown.

Point made, Finn walked over to the front door and pulled back the curtain that hung at the glass. Standing stock still, he perused the street in front of the bookstore. Little more than a single lane, the jumble of old-fashioned shops looked like something out of another time period.

While he had no proof, he had a gut feeling that Dixie and Johnny K's murderer was here in Paris. Somewhere. *And I aim to find him.*

'So long as the authorities don't get a hold of my ass,' Finn muttered under his breath, able to hear a police siren bleating in the near distance. Between the flight crew at Dover and the airmen at Mildenhall, too many people knew that he'd left the US in a *very* unusual manner. Some people would do anything for a buck. And that included ratting out 'a buddy'.

We can't blow this joint fast enough.

Finn let the curtain fall back into place. Turning on his heel, he walked back to the niche.

'A cup of tea. A little chitchat. Then we're getting the hell out of here,' he said to Kate in a lowered voice. 'And don't volunteer anything. Just follow my lead, okay?'

'Whatever,' she retorted testily, beginning to look and sound like a cranky kid on a long trip.

She wasn't the only cranky one. From the get-go, Finn had been opposed to bringing Kate Bauer to Paris. She was a distraction, plain and simple. But he knew that if he'd left her in DC, she'd likely wind up dead.

For better or worse, sickness and in health, she'd become a 115-pound anchor around his neck.

21

Musée de la Vie Romantique, Paris

Ivo Uhlemann slowly ascended the stone steps, his circumspect gait that of a white-haired septuagenarian. Physical debility a character flaw in a man of any age, he refused to use a cane. And he would rather put a bullet through his own skull than be pushed about in a wheelchair, his infirmities on public display.

Pausing at the top of the stone steps, he savoured the delicate scent of the pink roses that clung to the wrought-iron railing. The Museum of the Romantic Life boasted a magnificent garden and charming courtyard. Housed in the former residence of Ary Scheffer, a nineteenth-century artist, the mansion in its heyday had hosted the likes of Chopin, Dickens and Delacroix. He was there on that warm August morning to view the museum's new exhibition of drawings and watercolours from 'The Golden Age of the German Romantic Artists'.

No sooner did Ivo step through the museum's entryway than a pixie of a man rushed forward.

'Bonjour, Monsieur le Docteur!' Grasping Ivo by the shoulder, the museum curator warmly greeted him with the salutary cheek kiss. 'Such a pleasure! As always!'

Ivo suffered the *faire le bise* with a tight-lipped smile. It'd taken years of practice to train himself *not* to flinch at the overly familiar French greeting.

Taking a backward step, politely distancing himself from the other man, he said, 'I am greatly looking forward to viewing the new exhibition.'

'The French poet Nerval rightly claimed that Germany's Romantic artists were "a mother to us all",' the curator effused. With an ingratiating smile, he proffered a slim pamphlet. 'For your edification, I have prepared a pamphlet that contains the pertinent details for each work. It is my sincere hope that you enjoy the exhibition, Monsieur le Docteur.'

Ivo took the flyer. A generous donor, he'd earned the privilege of privately viewing the exhibition before the museum opened later that morning to the general public. Eager to see the show, he entered the adjacent hall.

Approaching the first framed piece of artwork, enthusiasm fizzled into disappointment at seeing a pen-and-ink drawing of a Gothic cathedral.

Bah! Religion. The great destroyer of all that is good and heroic.

Indeed, he'd often contended that one of the Führer's mistakes was *not* outlawing the Christian churches in Germany. A global pestilence, Christianity appealed only to those who were too craven to forge their own destiny. Although, to be fair, Christianity was no less abhorrent than the occultism that infected the Reich's high command, the two being the flipside of the same tarnished coin.

His father, in his letters, had bitterly complained about the farcical 'rituals' that took place at Wewelsburg Castle, the official headquarters of the SS. According to his father's firsthand accounts, incense was burned, Tarot cards were read, Sufi Muslim rites were enacted and astrological charts were carefully scrutinized. A travesty, all of it. One that deeply disturbed the original members of the Seven. Scholars and scientists, they secretly eschewed the patently absurd beliefs of the German high command.

To a man, the original Seven contended that occultism and Christianity were the twin cancers that destroyed the Reich from within.

Searching for a specific piece of art, Ivo impatiently made his way into the next room.

Ah, there it was. *The Schneegruben Massif Seen From the Hainbergshöh.*

A watercolour by Caspar David Friedrich, the most famous of the German Romantic artists, it was a stunning landscape that depicted a flat plain rimmed with plush clumps of shrub and bordered by towering mountains in the distance. Rendered with a poetic sensitivity, the work didn't rely on the false promise of Christian iconography.

'Such a sublime pleasure,' he whispered, the watercolour an unabashed celebration of the Fatherland.

Not surprisingly, it put Ivo in mind of the countryside in the Weserbergland where he spent the autumn of 1944 with boys from the Hitler-Jugend harvesting sugar beets. As part of the Blood and Soil programme, each year millions of children were sent to Germany's rural hinterlands to toil on large farms. Since the vast majority of the country's able-bodied adult males were away fighting, the Hitler Youth's labour was essential to the war effort.

The Blood and Soil programme not only cultivated the virtues of rural living, but sought to preserve Germany's farming communities from the deadening onslaught of industrialization. Unlike factory work, there was meaning and purpose to working the land. It engendered a sense of self-sufficiency that enabled one to resist the empty lure of materialism. More importantly, the programme recognized that the Germanic spirit was created by the pure blood that they collectively shared as a nation. And as a People. Blood is what nurtured love of the Fatherland. What better way to express that love than tending to the land?

Lost in the memories of that long-ago autumn, Ivo recalled how, in the evenings, after the boys had eaten their thick peasant sandwiches smeared with *zuckerrüben sirup*, they practised their military drills while they recited proverbs from the *Hávámal*, the famous poem in the Old Norse *Edda*. To this day, he could still recite the stanzas that recounted how Wotan, the great Proto-Germanic god, sacrificed himself by thrusting a spear into his own side as he 'hung on a windy tree nine long nights'. Unlike the effeminate Christian saviour, Wotan was a heroic god who refused to wait passively for his enemies to nail him to a cross. Instead, Wotan decided for himself the hour of his death.

Suddenly hearing a heavy footfall, Ivo peered over his shoulder, annoyed that his driver, Dolf Reinhardt, had entered the salon. The tailored black suit with its matching chauffeur's cap did little to disguise the man's massive build and brutish features. In the crook of his right arm, Dolf awkwardly clutched a miniature Schnauzer.

'Herr Doktor, forgive me for interrupting,' he said with a diffident nod. 'But there's been a new development.'

Ivo listened intently to the update.

Delighted to hear that McGuire was in Paris, one side of his mouth curved in a half-smile. 'Just as we thought . . . David has come to slay Goliath.'

Little did the commando know that this Philistine warrior was insuperable.

Two days ago, to the Seven's astonished relief, they had learned that Finnegan McGuire had stolen Fabius Jutier's laptop computer from the French Embassy. An ill-considered stratagem as the embedded GPS microchip had enabled them to track the American's every move.

If they could get their hands on the Montségur Medallion in the next few hours, they would still have three days to decipher the map and find the *Lapis Exillis.* It could be done.

It *had* to be done.

'I require the services of the Dark Angel.' Still smiling, Ivo smoothed a withered hand over the Schnauzer's salt-and-pepper beard. 'Wolfgang seems anxious. A walk in the Tuileries will do us both good.'

22

Shirt buttoned, shoes donned and red hair pulled into a ponytail, Aisquith entered the book nook carrying a silver tray.

Finn assumed the make-over was for Kate's benefit, not his.

'The alchemist Paracelsus claimed that lemon balm tea was the elixir of life. Although given that he only lived to the age of forty-eight, I wouldn't put much stock in the great alchemist's lofty claim,' the Brit said as he deposited the tray on an ornately carved Chinese tea table. Like everything else in the joint, it was covered in a dusty veneer.

Making herself at home, Kate tucked a leg under her hip. 'I once read that Paracelsus was the first to discover that goiters were caused by toxic levels of lead in the drinking water. A remarkable discovery for the early sixteenth century,' she added, clearly enthralled by the obscure topic.

Their host handed each of them a dainty cup and saucer.

Having no friggin' idea who Paracelsus was, Finn raised the cup to his nose and took a wary sniff. Unable to detect anything other than a faint lemony scent, he took a tentative sip.

'I hope the scones aren't too stale,' the other man said as he extended a chipped plate in Kate's direction.

'Yummy. Cherry scones are my favourite. And I don't care if they are stale.'

Smiling, Aisquith peered over his shoulder at Finn. 'I vividly recall the first time that I set eyes on our fair Kate at Oxford. She was sitting in a medieval oriel reading Spinoza, backlit by the morning sun streaming through three-hundred-year-old glass.'

Stunned by the jaw-dropper, Finn shot Kate a questioning glance. '*You went to Oxford?*'

'I was a, um, Rhodes Scholar,' she demurred. As though embarrassed by the admission, she smiled nervously.

A Rhodes Scholar? Hell, he knew she was smart. He just didn't know she was *that* smart. For some crazy-ass reason, it upped her appeal another notch. That he was even remotely attracted to Kate Bauer bothered the hell out of him. He was on a mission. He *did not* need a distraction. But there it was, all curled up in a wingback chair, nibbling on a cherry scone. The fact that he was attracted to Kate made him dislike Aisquith even more. Once upon a time, the two of them had had an intimate relationship. Something he only got to dream about.

Cup, saucer and scone in hand, Aisquith planted his ass in the vacant wingback. 'So, how may I be of assistance?'

'Actually, Kate and I are, um –' In need of a quick lie, Finn glanced around the dusty shop. Inspired, he said '– collaborating on a book.'

One red brow noticeably lifted.

'Yes! That's right!' Kate exclaimed, exuberantly latching on to the lie. 'And during the course of our research we discovered some interesting symbols that we hoped you might be able to decipher.'

'Indeed?' The brow lowered as blood-shot eyes narrowed suspiciously. While he looked like a skewered shit kebob, the Brit didn't miss a beat.

Stepping over to the tea table, Finn snagged a cherry scone off the plate. 'According to my writing partner, you're the go-to guy when it comes to symbols and myths. A real Oxford don.'

'Ghosts of genius past,' Aisquith mumbled as he took a sip of his tea. 'And what, may I ask, is the topic of this joint literary effort?'

'Like Kate said, we're still in the research phase,' Finn hedged. As he spoke, he shoved a hand into his left trouser pocket, retrieving his phone. Out of habit he always kept his cash and cell phone on the left side, freeing his right hand to reach for a weapon. Or to be used *as* a weapon if need be. 'This is a digital photo of a tattoo. Don't ask the name of the tattoo model; we never did get a positive ID.' He passed his cell phone to Aisquith.

'Mmmm . . . interesting. This tattoo is a Nazi design rooted in the esoteric,' Aisquith intoned, setting the cell phone on top of the Chinese table. 'While I get the odd request for books on esoteric Nazism, I refuse to stock them. Matter of principle. My grandfather was one of the prosecuting attorneys at Nuremberg.'

Finn spared a quick glance at his 'writing partner'. Back in DC, Kate had made the same claim about the tattoo, thinking it might have something to do with the esoteric. He thought now what he did then – *big crock of shit.*

'The horrific particulars of Nazi history are familiar enough,' Aisquith continued. 'In the aftermath of the First World War, the National Socialist Party rose to power, an embittered firebrand by the name of Adolf Hitler at the helm. The mustachioed Führer envisioned a new world order ruled by the Aryan master race. His egomaniacal ambitions led to the invasion of Europe; his demonization of the Jews led to the terrors of the Holocaust.' As he spoke, Aisquith reached for the teapot and freshened Kate's cup. 'When all was said and done, the death toll stood at sixty million. But there is another chapter to the story, one frequently absent from the history books. And that pertains to the little-known fact that a good many of the Nazi top command were adherents of the occult.'

Hearing the word 'occult', Finn barely repressed a snicker. *Time to roll out the aluminium foil.*

'Several years ago, I saw a documentary that claimed Hitler used a Foucault pendulum suspended over large maps to assist with military planning.' Kate raised the delicate teacup to her lips and took a ladylike sip.

'No surprise there. Hitler, Göring, Goebbels, Hess, they all had an obsession with the occult. Although none in the top echelon was as deeply devoted to the arcane mysteries as Heinrich Himmler.' Holding the teapot aloft, Aisquith inclined his head in Finn's direction.

Unimpressed with Paracelsus's secret elixir, Finn shook his head, declining the refill. 'You're talking about the bespectacled dude who headed up the SS, right?'

One side of Aisquith's mouth quirked upward in a blatant sneer. 'Yes, *that* dude.' Put-down issued, he turned his attention back to Kate, the sneer instantly reworking itself into a congenial smile. 'The SS, as you undoubtedly know, was an elite organization within the Nazi hierarchy responsible for the internal security of the entire regime.'

'And what the hell does any of this have to do with the tattoo?' Finn snarled, wishing the Brit would stay on point.

'As these symbols so vividly illustrate, Nazism is far more than a political doctrine.' Aisquith picked up the cell phone from the table. 'This symbol that dominates the centre of the design is unique to German occult beliefs. Known as the *Schwarze Sonne*, or Black Sun, it's a sun wheel comprised of zigzag sig-runes. While it harkens to the star Sirius, it's a mysterious orb often described in the esoteric literature as a *prima materia* mass.'

'How utterly fascinating.'

'Indeed.'

'Glad we got that settled,' Finn muttered under his breath. 'What about the skull? Nothing mystical about that bad boy.'

'On the contrary,' Aisquith retorted. 'The German *totenkoph*, or Death Head as it's more familiarly called in

English, connotes the willingness to lay down one's life to defend one's comrade. The *totenkoph* insignia always adorned the uniforms of the *Schutzstaffel*.'

'Just so I don't feel like I wandered into a German language class, can we stick with the mother tongue?'

'As you like,' the other man replied, oblivious to the fact that he was annoying as hell.

'So this tattoo has something to do with the SS. Is that right?' Kate enquired.

'The Ahnenerbe, to be precise; both the Death Head and the Black Sun emblem are significant to that organization. I suspect that this tattoo may have originally designated membership. That said, the individual in the digital photograph is obviously a twenty-first-century Nazi devotee.' Aisquith turned his head, pointedly looking in Finn direction. 'A personal acquaintance of yours?'

Finn's back straightened, his hands involuntarily clenching into fists. About to ask the Brit if he wanted to take it outside, Kate beat him to the punch.

'What's the Ahnenerbe?' she asked. Brows drawn together, her gaze dropped to Finn's balled fists.

Recognizing that grey-blue gaze as a silent entreaty, Finn uncurled his hands.

'All in all, the Ahnenerbe is a rather fascinating group,' Aisquith replied. 'After the Nazis seized power in 1933, Himmler subdivided the SS into numerous sections. The Ahnenerbe was the academic and scientific branch of the SS. What we today would refer to as a think tank. Unfortunately, the Ahnenerbe's vast archive disappeared in the waning days of the war. Whether destroyed or hidden is anyone's guess.'

'And how does the Black Sun relate to the Ahnenerbe?' Kate next asked, on the fast track to becoming the teacher's pet.

'Bearing in mind that the Ahnenerbe was the scientific corps of the SS, its members believed that an invisible universal force known as Vril could be created using the astral energy from the Black Sun.' Leaning towards Kate, making like a man about to impart a big secret, Aisquith continued in a lowered voice, 'During the last years of the war, Nazi scientists in the Ahnenerbe were desperately trying to generate the Vril force in order to weaponize it.'

'And what? Make an invisible ray gun?' Finn snorted derisively. 'Gimme a break! This just proves what I already knew about the Nazis: You can fool some of the people all of the time and those are the morons you want to actively recruit.'

'While I find Nazism a repugnant doctrine, no one can accuse their scientists of being anything less than brilliant,' Aisquith asserted, quick to defend himself. 'German physicists were convinced that if they could generate the Vril force, they could use it as an alternative energy source to power their war machine, the Germans fast running out of oil. Desperate, Nazi physicists were actively developing a technology to use the Vril force to power flying saucers and –'

'Hate to interrupt the lecture, but we've got a late-morning appointment on the other side of town,' Finn interjected, worried that if they stayed much longer, Aisquith would pull out his aluminium foil space suit.

'Oh, so sorry,' the other man mumbled disappointedly. 'Perhaps we can continue the conversation later in the day.'

‘That’s a wonderful –’

‘Unfortunately, we got a full schedule,’ Finn said over the top of Kate, effectively drowning her out.

‘Mmmm . . . a pity that.’ The Brit shoved a hand into his trouser pocket. Removing a chrome-plated key, he handed it wordlessly to Finn.

‘Let me guess? Key to the city.’

‘A motor scooter that’s parked in the back alley,’ Aisquith informed him. ‘I couldn’t help but notice that you arrived on foot.’

Beaming, Kate walked over and, going up on her tiptoes, kissed him on his unshaven cheek. ‘Thank you, Cædmon. That’s very generous.’

‘Yes, well, shame that you couldn’t stay longer. I hadn’t even got to the Nordic runes that rim the periphery of the tattoo.’

Finn pocketed the scooter key. ‘Another time.’ *Place. And century.*

23

'"I hope the *skahns* aren't too stale,"' Finn mimicked in an exaggerated English accent as they made their way to the alley behind the bookstore. 'Jesus, talk about a pompous ass.'

'Your rudeness knows no bounds,' Kate shot back, clearly miffed. 'Where do you get off saying those kind of things? You don't even know Cædmon.'

'Trust me. That guy was an open book. Yeah, pun intended. And who was being rude?' Finn raised an imaginary teacup to his lips, pinky finger crooked. 'One lump or two, Lord Percy?'

'You are such a Neanderthal!'

Just to prove Kate wrong, he cupped a gentlemanly hand around her elbow, ushering her down a dim alley. The sunless passageway was strewn with empty crates and bits of broken glass, not a soul in sight. Unless you counted the scrawny tabby who hissed its displeasure at the intrusion.

'My old Oxford pal, Professor Higgins, is a *serious* scholar. Isn't that what you told me back in DC?'

'Cædmon Aisquith is a highly educated man who –'

'Happens to be a wingnut. And if he's not a wingnut, then the guy is a hardcore, straight-shooting alki.' With his free hand, Finn hefted an imaginary liquor bottle to his lips. 'Glug, glug, glug. Bottoms up.'

‘Because a man opens the front door with an unbuttoned shirt and mussed hair, you automatically jump to a preposterous conclusion.’

‘All I know, it’s hard to play the lute when you’re on the juice. What do you wanna bet that last night Engelbert was three sheets, two pillowslips and a big blanket to the wind?’

‘And in case you didn’t notice, Cædmon has a brilliant mind. Certainly puts you to shame,’ Kate muttered under her breath as she shrugged off his hand.

‘I don’t need to be an Einstein. All I need is a loaded weapon and –’

‘A clear shot. I know. I’ve heard that line before.’

‘Excuse me for being redundant.’ Suddenly, without warning, Finn yanked Kate over to a nearby stone wall. ‘Shh,’ he ordered in a lowered voice, reiterating the command with a finger to the lip.

Hit with a creepy feeling – like maybe they were being followed – he cocked his head to one side and listened, trying to pick out the sound that didn’t belong. A footfall. An in-drawn breath. A gun being cocked.

On high alert, he silently counted to ten. Reaching ‘ten’, he relaxed slightly.

‘You said that the authorities didn’t follow us to Paris,’ Kate whispered, wide-eyed.

I only said that so you wouldn’t be scared.

Finn pushed out a deep breath. ‘All right, I think the coast is clear. Let’s roll.’

Seeing a rusty blue Vespa that looked like it’d seen better days, Finn headed in that direction, Kate following in his wake.

'So what's on the agenda?'

He shoved a hand into his pocket and removed the key. 'According to Fabius Jutier's calendar, tomorrow morning the Seven will be meeting at their headquarters at the Grande Arche. I intend to crash the party. All of this shit about mystical energy and mad scientists weaponizing Vril is a waste of my valuable time. I already know that I'm dealing with a bunch of fanatics. And, like any fanatic cult, the Seven probably has some crazy-ass agenda.'

'My point exactly.'

Standing beside the Vespa, they stood toe-to-toe, like two fighters at the opening bell. Decked out in a white cotton T-shirt, generic running shoes and khaki pants cropped at mid-calf, Kate more closely resembled a suburban soccer mom than a badass contender.

'Knowing the Seven's crazy-ass agenda isn't going to help me find the Dark Angel.'

'What if the Seven Research Foundation is a modern-day Ahnenerbe?'

At that close range, literally inches apart, Finn could smell Kate's 'perfume' – an uninspiring mix of Combat Bath and lemon balm tea – which, for some strange reason, he found oddly appealing.

He shrugged. 'I'd say big whup. I came to Paris to find the murdering scumbag who killed my two buddies. For Christ's sake, Kate! The guy was talking about flying saucers.'

'Not only was Cædmon a gracious host, he did us a very big favour,' Kate retorted with surprising force. 'There aren't many people who would drop everything and give us their full, undivided attention. But instead of being appreciative, the entire time we were at L'Equinoxe you behaved like a –'

'Neanderthal. I know. I've heard that line before. But don't give me an ass-chewing just because I wouldn't cross over to the dork side with you and Red Rover.' Admittedly pissed off, Finn held his ground. 'I don't think you get it, Kate. I did not cross the Atlantic in the hull of a supply plane so we could attend a tea party with your old buddy Aisquith. Back in Washington, I promised that I would protect you from harm. Provided you don't distract me from my mission. As far as I'm concerned, the Montségur Medallion is nothing more than a bargaining chip that I can trade for the Dark Angel.'

'So that you can clear your name.'

'No. So that I can get Corporals Dixon and Kelleher justice in a court of law.' Needing to make sure that she understood just how serious he was about doing that, he let her have it with both barrels. 'Those two guys selflessly did the dirty work that nobody else wants to do but has to be done to keep this freaking world safe from monsters, despots and terrorists. And they did their job not for glory or an attaboy pat on the back. They did it because they loved their country. So I'm going to make sure that they didn't die in vain.'

A guilty expression crept into her eyes. 'I know that you loved your friends and I promise that I won't do anything to distract you from your mission.'

Whether you know it or not, Kate, you've already become a damned distraction.

Wanting to close the book on that particular topic, Finn unzipped the canvas satchel strapped to his chest and shoved his hand inside. Rummaging through the bag, his fingers grazed his KA-BAR commando knife. And because he was one prepared son of a bitch, his Go Bag also contained a roll of duct tape, a ball of wire, a flashlight, a two-day supply of dehydrated meals, baby wipes and a can of Combat Bath.

'I gotta check our coordinates before we hit the road,' he informed her, purposefully changing the subject as he unfolded the Paris map.

Kate placed a restraining hand on his wrist. 'Actually, I was hoping that we could check into a hotel. I'm utterly exhausted and in desperate need of some sleep.'

He glanced at her face, forcing himself to ignore the dark circles that rimmed her exotic grey-blue eyes. 'Later. We gotta first take care of logistics.'

'What does *that* mean?'

'You'll find out when we get there.'

'No. I will find out right now.' The lady defiantly folded her arms over her chest. 'I'm tired of being dragged willy-nilly, absolutely clueless as to what we're doing or why we're doing it. I'll be happy to assist you with logistics if you would be so kind as to give me a mission brief.'

Finn conceded reluctantly with a nod. 'According to my buddy at Mildenhall, there's a military supply store near the subway station at Montparnasse. I also need to find the Paris equivalent of a spy shop. Some place that stocks surveillance equipment and high-end recording devices.'

'Thank you. And I would appreciate it if, from here on out, you kept me in the loop.'

Rather than reply, Finn raised his left hand and smoothed

away a silky skein of dark hair that had snagged in the corner of her mouth.

'Thank you,' Kate murmured again, this time noticeably blushing.

'You're welcome,' he replied, uncertain what to make of her reaction.

'I should probably get a, um, hair band to keep the fly-away strands out of my face.' Suddenly turning skittish, Kate gnawed on her bottom lip.

Groin tightening, Finn stared at those pearly-white teeth clamped down on that plump bit of flesh. 'I like your hair loose . . . it's pretty.'

Ah, shit! Did I really just say that?

Kate was right; he was a total Neanderthal. *Hubba-hubba. You pretty. Me strong.* Not like her old buddy Aisquith who, even in an alcoholic fog, could effortlessly recite lines of poetry.

Feeling like a tongue-tied teenager, Finn turned towards the Vespa. 'Hop on. We need to hit it,' he said gruffly, swinging his leg over the padded seat. 'I've got a long shopping list.'

24

'Writing a book, my arse,' Cædmon Aisquith grumbled uncharitably as he picked up the teacups and crumb-laden plates scattered about the snuggery. For the life of him, he couldn't imagine what Kate Bauer was doing with that muscle-bound Celt; the man was an absolute boor.

Although who am I to criticize?

He'd awakened that morning, head throbbing, stomach reeling, each and every movement requiring advance planning. Bumbling into the kitchen, he'd groped his way towards the kettle, intending to brew a pot of coffee. Only to grab the Tanqueray gin bottle instead.

Similia similibus curantur.

Like cures like. As good a reason as any for an early-morning stroll down gin alley. While admittedly a contemptible act, it did cure the malady. In fact, he'd just unscrewed the cap from the bottle when he'd heard the fateful knock at the door. An inopportune moment for Kate Bauer to pay her overdue respects.

Empty teacups and plates neatly stacked, Cædmon set them on the ridiculously ornate serving tray, an eighteenth-century relic he'd picked up at a Paris flea market. He'd yet to purchase a bottle of silver polish so the tray, like everything else in his life, was badly tarnished.

He finished tidying up and carried the tray to the small flat at the rear of the bookstore. Stepping through the door that separated retail space from residence, he entered the 'drawing room' – a cramped space that barely accommodated a sagging but comfortable tufted leather sofa. In front of the sofa, a scarred Edwardian coffee table was burdened with old issues of *The Times*, a half-full carton of takeaway, classical music LPs, a dog-eared copy of Marcus Aurelius' *Meditations* and a messy pile of clean laundry.

Hard to believe that at Oxford he'd been considered something of a neat nick.

Oh, sweet Kate. What must you think of me?

From the onset, he'd been attracted to Kate because, unlike so many of his one-dimensional classmates at Oxford who were experts in their chosen academic field but unable to converse on any other subject, Kate was interesting. Not only could she speak fluidly on any number of topics, she had an innate curiosity about the world that he found compelling.

Which is why it pained him that she'd severed the relationship, claiming he loved his studies more than he loved her. '*Still climbing after knowledge infinite.*' Another plagiarized line from her 'classy Dear John' letter. While the accusation stung, he couldn't deny that he'd been totally obsessed with the Knights Templar, the medieval order of warrior monks that was his chosen research niche. In the end, the Templars spelled his doom; the head of the history department at Queen's College refused to confer his doctoral degree because of unfounded claims he'd made in his dissertation regarding the Templars' exposure to the Egyptian mystery cults.

Hail and well met, Brother Knight. How the mighty have fallen.

Certainly, he didn't want to dwell on the maudlin. Didn't want to admit that Kate Bauer was little changed from Oxford, while he'd become the proverbial pale shadow. And he certainly didn't want to conjure from his memory that single sheet of watermarked stationery neatly inserted into the tissue-lined envelope. He wouldn't contest the Marlowe, but the line from Yeats still rankled.

Heading towards the kitchen, Cædmon sidestepped a pile of books stacked next to the sofa. As he did, the nestled teacups on the tray rattled, inciting a migrainous thunder.

'Christ,' he muttered. 'Sod all Irishmen.' Or Irish-Americans as the case may be.

Was there even a difference?

He had his doubts, the English and the Irish locked in mortal combat. It had been that way for eight hundred years. If the bastards in the Real Irish Republican Army got their way, it would be that way for another eight hundred.

So who the bloody hell was the morbidly named Finnegan McGuire?

Certainly no would-be writer. On that Cædmon would wager the entire bookstore.

Suddenly curious, he walked back to the cluttered Edwardian coffee table. Shoving the laundry on to the carpet, he set the tray down. He then strode over to the mahogany corner cabinet where he kept his laptop computer.

When he left Oxford, he'd promptly been recruited into service in Her Majesty's government. It was an interesting venture, his duties extending beyond the typical paper-pushing. Having recently severed his ties with his former employer, he still maintained a few valuable contacts with individuals who had access to every computer database in the United Kingdom. And a goodly portion of the rest of the world, for that matter.

He quickly typed in the request and hit the SEND button. Soon enough he would know if there was more to Finnegan McGuire than an impolite fellow who didn't speak German. Also desirous to know why Kate had attached herself to such a brute, he typed a second request for Katsumi Bauer.

'I apologize, dear Kate, but needs must.'

Retrieving the tray, he carried it into the kitchen. As usual, he braced himself for the onslaught – the sink full of dirty dishes, the countertop inundated with empty food containers. He set the tray on the counter, inadvertently knocking over a tonic bottle. Its evil twin, a green bottle of Tanqueray, remained upright. He could see that there were two fingers of gin left. Enough for a double.

He reached for an empty glass, unconcerned that it had a dirty smudge on the rim.

By his own admission, he'd succumbed to a pitiful paralysis of mind and spirit, having experienced grief in all its myriad forms over the course of the last two years. Indeed, there were many times when he'd been unable to utter the words 'Juliana is dead' without tearing up. And having to hear the 'I'm so sorry' speech was pure torture. While the condolences were well-intended, they couldn't resuscitate the dead.

At least Kate had spared him that torment. Clearly, she had no idea that he'd met Juliana Howe, an investigative reporter for the BBC who, one humid August evening, happened to be standing at a London tube station when a RIRA bomb detonated. He'd just 'celebrated' the two-year anniversary of that horrific event; the reason for the drunken binge.

He raised his glass in mock salute. 'To *Ars Moriendi*, the art of dying.'

A contrarian, he was clearly determined to end his own life in the most craven way imaginable, nothing quite as reprehensible as an unrepentant inebriate. Unless it was a cold-blooded killer. He had the dubious distinction of being both, having killed the man responsible for Juliana's death. Moreover, he'd stood by and watched as a nine-millimetre bullet ploughed through his enemy's skull. Rendering the bastard a graceless heap, arms and legs splayed like spokes on a blood-stained wheel.

Certainly, he'd had just cause.

Juliana Howe had been brilliant. And beautiful. And she did not deserve to die because a rebellious Irishman wanted to terrorize London. *Christ.* It'd been a scene right out of the Apocalypse, the bomb blast having turned the tube station into a fiery death trap. A maelstrom of twisted metal, chunks of concrete and deadly steel rods. In a frantic state, he'd shouldered his way past the dazed survivors, screaming her name. When his gaze landed on a familiar black high-heel shoe still attached to a foot, he'd lurched, heaved, then promptly vomited. His gut painfully turned inside out at the realization that Juliana had literally been blown to bits. Nothing to recover but that bloody stump.

Having vowed to find the perpetrators, he used his government contacts to track down the RIRA mastermind. In the days preceding the execution, he'd been so consumed with bloodlust that he had no recollection of the trip from London to Belfast.

How is it possible to forget the road from Gethsemane to Calgary?

Once he'd arrived in Belfast, he'd tracked Timothy O'Halloran to a raucous pub on the Catholic side of the peace wall. No surprise there, the Irish being fine ones for drinking and blathering *ad nauseam*. Committed, he waited in a darkened doorway for three hours and seventeen minutes. Legs cramped. Neck pinched. Finger poised over the trigger. And then the pub door swung open and O'Halloran, jolly smile plastered on his drunken face, blithely stepped across the threshold. Cædmon followed him down the rain-slicked pavement, until O'Halloran ducked into an alleyway to relieve himself. That's when he pulled the black balaclava mask over his face and removed the Ruger pistol from his pocket.

Having been obsessed with revenge, he'd not reckoned for the ensuing guilt that now clung to him like a second skin. Killing his enemy in cold blood was supposed to set him free. But, instead, he discovered that you take everything from a man when you kill him. And he, in turn, steals everything from you. Gin was simply the most expedient means of dulling the pain.

How pathetically trite. A man drowning his sorrows in a bottle of distilled spirits.

Knowing that his battle with the bottle trivialized Juliana's death, Cædmon ran his thumb over the glass rim, wondering if he should, *if he could*, pour the remaining contents down the drain. After two years, surely the time had come to put his life in order?

He raised the glass to his lips. *Shag it.* What was the point? So he could return to the infantile enthusiasm of his youth? At forty years of age, he was too jaded to believe in a Second Coming.

'Rack and ruin. The measure of this man.'

Hearing a chime emanate from his laptop, Cædmon, glass in hand, wandered into the other room. Curious about his old lover, he first opened the attachment marked 'Katsumi Rosamund Bauer'. *Rosa Mundi.* The Rose of the World, as he used to affectionately call her. He quickly scanned the particulars of the dossier. As he neared the bottom, his stomach clenched, horrified to read that two years ago Kate's infant son had died of SIDS, cot death.

We are kindred after all, Rosa Mundi.

Cædmon opened the next attachment.

'Shite,' he muttered, utterly astounded. While the ex-Delta Force commando didn't fit the typical stereotype of a RIRA terrorist, the connection was there. Even more worrisome, the man was a fugitive from the law, accused of committing two heinous murders.

The skin on the back of his neck prickled, as though a ghost from his old life had just flitted past.

Concerned for Kate's safety, Cædmon snatched his car keys out of the crystal bowl on top of the cabinet and stuffed them into his trouser pocket. That done, he opened the top drawer and removed a leather holster, quickly strapping it on to his shoulder. Spinning on his heel, he rushed out of the room, grabbing a tweed jacket off the arm of the sofa on his way to the door.

Just you wait, you bloodthirsty Irish bastard.

25

Finn turned the ignition key, the Vespa thrumming to life.

Clambering on to the back of the scooter, Kate adjusted her hips so that she wasn't pressed so intimately close to Finn's rear end.

'Since we can both use some shut eye, as soon as we finish buying the supplies I'll find us a secure hotel room.'

The offer came as something of a surprise, with Kate beginning to worry that Finn was the product of a clandestine military experiment, reprogrammed to function on little to no sleep.

'Thank you.'

'You're welcome, Katie.' Finn turned his head a few more inches in her direction, his whiskered cheek brushing against the side of her face. 'Okay. We're ready for takeoff.'

Warning issued, he steered the Vespa down the rutted alley, merging on to a narrow street jam-packed with parked cars and Greek cafés.

Kate glanced back at L'Equinoxe. At the gently swaying sign emblazoned with The Fool. She'd never dreamed that she'd see Cædmon again, had long since shoved recollections of their time at Oxford to the wayside of her youth. Seeing him after so many years brought it all back. So many endearing memories. The chiaroscuro light and early-morning mist that suffused Oxford. The silliness of trying to learn the meaning of a 'quid' and a 'crisp'. The challenging debates that lasted well into the night. The lazy Sunday afternoon picnics along the River Isis.

Hard now to imagine herself ever being that young. That naive about relationships. About love. Betrayal. The evil that men do.

With a forlorn sigh, Kate leaned her cheek against Finn's broad back. *So strong and dependable.* Her bulwark against all that evil. And while Finn McGuire was an unrepentant smart-aleck, he would never harm or demean her in any way.

Maybe her strange attraction to Finn McGuire wasn't a form of Stockholm Syndrome so much as an actual stirring of the heart. Not only was he a physically fit male, but he was honourable and courageous. And much smarter than he let on. The fact that he didn't preen or showboat made him even more attractive. Attractive like a standing stone. Or a towering oak tree. Beautiful and solid and wildly primitive.

But he is so not my type.

Having always dated 'academic' types, it made Kate think that it might be a case of opposites attracting. Like positive and negative poles on a magnet. Or the *Yin* and *Yang* of Chinese –

Finn elbowed her in the ribs. 'We've got a crotch rocket on our six!'

'*What?*' Kate had to screech to be heard over the top of the sudden roar of a loud engine.

'I'm going to make a sharp left up ahead.'

Uncertain who or what a 'crotch rocket' was, Kate tapped him on the shoulder. 'But, Finn, that's a one-way street. If you turn left, we'll be headed in the wrong –'

She grabbed his waist as the scooter suddenly made a very tight turn, the illegal manoeuvre inciting a loud horn blast from a passing motorist. Craning her head, Kate caught sight of a silver motorcycle about thirty yards behind them, its rider decked out in head-to-toe black leather.

Menacing? Yes. *Dangerous?* She hoped not.

Wrapping her arms around Finn's torso, Kate clutched her left wrist with her right hand, locking herself into place. Terrified, she couldn't tell if her heart was beating too fast or too slow.

Finn glanced in the side mirror, his expression grim. 'Hold on tight,' he ordered as he opened the throttle, the Vespa quickly picking up speed.

But not enough speed; the motorcycle was no more than fifteen feet behind them. And gaining.

Accelerating, Finn crossed the heavily-trafficked Boulevard Saint Germain to the accompaniment of blaring horns and foul-mouthed yells. Certain they were going to be hit by a delivery truck, its driver wildly gesturing at them, Kate wrapped her arms even tighter around Finn's waist.

Somehow, miraculously, they crossed the busy thoroughfare without incident.

Glancing behind her, Kate saw that the driver of the hotrod motorcycle had been the recipient of the same miracle.

Directly ahead of them, the view wasn't much better, a green street-cleaning truck hogging the entire lane. In a manoeuvre Kate didn't see coming, Finn jumped the kerb to the right of the truck and passed it on the pavement.

The motorcycle also jumped the kerb, its front wheel coming off the ground at least two feet as the driver gunned the engine. The sinister theatrics elicited a cacophony of terrified screams, pedestrians running pell-mell to escape the two vehicles.

Seeing a small cluster of people gathered around a vegetable stand, Kate hollered, 'Watch out!'

'I know!' Finn yelled back at her, both of them flinching as someone threw a head of lettuce, the green projectile bouncing off the scooter's windshield with a resounding thud.

Having successfully navigated around the vegetable stand, Finn took a hard right, narrowly missing a bicyclist. The sudden turn put them on a cobbled street, one of the tiny lanes that made up the labyrinth of pedestrian streets bordering St Séverin Church. Motorized vehicles were forbidden, but Finn clearly didn't care about Parisian road regulations.

The same could be said of the driver on the motorcycle, Kate glimpsing a silver flash to the rear of them.

'Oh, God! Don't hit the pigeons!' she screamed a few seconds later as they sped down a minuscule street that was little more than a fissure between two adjoining buildings.

Finn shot her a warning glance in the side mirror. Kate didn't have to be a mind reader to know she'd just been telepathically ordered to '*Shut up and stop back-seat driving!*'

Moments later, as they passed the Gothic St Séverin, she caught sight of the grotesque stone gargoyles that extended from the gables. For centuries they'd stood sentry high atop St Séverin, keeping evil at bay. She offered up a quick prayer, the silver motorcycle still 'on their six'.

As they approached the congested Quai St Michel, Kate knew Finn had only one option – turn left or end up in the River Seine. Leaning close as he made the approach, she braced herself for the sharp turn, the Vespa precariously lurching off balance.

Which is when it occurred to her that neither of them wore a helmet. Or any other form of protective clothing.

That realization made her pray all the harder.

No sooner did they make the turn on to Quai St Michel than Finn proceeded to weave in and out of traffic. The silver sports bike zigzagged right along with them, easily keeping pace with their every manoeuvre, the helmeted driver waving at her as she glanced at him over her shoulder.

'Hasn't your buddy Aisquith ever heard of a tune-up?' Finn complained. 'We'd have more power on a tricycle.'

Evidently their pursuer thought the same thing because suddenly he revved his engine. Where before there had been five feet between them, the distance was now reduced to five inches.

Like a high-speed battering ram, the motorcycle butted the back of the scooter.

'Finn!'

'I know! I can't go any faster!' he hollered, veering in front of a taxi.

The motorcycle pulled abreast of them.

Which is when Kate saw the driver remove a weapon from his jacket.

'He has a gun!' she screamed, every muscle in her body tensed, already anticipating rigor mortis.

What happened next was a visual blur as Finn abruptly

swerved to the right on to an exit ramp – an exit ramp that descended to the paved wharf that fronted the Seine. On one side of the pavement there was a two-storey retaining wall that abutted the multi-lane speedway; on the other side was the river.

Finn cut the engine on the Vespa and slammed his booted foot against the kickstand.

'Get off! Quick! He'll be here any second!'

Kate did as instructed, offering no resistance when Finn grabbed her by the hand and ran over to the water's edge. About a hundred yards away a grey-haired man seated in an aluminium deck chair was fishing, a dog asleep at his side. Fifty yards in the other direction were two parked cars, their owners nowhere in sight. For all intents and purposes, they were alone.

'Okay, it's show time,' Finn hissed, jutting his chin towards the silver motorcycle zooming down the concrete ramp. 'You let me handle this. No interfering. Understood?' As he spoke, he shoved her behind him, shielding her with his much larger body.

'What are you going to do?' Kate asked fearfully, wondering if there was anything he could do.

'I'll tell you what I'm *not* going to do . . . I am not going to retreat.' Unzipping the canvas satchel slung across his chest, Finn removed the Montségur Medallion from his bag, the gold disc brightly gleaming in the midday sun.

'Drop your weapon!' Finn shouted at the helmeted man on the motorcycle. 'Or the medallion gets hurled in the river!'

26

'And just so we're clear –' smiling mirthlessly, Finn tossed the Montségur Medallion into the air, catching it in his left hand – '*this* has no value to me whatsoever. One wrong move from you and I will not hesitate to fling it like a damned frisbee into the Seine.'

He hoped to God the bravado worked. If not, they were screwed. Other than the somnolent old man with the hook'n'line dangling in the water, there wasn't a soul in sight. He and Kate were in the open. Completely exposed. Even the old man wouldn't know what had happened until all was said and done; the bad guy's HK semi-automatic had a silencer on the end of it.

Which probably explained why Kate was quaking against his backside.

Or maybe she knew there was one really big chink in his armour – he had no weapon.

In those few seconds before the motorcycle roared on to the wharf, he thought about grabbing the KA-BAR knife. He had a deadly aim and to hell with the legal consequences. He always said he'd rather be tried by twelve than carried by six. But at the last moment *something* made him reach for the medallion instead. He wasn't altogether certain why he did it, other than he had a gut feeling it was the better weapon to draw from his holster.

The helmeted rider, his features obscured by the

black-tinted face guard, lowered his weapon, setting it on the ground. The bastard then did the unexpected and kicked the damned thing into the Seine, the gun hitting the water with a loud splash.

Cocky motherfucker.

Finn raised a quizzical brow. 'You know, I was fully expecting you to play a few more hands before folding. You must want this medallion *real* bad.' When his adversary made no reply, he said, 'I'll take that as a "Yes". Now that we've got that settled, lose the helmet, asshole. I want to see your face. *Slowly.* No sudden moves or the medallion will end up next to the HK at the bottom of the river.'

Clasping either side of the metallic grey helmet, the other man complied with the request.

The moment the helmet was removed, Finn sucked in a deep breath, completely blown away.

Holy shit!

Unhurriedly, well of aware of the effect, his adversary shook out a mane of long, silver-blonde hair. Hearing Kate's indrawn breath, Finn could only assume that she was equally stunned to discover that the person standing opposite them was a woman.

Quite possibly the most beautiful woman he'd ever seen.

'Who the hell are you?' he demanded to know, still getting over the shock.

'Some call me Angelika; others, the Dark Angel,' the woman calmly replied in a husky French accent.

The Dark Angel!

Fuck!

Finn glared at the leather-clad assassin. Although sorely

tempted to kill the bitch with his bare hands, he'd vowed that Dixie and Johnny K's murderer would stand trial. That meant he had to have her alive and kicking. She wasn't worth a damn to him dead.

'So, which do you prefer . . . the Dark Angel or Angelika?'

'I prefer the Dark Angel.'

'What is that, your alter ego?'

'*Mais, oui.* In the war between the Sons of Light and the Sons of Darkness, the Dark Angel will be triumphant.'

Finn snorted derisively. 'Thanks, Yoda. So, how about telling me how you tracked us. Hell, we haven't been in Paris but a few hours.'

'While you have many skills, you committed a glaring blunder.'

'Yeah? What was that?'

'You took Fabius Jutier's laptop from his embassy office.' Her lips curled in a gloating smirk. 'We surmised that you did so in order to mine the computer for information regarding our organization. Information which would have led you directly to our headquarters here in Paris.'

'I didn't steal a damned thing,' Finn said with a shake of the head.

'There's no sense lying. The misdeed is done. Since you are a decisive man, we knew that you would go on the offensive. Which is why we've been watching the airports and train stations around Paris.' The smirk morphed into a come-hither smile. 'If you must know, I had you in my gun sights earlier this morning at Gare du Nord.'

'Why didn't you pull the trigger?'

'Regardless of what you think, the Seven has no desire to see you dead.' As she spoke, the Dark Angel unzipped the pocket on the left arm of her jacket and removed a box of Lucky Strike cigarettes. 'If I wanted you dead, I could have killed you at any time.' She nodded at the Ducati 999R parked a few feet from where she stood. 'Mine is the more powerful vehicle. It would have been child's play to have caused a fatal accident.'

'And the only reason you didn't mow us over with your Italian crotch rocket is because you had no way of knowing whether or not I had the medallion on me.' For damn sure, she didn't spare their lives out of the goodness of her heart.

Opening the box of Lucky Strikes, the Dark Angel removed a gold lighter. She then shook a cigarette loose and extended her arm towards Finn. '*Fumez-vous?*' When he shook his head, she lit a cigarette, throwing her head back as she languidly blew out a perfectly shaped smoke ring.

'I'm curious: are you just a hired gun or are you a card-carrying member of the Seven?' he asked, admittedly having a hard time getting a handle on her.

Her brow wrinkled. Either she didn't understand the question or she was playing dumb.

'Okay, I'll put it another way . . . are you the proud owner of a Black Sun tattoo?'

'Would you like to see my tattoo?' Looking like a poster girl for sin city, the blonde started to unzip her Joe Rocket motorcycle jacket.

'Not especially.'

Affecting a pout, she released the zipper. 'Perhaps later I could tempt you into taking a peek.'

'Don't count on it,' he snarled, refusing to let himself be affected by his adversary's beautiful packaging.

Just then, Kate stepped out from behind him, taking up a new position on his left flank. 'What do you know about the connection between the Black Sun and the Vril force?' she asked in a quavering voice. Although scared, she didn't lack for gumption.

'*Ah, le petit souris avec les yeux bleus. Ou peut-être gris.*' Tilting her head to one side, the Dark Angel contemplatively assessed Kate. 'Blue. Grey. It matters not. To answer your question, little mouse, Vril is the force that allows us to escape the prison of the here and now.'

What the fuck did that mean?

'Okay, next question: who hired you to kill Dixie and Johnny K?' Finn asked, steering away from the mumbo-jumbo.

'I was sent by the Seven Research Foundation.' She lifted a shoulder in an elegant Gallic shrug. 'But then you already knew that.' With an impatient flick of the wrist, the Dark Angel flung her cigarette aside. 'You do realize, don't you, that we have a great deal in common?'

'News flash: We don't have a damned thing in common.'

'Don't fool yourself, Finnegan . . . We are both killers, *n'est-ce pas*?'

'I've only killed out of necessity.'

'And I kill for the sheer pleasure of it, but that doesn't change the end result.'

'What about Dixie and Johnny K? Did you enjoy killing them?'

She wistfully sighed as though recalling a fond memory.

'*Oui.* Very much so. They were both strong, their will to live immense. Their deaths brought me much pleasure.'

Jesus H! What a fucking psychopath.

A male assassin wouldn't have stood a chance getting through a Delta trooper's front door. But Angelika was the enemy a man didn't expect – a drop-dead gorgeous woman.

'I want names and I want them right now. Who hired you?' All he needed to squeeze out of her was one goddamn name.

The Dark Angel answered the demand with stony-faced silence.

Fine. Finn unclipped the phone from his waistband and handed it to Kate. Although he wanted to personally avenge the deaths of his two comrades, he knew that he had to turn the Dark Angel over to the authorities. Since they were in Paris, that would be the French authorities. They, in turn, could contact CID and arrange to have the bitch extradited to the US.

'Call the police for me, will ya?' he said to Kate.

'*Non!*'

Surprised by the blonde's frantic tone, Finn raised his hand, signalling Kate to hold off on making the call. 'Okay, you've got a temporary reprieve. Give me a name.'

Staring at the medallion, the Dark Angel extended an arm in his direction, a beseeching look in her eyes. 'The Montségur Medallion is the key to unlock the door to other worlds. We *must* have it returned to us. Soon the great star will rise with the sun. You have but to name your price.'

Not missing a beat, Finn said, 'You. *That's* my price.

And I also want a signed confession. When I get that, I'll gladly turn over the Montségur Medallion to whichever tattooed bastard wants it. That's my final offer. Take it or leave it.'

'*Ne soyez pas un idiot!*'

'Hey, I've been accused of worse things than being an idiot.' He took several steps in her direction.

'Don't come any closer!'

'Or what? You gonna chomp down on a cyanide –' Finn stopped midstream, suddenly catching sight of a black Citroën C4 barrelling down the quayside ramp, its tyres loudly squealing as the driver took a sharp left at the bottom of the incline – the speeding vehicle heading right towards them.

'What the . . . ?'

Seizing her chance, the Dark Angel charged forward, taking a nosedive into the River Seine.

'Oh, my God!' Kate screamed.

An instant later, the bitch had vanished from sight, cloudy water rippling in her wake.

Fuck!

The Citroën skidded to a stop a few feet from where they stood, the four-door hatch shaking on its frame from the sudden manoeuvre. Almost immediately, the dark-tinted front passenger window came down.

Finn caught a glimpse of dark-red hair.

'What the . . . ?'

'Get in!' Aisquith hissed.

'Fuck you!' Finn hissed right back at him.

'I think not.'

To Finn's surprise, the Brit, in a lightning-fast move,

whipped out a Ruger P89 semi-automatic pistol. Even more surprising, there was deadly intent in the other man's eyes. Like it wouldn't take much for him to pull the trigger. In that instant, Finn knew that Cædmon Aisquith *did not* play the lute at the Renaissance Festival.

But he'd bank that the other man was a player. *SAS*? *Counter Terrorism Command? The Royal Marines?*

Fuck.

Muttering under his breath, Finn opened the back passenger door and, ducking his head and crouching low, clambered into the not-so-roomy vehicle. He immediately slid across the leather bench seat, making room for Kate, who was right behind him.

Still training the gun on him, the Brit smiled nastily. 'You made a wise decision, Sergeant McGuire.'

27

'Cædmon! My God! Have you lost your mind?'

Indeed, there were days when he wasn't altogether sane. But this wasn't one of them.

'I can assure you that I'm not bonkers,' Cædmon quietly informed Kate. As he spoke, he debated whether or not to slide the Ruger back into the leather shoulder holster. If McGuire was armed, surely he would have already drawn his weapon. *Although he could be carrying a knife and is simply biding his time, waiting for an opportune moment to slit my throat.*

He placed the gun on his lap with the safety off.

Driving at a more sedate speed than when he arrived, Cædmon headed up the concrete ramp. He flipped on the indicator light, manoeuvring the Citroën into the fast-moving traffic on Quai D'Orsay.

'Does she know?' Cædmon directed the question to Sergeant McGuire.

Eyes narrowed, the commando glared at him; an infuriated bull ready to charge. 'About the two murders at Fort Bragg? Yeah. She also knows about the suicide at the French Embassy.'

'There was nothing in the dossier about the French Embassy.'

'Really? Huh. Guess your source isn't so reliable after all,' the American snickered.

'My *source* is British Intelligence.'

'Shit!' the other man exclaimed, clearly surprised. 'You're MI6?'

'I'm an intelligence officer in MI5. Or rather, I *was*,' Cædmon amended. 'My tenure with Her Majesty's Secret Service ended several weeks ago. However, I still maintain my connections at Thames House.'

'*You're a spy!?* Caedmon, how can that be? You studied medieval history.' Ashen-faced, Kate turned to her companion. 'Finn, I'm so sorry! I swear! I had no idea. I would never have taken you to –'

'Shh, Katie. It's okay.' The mastodon put his arm around Kate's shoulders and gave her a reassuring squeeze. 'Spooks are trained to keep secrets. I suspect his own mother doesn't know.'

Something about the familiarity of the gesture plus the pet name irked the bloody hell out of Cædmon.

Crossing the Seine at Pont des Invalides, he headed due east. Because the Seine so thoroughly separated the city, north and south, *la Rive Droite et la Rive Gauche* in the local parlance, it seemed that all one ever did was leapfrog across the watery divide. It was the reason why Paris boasted thirty-seven different bridges. This particular expanse was anchored on the other side by the flamboyant, glass-roofed Grand Palais, the building punctuated at each corner with flying horses and chariots sculpted in bronze. Although the colossal palace demanded one's attention, Cædmon barely glanced. Like most Parisians, he'd become anaesthetized to the majestic architecture that greeted every turn of the head. Yes, Paris was arguably one of the most beautiful cities in the world. But a man still had to buy toilet paper and mouthwash.

He spared a quick glance in the rearview mirror: Both passengers stared, unblinking, at the back of his head, Kate's brow furrowed, McGuire's jaw clamped. One baffled, one thoroughly enraged.

Navigating the Citroën towards the Isle de la Cité, he crossed the Seine at Pont Notre-Dame. To the left, L'Hotel Dieu, the city hospital; to the right, the black turrets of the Conciergerie, Marie Antoinette's prison before being hauled to the guillotine. He headed towards the fabled turrets. Neither of his passengers said anything as he drove past the line of outdoor stalls that housed the Paris flower market.

Well aware that the plot was about to thicken, he turned left on to Boulevard du Palais, the scenery changing dramatically, the streets and pavements teeming – not with tourists, but with sombre-suited bureaucrats. And a *very* visible police presence.

Reaching under his tweed jacket, Cædmon returned the Ruger to its leather holster. Out of sight.

'Where the hell are we?' McGuire hissed as they drove past two black-garbed riot police standing guard in front of an imposing building, automatic weapons at the ready.

'The Palais de Justice,' Kate whispered. 'It's the equivalent of our Supreme Court. Across the street is city hall and beyond that is the Prefecture de Police.'

'Jesus! You drove us right to the lion's den.'

'Merely to the gate,' Cædmon replied, having purposefully chosen the location. If the American commando made one wrong move, he wouldn't hesitate to summon the police. Given that there was a multitude of them within shouting range, he would have his pick.

Leaning forward, Kate grasped the side of his headrest. 'Are you going to the authorities?' There was no mistaking her distress. It was plain to see and hear.

Rather than answer, Cædmon tucked into an available parking spot on the tree-lined Quai du Marché Neuf and turned off the ignition. On the other side of the narrow street, a uniformed gendarme leaned casually against a parked motorcycle, a cigarette dangling from the corner of his mouth.

Shifting his hips, Cædmon turned towards his two passengers. He threw the question right back at Kate. 'Do you want me to go the authorities?' he asked, raising his voice to be heard over the blaring two-tone siren of a speeding police car.

'No! Absolutely not. Finn's been falsely accused of murder. That's why we're here, so he can find the real killer and avenge his comrades. Furthermore, Finn's a brave soldier who –'

'That's enough, Kate,' McGuire interjected in a lowered voice. 'The less he knows, the better.'

'It just so happens that I know quite a bit.' Deciding the time had come to divide and conquer, Cædmon directed his next remark to the scowling commando. 'Have you told Kate that your twin brother Mychal is a notorious gangster in Boston's Irish mob?'

'Fuck you!'

'I believe that we've already had that conversation,' he calmly replied.

'No, I . . . I had no idea.' Kate's eyes opened wide, the rose tint thoroughly removed from her glasses. 'A gangster . . . my God.'

Having successfully 'divided', it was now time to hand the commando his Waterloo.

'Even more worrisome, my intelligence report indicates that Mychal McGuire has, on more than one occasion, aided and abetted terrorist cells in Northern Ireland, providing them with cash, arms, bomb-making devices and moral support.'

'That's Mickey for ya.' The American smirked, proving that he was not yet vanquished. 'Always had a generous streak.'

The callous remark incited a silent rage, a fury so dense, so potent, Cædmon's hands noticeably shook. After the bomb blast in London, there had hardly been enough left of Juliana Howe to even bury.

Cædmon blinked and took a deep breath, clearing the gruesome image from his mind's eye.

'British Intelligence would very much like to question Sergeant's McGuire's brother,' he continued. 'I mention this, Kate, because I'm deeply concerned that you may have unwittingly aligned yourself with a very dangerous cohort.'

Kate opened her mouth to speak, but it was her 'cohort' who returned the salvo.

'Listen, asshole! I'm only going to say this one time: Mickey's business is just that, Mickey's business. Look at your friggin' dossier, will ya? The McGuire brothers took radically different paths. I've spent the last seventeen years risking my life in places with names that I can't even pronounce to keep people *safe* from terrorism. Not that it's any of your business.' Folding his arms over his chest, McGuire turned his head and stared sullenly out of the window.

‘Oh, but it *is* my business.’ MI5 was responsible for intelligence gathering related to terrorism in Northern Ireland. The official tie may have been severed, but the bond with Five still ran deep. ‘While you claim not to be your brother’s keeper, I suspect that you’re very good at keeping the family secrets. And that makes you complicit.’

‘In *your* book.’

‘In a great many books, I daresay. Poisoned fruit falling from the same tree and all that.’

Swivelling his head, the commando glared at him. ‘Hey, Aisquith. Go fuck my left nut.’

‘Stop it! Just stop it! The both of you!’ The normally placid Kate shot each of them a look that powerfully conveyed the message ‘Cease and desist’. ‘Okay, I get it. You don’t like each other. But that’s no reason why we can’t act like grown adults. That said, I can personally attest to the fact that Finn McGuire did not kill *anyone*.’

‘That you know of,’ Cædmon retorted. Despite the fact that he had once deeply loved Kate Bauer, he would not concede the field to a cold-blooded killer.

‘I told you: we came to Paris so that Finn can apprehend the assassin hired to kill his two slain comrades.’ Chest heaving, Kate placed a hand on the commando’s shoulder. A show of good faith. ‘The individual whom you undoubtedly saw dive into the Seine freely confessed to the murders. And I was a witness to that confession.’ Removing her hand from McGuire’s shoulder, she leaned forward and grabbed hold of Cædmon’s upper arm. ‘Please, Cædmon. I’m begging –’

‘No way am I begging anything from this guy,’ McGuire gruffly said over the top of her.

'If you let your pride intervene, you won't be able to get justice for your two friends. They were both brave soldiers who didn't deserve to be tortured to death. You know full well that you're the *only* person who can avenge those brutal murders.' Kate shot McGuire a meaningful glance. 'But you won't be able to do that if you're apprehended by the authorities.'

Cædmon watched the exchange, glimpsing a moment's hesitation in the other man's eyes. Unknowingly, Kate had brought up the rear and struck a nerve, all in one fell swoop.

I might yet win the battle.

Having no qualms about kicking the commando when he was down, Cædmon said, 'For Kate's sake, I won't turn you over to the police . . . provided you make a full confession to Father Cædmon.'

28

'I need some fresh air.' Purposefully testing his jailer's limits, Finn didn't wait for a reply. Opening the back door on the Citroën, he got out, slamming the door behind him. To his surprise, Aisquith made no move to stop him.

Why expend the energy? It wasn't like he could fly the coop. The place was crawling with cops, one of 'em propped against a dark blue Yamaha bike no more than thirty feet away.

Strolling to the back of the vehicle, Finn leaned against the Citroën's hatch, crossing his feet at the ankles and his arms over his chest. The cop glared at him; he glared right back.

The English bastard was clever, he'd give him that. But goddamn the man. Just when he'd been so close to apprehending the Dark Angel. *Shit!* Back to square one. Except he now had Aisquith trying to nail his dick to the wall.

Thank you, Mickey.

Because *that's* what really had Aisquith up in arms, the fact that his brother had 'aided and abetted' Irish rebels who refused to accept the Good Friday Peace Agreement.

Hearing a car door open, he didn't bother to turn his head. A few seconds later, just as he figured, Kate materialized at his side. Anxious expression a given.

'Don't worry. I'm not planning a prison break,' he

assured her. 'Just taking a breather while I consider the Scarlet Pimpernel's magnanimous offer.'

Kate sidled next to him, the curve of her outer hip brushing against his leg. 'Is it true?'

'That I have a twin brother? Guilty as charged. Although Mickey's the one with the goatee. That's how you can tell us apart.'

'That's not what I meant, Finn.'

Don't I know it? Little Katie wanted to know if Mychal McGuire really was a gunslinging gangster.

Always uncomfortable when the topic of family came up, he stared at his boot tip. On the plus side, his brother loved Irish music, beautiful women and shooting the breeze. But in the debit column, he loved robbing banks, running guns and snorting coke. Which made Mickey a big-league criminal. His mother used to say that Finn got the brawn and Mickey got the brains. *What a crock.*

He shrugged, not sure what, exactly, Kate wanted to hear. 'In all honesty, I have no friggin' idea if Mickey did the things that Ass-wipe –'

'*Aisquith.*'

'– accused him of. Although . . .' He hesitated, his gut churning, forced to admit that Mickey had taken his criminal activity to the next level. 'There's probably more than a little truth in Aisquith's accusation. I won't lie. My parents raised us to hate the English. What can I say? They were Irish Catholics from Derry. For the last seventeen years of his life, my old man carried a piece of lead in his back courtesy of a British soldier firing into an unarmed crowd of demonstrators.' Finn shook his head, having heard the story so many times he could recite it in his sleep. 'Fourteen people lost their lives on that Bloody Sunday. So I guess Da got off lucky.'

'I can understand why your brother would harbour antipathy towards the English,' Kate said quietly.

'But that doesn't give him a free pass to aid terrorists. Which I suppose makes him one of 'em,' Finn added, refusing to split the difference. 'And just so you know, I haven't seen or spoken to Mickey in the last five years.'

'We all have skeletons in our closet.'

'Yeah, but mine are scarier than most.'

'Change of subject –' Kate glanced expectantly at him – 'I actually do think it's a magnanimous offer.'

Finn made no reply. Instead, he checked his watch, stalling for time. He then craned his neck and peered through the Citroën's rear window; his jailor was busy rummaging through the glove compartment. *Probably searching for a flask.*

'I don't trust him,' he said flatly, turning his head back in Kate's direction.

'But I do.' Pivoting on her heel, she stepped directly in front of him. 'For all his faults, past and present, I know that Cædmon Aisquith is a man of integrity. He *will* keep his end of the bargain.' Kate put a placating hand on his crossed arms. Smiling wistfully, she said, 'What choice do we have?'

Maybe it was the fact that she used the word 'we'. Or that she'd been like a fierce lioness defending him to Aisquith. Maybe he just needed to make a physical connection. Whatever the reason, Finn pulled her towards him. To his surprise, Kate wrapped her arms around his waist and rested her cheek squarely against his pectoral muscle.

For several long moments they held each other. Neither spoke. Neither moved. If Aisquith hadn't been sitting a few feet away, Finn would have kissed her. If for no other reason than to find out if her lips were really as soft as he imagined.

I am a soldier on a mission. I do not need this kind of distraction.

Yeah, now tell that to a certain male organ.

Kate tipped her head to meet his gaze. 'Well . . . ?'

The battle lost, Finn acquiesced with a brusque nod. 'All right. Let him know that I'm ready to talk. And Kate –' he grabbed her by the arm as she turned to leave, stopping her in mid-spin. 'Let *me* do the talking. All right?'

'Afraid I'll steal the show?' she teased, pulling her arm free.

That or tell the truth.

Stepping away from the Citroën, Finn waited for Aisquith to get out of the car, his gaze zeroing in on the slight bulge of tweed fabric under the other man's left arm. Still pissed off, he recalled the bastard's fast draw.

'Okay, you win,' Finn said grudgingly, the concession leaving a bitter taste in his mouth. 'I'll tell you about the murders.'

'And the Black Sun tattoo?'

'Yeah, that too. But I've already said *everything* that I'm going to say about my brother. *Capiche?*'

Aisquith was silent for several seconds. Then, eyes narrowing, he nodded his consent. 'Agreed. Shall we adjourn to the café across the street?'

'I think that's a great idea,' Kate said, hers the only smiling face. 'I certainly could use a cappuccino.'

Turning his head, Finn sized up the joint. 'Yeah, all right.'

Decision made, the three of them trooped across the street. Playing the gallant, Aisquith opened the door to the café, motioning Kate through.

At a glance, Finn could see that the establishment was low-key; a couple of suits, a couple of touristos, a couple of waiters. On the far left, behind the bar, was a back exit. About to bolt in that direction, he pulled up short when Aisquith slid his right hand under his tweed jacket, having gauged his intentions.

Finn figured Aisquith would like nothing better than to lay him low with a nine mil.

Already a disgruntled customer, Finn walked over and seated himself in the rickety cane chair next to Kate. The Brit took the vacant chair across from them.

A waiter approached. Not bothering to ask Finn what he wanted to drink, Aisquith rattled off an order.

No sooner had the waiter left than he jutted his chin at Finn. 'It's your turn at bat, I believe.'

Ready to hit one out of the park, Finn got right to it. 'There's a group headquartered here in Paris called the Seven Research Foundation that's convinced I found a gold medallion during a black-ops mission in Syria. They're so convinced that I have this damned medallion that they sent an assassin called the Dark Angel –'

'That's the blonde-haired woman at the quay,' Kate said in a quick aside.

'– to take out two Delta Force troopers. Which she

obligingly did. She was even kind enough to leave evidence making it look like I wielded the knife.'

'To what purpose?'

'To force my hand. Fabius Jutier, a bigwig at the French Embassy, offered me a *very* sweet deal: I give him the medallion and the Seven gives me one million dollars and a "Get Out of Jail" – *Shit!*' Finn muttered under his breath as two uniformed police officers entered the café.

'*Oh, God . . .* they're looking for someone,' Kate anxiously hissed.

Reaching under the table, Finn squeezed her leg, wordlessly ordering her to remain calm. No easy feat given that both cops were scoping out the joint. Kate was right; they were obviously searching for someone.

'Did you use your own passports to enter France?' A cool customer, Aisquith didn't even glance at the uniformed pair.

No point in lying, Finn said, 'We came in through the back door with forged papers.'

'Who knows that you're in Paris?'

'No one.'

'Insurance of a sort. However, because you're a member of the US military, your photo is on a computer database. For Kate's sake, let us hope that the authorities don't employ photo recognition software to track you.'

'Yeah, let's hope they don't do that.' *Bastard.*

Just then, the owner of the café rushed out of the kitchen, greeting the two cops effusively. It was obvious from the exchange that they were regulars. Finn marginally relaxed. Kate one-upped him, visibly slumping in her chair.

'To get back on point, where is the medallion now?'

Trained to lie under pressure, Finn stared the Brit right in the eye and said, 'How the hell should I know? Still in Syria, I figure. I'm a soldier, not a treasure hunter.'

On hearing that whopper, Kate immediately straightened in her chair. If she had laser vision, she would have bored a hole right through his cheek.

'And the tattoo?'

Gathering that his lie passed muster, Finn folded his arms over his chest and said, 'That beaut was emblazoned right over Fabius Jutier's heart. Sweet, huh?'

'Mmmm . . . I take it the man is no longer among the living?'

'See, it's like this –' Finn lowered his voice, forcing Aisquith to lean towards him. 'I was in the middle of questioning Jutier – and, yeah, I admit, I was using an *enhanced* interrogation technique – when the weasel chomps down on a cyanide capsule.'

'How interesting. Cyanide was the preferred suicide method for many of the Nazis.'

'Except Jutier was French, not German,' Kate pointed out.

'We need to get to the bottom of this.' Reaching into his breast pocket, Aisquith removed a BlackBerry phone.

'What are you doing?' Finn hissed, suddenly worried that Aisquith had duped him.

The other man glanced up from the device. 'Requesting dossiers on Jutier and the Seven Research Foundation.'

'But, Cædmon, you said that you wouldn't contact the authorities.' Reaching across the table, Kate tried, unsuccessfully, to snatch the BlackBerry out of his hand.

'I would think that you and Sergeant McGuire would want this information.'

Hearing that, Finn was taken aback. 'Are you saying that you'll actually share the dossiers with me?'

'Yes, of course. Why else would I request them?' Aisquith snapped irritably. 'Ah! Our order has arrived.'

Their unsmiling waiter plunked three cups of cappuccino and a wire basket of croissants on the table.

'At this point we should mention that Finn and I don't know if there's a connection between the Black Sun tattoo and the Montségur Medallion,' Kate remarked as she unwrapped a sugar cube.

In the process of stirring his cappuccino, Aisquith let go of the spoon. 'Good God! *That's* what all this murder and mayhem is about, the Montségur Medallion?'

Kate's eyes opened wide. 'You've actually heard of it?'

'There are few medievalists who've not heard the rumours about the doomed Cathars and their fabled gold medallion. Their days numbered, the Pope's army having laid siege to their last bastion at Montségur, the Cathars supposedly smuggled a treasure out of their mountaintop stronghold.'

Having just snatched a croissant from the basket, Finn glanced up. 'You're talking about the medallion, right?'

'No. The medallion is simply an encrypted map that reveals the location of the treasure. And before you enquire, no one knows what comprised the fabled treasure. Some claim it's a sacred text, others a biblical relic.' Aisquith dunked a croissant into his cappuccino. 'Truly one of the great mysteries of the Middle Ages.'

'Then we have to assume that the Seven Research

Foundation wants the medallion so they can find the Cathar treasure trove.'

Still in the process of dunking, Aisquith nodded. 'Jutier's tattoo suggests that the Seven Research Foundation is somehow connected to the Ahnenerbe. Who, I might add, were obsessed with the Cathars. No doubt the Ahnenerbe also searched for the Montségur Medallion. The Nazis were quite intent on finding ancient relics.'

'Speaking of Jutier's tattoo, I asked the Dark Angel about the Black Sun and the Vril force.' Kate raised her cup. Before taking a sip, she said, 'Although Angelika gave a vague reply, she clearly knew what I was talking about.'

'Mmmm . . . interesting. More than a few historians have speculated that Adolf Hitler decided *not* to destroy Paris because there was something in the city that he very much wanted.'

'I take it it wasn't the Eiffel Tower.' Holding a half-eaten croissant in his hand, Finn glanced at his crumb-littered chest. *Not exactly the breakfast of champions.*

'While I have no proof, I suspect the Führer was very keen to generate the elusive Vril force.'

'To power his flying saucers?' Finn couldn't help but snicker.

'Fighter planes and Panzer divisions more than likely,' Aisquith replied, refusing to pick up the gauntlet.

'I'm confused, Cædmon. What does the city of Paris have to do with the Vril force?'

The Brit smiled fondly at Kate. 'More than meets the eye. In that it's *invisible* to the naked eye. But the best way to explain the connection is to *show* rather than tell.

Assuming, of course, that I'm not keeping you from a prior engagement.'

'Do we have time, Finn?' Kate peered anxiously at him.

Figuring he needed to play along in order to get Aisquith to share the dossiers with him, Finn shrugged and said, 'Yeah, why not? I've never seen a flying saucer.'

29

Tipping her head, Angelika Schwärz slowly blew a smoke ring, the diaphanous spiral floating towards the coffered ceiling. Somewhat moodily she stood at the open French doors that led to a small Juliet balcony. Below her the Seine flowed past the Île St Louis, the posh island enclave where she maintained an apartment.

Like her alter ego, she'd managed to fly away at the last moment. Or, in this case, swim away.

The Dark Angel.

A play on her birth name, the *nom de guerre* suited her. For she *was* the bringer of death and destruction. The one who liberated man's soul from his physical body. Life or death. Good or evil. Sacred or profane. She could be any or all of them. Today, she'd been good. Merciful, even. She could easily have pulled the trigger and ended it at the quay. But instead she'd decided to play with Finnegan McGuire. Taunt him with innuendo. Mystify him with shadowy allusion.

She already looked forward to the next bout.

Suddenly losing her taste for the Lucky Strike, Angelika smashed it into a crystal ashtray. As she did, a man approached from behind. Wordlessly, he pulled aside the right lapel of her red silk kimono and cupped her bare breast in his hand. Several passengers sitting on the upper deck of a *bateau-mouche*, one of the many tourist boats that routinely cruised the Seine, stared in slack-jawed amazement. One or two turned away, overcome with Puritanical outrage. A few pointed excitedly to the French doors where she stood, two storeys above them. Someone else aimed a video camera.

Well aware of the effect that her beauty had on men and women alike, Angelika graced them with a smile.

'You're quite the exhibitionist, aren't you?' the man whispered in her ear, tweaking her nipple between his fingers.

Thinking the answer rather obvious, she arched into his calloused hand. 'Ah, Finnegan, a little harder.'

'I told you, my name is Ryan,' he whined petulantly, even as he twisted her turgid nipple that much harder.

'Umm . . .' She luxuriated in the pain, feeling every agonized jolt. 'No. Today your name is Finnegan.'

The young man knew better than to argue. He was an American in Paris. A polite way of saying that he was a male escort, a gigolo who plied his trade to bored upper-class women with money to spend. Without being told, she knew that he was an exchange student at the Sorbonne who turned tricks to pay the rent. Not that she cared about the particulars of his life. She'd picked him because he bore a striking resemblance to Finnegan McGuire. While the accent wasn't quite right, the colouring – brown hair, brown eyes, bronzed skin – was identical. All in all, a good match.

Finnegan McGuire.

An uncommon name for an uncommon man. When she and Finnegan had faced one another on the quay, she'd found herself sexually aroused by his rugged features and cocky self-assurance. So rough around the muscular edges.

The gigolo raised a hand to the still wet hair that was twisted in a chignon at the back of her head. Realizing he was about to remove the etched silver hair pin, she pulled away from him.

'I just wanted to –'

'I have paid you a generous sum of money to tend to *my* wants,' she interrupted, annoyed with his presumption.

He threw up his hands in a show of surrender. 'Hey, no problem. Like you said, you're calling the shots.'

Actually, when she went for the kill, she preferred more silent methods. But she doubted that her paid paramour would be especially interested in the dark particulars of her life.

'Are you thirsty?'

'For you, baby. I'm thirsty for you.'

Angelika resisted the urge to laugh at his sophomoric repartee. Instead, she shoved him aside. 'I was asking if you'd like a drink,' she said over her shoulder as she strolled across to the bar.

Like a lost puppy, the gigolo trailed on her heels. 'A drink. Yeah, sure. What have you got?'

'*La Fée Verte*,' she said, lifting a bottle for his inspection.

His brow wrinkled. 'The green fairy?' He took the proffered bottle and read the label. A moment later, a look of near-comical shock on his face, he said, 'Absinthe! Is this shit even legal?'

'More or less,' she equivocated. French distilleries still brewed the mythical green liquor despite the fact that the original 1915 ban on absinthe had yet to be revoked.

'I thought this stuff was outlawed for, you know, making people go insane.'

'I don't think you need to worry about that happening.' Not bothering to ask if he wished to imbibe, she poured the absinthe into two hand-blown glasses. She then placed a slotted silver spoon over one of the glasses and, reaching into a sugar bowl, removed a cube.

'Are you going to set it on fire? I once saw Susan Sarandon do that in a movie.'

Although Angelika had not seen the movie in question, she knew that he referred to the modern ritual of setting the sugar cube aflame. While dramatic, she preferred the Zen-like simplicity of the old ways.

'The fire will come later,' she promised.

'I bet. I mean, man alive, you're one hot babe. Usually my clients are, you know, older women who schedule me between morning shopping sprees on the Champs-Élysées and afternoon tea at the Ladurée Salon.'

'Poor *bébé*. Such a difficult life,' she said with a taunting sneer.

Reaching for a decanter, she slowly drizzled cold water over the sugar cube, the green liquid replaced with an opalescent cloud. Within moments, a strong liquorice aroma wafted from the glass.

'Way cool!' her companion enthused, his earlier hesitancy about drinking absinthe having vanished.

Angelika repeated the ritual with the second glass.

'*A votre santé*,' she said, handing him the milky green beverage.

Doing a fair imitation of a thirsty man in the desert, he quaffed half the contents of the glass in one swallow. Like most Americans, he drank to get intoxicated, the subtlety of the honeyed herbs and floral bouquet beyond his appreciation.

Wearing an asinine expression, he giggled. 'I can't feel my tongue. Jeez, no wonder Van Gogh cut off his ear. Talk about a buzz.' Two gulps later, he'd finished his drink.

Ah, 'The ceremony of innocence is drowned'.

Wordlessly, Angelika turned away from the bar and walked down the hall to her bed chamber.

'Nice digs,' her companion remarked as he stepped into the bedroom, the stark space a study in white fabric and ebonized furniture. 'It's like, what, contemporary Asian?'

Not in the mood for chit-chat, she impatiently waved a hand in his direction. 'Remove your clothes. I wish to see what I paid for.' She sat down on the white leather chaise adjacent to the bed, her kimono fanning out from her bare legs like a giant blood stain.

'Whatever the pretty lady wants. I'm not one to brag, but I think you'll be pleased,' the young man said with a brash smirk as he unzipped his Levi jeans. 'I work out five times a week.'

'Very nice,' she complimented once he'd removed all of his clothing. Not nearly as impressive as Finnegan McGuire, but more than satisfactory. She jutted her head towards the king-size platform bed. 'On the bed. Spread-eagle.'

'A lady who knows her mind. I like that. Most of my clients aren't nearly so assertive.'

Because I'm not like any of your other clients, she silently mused as she got up from the chaise. Taking a last sip of her absinthe, she placed the glass on the Tansu cabinet before walking over to the bed. Pleased to see that he was fully aroused, she let the red kimono slide off her shoulders and drop on to the white carpet.

The young man's eyes opened wide. 'What's that tattooed on your left tit?'

She glanced at the circular tattoo with the Black Sun symbol. '*That* is my talisman,' she said as she straddled his hips. Grasping his erection in her right hand, she pulled it towards her, impaling herself with one quick plunge.

'Oh, babe, that's good!' her paramour crooned, moving his hands towards her waist.

She slapped at his groping hands. 'I want you spread-eagled.'

'Just like Da Vinci's *Vitruvian Man*, huh?'

Annoyed with his non-stop banter, she quickened the pace.

'You need to slow down,' he moaned. 'I'm about to come.'

'I sincerely hope so,' she quietly remarked. Reaching behind her head, she removed the ornately incised stiletto from her rolled chignon, damp locks tumbling past her shoulders.

She spared a quick glance at the silver emblem of the sacred *Irminsul*, the ancient Saxon tree of life that adorned the slender hilt. Her lips curved into a smile.

Closing her eyes, Angelika conjured Finnegan McGuire's image in her mind's eye, able to see his brown eyes roll to the back of his head as he writhed beneath her. Able to feel his strong, muscular hips buck to and fro. Pleased with the image, she grasped the stiletto in her fist and, just at the moment of mutual orgasm –

– plunged it into the young man's heart. Then across his throat. His face. His chest.

Warm blood splattered her bare breasts, Angelika gasping with pleasure.

Die, Finnegan McGuire, die. A thousand deaths. Each more painful than the one before.

30

'How the hell did I get roped into coming to an art museum?' Finn grumbled. 'If you ask me, this is just a waste of time.'

'I didn't ask,' Kate promptly retorted.

Ten minutes ago they'd arrived at the Musée du Louvre, Cædmon silent as to the reason for the visit. In that short time span, they'd climbed two flights of marble steps, waded through throngs of yammering tourists and seen centuries of art and antiquities pass in a surreal blur. Like billboards on the interstate.

A general leading his war-weary troops into battle, Cædmon strode into the high-ceilinged Salle des Bronzes. A cavernous gallery, it benefitted from the abundant natural light streaming through a bank of tall windows. Glass display cases affixed to the walls and lining the centre of the salon contained exquisite pieces of metalwork from the Classical period.

Originally a sturdy but simple medieval fortress, over the centuries the Louvre had undergone numerous renovations and expansions, evolving into the palatial residence of the kings of France. Through conquest and outright theft, those same kings amassed one of the most impressive art collections in all of Europe. Confiscated during the Revolution, the royal palace officially opened its doors as a public museum on 10 August 1793. Ironically, the event coincided with the one-year anniversary of the monarchy's downfall.

'Jesus, this place is at least twenty times bigger than anything Saddam built.'

Exasperated, Kate shook her head. *Always trust Finn to be utterly irreverent.*

But also trust him to be incredibly valiant. During the standoff with the Dark Angel, he'd actually shielded her with his own body, fully prepared to take a bullet for her. Kate was still awestruck at his incredible bravery. Even at the beginning of her disastrous marriage, during the 'happy years', she somehow doubted that her ex-husband would have gone to such extraordinary lengths to protect her. And while Finn liked to play the foul-mouthed commando, she knew that he had true courage and conviction. In a word, he *was* an unsung hero.

But she wasn't about to sing his praises or reveal her feelings. Finn was on a mission to avenge his slain comrades and did not need or want any distractions. Earlier today, he intimated that she was just that, an unwanted distraction that he was obliged to protect.

Because she so greatly admired Finn's loyalty to his two friends, she wanted to help, not hinder him.

Having yet to explain the purpose of the excursion, Cædmon headed for the last window in the salon. 'From this vantage point, we can see the spectacular Axe Historique de Paris,' he said over his shoulder, motioning them to join him.

Sandwiched between her two taller companions, Kate peered through the window; directly below them was the crowded Cour Napoléon and I. M. Pei's famous glass pyramid.

'As you can see, the Historic Axis runs in a westward trajectory from the apex of the glass pyramid, through the middle of the Tuileries Gardens and the Place de la Concorde.' Cædmon tilted his chin at the two famous landmarks, visible in the hazy distance. 'The axis then continues along the Champs-Élysées, dramatically terminating at the ultra-modern Grande Arche. Without a doubt, one of the most beautiful stretches of real estate in the world. While lovely to behold, most people are unaware that this famous axis is *identical* to the Sacred Axis in ancient Thebes that connected the Temple of Luxor to the Temple of Karnak.'

Finn glanced out of the window. 'Oh, yeah. I'm sure that King Tut had a glass pyramid just like the one down there on the concourse.'

'By "identical", I meant that both axes were constructed on an alignment twenty-six degrees north-of-west in one direction and twenty-six degrees south-of-east in the other. Fascinating, don't you think?'

Intrigued, Kate asked the obvious: 'Identical by design or accident?'

'The layout of the Axe Historique is quite intentional.' As he spoke, a lock of red hair fell on to Cædmon's brow.

Something about those errant strands called to mind a long-forgotten memory of Cædmon, sprawled on a rumpled bed, hands wrapped, not around her, but around a leather-bound history book. Utterly enthralled. That was when Kate realized that Cædmon Aisquith loved the mysteries of history more than he loved her. Soon thereafter, she sent the infamous '*lettre de rupture*'.

Unnerved by the memory, Kate refocused her attention on the axis. 'The Egyptian obelisk that's located at Place de la Concorde, wasn't that brought to Paris from the Temple of Luxor?'

'Hauled from Egypt to France in the nineteenth century, the obelisk originally stood sentry along the Sacred Axis at Thebes. And just like its Egyptian twin, the Paris axis is orientated to the Heliacal Rising of Sirius.'

'Sirius is that big bright star in Canis Major, right?'

Pleased that Finn was making an effort to participate, Kate enthusiastically nodded. 'Big and bright because Sirius is twice the size of the sun and approximately twenty times more luminous.' She'd always attributed her avid interest in astronomy to the fact that her father was an astrophysicist.

'Sirius is also the celestial abode of Isis, the queen of the Egyptian pantheon,' Cædmon added. 'Marking the beginning of the Egyptian New Year, or *Prt śpdt*, the heliacal rising of Sirius was heralded as a sacred event.'

'Wouldn't the heliacal rising of Sirius happen *every* morning when the sun came up?'

Although Finn's question had merit, Kate shook her head, disavowing him of the notion. 'You'd think so. However, in the spring, Sirius drops below the horizon, vanishing from sight for a seventy-day period. During that time, it drifts approximately one degree each day as it hovers near the Pleiades. The heliacal rising refers to the star's re-emergence after its lengthy absence.' She thoughtfully tapped her finger against her lip. 'Cædmon, what exactly did you mean when you said that the Axe Historique and the Sacred Axis in Thebes are both orientated to the heliacal rising?'

'I meant that at dawn on the morning of the helical rising, if you were to stand on the Axe Historique and gaze due east –' turning, he extended his arm towards the wall behind them – 'Sirius would be in your direct line of sight. But, even more amazing, that evening at sunset, if you stood in the same spot and looked due west –' he pivoted, resuming his original stance – 'you would see the setting sun perfectly framed within the open cube of the Grande Arche.'

'Wow. I bet that's an awesome sight,' Kate murmured.

'Truly magnificent. And while we can only assume that the Egyptians contrived an equally stunning spectacle, the Sacred Axis at Thebes was designed for one specific purpose: at the heliacal rising, the temple priests would draw the astral energy emanating from Sirius along the axis that connected the two temples.'

Hearing that, Finn said, 'All right. I'll bite. What's astral energy?'

'All stars emit electromagnetically charged energy,' Cædmon replied. 'The Egyptians believed that at the heliacal rising of Sirius, an opening was created in the cosmos, an aperture through which the energy of Sirius could be accessed and manipulated.'

'And what does *that* have to do with the Dark Angel or those bastards at the Seven Research Foundation?'

'I would think a great deal. German scholars in the Ahnenerbe referred to Sirius as the Black Sun. That being the same Black Sun depicted on the tattoo that you earlier showed me.'

Surprised, Kate's eyes opened wide. 'Which suggests that there *is* a connection between the Ahnenerbe and the Seven Research Foundation.'

Cædmon concurred with a nod. 'Obsessed with Egypt, the Ahnenerbe was convinced that the origins of physics, chemistry and biology were encoded in the Egyptian glyphs, texts and sacred monuments. Whole divisions within the Ahnenerbe were dedicated to recovering the lost sciences of the ancient world.'

'And wasn't *that* a waste of time,' Finn muttered disagreeably under his breath. 'Talk about a bogus load of malarkey.'

'Why is it so difficult to accept that the ancients may have possessed scientific knowledge that was equal, if not superior, to our own?' Exhibiting the unflappable calm for which the English were famous, Cædmon stood his ground. 'One need only examine the pyramids to know that the Egyptians were brilliant engineers.'

'In fact, modern engineers still haven't figured out how they built those darned things,' Kate informed her sceptical companion.

'And let us not forget that many of those pyramids were orientated to the constellations in the night sky. A notable achievement in any century.'

'That reminds me, Cædmon.' Kate suddenly recalled a remark made earlier in the day. 'When we questioned the Dark Angel, she made a passing reference to "the great star rising with the sun".'

'Indeed? Then we must presume that the Seven Research Foundation knows about the heliacal rising of Sirius.'

'Which leads to my next question: what was the purpose of drawing the astral energy from Sirius along the Sacred Axis?'

'Ah! We finally get to the marrow.' Blue eyes glittering, the man clearly in the know about *something*, Cædmon stared intently out of the window. 'The purpose of the exercise was to create the Vril force by fusing astral energy to the telluric currents deep within the earth. And, according to the foremost Freemason of the nineteenth century, Albert Pike, the man who can glean *that* lost science can control the world.'

31

Jardins des Tuileries

'I am grateful, Herr Doktor, for this opportunity to prove my worth,' the chauffeur energetically affirmed. 'And *I* will succeed where the Dark Angel failed.'

Ivo Uhlemann lightly patted Dolf Reinhardt on the chest, pleased that he relished the upcoming assignment. Although a coarse bully boy, he was dependable, a truncheon now in order. Time was running out with the heliacal rising of Sirius only three days away. Since Finnegan McGuire refused to surrender the Montségur Medallion, they must resort to brute force. *Pity the poor Americans.*

'I have every confidence in your abilities,' Ivo replied.

'Would you like for me to drive you home beforehand, Herr Doktor?'

'A bit more sunshine will do us both good, I think.' Ivo glanced at the Schnauzer obediently sitting at his feet. 'Since I've a yen for wild duck with chutney, I'll have Boris drive me to Le Meurice when I'm ready to depart.'

With a blank expression on his doughy face, Dolf stared, uncomprehending. A man of plebeian tastes, he ate sausage by the pound and sauerkraut by the crock.

Suddenly annoyed, Ivo waved the chauffeur on his way.

Clucking his tongue, he signalled to Wolfgang that he was ready to continue the stroll through the Tuileries.

Attentive, as always, the Schnauzer walked sedately beside him. While Ivo wouldn't go so far as to claim that the beast was his best friend, the little salt-and-pepper dog had been a loyal and uncomplaining companion for the last twelve years.

Several minutes later, energy flagging, he sat down in one of the vacant chairs located near the model boat pond. Snapping his fingers, Ivo motioned Wolfgang to the shady spot beneath the metal chair. The pain in his abdomen severe, he took several slow deep breaths. As he did, he noticed the nearby statue of *La Misére* by Jean-Baptiste Hugues, a monumental nude whose limbs and torso were entwined with a constricting serpent. Ivo thought it cruelly apropos.

How the gods must be laughing.

Adjusting his panama hat to better shade his face, Ivo glanced around the pond, appalled at seeing scores of young people chattering on their phones or jabbing their thumbs across ridiculously small keypads. True narcissists, they were busily engaged in disseminating the petty details of their lives. To anyone and everyone.

Twenty years ago, these same youths would have each had their nose in a book. But, sadly, they'd had the capacity for wonder bred out of them. In its stead was a collective ennui that demanded an endless stream of mindless stimulation. While able-bodied, these loafers had no higher purpose. If they continued in this vein, they would not be able to meaningfully contribute to society. Once that happened, it would be difficult to justify their existence.

Determined to create a better world, Ivo knew that it

was simply a matter of purging the horde. Certainly, there were capable and competent individuals. But too often they were held back by those of lesser intelligence. For years now, the imbeciles had been convinced by well-meaning do-gooders that their answer mattered. Their opinion counted. And, exacerbating the situation, the digital age had empowered these cretins, reinforcing the great deceit. The fact that the imbeciles reproduced at an alarmingly fast rate was a grave concern. Eventually, their escalating birthrates would enable them to conquer Europe without ever firing a single bullet.

Because that was a very real danger, those who did not meet requisite IQ standards must be sterilized. While the do-gooders would decry it as a drastic measure, Ivo contended that it was nothing less than scientifically controlled evolution aimed at improving the collective gene pool. A social theory that originated in the late nineteenth- and early twentieth-century, eugenics had been championed by such luminaries as Henry Ford, Theodore Roosevelt and Linus Pauling. Their opponents claimed that the criteria for determining a 'defect' was too subjective. Again, he would argue that a standardized IQ test was an objective measure.

And who among them would dare claim that ignorance was a virtue?

In point of fact, low intelligence had been scientifically linked to a host of medical and social defects such as morbidity, schizophrenia, criminal behaviour, sexual deviance and dementia. The evidence was glaringly clear: individuals with a low IQ were destined to become a burden to society. This could not, and would not, be tolerated.

Through selective breeding, the dangerous trend towards mediocrity could be reverted, creating a nation of exceptional citizens.

A humane man, he'd always favoured eugenics rather than extermination. Which is why the Seven Research Foundation had spent years formulating a Universal Intelligence Quotient Policy, consulting with a wide range of experts that included social scientists, geneticists, neurologists and psychologists. Several standardized tests had been designed to measure both intelligence and aptitude. These tests would be administered to every man, woman and child, the results stored in a central data bank. Additionally, all citizens would be implanted with a microchip that not only indicated their IQ test scores, but pertinent medical and genetic screening data. Those who refused to take the IQ test would be summarily sterilized. To enforce the policy, the police would have broad authority to use a hand-held digital scanner which would quickly determine if a citizen was microchipped.

Those with an IQ less than 100 would be sent to a Eugenics Centre where they would be sterilized before being assigned to a Work Detention Programme.

The last thing that anyone wanted was another holocaust; a disastrous policy that cost the Third Reich its true place in history. Besides, he had nothing against the Jews and admired a good many of them. An enlightened plan, the Universal IQ Policy would create a society of *Übermensch*, Supermen, fit of body and mind, who would populate their glorious new Reich.

Hearing a sudden childish peal of laughter, Ivo glanced at the shallow pond. A colourful regatta of toy yachts gracefully bobbed and weaved on the glistening surface. A charming sight, it put a smile on his face.

With good reason, this was his favourite spot in the park. From where he sat, he could see the Arc de Triomphe du Carrousel to the east and the Obelisk at Place de la Concorde to the west. Both monuments were part of an elaborate blueprint originally devised by the Knights Templar that could unlock the entire scientific mystery of the universe.

Provided they find the *Lapis Exillis.*

'And we *will* find it,' Ivo rasped, not about to let Finnegan McGuire – or any man for that matter – stand in his way.

32

'. . . but, of course, the trick is to maintain that power once it's been seized,' Cædmon Aisquith continued, having just dropped a bombshell about Freemasons controlling the world. 'That said, I should preface my next remarks by saying that I'm about to go out on a limb –'

'Buddy, you've been hanging from a twig since we got here,' Finn muttered under his breath.

'– but I believe the Axe Historique in Paris was constructed so that some unknown group could harness the astral energy that emanates from Sirius at the heliacal rising and fuse it to the telluric energy that emanates directly beneath the axis.'

A thoughtful expression on her face, Kate took a moment to digest Aisquith's assertion. 'When you say "telluric" energy, you're referring to the earth energy that moves underground along the Earth's crust and mantle, right?'

Aisquith smiled fondly at his favourite pupil. 'Telluric energy is derived from the primary water system that exists inside the Earth as hydrated minerals. It's considered a geophysical phenomenon which emits radiation and can be enhanced when there are changes in the magnetic field. In fact, telluric energy was used during the nineteenth century as a type of earth battery to power the early telegraph grids. Although little understood, some scientists believe that the power potential of telluric energy is far greater than the electricity we generate above ground.'

'Begging the question: how do you fuse astral and telluric energy?'

'By building a ley line.' Just warming up, Aisquith's smile broadened. 'Which is exactly what the ancient engineers constructed at Thebes. And, no coincidence, it's what their French counterparts have constructed on the Axe Historique.'

Half tempted to tell the Brit to pull the wine cork out of his ass, Finn instead said, '*That's* a ley line?' As he spoke, he jutted his chin at the chaotic scene below, tourists milling around as far as the eye could see.

'Ley lines are man-made energy conduits. Built over the top of telluric currents, the stones used in ley lines can carry electromagnetic energy for hundreds of miles,' Aisquith replied. 'This particular ley line is comprised of five monuments: the Pyramid, the Arc de Triomphe du Carrousel, the Obelisk, the Arc de Triomphe l'Étoile and the Grande Arche. Not surprisingly, during the Paris Occupation, the Ahnenerbe spent an inordinate amount of time mapping and measuring the Axe Historique.'

Clearly on board, Kate's head energetically bobbed up and down. 'Let me make certain that I comprehend how the pieces fit together: there's astral energy radiating from Sirius and telluric energy radiating from beneath the ground. But in order to fuse these two different forms of energy, a ley line must be constructed.' She pressed her palms together to illustrate the point.

'Precisely. As above, so below.'

'And then what?'

'Then, if all the pieces of the puzzle have been properly placed, you can now create the Vril force. Vril, chi, orgone, mana –' as he reeled off the list, Aisquith waved his hand in the air – 'they're all names for the same fused energy force.'

'How very interesting,' Kate murmured. 'Were the ancient Egyptians able to fuse astral and telluric energy and create the Vril force?'

'The Germans were convinced that the megalithic structures built along the Nile delta enabled the Egyptians to do just that. Determined to resurrect this lost science, the Ahnenerbe spent a small fortune studying the texts and monuments of ancient Egypt. As I said earlier today, the Ahnenerbe were desperately trying to devise military applications for the Vril force.'

'Just a pie-in-the-sky theory,' Finn said dismissively, certain he was the only one in the group able to distinguish fact from fantasy.

'All great ideas begin with a theory,' Aisquith was quick to assert. 'If the Vril force could be harnessed, it would create a powerful biodynamic comprised of magnetic, electromagnetic and electrical energy.'

'Yeah, whatever.'

Needing to clear his head – having reached his bullshit quota – Finn strode over to a nearby display case and peered inside. For several seconds he stared at a little bronze statue of a nude dude hefting a weird-looking beast on to his shoulders. He read the neatly typed tag: 'Anonymous; Archaic Period; Around 530 BC.' *Guess that was before they invented pants.*

Bored, he glanced at his watch. *1203 hours.* Jesus. How

long was it going to take for Aisquith to get the dossiers? He still needed to buy supplies and find a hotel room so he and Kate could hunker down and get some shut-eye. Tomorrow the mission would kick into full gear and they needed to be bright-eyed and bushy-tailed. *And here I am fucking around at the Louvre.*

Just then, Kate looked over and smiled shyly at him. As though his eye muscles had a mind of their own, Finn winked at her. A split-second later, self-consciously aware of what he'd done, he lowered his head and feigned an interest in the display case.

Not for the first time, he was surprised that he could be turned on by Kate's winsome personality. In the past, sexual arousal had always been linked to lots of cleavage, swaying hips and pouty lips. But Kate roasted his nuts because her dainty femininity was wrapped around a steel core of quiet strength. And, yeah, he found that sexy as hell. He also found that scary as hell. If he lost his focus for one moment, the Dark Angel could blow them away. Or the French authorities could catch him in a dragnet, allowing CID to extradite his ass to the US. *Who would protect Kate if that happened?* Though he'd never admit it to Aisquith, that business about the photo recognition software spooked him. Just one more thing to worry about.

Still standing next to the display case, Finn watched as Aisquith placed a hand on Kate's shoulder. Obviously, the Brit still carried a torch. *Well, fuck that shit.*

Finn strode over to where the pair stood at the window.

'And another thing,' he announced without preamble, determined to break up their little exchange. 'You don't have one scrap of evidence to prove any of your theories.

You keep yammering about something that I can't see, touch or smell. Just how the hell do you use the ley line that's on the axis to create this all-powerful Vril force?' Monkey wrench hurled, he belligerently put his hands on his hips.

Aisquith shrugged. 'I have no idea.'

'Finally! An honest answer.'

'Cædmon, do you by any chance know when the heliacal rising of Sirius will take place?' Kate enquired, still riding the Vril bandwagon.

'Unless I'm greatly mistaken, it will occur on the seventh of August.'

Kate's jaw visibly slackened. '*Oh, my God* . . . that's just three days away.'

33

'*Scheisse!*'

Annoyed that the dresser drawer had jammed, Dolf Reinhardt yanked it off the runner, several pairs of rolled socks bouncing free and rolling across the bare floor.

In a hurry, he deposited the drawer on to the nearby bed. Hearing the pulsating beat of loud music emanate from the next-door apartment, he strode over to the adjoining wall and roughly banged it with a balled fist.

'*Halt die fresse, drecksau!*'

Uncertain if what he was hearing was rap or hip-hop, Dolf was absolutely convinced that the Senegalese family who had recently moved into the flat was a gang of dirty pigs. Ear to the wall, he listened as a female berated someone in a foreign language. Whatever was said, it had the desired effect, the offending music turned down. Satisfied, Dolf gathered his small bundle of clean clothes and headed into the bathroom.

Over the last three years, his Oberkampf neighbourhood had become infested with dark-skinned foreigners and homosexuals. Dolf was repulsed by the sight of them. Willing to put up with leaky plumbing and having to climb six flights of steps, he could not tolerate living in a mixed apartment building. Unfortunately, Paris was a rich man's city, the lower-class enclave all that he could afford.

Squeezing his six-foot-two frame into the ridiculously small bathroom, he set the pile of clothing on the toilet lid. He then peered into the cracked mirror above the sink, ignoring the incessant *plop plop plop* that emanated from the tap. Examining his bald pate, he detected a slight golden shimmer. His light blond hair made him look like a gargantuan baby chick – the reason why he kept his head shaved. Striking a bad-ass pose, he flexed both arms, pleased, as always, at seeing the veined muscles. *Check out these gunz!* Although it'd been twenty years since he'd been crowned the European Junior Boxing Champion, Dolf still had the arms of a heavyweight contender.

Born in East Berlin, he'd been recruited from elementary school into the world-renowned *Sportvereinigung Dynamo.* Only the most talented athletes were placed into the state-run sports programme. His mother predictably baulked at the idea of her eleven-year-old son living away from home but, with a bit of coaxing, soon relented. Dolf assured her that he would bring honour to the family and, more importantly, to the German Democratic Republic. Since the 1970s, the GDR had dominated the Olympic games, their athletes the best trained in the world.

When, on a rainy October morning, Hedwig Reinhardt signed the official paperwork, she in effect legally turned her only child over to the Stasi, the secret police who were in charge of running the Sports Dynamo.

For the next six years, Dolf's life was strictly regimented, the sports ideology of the GDR relentlessly hammered into him. Training, teamwork, good hygiene, healthy nutrition and self-discipline were the core principles of the elite sports programme. Because of his size and strength, Dolf quickly came to the attention of the boxing coaches. As his training intensified, Dolf, like many of the top-tier athletes, was constantly monitored. Whenever he left the dormitory, he had to sign a register, indicating what time he would return. If, for whatever reason, he was tardy, a Stasi agent would be sent to locate him. At international boxing matches, he was instructed by these same Stasi agents not to speak to foreigners, especially members of the press.

In 1988, at the age of seventeen, he became the European Junior Champion in his weight division. His coaches were ecstatic, certain that Dolf would be a medal contender in the 1992 Barcelona Olympic Games.

And then, in 1989, the fucking wall came tumbling down, *literally*, the tide of history turning very much against him.

Within days of the collapse of the Berlin Wall, the Sports Dynamo was closed; all of the athletes put out on the street. Hopes dashed. Dreams destroyed. While thousands cheered throughout the city, Dolf sat huddled in a locker room sobbing. Everything he'd known had just been robbed from him. *The glory, the greatness, of being an East German athlete.* How many times had he dreamed of carrying the GDR flag in the opening ceremony at Barcelona? Head held high. The pride of his country. The envy of the world.

Grief soon mutated into confusion when, several weeks after his training abruptly ended, he began to notice unusual changes in his body, horrified that his testicles were shrinking. But, even more worrisome, he was starting to develop breasts! Too humiliated to tell his mother, he began to wear baggy shirts. Finally, afraid that he might actually be morphing into a girl, he went to a health clinic on the west side of Berlin. Where no one knew him.

The doctor took one glance at his plump boobies and, like he was a mind reader, said, 'You were an athlete at the Sports Dynamo, weren't you?'

Dolf hesitantly nodded his head, too afraid to do anything other than admit to the truth.

'You have a condition known as gynaecomastia. In your case, it's the result of having been administered androgenic steroids.'

Vehemently shaking his head, Dolf denied the charge. 'That is a lie! We were only given vitamins and regeneration tablets.'

'Yes, so they all claim,' the doctor replied wearily. 'I can refer you to a specialist who'll remove the breast tissue.'

Although a surgical referral was made, Dolf never went to the appointment. He was terrified that, once it was revealed he'd been doped with steroids, his Junior European Championship medal would be stripped from him.

Still standing at the bathroom sink, Dolf glanced at his breasts. They weren't huge, thank God. But they were decidedly feminine, the skin soft, the nipples enlarged. Over the years, he'd often contemplated having the breast tissue removed. But, just when he'd be on the brink of making an appointment, thinking it was finally safe, there would be a new media story about the East German doping scandal – usually triggered by some emotionally traumatized ex-athlete who felt betrayed by the old regime.

Why the hell can't they keep their mouths shut?

It'd been twenty years! Who gave a shit if those female

athletes had been turned into hairy-assed infertile Amazons?

Knowing that the details of the 1988 European Junior Championship were readily available on the Internet, Dolf feared some nosy surgeon would key his name into a search engine. Twenty years may have passed, but they could *still* take his medal from him. Better to live with a pair of boobies than the shame of having his one glory in life wrenched from his grasp.

Pulling the oversized black T-shirt over his head, Dolf slightly hunched his shoulders, making the telltale bumps barely noticeable. Finished dressing, he headed back to the small bedroom and rifled through the drawer on the bed, removing a twelve-inch painted truncheon decorated with the SS *Totenkampf* Death Head. The impressive cudgel had belonged to his grandfather, Josef Krueger, an SS officer in the elite Reich Security Service. It was his second most prized possession after his championship medal. Dolf slid the smooth wooden truncheon into his jeans belt loop. A perfect fit.

He then walked over to the wardrobe and retrieved an oversized black satin jacket, emblazoned on the back with Iron Maiden's famous 'Evil Eddie' emblem. Jacket donned, he removed a cardboard shoebox from the top of the wardrobe. Inside was a Heckler & Koch Mark 23 pistol with laser device and an attached silencer; a beautiful piece that he'd bought from an unscrupulous American soldier stationed at the Bamberg military garrison. He shoved the pistol into the back of his waistband. Gangsta-style.

Ready to depart, Dolf walked down the narrow hallway to the second bedroom. Opening the door, he peered inside. A woman with braided grey hair sat at the window, staring at the Paris rooftops.

'I will be back later. We're having pickled ham hocks for dinner. Your favourite,' he added, hoping to elicit a response. When no reply was forthcoming, Dolf sighed wistfully. '*Auf wiedersehen, Mutter.*'

34

'*La Pyramide Inversée*, as you can see, is the inverted twin to the glass pyramid directly behind us,' Cædmon said in passing, as the three of them trooped across the street.

'As above, so below,' Kate sagely remarked.

'Indeed.'

Set in the middle of the four-lane thoroughfare, the inverted glass pyramid could only be viewed underground – the reason why the architectural curiosity was often overlooked by tourists strolling in the Cour Napoléon.

Taking a deep breath, Cædmon filled his lungs with muggy air. Despite the sun beating down on his head, neck and face, he'd had his fill of the Louvre. During the summer months, jam-packed with tourists, the museum often felt like a lavish sardine can, which was why he had suggested that they adjourn to the outdoors and view the Axe Historique in situ.

He cast a sideways glance at the grim-faced Finnegan McGuire. Since leaving the museum, the commando had gone on high alert. Although outwardly calm, the man's gaze constantly shifted from person to person. The roving eye of a fugitive at large. Should the police try to apprehend him, he suspected McGuire would retaliate rather than run, the man a natural-born fighter. Not to mention a cocky son of a bitch.

Whatever does Kate see in him?

Leaving the Pyramide Inversée in their wake, they approached the blush-hued Arc de Triomphe du Carrousel, the second monument on the Axe Historique. 'War and peace have never been so powerfully articulated,' he commented, having always been drawn to the magnificent landmark. 'Derived from the triumphal arches of the Roman Empire, the memorial was commissioned by Napoleon to commemorate his stunning victory at Austerlitz. Composed of not one, but three arches, it's surmounted by a quadriga that depicts Peace holding the reins of a horse-drawn chariot. Flanked by the gilded Victories, the group perpetually gleams. Rain or shine.'

'I've always thought that the rose marble on the columns and front panels softens the lines, adding a surprisingly feminine aura to a monument designed to celebrate the unabashed pursuit of war,' Kate remarked as the three of them strolled through the centre arch of the monument.

'Our thoughts run a similar course.'

'This arch looks a lot like the big one down the road.' McGuire's aside was made in his typical blunt fashion.

'You refer, of course, to the Arc de Triomphe de l'Étoile, the Triumphal Arch of the Star,' Cædmon said in response. 'Seen from the sky, the twelve evenly spaced avenues that radiate from the larger arch create a star pattern. I would posit that the star in question is none other than Sirius.'

'An interesting premise.' Kate raised her right hand, shielding her eyes from the afternoon glare. 'But why do you think that?'

'Because here –' raising his arm, Cædmon gestured to

the monument before them – 'at the smaller Arc de Triomphe du Carrousel, the thick lines of hedgerow that you see radiating from the arch and extending into the adjacent garden have been carefully manicured to resemble the rays of the sun.'

Eyes opened wide, Kate's head slowly swivelled from side to side. 'Ohmygosh. You're right. The summer I spent in Paris, I walked along this path quite a few times and never noticed that.' Using her finger as a pointer, she counted the number of 'rays'. 'What do you know? There're twelve of them.'

'Every day, hordes of tourists rush past these monuments, digital cameras madly clicking, and not one of them *truly* sees what has been depicted in the landscape, the sun and the star harkening to the heliacal rising of Sirius. Indeed, the cloak of invisibility was part of the original blueprint,' he said with added emphasis, Kate having ably made the point for him.

'Were there any arches on the Egyptian axis at Thebes?' Kate asked thoughtfully,

'Instead of arches, the ancients built a series of pylons that were set along the Sacred Axis. The rectangular gateways served the same purpose as the arches in Paris; they created an enormous horizontal telescope through which astral and telluric energies were funnelled.' Cædmon turned towards the Egyptian obelisk, clearly visible just beyond the garden. 'What's so utterly fascinating about the Axe Historique is that, from this position, as you head west along the axis, the distance between each monument precisely doubles. Even more astounding than that, the size of each of the three arches doubles as well.'

'I'm wondering just how long it took to build this damned thing?' McGuire enquired gruffly.

'The Axe Historique was a project several hundred years in the making,' Cædmon replied, surprised that the commando had even asked the question. 'Officially it was begun in 1564 when Catherine de Medici ordered the planting of the Tuileries Gardens. It then took another four hundred years for the axis to finally be completed, the last monument, the Grande Arche, erected in 1989. All in all, the Axe Historique is a sophisticated piece of ancient technology.'

Kate's brow wrinkled. 'It certainly makes you wonder who's got the instruction manual.'

'Which brings up my next question: so far, you've given the "where", the "why" and the "when". Call me crazy, but I'm still waiting for the "who".' Point made, McGuire unhooked a pair of black sunglasses from the neck of his T shirt and slipped them on.

Carefully considering his reply, Cædmon shoved his hands into the pockets of his well-worn trousers. 'Throughout history, there has always been a tight-knit cadre that operates in the shadows. Powerbrokers. King-makers. These men wield enormous influence. They do so because they are the keepers of the secrets. Secrets that they share only with the initiated few.'

'In other words, you don't have a friggin' idea who's responsible for building this axis.'

'The Knights Templar, the Rosicrucians, the Freemasons, the Illuminati.' He shrugged, McGuire having posed a thorny question. 'I assume that at one time or another, each group contributed a piece to the axis. And while seemingly separate, all were germinated from the same seed. Indeed, these sects, orders and secret societies form an esoteric matrix that spans the ages. The names may change, but the agenda remains the same.'

'I think you can guess at my next question . . . What's the agenda?'

Cædmon took a moment to consider his reply, Kate's query no more easily answered than her cohort's.

'These shadow groups are the designated guardians of a body of sacred knowledge which includes the Lost Science of the ancient world,' he said, admittedly sloshing in murky water. 'Over the centuries, that knowledge has been transmitted from one group to the next. The agenda, simply put, was to safeguard this knowledge so that it wouldn't fall into the hands of a despot who would use it for maniacal ends. And then, of course, one must always stay two steps ahead of the black-robed gents in the Inquisition, jolly fellows who wouldn't hesitate to consign the whole of ancient knowledge to the bonfire.'

'That's rather damning, don't you think?'

'Is it? In the thirteenth century, the Church not only exterminated the Cathars, but they managed to destroy all of the Cathars' written texts and documents. Only the legend remains.'

Sliding a black rucksack off her shoulder, Kate unzipped the front pocket and removed a pair of blue-tinted sunglasses. The eyewear did little to hide the fact that her cheeks had suddenly flushed a bright shade of crimson red.

Jaw locked tight, McGuire wordlessly took hold of the rucksack and swung it on to his own shoulder. Then, taking her by the arm, he escorted Kate into the shadows of a nearby tree.

Watching them, Cædmon grudgingly acknowledged that the man's only saving grace was the care he took with Kate.

'The design and construction of the Axe Historique is one of the great mysteries of Paris,' he continued, joining the pair in the shady patch. 'A massive building project, the construction of each monument required an enormous outlay of cash, funds the French government didn't always have at its disposal. Just when a project seemed doomed to failure, an anonymous largesse would suddenly be made and – *voila!* – the project would miraculously be saved.'

'Do you mean that all of this –' McGuire swept his arm from the pyramid to the obelisk – 'was created by a secret sugar daddy?'

'Some would say that it's a centuries-old conspiracy.'

'And you wanna know what I say? All of this was built to give Parisians something pretty to look at as they trudge to and from work every day.'

'Oh, ye of little faith,' Kate chided playfully, nudging McGuire with her shoulder.

Feeling a vibrating pulse, Cædmon unclipped his mobile from his waistband and checked the display screen.

'I've just been emailed the dossiers on Fabius Jutier and the Seven Research Foundation,' he informed them. 'If we head back to the bookstore, I can open the attachments on the computer.'

'No need.' Kate patted the side of the rucksack that

was slung over McGuire's shoulder. 'We've got a laptop with a wireless Internet connection.'

Ah, perfect.

'I see a vacant bench on the other side of the hedgerow. Shall we?'

35

Dolf Reinhardt glanced at the hand-held transmitter, squinting to better see the small map.

Unknown to Finnegan McGuire, the laptop computer that he had stolen from the French Embassy had a GPS tracking device embedded in the hardware. For the last two days, the Seven had been waiting for the commando to arrive at their lair – from where there would be no escape, the jaws of death *very* sharp.

While he didn't know where precisely his quarry was located, Dolf knew that the pair was in the near vicinity. Because of the hundreds of milling tourists, he'd not yet caught sight of them. But since their position updated every five seconds on his transmitter, there was no chance of losing them. They were here. *Somewhere.*

As he studied the map screen, trying to orientate his position with the landmarks indicated, a gaggle of laughing, half-dressed teenage girls strolled past. Legs, midriffs and cleavages all on eye-popping display. One of them, a curly-haired hussy, glanced over at him and snickered.

'*Schlampe*,' he muttered under this breath, the little tramp a disgrace to her sex.

Hard as a rock, he watched their hips provocatively swing in shorts so tight he could see the cracks in their asses. He wanted to fuck them all. Make them go down on their knees and suck him dry. That would teach them a lesson. That's all they were good for. He couldn't respect a woman who didn't behave like a lady.

Dolf swiped at a bead of sweat that trickled down the side of his face. *Scheisse.* He hated the summer, the heat and humidity an uncomfortable reminder of what *didn't* happen the summer of '92. That was when the Barcelona Olympics took place. The summer that he *should* have represented East Germany. Instead, he was on the dole. Twenty-one years of age. No job and no prospects. Since he couldn't find steady work, he couldn't afford to train at the boxing gym. Everything in the fucking West cost money. And without the regulated discipline of the Sports Dynamo, his life had fallen into a tailspin.

His mother, Hedwig, who lost her former job with the state-run utility, earned a pittance cleaning toilets at the Alexanderplatz train station. When she came home after working a double shift, haggard, barely able to put one swollen foot in front of the other, Dolf would slink off to his bedroom and put on his headphones. Losing himself in heavy metal music. Forgetting, at least temporarily, that he was a useless excuse for a man. Even more useless than his father who'd dropped dead from a heart attack at the age of thirty-seven.

Like so many former East Germans, Dolf felt lost after Reunification. From the brands of cigarettes and beer to the programming on television, nothing was as it had been. In the GDR, there had been full employment. Not only did every citizen have a job, they each had a sense of purpose that came from knowing their specific place in the regime.

Although he didn't believe in God, Dolf would have cut a deal with the devil to keep the Berlin Wall in place.

The only good thing that came out of that miserable summer of '92 was that he met Stefan and the *Blut Brüder*. Although his mother didn't approve of his new acquaintances, claiming the Blood Brethren were all unemployed hooligans, Dolf liked hanging out with his tough-talking pals. Liked the fact that people gave the twelve 'hooligans' a wide berth. According to Stefan, their shitty lot in life was due to the influx of immigrants into Germany, the government allowing any dark-skinned foreigner into the country.

One night, drunk on schnapps, the *Blut Brüder* decided to torch a local hostel overrun with Turkish immigrants. Excited by the prospect of taking back their country, they tossed Molotov cocktails into the building then chained the exit doors. Soon the fun began, Stefan and Dolf laughing their asses off as they watched those filthy foreigners toss their screaming brats out of the windows. By night's end, there were three less Turks to steal jobs from native Germans. Not bad for a night's work.

Anxious, Dolf glanced up from the hand-held transmitting device and scanned the vicinity. *Where the hell was McGuire?* Like a never-ending plague of locusts, big buses kept dropping off tourists. He walked away from his position near a metal lamp post and headed towards a long line of neatly clipped hedgerow. The Mark 23 pistol, plastered against the small of his back, was an uncomfortable reminder that he'd not yet bagged his prey.

When he did find them, Herr Doktor Uhlemann had been adamant: the kills must be quick and quiet. No advance warning. Pull the trigger, grab the dead commando's canvas bag and immediately leave the vicinity.

The dense crowds of tourists would give him cover as he made his escape. *No running. No furtive glances.* Instead, walk calmly to the nearest Metro station and board a crowded car.

Scanning the crowd, Dolf *finally* caught sight of the American commando, recognizing him from the photo that he'd earlier been given. A muscular hulk, Finnegan McGuire looked like he could hold his own in any ring. The Bauer woman was approximately thirty feet from him, seated on a low retaining wall. A second man, with red hair, stood beside her.

Dolf did a double-take.

Who the fuck was that?

There were only supposed to be two targets. Not three.

Bewildered, Dolf wondered if he should apprise Herr Doktor Uhlemann of the situation and ask for revised instructions.

No sooner did the idea pop into his head than he nixed it, worried that he'd come off looking incompetent. The last thing he wanted was for Herr Doktor to think that he was a plodder who couldn't move his feet and fists fast enough.

He had enough bullets to deal with the problem.

What was one more dead body?

36

In dire need of a drink, Cædmon glanced at his watch.

Mmmm . . . wonder if it's too early to suggest an aperitif at a nearby café?

'We're not keeping you from anything, are we?' Kate enquired pleasantly.

'No, no,' he assured her. 'Although I was wondering if –' Hit with a sudden change of heart, he waved the errant thought away. 'Never mind.'

On edge, Cædmon paced in front of the granite retaining wall where Kate had set up a makeshift office beneath a towering maple tree. Uncertain as to the cause of his unease, he glanced to and fro. In the near distance, the Louvre's two Neoclassical wings flamboyantly defined the open-ended courtyard. A typical August afternoon, the Cour Napoléon was a veritable hive, hundreds of people swarming about in the sweltering heat. Nothing out of the ordinary.

Then why the bloody hell am I so apprehensive?

'Cædmon, sit down.' Kate smiled winsomely. 'You're making me nervous.' Prising the laptop open, she pressed the 'on' switch.

'My apologies.' Hoping he didn't appear as anxious as he felt, he obediently sat beside her.

Kate playfully nudged him with her elbow. 'Much better.'

'Is it?' He held her gaze. Only to sheepishly glance away an instant later, afraid that Kate would suddenly see him for what he was – a wreck of a man who lacked the wherewithal to put his life in order.

Standing sentry some thirty feet away, Kate's brooding mastodon openly glared at him.

Soldier and spy . . . never the twain shall meet.

'Pardon me if I'm out of line –' Cædmon lowered his voice to a conspiratorial tone – 'but he doesn't seem your type.'

'Wh-why would you say that?' Kate stammered, clearly taken aback. 'Have you lost your mind?'

'Still intact last time I checked.'

'Then why would you ever think that Finn and I –'

'What else was I to think? The two of you seem rather chummy.'

'Like you said, he's not my type.' The telltale blush belied the denial.

'I see,' Cædmon replied, thinking 'the lady doth protest too much'. Particularly since he'd caught Kate and McGuire sharing more than a few sly glances. Although he was rusty when it came to affairs of the heart, those telltale exchanges implied a mutual attraction. One which Kate was taking great pains to refute.

'So, I would greatly appreciate it if you, um, not mention anything to Finn about this conversation. He doesn't need the distraction. As for me, without going into the details, what happened in Washington was –' Kate paused, a shadowed expression on her face – '*harrowing*. So I thought it might be a good idea to have my own personal bodyguard. In case you haven't noticed, Finn McGuire is a human predator drone.'

'Yes, well, he's a trained commando. Quick to grab the battering ram. Sleeping with one eye open. All that.' Concerned that she captained a listing ship, he placed a hand on her shoulder. 'I imagine that McGuire has a full plate, what with being a fugitive-at-large. If the authorities try to apprehend him, you could find yourself in a very dangerous predicament. I can have you placed in an MI5 safe house,' he offered, hoping to lure her away from the shoals.

'But you can't give me a trained commando who will lay down his life to protect me.' Kate set the notebook computer on his lap. 'All booted up and ready to go,' she said, effectively changing the subject.

As he accessed his email account, Cædmon noticed that McGuire, a belligerent swagger to his step, was headed in their direction. He gave the man full marks for ably toting his gargantuan chip.

'All right, so what's in your little spy report?'

Determined to prove himself the better man, Cædmon strove for a civil tone. 'I've been sent two dossiers: one for Fabius Jutier, the other for the Seven Research Foundation.'

'Since the French dude's dead, let's first check out the foundation.'

'Right.' Opening the attachment, he obligingly read the summary bullets aloud. 'Founded in 1981 by Dr Ivo Uhlemann, a German national, the Seven Research Foundation is headquartered in Paris. My, my, I'm impressed.

Uhlemann has a doctorate degree from Göttingen University in theoretical physics.'

'The group of physicists that my father always refers to as the mathematical daydreamers.' Turning to McGuire, Kate said in a quick aside, 'It's a branch of physics that relies heavily on mathematical equations rather than physical experimentation.'

'Albert Einstein, also a theoretical physicist, might take exception to that characterization,' Cædmon remarked before continuing with the particulars. 'A nonprofit foundation, the Seven awards academic grants across a diverse research spectrum. Everything from physics to electrical engineering to archaeology.'

'No smoking gun there.' Leaning close, Kate propped her cheek against his jacket-clad arm as she peered at the dossier. 'Downright respectable, actually.'

'Yeah, that was real respectable what they did to my two buddies.' Punch-line delivered, McGuire yanked a leafy sprig from the imposing hedgerow that grew just behind the retaining wall.

Ignoring the other man, Cædmon skimmed through the next few paragraphs. 'Now this *is* interesting. Not only do they maintain office space in the Grande Arche building, but the Seven Research Foundation was instrumental in getting the building project off the ground.'

Kate's eyes opened wide. 'Then all of this murder and mayhem *does* have something to do with the Axe Historique.'

'Moreover, a cloud of suspicion still hovers over the Grande Arche and its design,' he told her, assuming she'd be more interested in the information than her surly companion.

'Although no proof has ever been tendered, that hasn't stopped the chattering café classes from claiming that a secret esoteric group was involved in the construction project.'

'That's scary.'

'That's bullshit,' the commando muttered.

'That's the least of your worries.' Cædmon glanced up, stunned by what he'd just read. 'According to the dossier, each and every member of the Seven's Board of Trustees is a direct descendant of an SS Ahnenerbe officer.' He paused, assailed with a dark foreboding, his earlier anxiety having come full circle. 'I fear that you're dealing with a very dangerous enemy.'

McGuire shrugged and said, 'Tell me something I don't know.'

Troubled by a niggling thought, Cædmon ran a hand over his unshaven cheek. 'There's a piece of the puzzle that we've not yet considered. The Seven Research Foundation is desperately trying to recover the Montségur Medallion on which, reputedly, there's an encrypted map that leads to a long-lost Cathar treasure. How does that come into play? And, more importantly, is there a connection between the Axe Historique and the Cathar treasure?'

Cheeks noticeably flushed, Kate grabbed hold of McGuire's wrist. 'Finn, I think you'd better show him.'

'I'm not showing him jack.'

'You've been falsely accused of killing two men. Do you next want to be falsely accused of associating with a bunch of latter-day Nazis?'

'Pardon me for interrupting your tête-à-tête, but what the bloody hell is going on?' Cædmon demanded to know, the two of them behaving like criminals in the dock.

'If you won't do it, I will.' Ultimatum issued, Kate made a futile grab for the canvas satchel that McGuire wore, bandolier style, across his chest.

'Shit.'

With that muttered oath, McGuire capitulated. Unzipping the canvas satchel, he shoved his hand inside. When, a few seconds later, he pulled out a gleaming gold pendant, Cædmon's eyes opened wide.

Shite.

'You actually stole the Montségur Medallion. You lying bastard!' Shoving the computer on to Kate's lap, Cædmon lurched to his feet. Fists clenched, he was sorely tempted to bash McGuire in the face.

'I can assure you that Finn had the noblest of intentions,' Kate exclaimed, quick to defend her mastodon. 'The only reason he took the medallion was to keep it out of the hands of men who would profit from it.'

Pitying Kate for being so sadly deluded, Cædmon thrust out his hand. Glaring at McGuire, he silently dared the commando to refuse the request.

Wearing his trademark sneer, McGuire dropped the medallion into his palm. 'Read it and weep.'

For several long moments Cædmon stared at the relic, the gold pendant divided into four separate quadrants, each containing a unique image.

'You do know that *this* may actually be the Cathars' only material legacy, making it an incredible historic find?'

'Well, don't get any ideas about putting it in a display case at the Louvre,' McGuire shot back.

'Any guesses as to what it means?' Kate enquired in a conciliatory tone.

'No need to guess. Its meaning is perfectly clear. These symbols are a hieroglyph of the heliacal rising of Sirius. Viewed as a pictorial depiction of the cosmos, the setting sun is seen in the west with the star, Sirius, in the east and the moon directly overhead. Clearly, the medallion is connected to the Axe Historique.'

'What about these four As?' Kate pointed to the fourth quadrant. 'Instead of the usual horizontal cross bars, they all have an angled crossbar.'

'A stylistic flourish, and as such, inconsequential. As to what they mean, I'm no expert on the Cathar religion, but the "A"s may represent the Four Ages of Man. Difficult to say.' He flipped the medallion over to examine the back.

'We were hoping you could translate the inscription.'

Cædmon tapped the first two incised lines with his index finger. 'These are inscribed in medieval Occitan, the *lingua franca* of the Cathars. The inscription reads "In the glare of the twelfth hour, the moon shines true." The last line, *Reddis lapis exillis cellis*, is written in Latin.' Belatedly realising the meaning of what he'd just said, his heart slammed against his breastbone. 'I don't bloody believe it!'

'Believe what?'

He brought the medallion several inches closer to his face. Squinting, he reread the inscription, verifying the translation.

'The inscription is written in grammatically incorrect, corrupted Latin. That said, it roughly translates, "The Stone of Exile has been returned to the niche."'

'What the hell does *that* mean?' McGuire asked gruffly.

'A great deal to anyone who has read Wolfram von Eschenbach's *Parzival*. In that classic medieval tale, von Eschenbach refers to the Grail as the *Lapis Exillis*. The "stone in exile".'

Hearing that, Kate gasped. Even the dour-faced commando seemed genuinely taken aback.

'As in the Holy fucking Grail?'

'Yes, *that* Grail. Which means –' Suddenly noticing a pinprick of light in his peripheral vision, Cædmon stopped in mid-stream. Glancing down, he was horrified to see a red laser dot on his chest, centred over his heart.

Jesus!

37

'Christ!'

His reflexes honed from three wars, Finn roughly shoved Cædmon Aisquith in the shoulder, knocking the other man off-centre. The bullet, intended for the Brit's heart, ploughed into a maple tree instead, a chunk of sheared bark blasted into the air.

The next instant, seeing a red laser light bounce in Kate's direction, Finn spun on his booted heel and dived straight at her, lifting her up and over the retaining wall. The two of them crash landed in the narrow gully behind the concrete barrier – just as another piece of bark chipped off the tree trunk.

Finn clamped a hand over Kate's mouth, muffling her in mid-scream.

'We're under fire!' he hissed. 'I need you to stay calm. Got it?'

Grey-blue eyes wide with fear, Kate nodded. Finn removed his hand from her mouth.

'Where's Cædmon? And why didn't I hear any gunfire?'

Her questions were asked with the *rat-a-tat-tat* rapidity of automatic weapons fire.

'The shooter's got a silenced weapon.' Finn raised up slightly and peered over the top of the retaining wall. Aisquith was nowhere in sight, the man smart enough to turn tail and run. He also didn't see anyone who looked like a cold-blooded killer on the prowl. In fact, none of the milling masses was even aware that there was a gunman in their midst.

Fuck.

He slammed shut the upended laptop computer. Then, snaking his hand over the top of the retaining wall, he snatched Kate's knapsack and dragged it down into the gully.

'Quick! Stick this inside the knapsack.' He shoved both items at Kate.

No time to lose, he scoped out their position – hunkered behind the three-foot-high retaining wall, with a four-foot-high hedgerow to the other side of them, they didn't have a whole helluva lot of options. Just the one, actually. Seeing a narrow gap in the hedgerow, he looped his left arm around Kate's torso.

'*Carpe diem*,' he muttered, dragging her through the leafy breach, branches snapping in his broad-shouldered wake. While the thick bushes wouldn't stop a bullet, they'd camouflage their whereabouts. An expert marksman, he knew that you gotta be able to see the target in order to shoot at it.

Aisquith, crawling on all fours, came barrelling through the bushes about ten feet away. Moving surprisingly fast for a tall man, he scurried over to their position.

He removed the Montségur Medallion from his jacket pocket and handed it to Finn. 'You left your trinket behind. Tad close for comfort. My heart is still racing.' Obviously, the Brit referred to the fact that he'd narrowly escaped the grim reaper and his laser-guided pistol. 'Unless I'm greatly mistaken, our gunman is a bald bloke in a black jacket. He's positioned approximately sixty-five metres away, standing behind the statuary just south of the Arc de Triomphe du Carrousel. I saw him dash in that direction after he fired his weapon.'

'I think I know the dude that you're talking about,' Finn said, quickly searching his memory bank. 'I saw a bald-headed guy earlier, staring at his iPod or cell phone or something. A big-ass cue ball who didn't strike me as the artsy-fartsy let's-do-lunch-at-the-Louvre type. I'd peg him at six two, two twenty.'

Aisquith nodded tersely. 'That's our man.'

Unzipping his Go Bag, Finn deposited the gold medallion. He then pulled out a pair of Bushnell binoculars, aiming them at the statue on the other side of the Arc de Triomphe. 'Got him. The bastard hasn't moved to a new position.' He handed the binocs to Aisquith.

'Which tells me that our shooter is a rank amateur.'

Finn didn't bother informing Aisquith that even a rank amateur could pull a trigger and kill a man. 'I'm guessing he's packing a forty-five outfitted with laser-aiming device and a sound suppressor.'

'That or an invisible ray gun,' Aisquith deadpanned, returning the Bushnells to him.

'Since you know the lay of the land better than I do, what are our escape options?' Finn already knew they could rule out the Citroën; it was in the museum's underground car park, the Ruger locked in the glove box.

Using the tip of his finger, Aisquith drew an open-ended rectangle in the dirt. 'The Cour Napoléon is enclosed on three sides by the Louvre which is shaped like a massive horseshoe. Our position is here.' He tapped a spot centred near the open end of the horseshoe. 'There are three escape routes. The first option: we can dash seventy metres to the open end of the horseshoe and flag a passing motorist on the Avenue du Général Lemonnier.'

Finn impatiently made a rolling motion with his left index finger. 'Next option,' he ordered, figuring that Door Number One would get them mowed down the fastest with the hedgerow the *only* cover in those seventy metres.

The Brit pointed to the two long sides of the horseshoe. 'On the north and south wings of the Louvre, there are *guichets* –'

'*What?*'

'Wickets,' the other man translated.

Finn shook his head, still in the dark. 'Try again.'

'Archways,' Kate said. 'Actually, they're huge portals cut into each wing of the Louvre, enabling traffic to pass through the Cour Napoléon.'

Finn raised the Bushnells and took a gander, first at the gunman, still hunkered behind the statue, then at the arched portals. He'd earlier noticed the archways when they crossed the thoroughfare that passed between the Louvre's inner courtyard and the Arc de Triomphe plaza. From their current position, the two sets of archways were equidistant, each about two hundred metres away. On the plus side, there were trees, shrubs and statues to give them cover. In the minus column, there were hundreds of tourists strolling about.

'Okay, here's the plan,' he announced, stuffing the Bushnells in his Go Bag. 'I'm going to make the first prison break through the archway on the southern wing. That will draw the shooter in my direction. Before I reach the archway, I'm going to create a loud commotion. That'll be your signal to haul ass towards the opposite archway on the north wing.'

'What sort of commotion?' Aisquith enquired.

'I haven't thought that far in advance. Don't worry. I'll devise something.'

'Finn, have you lost your mind?' Kate hissed, frantically grabbing him by the forearm. 'You can't go out there! You don't have a weapon.' Because of tight security inside the Louvre, he'd had to leave his KA-BAR knife locked inside the Citroën.

Finn held up his two hands. 'Kingdom Come or the fiery pits of hell. I can send the bastard to either locale with these two babies.'

'This is no time for do-or-die theatrics. What if –'

'Kate! Leave be!' the Brit interjected in a lowered voice. 'The man is a trained commando. He knows what he's doing.'

'I'll meet you two jailbirds at the Eiffel Tower in thirty minutes.' Finn purposefully picked that location because it was the one spot in Paris that he didn't need a map to find, the damned thing visible from just about everywhere.

'There's a café on the corner, one block due east of the tower,' Aisquith said, jutting his chin towards the famous landmark on the other side of the Seine. 'We'll wait for you there.'

'Gotcha.' Swinging his Go Bag behind him, Finn went into a sprinter's stance. 'Time to do or die.'

38

How could I have missed both shots!?

Standing in the shadow cast by a stone sculpture, Dolf Reinhardt stared at the offending Heckler & Koch Mark 23, ready to hurl the piece of shit across the Jardin du Carrousel. The American soldier who sold it to him had claimed that with the laser-aiming device, hitting the target would be child's play.

Humiliated by his ineptitude, Dolf shoved the pistol into his waistband. He then wiped his palms on the leg of his jeans. That's why he'd missed both shots: his hand slipped on the gun handle because of his excessively clammy palms. *Palmar hyperhidrosis.* Another side effect of all those fucking steroids he'd been force-fed at the Sports Dynamo.

I should have worn gloves.

But it was ninety degrees in the shade. And Herr Doktor Uhlemann had been adamant that he not draw any attention to himself. People would have noticed a big bald-headed man wearing gloves in August.

'*Scheisse!*' How was he going to make this right? The trio had dived into the bushes, vanishing from sight.

Removing the GPS transmitter from his pocket, Dolf stared at the minuscule screen. According to the map, they were somewhere in the bushes southwest of his current position.

Yes! But which fucking bush?

And what if they were armed? It would be three against one. They could shoot him dead, piss on his corpse, and walk away with no one the wiser. Then who would take care of his mother? He couldn't take that kind of chance.

Overcome with shame, his chin dropped to his chest. Unable to think straight, he stared at the ground. A few feet from where he stood, two tottering pigeons fought over a discarded crumb. *Flying rodents, the city should poison them all*, he thought, tempted to blow the heads off of the squabbling pair.

Instead, he shoved the transmitter back into his jacket pocket and retrieved his cell phone. For several long seconds, he stared at it, vacillating. He *wanted* to call Herr Doktor and ask whether he should remain in the Jardin du Carrousel or leave the vicinity.

But if I make the call, I'll have to own up to my colossal failure.

Dolf bit his lip, well aware that he was knee-deep in shit without a shovel.

It was like the summer of '92 when his thirteen-year-old sister, Annah, had been raped. While Annah refused to go to the police and identify the bastard who attacked her, Dolf had been certain that her rapist was the Turkish fruit vendor down the street. Dolf had seen the bastard eyeing his sister. Blonde-haired, blue-eyed, she was like an angel, and the rape was retaliation for the apartment fire.

Determined to avenge his sister, Dolf had waited in the dark alley behind the market where the Turk sold his overpriced produce. When the Turk hauled a crate of rubbish out to the metal dumpster, Dolf sneaked up from behind and bashed him on the head with his grandfather's truncheon. Gasping for breath, the Turk had peered at Dolf, a pleading look in his limpid brown eyes. 'Please, who will take care of my wife and four children if you kill me? I beg you, sir! Have mercy!'

About to bash him again, Dolf hesitated. Confused. Uncertain what to do. When he had earlier fantasized about killing the Turk, it had been quick and easy. Like in the movies. He hated the fact that his enemy, the man who raped his sister, had just caused this minefield of doubt. Enraged, Dolf ended up pummelling the man with his bare fists, swinging with all the might of his 223-pound body.

The long-ago memory caused Dolf's gut to twist into a painful knot. Afraid that he might actually puke the contents of his stomach on to the pavement, he removed a roll of antacids from his pocket.

Just as he was in the process of peeling the foil away from a pink tablet, he saw Finnegan McGuire emerge from the hedgerow and sprint towards the plaza.

Stunned by the miraculous sight, Dolf dropped the roll of antacids.

He could now make things right!

And when he did, that bastard McGuire would pay dearly for the earlier humiliation. This time Dolf would shoot the American in the kneecaps. Then, when he was incapacitated, he would beat the bastard to death with his bare hands.

Just like he did to that Turk back in Berlin.

39

Planning to do rather than die, Finn ran across the open plaza in a zigzag pattern, a moving target being more difficult to hit.

When he reached the first goalpost, the Arc de Triomphe du Carrousel, he put on the brakes. Standing in the shadow of an ornately carved archway, he scanned the terrain behind him. *No Cue Ball.*

'Where is he?' Finn muttered under his breath, worried that the gunman may have decided to go after the soft targets, Aisquith and Kate, instead.

Catching a fast-moving blur out of the corner of his eye, he swung his head to the left. Relieved, he saw the bald gunman, approximately sixty-five yards away, scurrying towards the monument.

Hurriedly plotting his course, Finn craned his head in the other direction, sighting an enclosure about fifty yards beyond the archway, completely surrounded by an eight-foot-high hedge. *Perfect.* All of the touristos were focused on one of three things: the Arc de Triomphe, the glass pyramid or the Louvre. Nobody gave a rat's ass about a bunch of shrubs on the far side of the plaza.

He purposefully stepped away from the niche, putting himself in Baldy's direct line of sight.

Bear baited, Finn took off running.

No sooner did he pass through the narrow opening in

the hedges than he realized that he'd entered an eight-foot-high maze. Going with the flow, he cut to the left and ran to the end of the aisle. Flanked on both sides by towering shrubs, he was completely hidden from view.

At the end of the aisle, Finn hung to the right. He then dodged into the first cutaway that led to the interior of the maze. Coming to an abrupt halt, he flattened his spine against the manicured shrub. A quick peek verified that the goon, silenced gun now gripped in his right hand, was warily venturing down the aisle.

Reaching into his trouser pocket, Finn removed a coin and – aiming for a spot ten yards away – he tossed it up and over the hedge. Even with all the noise emanating from the plaza, he could hear the slight rustle as the coin landed. Well worth the two euros if it fooled the gunman into thinking that he was somewhere other than his current position.

Trap set, he waited until . . . he glimpsed the gun's silencer.

Springing out of the shadows, Finn pounded the other man's right wrist with spine-jangling force. Stunned by the blow, the big bruiser dropped the gun.

A bullet discharged.

Grunting, the goon automatically stooped to pick up his downed weapon. Finn beat him to the prize, kicking the pistol into the hedges. He then threw his weight into a powerhouse right jab, his balled fist connecting with the other man's face. A thunder punch that induced a sickening *crunch!* of broken bone and busted cartilage. The bald head instantly whipped to the left, spewing blood spray-painting the nearby bushes crimson red.

A painful blow, it would have felled most men. But the big Neanderthal simply shrugged it off.

That was when Finn noticed the scar tissue around the other man's eyes, the beefy fists and cauliflower ears: the telltale marks of a trained boxer.

Fuck.

Sneering, the other man whipped a foot-long truncheon out of his belt loop.

Double fuck.

Not about to let the bastard knock him out, Finn lurched towards his adversary, using his raised forearm to block the other man's swing in mid-air.

Which was why he didn't see the uppercut aimed at his left jaw.

Thrown off his stride by the intense burst of pain, Finn staggered backward. The bald dude, no doubt figuring his fists were the better weapon, hurled the truncheon aside and came at him fast and furious. *Power jab. Straight right. Left hook to solar plexus.*

Grateful for the six-pack abs, the best armour a man could have in a no-holds-barred contest, Finn retaliated with a quick left to the jaw and a right shovel to a less than rock solid gut.

Wham, bang, thank you, ma'am!

Dazed, the other man swung wild.

Seizing the advantage, Finn slammed the heel of his hand against his adversary's chin. The money shot.

Like a giant Weeble, the other man swayed to one side . . . just before the part of his brain that controlled autonomic function temporarily shut down. Causing the bruiser to collapse in a shuddering heap.

Mass times acceleration equals K.O. Simple physics.

Finn ran over and retrieved the discarded truncheon. Unzipping his Go Bag, he shoved it inside. The gun, having been kicked into the hedges, was a lost cause. He spared a quick glance at his unconscious adversary. If it had been a combat situation, he would've neutralized the target. But given that he was already wanted for two murders, he wasn't about to up the ante. It was enough that he'd disarmed the big bastard.

'Count your blessings, Baldy.'

No time to gloat, Finn retraced his steps. He guesstimated that he had no more than fifteen seconds before the goon revived.

Reaching the entrance to the maze, he could see that the *guichet* was sixty metres away. Between Point A and Point B, there were scores of gawking sightseers, some bozo on rollerblades and one dipshit pulling a red wheeled suitcase.

The perfect props to create a diversion that would confuse the hell out of his attacker.

To that end, Finn charged through the plaza, grabbing purses, backpacks, camera bags, shopping totes – whatever he could snatch – flinging each, in turn, into the air. A mad man run amuck, whipping docile bystanders into a frenzied horde.

Sparing a quick glance over his shoulder, he saw that Cue Ball had revived. Face smeared with blood, the big brute stood at the entrance to the maze, staring at the melee.

Time to haul ass.

Arms pumping, Finn sprinted towards the roadway,

leaping over the front-end of a baby stroller, in too big of a hurry to sidestep it.

Needing an escape vehicle, he scanned the southbound lane of traffic that had stopped at the red light. His gaze settled on a canary-yellow Yamaha motorcycle.

Just then, the light turned green.

Worried that he was going to miss his ride, Finn ran over to the dipshit with the wheeled luggage. Bending at the waist, he grabbed hold of the bright red suitcase and hurled it towards the southbound lane, the red suitcase bouncing off a sedan's front bumper, creating a clamour that caused the moving traffic to come to a sudden halt.

Finn ran up to the yellow motorcycle that had slowed to a stop near the kerb. Not bothering to ask for a lift, he clambered on to the passenger seat. To make certain the biker cooperated, he shoved the truncheon into the driver's ribs.

'Make like the wind, asshole!'

40

Standing in the midst of the chaos, Dolf watched impotently as Finnegan McGuire escaped on the back of a motorcycle.

Unable to think straight, he staggered to a nearby bench and collapsed. Head clutched in his hands, he felt as though he'd just wandered into an asylum. So much was going on – people shouting and rushing about – the only thing that he could process was the fact that the motherfucker McGuire had stolen his grandfather's truncheon. That and he'd bested Dolf in a fist fight.

I should have won that bout.

Just then a black Scottish terrier darted over to the bench. Curious, the dog sniffed at him. A few seconds later, it growled ferociously.

'Get lost!' Dolf hissed, ready to hurl the shaggy beast across the plaza if it came any closer.

The owner, a leash dangling from her hand, breathlessly rushed up to him. 'I'm awfully sorry, but in all the madness, Sadie flew the coop and I – My God! There's blood all over your face! Do you want me to call an ambulance?'

'I want you to take your furry piece of shit out of my sight! I hate dogs!' Dolf glared at the annoying American woman with the sing-songy accent. 'In my country, we grill little dogs on a spit.'

Bending at the waist, the woman hurriedly scooped the squirming animal into her arms. 'Aren't you a miserable excuse for a human being!'

Tell me something that I don't know, bitch.

Lacking the enthusiasm to hurl a parting insult, Dolf unzipped his jacket and, raising the hem of his cotton T-shirt, wiped the blood from his face. Like most former boxers, his nose had been broken so many times, he'd lost count.

Bewildered, events having transpired too rapidly, he wondered how he was going to explain the debacle to Herr Doktor.

Per usual, his life was a big fucking catastrophe, this just one in a long series of disasters. Every time he thought he'd done the right thing, he'd later discover he'd fucked everything up. Just once, he wished things would go *his* way. But they never did. Always things went left instead of right. Like what happened with that fucking Turkish fruit vendor.

Three months after his sister Annah had been raped, she'd slashed her wrists in the bathtub. In her suicide note, she claimed that Stefan, Dolf's best friend in the *Blut Brüder*, had entered her bedroom one afternoon while she was getting dressed and sexually assaulted her. Dolf felt as though a sledge-hammer had been swung at his head. *Why couldn't Stefan have raped someone else's sister?* Why his? And why did Annah have to ruin his life with her tell-all suicide note? He'd already killed the Turk.

Having been the one to find his sister floating in a tub of bloody water, he tore up the piece of lined notepaper and threw the shreds into the incinerator.

Betrayed by Stefan, he left the *Blut Brüder* gang. That's when he started to hang out at the boxing gym. Since he was on the dole, he offered to wipe down the ring, get equipment, hold the punching bag, whatever odd chore needed to be done. In exchange, he could work out at the gym free of charge. Eventually, Dolf was asked to be a sparring partner for some of the up-and-coming boxers. Excited, he saw this as his big chance to catch the eye of a boxing promoter. But it never happened. He'd lost his touch. Without his 'vitamins', he was just an average boxer with a strong punch, lacking the speed and agility of a prize fighter.

A big fucking catastrophe.

Reaching into his pocket, Dolf removed the GPS transmitter. According to the data on the small screen, the tracked target had yet to move from the hedgerow.

How could that be? With his own eyes, he'd seen McGuire leave the plaza.

Either McGuire had discovered the tracking device on the computer and left it by the hedgerow or his two companions now had the laptop.

Although he'd been ordered to kill McGuire and commandeer the medallion that he carried in his canvas bag, *what if he killed the red-haired man and abducted the woman*? Herr Uhlemann could ransom her for the medallion.

Dolf stared at the transmitter. It was a good plan. Better to kill someone than no one. And when he returned to the foundation's office suite with the bitch in tow, everyone would see that he was a valuable asset. Then, finally, he would get his due. Prove to all of the naysayers that he was more than a mere chauffeur.

He just needed to find his Mark 23 pistol, the motherfucker McGuire having kicked it into the bushes.

Fully prepared to crawl on all fours and dig through the dirt with his bare hands, Dolf lurched to his feet and ran back into the maze.

41

'Do you think Finn's all right?' Kate worriedly asked, pandemonium raging on the other side of the Cour Napoléon.

'Ours is not to reason why,' Cædmon replied. Snatching hold of her elbow, he pulled her upright. 'Your commando has created the necessary diversion so that we can escape undetected. I suggest that we do so immediately.'

'I'm ready when you are.'

Stomach butterflies in a tumult, Kate ran faster than she would have thought possible, Cædmon pulling her through a cutaway in the hedgerow. She didn't resist. She trusted him implicitly. They then sprinted along the line of shrubs, dodging a group of squatting backpackers sharing a joint.

A few moments later, they emerged from the hedgerow, the arched *guichets* no more than two hundred and fifty feet away. Closer at hand, approximately twenty metres from their position, a swarm of people hurriedly rushed towards them, led by two men attired in blue uniforms. *The Paris police!*

'Do you think those gendarmes are looking for Finn?'

'No need to worry. They're simply directing the crowd to the northern end of the courtyard,' Cædmon said, slowing to a more sedate speed.

Within seconds, the two of them were suddenly engulfed

by a crowd of jostling tourists, all excitedly chattering and gesturing about what they'd just witnessed on the far side of the plaza. Overhead, fast-moving clouds malevolently cast a dark shadow, a summer storm about to break.

As if on cue, soft raindrops pelted the ground.

Worried that Finn might not have successfully escaped, Kate peered behind her. As she did, she caught sight of a red-faced, bald-headed man, fifty yards away, stridently moving in their direction. Hit with a burst of raw terror, she opened her mouth to sound an alert but her larynx produced a sound more akin to a high-pitched wheeze. Unable to speak, she yanked on Cædmon's tweed jacket.

'What's the mat– Bloody hell!'

Cædmon's expletive confirmed her worst fear – the gunman and the great hulk of a man charging towards them were one and the same.

'Hurry!' Cædmon's hoarse command was punctuated with a loud clap of thunder. 'We need to reach the portal!'

A split-second later, the skies opened up, soft raindrops instantly transformed into stinging pellets that fell at a furious rate.

Another ear-splitting boom of thunder reverberated in the Cour Napoléon.

The ominous sound triggered a mad dash towards the *guichet*, at least two hundred people rushing, en masse, in that direction. A long tunnel cut into the massive north wing of the Louvre, the narrow pedestrian *guichet* was the only shelter to be had in the near vicinity.

Kate spared a furtive glance over her shoulder, relieved to see that their assailant was completely enveloped by a large group of Japanese tourists, a human dragnet having been thrown around him.

'*Arigato*,' she whispered, grateful for the reprieve. Even if it was accompanied by a driving rain. And even if it was only temporary.

Cinching his left arm around Kate's shoulders, Cædmon pulled her close to him as he navigated through the horde.

Up ahead, a bottleneck had formed at the entrance to the *guichet* as a veritable mob descended on the single six-foot-wide opening. While there were a total of six *guichets* on the northern wing of the Louvre, the four large wickets in the middle were strictly for vehicular traffic. Conversely, the two narrow portals flanking either side of the thoroughfare were designated for pedestrians. At a glance, Kate could see that there was a similar log jam across the street in front of the second pedestrian portal.

With each boom of thunder, the soaking wet crowd to the rear of them became more insistent. Pushing that much harder. A living, breathing battering ram. Stuck in the middle of the pack, she feared they might not make it through the *guichet*.

But even if they did reach it, then what? Their assailant was a mere fifty metres behind them. He had a gun with a silencer. No doubt he intended to follow them through the portal. Then pull the trigger with no one the wiser.

'I th-think we should s-summon the g-gendarmes,' she stammered, grasping the front of Cædmon's jacket to get his attention.

Barely glancing at her, Cædmon scotched the idea with a terse shake of the head. 'Too much is at stake. If we go to the police, the Montségur Medallion will end up in the bloody Louvre.'

'B-better that than the two of us ending up in the grave,' she retorted.

Cædmon made no reply.

Fear level spiking, Kate took a deep stabilizing breath. In through her nostrils, out through her mouth. She kept a mental count until *finally* they reached the *guichet*.

'Quickly! Take the lead!' Cædmon ordered, pulling her in front of him.

Shoving wet hanks of hair out of her face, she did as instructed, belatedly realizing that Cædmon was shielding her with his own body, protecting her from the monster to the rear of them.

Although a full storey in height, the dimly lit *guichet* was stifling. Kate was pressed in on all four sides. The crowd's mood having noticeably soured, the thick stream of soaking wet tourists trudged through the dank chasm.

Craning her neck, Kate caught Cædmon's eye. 'Is he still –'

'Yes. About forty metres back.'

'How are we going to elude him?'

'I'm not altogether certain.'

Seconds later, like projectiles fired from a cannon, they burst free of the *guichet*, the summer tempest no less severe on the other side. Many in the throng rushed across the street, taking shelter under the covered arcade that ran parallel to Rue de Rivoli.

'We mustn't tarry. Our assailant will emerge from the portal at any moment.' Snatching hold of her hand, Cædmon turned to the right and ran up to a middle-aged man holding a large black umbrella over his head.

Tapping the bespectacled gentleman on the shoulder, Cædmon, speaking in flawless French, told the stranger that he'd give him fifty euros for his umbrella.

Brown eyes opened wide. '*Mais, oui!*'

Ten seconds later, the transaction complete, Cædmon shepherded the two of them, now huddled under the umbrella, down Rue de Rivoli.

'Cædmon, have you lost your mind?' Kate hissed. 'You just paid that man the equivalent of sixty-eight dollars. *For an umbrella!*'

'I didn't think that twenty euros would seal the deal. Trust me. There's a method to my madness.'

'Who cares if we get – Oh, I get it,' she said abruptly, noticing that the pavement teemed with people carrying umbrellas, most of which were basic black. Just like the one that Cædmon now held over their heads. 'The black umbrella isn't to keep us dry. It's to camouflage us.'

'Our assailant will, hopefully, assume that like everyone else who doesn't have an umbrella, we sought dry shelter under the arcade.'

'So, what's our next move?' she huffed, barely able to speak and draw breath at the same time.

Cædmon jutted his chin towards the taxi stand a block away. 'Do you have enough energy left for one last sprint?'

Despite the fact that her shins ached and the sides of her abdomen were painfully cramped, Kate gamely nodded. She hoped fear would make her fleet of foot. Or at least keep her on her feet.

Hand in hand, they sloshed down the pavement.

A few moments later, her lungs on fire, they reached the taxi stand. Opening the door of the cab, Cædmon motioned her into the back seat. He then closed the umbrella and sidled next to her.

Red hair plastered to his skull, Cædmon leaned forward and said, '*À la Tour Eiffel, s'il vous plaît.*'

42

'*. . . avec le citron.*'

Nodding, the waiter scribbled the drink order on to a notepad before heading back into the café, muttering under his breath about the crazy Englishman who insisted on sitting outside during a deluge.

What the sulking Frenchman failed to mutter was that Cædmon and Kate were protected from the rain, their small table situated beneath a canvas awning.

'Where is he?' For the fourth time in as many minutes, Kate anxiously glanced at her wristwatch.

About to inform his overwrought companion that he didn't know and, moreover, he didn't give a monkey's, Cædmon thought better of it at the last. 'He's only six minutes late. Let's not sound retreat just yet, eh?' *At least, not until my G&T arrives.*

'What if Finn didn't make it? Maybe the gunman shot him at the Arc de Triomphe plaza. If that happened, he could be injured or –'

'But he's not,' Cædmon interjected in a firm tone, alarmed by Kate's runaway imagination, concerned that she might be suffering from a mild case of hysteria. An understandable enough reaction given the recent hair-raising episode.

In truth, the skin on the back of his neck *still* prickled, his senses in a heightened state of awareness.

Feigning an interest in the large potted palm diagonally

opposite their table, he surreptitiously scanned the bustling cityscape; the driver of a panel truck parked directly across the street was in the process of delivering plastic tanks of bottled water; motorists weaved in and out of traffic; pedestrians, huddled beneath their brollies, scurried down the pavement.

Nothing out of the ordinary.

So, why this dread feeling in the pit of my stomach?

The waiter, lips turned down in a classic Gallic sneer, returned with their drinks. Cædmon, accustomed to the French and their infernal bad manners, wordlessly handed the man ten euros.

Reaching for the white ceramic cup set in front of her, Kate smiled weakly. 'If I didn't need the caffeine fix, I would have joined you.'

She referred, of course, to the fact that he'd ordered a gin and tonic. And a double, at that.

Unable to meet her gaze, Cædmon squeezed the wedge of lemon before dropping the mutilated piece of fruit into his glass. 'Having successfully outwitted the evil ogre, a celebratory drink is in order.' Affecting a jovial air, he toasted the sentiment with a raised glass. *A glass punctured with a red light beam.*

No sooner did the unexpected image hit his ocular nerve than the glass shattered in his hand.

'Shite!'

In the next instant, a green bottle of Perrier exploded.

Lurching at Kate, Cædmon none too gently yanked her out of the bistro chair, pulling her under their table. Hunched over the top of her, he grabbed the nearby potted palm and dragged it in front of them. Because of the rain, all of the outdoor tables were vacant. Because the gunman's weapon was suppressed, no one inside the café was even aware of what was happening, the bullets silently lodging in the stucco wall behind them.

'Oh, God!' Kate moaned, her body contorted into a quivering ball.

Acid churning like mad in the pit of his gut, Cædmon ventured a glance across the street. *The gunman had to be hiding behind the delivery van parked on the other side of the road!*

Just then, a taxi pulled up to the front of the café. Both rear doors, as well as the front passenger door, flung open. Four tall Swedes, businessmen on a working holiday from the looks of them, got out of the cab.

Cædmon, seizing what might be their one and only chance to escape unscathed, quickly stood up. Extending a hand, he helped Kate to her feet. 'She lost a contact lens,' he said to one of the men in the group who glanced quizzically at them.

'Found it.' Raising an index finger, Kate displayed a nonexistent lens.

Explanation offered, Cædmon immediately insinuated himself into the middle of the foursome, dragging Kate along with him, purposefully sandwiching her between his chest and a hefty blond bloke. Tightly clustered, the six of them entered the café. Once they were safely over the threshold, Cædmon splintered off, pulling Kate towards the polished bar that ran along the back wall of the café. Out of the gunman's line of sight.

'Are you all right?' As soon as he asked, he shook his head. 'Yes, I know, an asinine question.'

'H-how is this happening?' she stammered. 'How does he k-keep f-finding us?'

'That is a damn good question.' His gaze trained on the truck still parked across the street, he said matter-of-factly, 'The situation being what it is, we can no longer wait for your mastodon.'

'My *what*!?'

'I refer, of course, to McGuire, who is –'

'Right here. I came in through the back exit.'

Hearing that raspy baritone, Kate spun around, throwing herself at Finnegan McGuire's chest. Drenched from head to foot, the commando hesitated a moment before wrapping his wet arms around Kate's backside.

'I was so worried about you, Finn! I thought . . . thought that something terrible had –'

'Hey, Katie. *Shhh.* I'm here now. It's all right.' His movements curiously tender, McGuire smoothed his hand over Kate's flushed cheek.

'Actually, it's not all right. We just came under fire,' Cædmon informed the other man in a lowered voice. 'I suspect our gunman is positioned behind the delivery truck that's parked across the street.'

Eyes narrowed, McGuire stared out of the bank of plate-glass windows. 'I *know* that the bastard didn't follow me. Hell, my own shadow couldn't keep up.'

'I assume that our assailant is using some sort of GPS device.' Cædmon grabbed a handful of paper napkins from the top of the bar, ignoring the waiter's furious glare. As he dabbed at his jacket, trying to soak up the spilled gin and tonic as best he could, he turned to Kate. 'I need the laptop computer that's in your rucksack.'

'We've got a gun-toting Oom-pah-pah on our six and you're worried about a damned computer!'

Cædmon shoved the saturated napkins on to the bar, halfway tempted to stuff the wad into the commando's mouth. 'You earlier mentioned that it was Fabius Jutier's laptop, did you not?' When McGuire nodded warily, he said, 'I believe that's how the Seven Research Foundation tracked you from Washington to Paris.'

'How can you be so sure?'

'Commandos attack, snoops track. Trust me, there's a microchip implanted on your pilfered laptop.'

McGuire snatched the laptop out of Kate's hands. 'If that's the case, I'm going to use this sucker to throw the hound off the scent. While I'm doing that, I want the two of you to exit out the back alley.'

'I have a better idea.' Cædmon reached for his mobile phone. 'While I may not have battlefield experience, I know how to escape the enemy.'

'What are you doing?'

'Calling for an ambulance.'

'Hey, grow a pair, will ya? I'm planning on all of us getting out of here alive.'

'As am I.' Turning his back on McGuire, Cædmon informed the emergency operator that an ambulance was immediately required at the Bistro de la Tour Eiffel, an older gentleman having just gone into cardiac arrest in the men's WC. Call made, he redirected his attention to McGuire. 'Take the laptop and hide it behind the commode in the gents. When you leave, make certain that the door is locked from the inside.'

Scowling, the commando strode towards the back of the café.

Her delicate features marred with anxiety, Kate sidled

next to him. 'What are our chances of getting out of here alive?'

Unable to offer false comfort, Cædmon told the truth. 'The situation is extremely fluid. The dynamics could change in an instant.' He jutted his chin, first at the crowded café with its harried waiters and boisterous clientele, then at the congested streetscape beyond the plate-glass windows.

'But as long as we stay inside the café, we're safe, right?' There was no mistaking the hopeful glimmer in Kate's eyes.

'The danger is that our gunman will simply charge through the front entrance, gun barrels blazing.' Glancing at his right hand, Cædmon noticed that it was visibly shaking. *Bloody hell, but I need a drink*. 'However, you mustn't dwell on –'

'The laptop is out of sight, stuffed behind the water tank,' McGuire interjected. 'Now what?' He had to raise his voice to be heard over the shrieking siren, a bright-red ambulance having just pulled up to the front door of the café. 'I hope to God that you're not expecting me to fake a heart attack.'

'I'm not. That said, follow my lead.'

Just as he expected, the atmosphere inside the café instantly changed with the arrival of the ambulance, patrons frantically glancing about, huddled waiters pointing to the front entrance. Everyone wondering for whom the sirens blared.

A suitably worried expression affixed to his face, Cædmon rushed over to the entrance, holding one side of the double doors open as the emergency crew hauled their stretcher and equipment into the café. With an air of heightened excitement, he directed them to the WC, which was located down a narrow hallway.

As soon as the crew was out of ear-shot, he motioned McGuire and Kate through the open door. 'Hurry! There's no time to lose!' Espying a folded umbrella propped near the entry, Cædmon pinched it before stepping across the threshold. He then closed the door and slid his purloined brolly through the metal handles, effectively barricading the entrance.

Since the parked ambulance completely blocked the front of the café, the gunman across the street couldn't see that they had departed the premises. And, if he was tracking them on a GPS system, he would erroneously assume that they were still inside.

Having correctly guessed the game plan, McGuire opened the passenger door on the ambulance. 'There are no keys in the ignition.'

'Ambulances are always equipped with an emergency starter button located under the driver's seat,' Cædmon informed him as he climbed into the vehicle. Folding his legs, he awkwardly manoeuvred to the driver's side.

Taking the co-pilot's seat, McGuire slid his hands under Kate's arms and unceremoniously hauled her on to his lap. To say the woman was shell-shocked would be putting it mildly.

'Let's haul ass.'

'Right.' Reaching under his seat, Cædmon pushed the protruding knob, the engine immediately turning. Yanking the gear lever down, he slammed his foot on the accelerator and pulled away from the kerb at a frighteningly fast speed, city blocks passing in a blur.

'All in all, not a bad idea,' McGuire grudgingly complimented as he forcefully ripped the satellite navigation device off the front dashboard. Rolling down the window, he hurled it to the kerb.

'Bloody brilliant, I'd say.'

Craning his neck, McGuire peered into the wing mirror. 'I figure we got another forty-five seconds before we run into a cop car.'

'If that.' Pulling over to the kerb, Cædmon braked to a stop. 'There's a Metro station around the corner. I suggest that we jump into a crowded subway carriage post-haste.'

Kate, still wearing a stupefied expression, reached for the door handle. 'I can't get out of this stolen ambulance fast enough.'

'Er, McGuire.' When the other man glanced over at him, Cædmon cleared his throat. 'Earlier today, you saved my life . . . I'm indebted.'

One side of the commando's mouth curved in his trademark sneer. 'Gee, don't know what got into me.'

43

A gasoline-laced breeze wafted through the open French doors, carrying with it the discordant blare of honking horns, traffic heavy this time of day in the Marais district. From where he stood, Cædmon could watch the building entryway. An excellent vantage point. Even the commando had acknowledged that the St Merry Hotel was a good choice.

'"To be of no church is dangerous,"' he murmured, letting the drapery fall into place as he stepped into the room. *Let us hope this one proves a safe haven.*

Shoulders drooping, Kate deposited her rucksack on the Gothic-style desk across from the bed. 'I was thinking more along the lines of "Get me to the church on time". Normally, I'd be bowled over by the fact that we're staying in a restored seventeenth-century presbytery which is next door to an equally old church. But after everything that's happened today, I just can't drum up a whole lot of enthusiasm.' Peering in his direction, she graced him with a weary smile. 'Although I'm greatly relieved to be here. And for that we have you to thank.'

'Flying bullets will make any man quick on his feet.'

'Luckily, you're quicker than most.'

Clearly fatigued, Kate plopped into a high-backed chair. Like everything else in the room, it was fit for a feudal lord, the room's stone-block walls enlivened with oak quatrefoils and tracery cutouts, the centrepiece being a massive bed with an intricately carved seven-foot-high headboard. Fit for the feudal lord and his lady love. Despite the fact that Kate had vehemently denied a romantic involvement with McGuire, Cædmon couldn't help but wonder at their sleeping arrangements.

'This wood-beamed ceiling reminds me of your room in Oxford,' Kate remarked, tilting her head to glance upward.

'The hearty souls were housed in the medieval wing of the college; those able to withstand winter chill, summer heat and leaky pipes. Punishment for crimes yet committed,' he deadpanned.

'Faulty plumbing aside, I used to think that there wasn't anything quite as beautiful as when the setting sun tinted your centuries-old window a rich shade of tangerine.' As she spoke, Kate girlishly tucked a loose strand of hair behind her ear. 'Such a lovely memory.'

Cædmon seated himself on the opposite side of the desk. Surprised that Kate harboured warm memories of their time at Oxford, he was at a loss for words. Sixteen years had come and gone since they'd last seen one another. A lifetime. And yet he could easily envision her studiously bent over an open book. Claude Lévi Strauss's *A World on the Wane*. Or some other anthropology tome. Committed scholars, they used to spend hours in that medieval room, each engrossed in their separate studies. Each oblivious to the other's presence. Until one of them would look up and catch the other's eye. A come-hither smile later, they'd end up under the duvet. *Now that was a lovely memory.*

'Do you realize that I wouldn't know how to ride a

bicycle if it wasn't for you,' Kate remarked, unaware that his thoughts were running along a more lurid path. 'Since my parents were both academics, they didn't consider riding a bike a necessary life skill.'

'Don't know if it's necessary in the larger scheme of things, but certainly essential at Oxford.' Still stuck under the duvet, he smiled fondly. 'Indeed, you were so enamoured with your newly acquired skill that you would drag me out of bed at an ungodly hour for early morning rides in the mist.'

'You can't deny that there was a surreal beauty to it. As though we were trapped in a medieval dreamscape. Just the two of us peddling through a heavenly realm.' She closed her eyes; a woman lost in reverie.

'I also taught you how to drink sherry.'

Hearing that, her eyes popped wide open. 'Dry, chilled, served in a hand-blown *copita* glass, and –' an animated gleam in those greyish-blue eyes, Kate raised an imaginary glass – 'accompanied by your favourite toast –'

'Bottoms up and knickers down,' he chimed in, chortling.

No sooner did the shared chuckle fade into silence than a furrow appeared between Kate's brows. 'Were you really that upset by my *lettre de rupture*?'

Take aback by that unexpected query, he was tempted to play the cavalier. To make light of the whole affair.

'Utterly destroyed,' he confessed at the last, hoping the truth would finally set him free. 'I'd given you my heart.'

'As I recall, you were quite obsessed with the Knights Templar. I was tired of playing second fiddle to a bunch of dead monks.'

His regret real, Cædmon penitently bowed his head and stared at his hands. 'Like most men, I didn't realize what I had until I lost it.'

'And when we lose that thing that we hold so dear, it never comes back.'

Hearing a husky catch in her voice, he intuited that Kate was referring to her own life. Her own painful loss.

Raising his head, he gazed intently at the sad-faced woman seated across from him. He knew from Kate's dossier that life had flung her to the cement pavement. And from a very high rooftop. Her only child, a baby boy named Samuel, had died from SIDS. An unfathomable loss.

'I know about Samuel.'

Eyes welling with emotion, Kate flinched. A terrified animal caught in the headlights. 'Oh, God,' she moaned.

He reached across the desk and cupped her cheek in his hand. Gently, he swiped the pad of his thumb under her eye socket, catching a runaway tear. 'You probably loathe the "I'm so sorry" speech, but I understand, Kate. There's a gaping hole in your heart. I know . . . I, too, lost someone,' he confessed, words and sentiments jumbling together. 'And when Juliana died, it devastated me.'

'Oh, Cædmon . . . I . . . I'm so very sorry . . . there, I said it.' Turning her head, Kate lightly pressed her lips to his palm. She then gazed at him, eyes clouded with concern. 'If you need someone to talk to . . . or a shoulder to cry on . . . I can help you get through this. Maybe that's why we've re-connected after all these years. Because we need each other.' Clearly empathizing with his pain, she placed her hand over his. 'Was Juliana your wife?'

He dolefully shook his head. 'But I had given great thought to asking –'

'Sorry to interrupt the canoodle fest.'

Hearing that deep-throated voice, Cædmon and Kate quickly and gracelessly pulled apart. McGuire, an old-fashioned skeleton key in one hand and two plastic shopping bags dangling from the other, stood in the doorway. 'I bought some refreshments. Not that you two lovebirds would care.' He stomped over to the desk, managing to look more intimidating than usual.

'We were just reminiscing about old times at Oxford,' Kate assured her surly companion, cheeks guiltily stained a vivid bright red. 'Cædmon, do you remember Sidney Hartwell?'

'Pudgy Classics major prone to drunken stupors,' he replied, playing along with the game. 'Liked to wave his trousers in the air while he shouted obscene profanities.'

'In Latin and in the middle of the night, no less.' Never good at subterfuge, Kate nervously giggled.

McGuire dragged a chair over to the desk and set it inches from Kate's Gothic monstrosity. A man staking his claim. He then proceeded to remove a six-pack of beer from one bag and a litre bottle of water from the other. 'Choose your poison – Kronenbourg or H_2O. And just so you know, I cannot abide a country that doesn't sell cold beer at the grocery store. Here. You look like you could use one of these.' McGuire pulled a can free from the plastic ring and slid it across the desk in Cædmon's direction.

'An Irishman who would refuse a pint of warm Guinness. Well, well, wonders never cease.'

'You'd turn your nose up, too, if you'd ever seen how

my Da downed the black stuff. Surprised I'm able to enjoy a brewski.' Shaking his head, McGuire rolled his eyes. 'If *only* he'd waved his trousers in the air.'

Cædmon wondered at the startling admission. *Perhaps the earlier brush with death is causing the three of us to come apart at the seams.*

Seams ready to burst, he rapaciously eyed the unopened can. Like McGuire, he didn't much care for warm beer. A G&T on ice would be better. *But this might quell the pang.*

He reached for the Kronenbourg.

Only to retreat at the last.

Then, not fully trusting himself, he slid the proffered can back in McGuire's direction.

'No, thank you.' Jaw tight, those three simple words sounded unnaturally clipped. Probably because he'd recently come off a three-day binge. A bender, as the Yanks called them. Usually his drinking bouts lasted no more than a few days. Although the first, after the 'incident' in Belfast, extended to a full two weeks. The boys from Thames House found him slumped over a bar in Budapest. According to his passport, he'd been to six different countries in those two weeks. To this day, he had no recollection of that drunken fortnight, although it was his lone act of vengeance in Belfast that angered the powers that be at Thames House more than the drunken spree. In the two years since, he'd paid heavily for the transgression. Seconded to MI6, he'd been made to run a safe house in Paris. A humiliating demotion.

'You know, I've been thinking about it –' McGuire popped the lid on his can, misting the air with the tang of Strisselspalt hops and a light citrus aroma – 'and no way in hell can I accept that the Holy Grail is "the stone in exile". Sister Michael Patrick, a woman whose authority even a smart aleck like me didn't dare question, taught us that the Grail is the chalice that was used at the Last Supper. And when Jesus was on the cross, that same chalice was used to collect his blood. That's how it became the *Holy* Grail.'

Dissertation delivered, the commando raised the can to his lips and drank deeply.

Astonished that the other man had deliberated on the matter, Cædmon countered by saying, 'Don't know how "holy" it is. According to Wolfram von Eschenbach's *Parzival*, the *Lapis Exillis* was the stone knocked free from Lucifer's crown when he was cast from heaven. As you undoubtedly know, Lucifer had originally been God's favourite until he committed the grave sin of putting himself on a par with the Almighty. A heavenly insurrection ensued, the angelic legions battling for supremacy. In the end, Lucifer was tossed on his arse.' As he spoke, Cædmon belatedly realized that he shared a common bond with the ousted angel, having taken upon himself the power of life and death. *And look where it landed me.*

'Given its ignominious provenance, I'm surprised that the *Lapis Exillis* would be deemed sacred,' Kate said, twisting the lid on the water bottle. 'And Finn raises a valid point: most people believe that the Grail is a chalice.'

Getting up from his chair, Cædmon walked over to the other side of the room and retrieved a water glass from the bedside table. 'During the Middle Ages, there were three different Grail camps: those who believed the relic was a chalice; those who were convinced that it was a stone; and the peacekeepers who, through a convoluted twisting of both tales, declared that the Grail had been a stone that became a chalice.' Reseating himself, he handed the glass to Kate. 'Although what's not in dispute is the fact that the Grail, whether it be stone or chalice, has miraculous power. And what is power if not energy?'

'So you're thinking that the Grail has something to do with the Axe Historique and the Vril force,' Kate said, quick to catch his drift.

'Depictions of the Grail often render it shrouded in a brilliant burst of light.' Vexed, Cædmon shook his head. He had a gut feeling that the *Lapis Exillis* was connected to the Paris axis, but not a shred of evidence to prove it. 'Mind you, this is mere speculation, but it could be that the Grail is some sort of transducer that can convert one type of energy into another.'

'How do the Cathars fit into the Grail story?' Kate poured herself a glass of water, then, holding the bottle aloft, silently enquired if he cared for some.

'Difficult to say,' Cædmon replied, politely shaking his head, water no substitute for alcohol. 'The Cathars were dualists who believed that there were two gods, not one. The god whom they referred to as *Rex Mundi*, the king of the world, they associated with Lucifer who ruled the material realm. Conversely, the good god was the Light that illuminated the heavenly sphere. How the Cathars came to be in possession of a uniquely Christian relic is anyone's guess.' He paused, well aware that the conversation was about to veer off course. 'Although it's abundantly clear from the Latin inscription on the Montségur Medallion that the Cathars were the Grail Guardians.'

'But I always thought that the Cathars were a Christian

sect.' Kate's brow furrowed, having jumped to the same erroneous conclusion that most people made.

'While the Cathars thought of themselves as upright Christians, their rituals did not include the traditional Catholic sacraments. And, of course, there was that heretical business about Jesus being a divinely inspired prophet rather than the divine Son of God.'

One side of McGuire's mouth quirked in a wry half-grin. 'Reason enough for Sister Michael Patrick to pull out a box of Diamond matches and light a pyre.'

'How strange that you should make reference to the Inquisitors' funeral pyre since I'm about to throw caution aside and leap into the fire. After due deliberation . . .' Cædmon paused, on the cusp of a decision that could well change his life. 'I've decided to search for the Grail.'

44

'Jesus H!' Finn's shoulders jack-knifed off the back of the chair. 'You are off your freakin' English rocker if you think you can find the Holy Grail!'

'Thank you for that resounding vote of confidence,' Aisquith deadpanned, unfazed by the criticism.

'Finding the Grail is like putting toothpaste back in the tube. It ain't gonna happen. And didn't you see the movie? Indiana Jones already beat you to it,' Finn taunted, beginning to think the Brit needed to be knocked on the head with a 2 x 4. *Drastic?* Maybe. But he didn't know what else besides a wood kiss would knock sense into the guy.

'Do you have any idea what these people are capable of?' Folding his arms over his chest, Aisquith patronizingly looked down his nose. Like he was the school master and Finn the class dunce.

'They butchered two good buddies of mine, so, yeah, I think I know what I'm up against.' Raising the beer can to his lips, Finn polished it off.

'And before that, they *butchered* as many as seventeen million innocent people.'

'Cædmon, have you really thought this through?' Kate enquired in concern, having remained silent up to this point. Probably in a state of shock. 'The Seven Research Foundation could easily target you.'

'If memory serves correctly, they already have.' He

glanced down at the spot on his chest where he'd almost taken a bullet to the heart. 'Although not to worry. I'm well armed. *Fortis est veritas.*'

Kate smiled wistfully; the phrase obviously meaning something to her. 'And just as truth is strength, *scientia potentia est.*'

'Knowledge is power,' Aisquith replied.

'Hey, excuse me. I didn't get to go to *Awxford.* I got my education at Boot Camp U. So, can we all stick to English?'

'Very well. Here is a fact that requires no translation: the Ahnenerbe was obsessed with finding the Holy Grail. Their descendents seem no less fanatical. While I don't know the foundation's reason for coveting the relic, I'm certain that it pertains to the Axe Historique and the creation of the Vril force.' Doing a fair imitation of a traffic cop, Aisquith held up his right hand. 'And please spare me the stale refrain about flying saucers and Nazi ray guns.'

'Fine,' Finn muttered, having been two seconds shy of throwing a zinger. 'But do you actually expect me to believe that a bunch of Nazi descendants are planning a comeback? There's nothing left of the Third Reich. My great-uncle Seamus and all the other men who kicked Nazi ass sixty some years ago saw to that.' Point made, he reached for another beer.

'And my grandfather, who was a prosecuting attorney at the Nuremberg trials, was appalled that the high-ranking members of the Nazi Party considered themselves avatars, gods in the making. Indeed, he said on more than one occasion that it was impossible to reason with them. It's naive to think that the evil was completely eradicated at war's end. We must assume that the Ahnenerbe's spawn have been indoctrinated in this dark belief system.'

Finn lifted a disinterested shoulder. 'That was then, this is now.'

'Is it?' For several long seconds Aisquith stared at him, grim-faced. 'Many of the same global crises that gave rise to National Socialism in the 1930s again threaten to cripple world governments. This is a movement that thrives on despair and discontent. Pick up any newspaper; there's plenty of that to go around.'

'As a cultural anthropologist, I can attest to the fact that Western Europe and America are both in the midst of a social upheaval,' Kate remarked, throwing in her lot with Aisquith. 'Xenophobia and religious intolerance are rampant and could easily reach a dangerous tipping point. It's happened before. It could happen again.' Lips slightly quivering, her voice dropped to a husky whisper. 'Although a proud American citizen, my grandfather was forcibly imprisoned in a Japanese internment camp.'

Jesus. I had no idea. Finn stared at his beer can, wanting to give comfort, but uncertain how to act on the impulse.

'Lest we forget,' Aisquith said consolingly, reaching across the desk to squeeze Kate's hand. Then, his voice more strident, 'My aim is to destroy the enemy's arsenal. And, yes, I believe that the Vril force, if harnessed, could be used as a weapon. Had Nazi physicists been successful in their quest to weaponize the Vril, there would have been a far different outcome to the Second World War.'

'Hey, I can't get bogged down by something that didn't happen. If it doesn't relate to my mission op tomorrow at the Grande Arche, I'm not interested.' Beer can in hand,

Finn jabbed it in Aisquith's direction. 'And don't get any funny ideas in your head about borrowing the medallion. That sucker is the only bargaining chip I have to get the Dark Angel.'

'A digital photo of the Montségur Medallion will suffice. If you would be so kind.'

'Whatever.' Unzipping his Go Bag, Finn extracted the medallion and handed it over, figuring it was the quickest way to get rid of the other man.

The Brit wasted no time whipping out his BlackBerry, Kate getting up from her chair to play photographer's assistant. Annoyed that they kept making goo-goo eyes at each other, Finn stood up and walked over to the French doors, almost stumbling on the bed's footboard en route. The damned thing was enormous and, try as he might, there was no escaping it.

Opening the set of doors, he purposefully turned his back on the king-size mattress with the silky royal blue spread. While women needed a reason to have sex, men just needed a place. A bed. The back of a truck. A concrete floor. Didn't much matter. Although the floor was probably where he'd end up spending the night while Kate, sacked out on that huge mattress, dreamed about the Scarlet Pimpernel.

In a foul mood, Finn scanned the streetscape below, on the look-out for unfriendlies, cops or the Dark Angel, his enemies fast mounting. Aisquith had assured him that the hotel was secure, but his trust only went so far. Which was the reason why he had the floor plan for all five storeys of the hotel committed to memory and had checked out all of the exits before making his beer run.

Ignoring the murmured conversation taking place behind him, Finn watched as a grey Peugeot taxi sped down Rue de la Verrerie like it was in a Formula One time test. Not seeing anything suspicious, he closed the doors.

Still fuming, he headed back to the desk. Standing side-by-side, Aisquith and Kate were staring intently at the digital photos that they'd just taken of the medallion.

'Do you think the encoded map is contained within the pictorial symbols or the inscription?' Kate asked.

'The clues to the Grail's whereabouts could be embedded in the inscriptions as well as the symbols. A two-prong encryption code.' As he spoke, Aisquith fingered the rim of the medallion. 'Deciphering an esoteric mystery is akin to finding one's way through a Georgian maze. You spend hours aimlessly wandering, hitting one dead-end after another, only to find yourself standing at the very spot where you began.'

'Which begs the question: where are you going to begin the search?'

Not particularly interested in hearing Aisquith's reply, Finn reseated himself at the desk. Forced to take a back seat, he took a swig of warm beer, wondering if there was anything he could do to get Aisquith out of the door – other than the time-honoured boot to the ass.

'The legends state that the Cathars smuggled a treasure from their mountaintop citadel at Montségur several days before the fortress fell to the Pope's army,' Aisquith pontificated in his snooty *Awxford* accent. 'Making Montségur the logical place to begin the hunt. That said . . . ?'

Finn watched as Aisquith looked expectantly over at Kate. A silent invitation.

One second slipped into the next, Finn's hand tightening around the beer can.

'It's, um, probably best if I stay in Paris.'

Hearing that, the bottom half of him – that being the part between his hips – was relieved that Kate had rejected the Brit. But the top half – the part between his ears – was annoyed as hell. Kate Bauer was a complication. And a physical distraction. He had three irons in the fire. He didn't need a fourth one scorching his pants.

Aisquith glanced at his watch. 'I have just enough time to pack a bag and catch a southbound train.' Turning towards Kate, he cupped her face between his hands and quickly kissed her on the lips.

'Goodbye, Cædmon and . . . please be careful,' Kate whispered, clearly upset by the other man's imminent departure.

About to take another swig of his beer, Finn glanced at Aisquith. 'Needle. Haystack,' he said, summing up the crazy-ass, half-baked quest. 'That said, good luck, Sir Prancelot. And may the Force be with you.'

Aisquith's mouth contorted into a snide smile. 'You do realize, don't you, that if I find the Grail, your little gold trinket will be utterly worthless?'

45

Ivo Uhlemann raised the china cup to his lips and took a sip of green tea.

Without the tracking device, finding Finnegan McGuire in a city of two million inhabitants would be next to impossible. Particularly since they only had three days until the heliacal rising of Sirius. Although they had managed to track down McGuire's cohort, Cædmon Aisquith, the owner of L'Equinoxe bookstore.

The day's events having taken their toll, he'd sought his favourite sanctuary, the secluded alcove that overlooked the Seven's research facility. Constructed underground, the installation was designed around a three-storey faux atrium. Multiple laboratories, work stations, a well-stocked library and several conference rooms lined the top two storeys. With its full-spectrum illumination, banks of frosted glass and lush plants, it was a visually appealing environment.

Cathedral-like, it was here that Ivo prayed daily to the gods of Galileo, Copernicus, Newton and Planck.

Peering over the railing, he was pleased to observe the researchers, scientists and scholars seated at various tables on the mezzanine level. In order to maintain secrecy, they endeavoured under the false belief that they were working on a covert government project. To further the deceit, they'd been forced to sign an 'official' confidentiality disclosure agreement. Should they reveal the nature of their work to anyone outside of the foundation, they would be hit with heavy monetary fines and possible imprisonment. Or so they believed. If, in fact, any of the researchers ever did violate the terms of the agreement, a far more severe penalty would be meted out. Administered by the Dark Angel.

The sight of so much industry, of virtuosi working for a common cause, was a soothing balm for Ivo's frazzled nerves. An organized collective, all of the researchers at the Seven Research Foundation were in pursuit of the same primary objective – to analyze the effect of fusing astral and telluric energies to create the Vril force.

The Lost Science of the ancient world.

While they'd had great success engineering a special generator to create the Vril force, they were missing the unique integral component that would operate the device – the *Lapis Exillis.*

Once they found the *Lapis Exillis*, and they *would* find it, *das Groß Versuch*, the Great Experiment, could be conducted. In Stage One of the experiment, they would generate the Vril force. In the next stage, the Vril force would be used to do the unimaginable . . . to create a loop in the space–time continuum.

The ultimate physics experiment.

Glancing dismissively at his tepid cup of tea, Ivo hoped that he lived long enough to witness that history-altering event.

The pain having become more than he could bear, he gracelessly lumbered to his feet. The metastasized tumour in the back of his abdominal cavity pressed against his spine, creating near-constant pain. According to his oncologist, he had no more than four months to live. Even if he underwent the gruelling treatments, it would only add an extra two or three months to his life. Preferring pain to debilitating nausea and uncontrollable diarrhoea, he'd elected not to undergo the chemotherapy and radiation treatment. At least the pain could be managed.

Slowly shuffling to a locked door on the other side of the alcove, Ivo keyed a numeric code into the security pad, the door unlocking with a soft *pong!*

A private lavatory, it was painted and tiled in neutral shades of brown, the cabinetry stained a dark espresso. An elaborate dried floral arrangement, an upholstered high-backed chair and several pillar candles created a tasteful décor.

Ivo stepped over to the basin and washed his hands. Seating himself on the edge of the chair, he opened a drawer and removed a small bottle of white powder, a second bottle of sterile water, a tiny piece of cotton, an alcohol swab, a tourniquet, a wrapped syringe and a spoon. Hands shaking, he lit the nearby candle. He deemed it a bitter irony that his pain medication derived its name from the German word *heroisch* meaning 'heroic'.

From his perspective, there was nothing heroic about dying from cancer or shooting up with heroin.

However, he'd long since got over the shame of the latter. For him, it was a matter of simple expedience; heroin crossed the blood–brain barrier faster than morphine and was a far more potent analgesic.

Removing the needle from his vein, Ivo leaned back in the chair and closed his eyes, able to see a luminous fire burning in the dark void. An instant later, Wotan appeared, hanging from a gnarled oak tree.

Pain dissipating, Ivo softly cackled.

The fallacy of religion was that the Church Fathers adamantly asserted transcendental experiences proved the existence of God. *How trite.* One had only to inject a small amount of heroin into a vein to induce a spiritual euphoria.

Ivo savoured the bliss as the bright ball of fire travelled to his left breast, burning a hole through the middle of his tattoo.

Yes!

They *would* find the *Lapis Exillis.* He was certain of it. Then they would put his father's theory to the ultimate test. Transform the past into the present. And when they did, they would restore *das Dritte Reich* . . . the Third Reign . . . one that would indeed last a thousand years.

How amazing to ponder that the course of all their lives could be dramatically altered by fusing different types of energy. Creating an invisible force that had no intelligence, no scent, no taste and made no sound.

Yet, despite all that, a force to be reckoned with.

46

What was the Grail if not the Mysterium cosmographicum? Cædmon silently mused.

Excited by the prospect of finding the 'secret of the universe', he had nonetheless taken the time to shave, shower and don fresh clothing. Keys in hand, he swung the leather tote bag on to his shoulder. For some inexplicable reason, he felt like a new man.

Ready to depart, he shut the bedroom door and headed into the flat's cluttered sitting room. Opening the top drawer on the corner cabinet, he reluctantly deposited his holster. As he did, his gaze landed on a smudged glass with a finger's measure of gin, in plain sight where he'd left it earlier that morning on top of the cabinet.

For several long seconds he stared, his old self tempted.

'"And every spirit upon earth seemed fervourless as I,"' he muttered, well aware that he'd become a predictable bore.

Tuning out the Siren, he purposefully hitched the satchel a bit higher on his shoulder and strode out of the room.

A few moments later, alarm set and shop door locked, he departed L'Equinoxe bookstore. The gaily painted shop sign swayed ever so slightly in the breeze, rusty hinges jangling. He'd designed the signage, which depicted the Fool, the first card in the Tarot deck, as a satirical self-portrait.

The innocent young man blithely setting forth on an adventure. So consumed in his *joie de vivre*, it rendered him oblivious to the fact that he was about to step off a cliff and break his bloody neck.

Although, strangely enough, today the image bespoke a deeper meaning. In truth, he felt uplifted. Invigorated, even. Certainly a departure from the self-loathing he'd experienced upon rising. For what began as a day like any other had unexpectedly turned into an odyssey. A mental challenge had presented itself, wrapped in the tantalizing ribbons of a centuries-old mystery.

However, unlike the Fool, he wasn't naive. The Seven Research Foundation sought the Grail so they could put a dark plan into play. The progeny of monsters, God only knew what they intended. The Cathars would claim, and rightly so, that the Seven owed allegiance to none save *Rex Mundi*, Lucifer, the god of the material realm. The evil one who lured young fools from the straight and narrow path.

As he hurriedly made his way down Rue de la Bûcherie – feeling very much like a newly released penitentiary inmate – it dawned on Cædmon that all of the cock-ups in his life had transpired after he'd veered from the straight and narrow. His father, were he still alive, would maintain that he'd taken his first misstep when he'd journeyed down the birth canal. Indeed, he held Cædmon personally liable for the fact that Helena Aisquith died while she laboured to bring their first child, a squalling baby boy, into the world.

Because of that tragic misfortune, he'd been raised in a cheerless household. When he turned thirteen, his father shunted him off to Eton College. A malicious contrivance, Cædmon was forced to bear a whole new torment, pecking order at the hallowed public school determined by one's lineage. Lacking the ancestral prestige of his classmates, he had to best them with the only tools in his arsenal: a sharp mind and a well-honed body. By the time he left Eton, he boasted membership in the elite Sixth Form Select and had captained the cricket team that victoriously took the field against Harrow. For five arduous years he had stayed true to the straight path until, finally liberated, he set forth for Oxford.

In no time at all, he veered on to a crooked lane.

For the first two years he ran with a fast crowd who fancied themselves latter-day libertines, 'Mad, bad and dangerous to know.' When the late-night revels became old hat, his scholastic passions revived. However, craving academic excitement, he did the unthinkable and changed from Egyptology to medieval history, the Knights Templar *far* more thrilling than mummified pharaohs. Earning a reputation as a rogue scholar, the impulsive move eventually resulted in his ousting from Queen's College. 'The Manifesto', as he jokingly referred to his dissertation, was summarily dismissed as a 'harebrained hypothesis that could only have been opium-induced'. When, a few months later, MI5 came knocking at his door, it seemed a blessing in disguise.

Little did I know . . .

But the overlords at Thames House had not deadened his spirit. Nor had the dons at Queen's College blunted his academic passion. The fact that he was setting off for Montségur proved that he was still curious. Still intrigued by those questions that had no answers.

In a hurry to get to the Metro, Cædmon sidestepped a group of tourists who, maps and cameras in hand, huddled on the pavement. He glanced at his wristwatch. The high-speed TGV train for Marseille was scheduled to depart Gare de Lyon in forty-five minutes. Giving him just enough time to arrive at the train station and purchase a ticket. According to the schedule, they would arrive in Marseille by mid-evening. He intended to use the three-hour train ride to devise a plan of action. Wi-Fi Internet access would enable him to begin his preliminary research.

He knew that the trip might prove a fool's errand. Many men had sought the Grail. Many had met their death in the ill-fated quest. Be that as it may, he felt compelled to join the hunt.

Making his way across the Square René Viviani, the small park adjacent to St Julien-le-Pauvre Church, Cædmon sensed an unseen presence following in his wake. The nape of his neck prickled as he ducked into a church doorway.

Hidden in a dark alcove, cheek pressed to the fluted limestone, he surreptitiously peered around the corner. This time of day the tree-lined park brimmed with harried mothers chasing tots and pushing prams. From where he stood, he had an unobstructed view across the Seine to the much larger, and more magnificent, Notre-Dame.

Eyes narrowed, Cædmon searched for the telltale person who did not belong. The anomaly in the endless stream.

Nothing seemed out of the ordinary.

As a precaution, he waited a few seconds more. Because

all train passengers had to pass through a metal detector, he'd been forced to leave his Ruger pistol back at the flat.

He released a pent-up breath. 'I'm seeing fiends where none exist.'

Stepping away from the portal, he continued on his way. He quickened his pace as he glanced at the western horizon and noticed a strange chartreuse cast to the sky.

A warning that a violent storm was brewing.

Part III

'The real voyage of discovery consists not in seeing new landscapes, but in having new eyes' – Marcel Proust

47

Montségur Castle, The Languedoc

0914 hours

Could anything be more ridiculous than a middle-aged man on a Grail quest?

'Only the Fool about to blithely step off a steep cliff,' Cædmon muttered under his breath.

To prevent a fatal mishap, he braced both hands on the ruined battlement as he set his gaze on the Pyrenees. Perched atop a limestone and granite outcrop that rose an impressive three thousand feet into the air, Montségur commanded a panoramic view that left one awestruck. Ragged peaks. Colossal mountains. Sheer precipices. Set against a cerulean blue sky, the ancient mountains seemed impregnable.

Although appearances could be deceiving as the doomed Cathars discovered when their 'impregnable' citadel was besieged by the Pope's army.

According to legend, just before the fortress capitulated, on a frigid and moonless night, four brave Cathars scaled Montségur's western cliff. Managing to sneak past the enemy line, they travelled under cover of night to the Templar preceptory located twelve kilometres away. To persuade the warrior monks to fight on their behalf, the four Cathars bore a gold medallion with an encrypted map that revealed the secret location of the greatest treasure of the Middle Ages, the Holy Grail. Having presented the medallion to the Knights Templar, the Cathar emissaries promised that the encryption key would be turned over as soon as the Templars took up arms. The prize too tempting to resist, the Templars saddled their war horses and set off for Montségur.

By the time they arrived, the citadel had already fallen, the last two hundred and fifty Cathars forcibly marched through the barbican gates. They were put to the torch by order of the Pope's envoy, a white-robed Dominican priest, thus bringing to a fiery close the thirty-year-long Albigensian Crusade.

As had happened on all of his previous visits to Montségur, Cædmon found himself contemplating the tragedy with renewed vigour. Everywhere he looked the ghost of those humble heretics hovered amidst the ruined ramparts and shattered curtain walls, all that remained of the Cathars' mountaintop eyrie. A limestone monument to the dead, it invoked the memory of that other doomed mountaintop fortress, the Jewish bastion at Masada. Which no doubt explained the heart-rending aura that clung to the citadel like a finely spun burial shroud.

Opening the flap on his field jacket, Cædmon removed his BlackBerry. Because of the precipitous hike up the winding mountain trail from the village below, he'd dressed in khaki cargo pants, a practical long-sleeved shirt and rugged boots. Accessing the photo log on the BlackBerry, he stared at the symbols incised on the medallion: star, sun, moon and four strangely-shaped 'A's arranged in a cruciform.

His gaze zeroed in on the four 'A's.

Yesterday, on the train ride from Paris, he'd carefully examined a map of the Languedoc. With numerous place names in the region beginning with the letter 'A', it would take a lifetime to search each and every one. Moreover, the

Languedoc encompassed an area that measured nearly sixteen thousand square miles. Most of it, mountainous terrain. The disheartening reality was that the Grail could have been hidden *anywhere* within those sixteen thousand square miles.

He skipped to the next photograph, a close-up of the engraved text on the medallion's flipside. The first two lines, written in the Occitan language, read: 'In the glare of the twelfth hour, the moon shines true.' A curious turn of phrase since the moon was most often associated with the night sky. The last line of text had been scribed in Latin. *Reddis lapis exillis cellis*. 'The Stone of Exile has been returned to the niche.' While the meaning was obvious, it was also frustratingly vague, no mention made of where 'the niche' was located.

The mystery compounding, Cædmon took a deep breath, filling his lungs with the pine-scented air as he stared at the craggy mountains in the near distance. *Terra incognita.*

Worried that he'd journeyed to Montségur in vain, he gazed at the barren courtyard beneath the ramparts. Two blokes who'd hauled surveying equipment to the citadel were toying with a transit-level. Another pair, who were filming a documentary, had just set a very professional-looking video camera on to a tripod. A tour group on the far-side of the courtyard was taking turns reading aloud from Wolfram von Eschenbach's *Parzival.*

Cædmon suspected that, like him, they were all attempting to solve the mystery of the Cathars' mountaintop –

Mountain!

'Bloody hell,' he whispered, hit with a sudden burst of inspiration.

Sliding his rucksack off his shoulder, he hurriedly loosened the drawstrings, retrieving a small leather-bound journal and a sharpened pencil. His hand visibly shaking, he opened the journal to the first blank page and drew one of the 'A's from the medallion cruciform.

His breath caught in his throat.

It's not an 'A' . . . it's a mountain peak!

Taken aback by the revelation, Cædmon hitched his hip on to the battlement as he examined the digital photos on the BlackBerry with fresh eyes. If he was right, it meant that, rather than four 'A's, there were four mountain peaks depicted on the medallion. A pictogram of the landscape visible from Montségur. Hope renewed, he stared intently at the other engraved symbols.

Certain that the star and the sun represented the heliacal rising of Sirius, that left the moon in the top quadrant to decipher. An age-old symbol found in almost every culture, its meaning and significance was myriad. Birth. Death. Resurrection. Cyclical time. Spiritual light in the dead of night.

But how did any of that relate to the four mountain peaks?

'"In the glare of the twelfth hour, the moon shines true,"' he quietly recited, the moon not only depicted on the medallion, but specifically mentioned on the reverse inscription.

Could the 'moon' be the key to unlocking the riddle of the Montségur Medallion?

Again, he was struck by the strange reference to time. Noon, the twelfth hour of the day, was the apogee of light, when the sun, not the moon, shone at its brightest. Traditionally, 'noon' also correlated to the cardinal direction of 'south'. To this day, the French word 'midi' meant 'noon' *and* 'southern'. As in the Midi-Pyrénées, or southern Pyrenees, where Montségur was located.

What if the 'moon' referred to a specific mountain located south of Montségur?

Anxious to test the hypothesis, Cædmon quickly checked the online map feature on his BlackBerry.

'Damn,' he muttered a few moments later, not getting a single hit.

On a twenty-first-century map.

Undaunted, he next pulled up an Oxford University search engine for the map collection at the Bodleian Library. Just as he'd hoped, the Bod had a thirteenth-century map of the Languedoc archived online. Heart beating at a brisk tattoo, he clicked on it.

'Christ.'

Shaking his head in disbelief, Cædmon double-checked the crudely rendered chart. He then lurched to his feet and turned about face, towards the granite peak that loomed on the southern horizon. *Mont de la Lune.*

'Moon Mountain' as it had been called eight hundred years ago.

He barely suppressed the urge to rear his head and shout a joyful *hosanna.* While the clue might not lead to the Grail, it was a signpost. A new direction in which to venture forth.

On a wing, and even a prayer, so goeth the intrepid Fool.

Anxious to be on his way, Cædmon hurriedly shoved the BlackBerry into his jacket pocket and returned the journal to his rucksack. He then rushed towards the stone steps that led from the ramparts to the courtyard below, an unshaven, khaki-clad wayfarer ready to embark on *la quête du Graal.*

God help him.

48

Grande Arche Belvedere, Paris

1059 hours

'Hey, Katie. What's the matter?' Finn slid his Oakley sunglasses on to the top of his head. 'And please don't tell me that you're scared of heights.' Standing on the rooftop of the Grande Arche building, at the eastern side of the belvedere, they had a bird's-eye-view of the Axe Historique, a.k.a. the Champs-Élysées, thirty-five storeys below. With all of the ultra-modern architecture in the near vicinity, the area resembled a cityscape from a sci-fi movie.

Although Finn didn't consider it much of a tourist attraction, a crowd nonetheless shuffled along the barricaded perimeter of the rooftop. Bright-blue telescopes were set up every ten feet or so, tourists plopping coins into the slots so they could *ooh* and *ahh* over the wonders of Paris magnified umpteen times.

Kate seated herself on a nearby bench. 'I'm concerned about this so-called "mission op",' she told him in a subdued tone of voice. 'After everything that happened yesterday, is it prudent to go on the offensive?'

'Grabbing the bull by the balls is the only way that I can get justice for Corporals Dixon and Kelleher. The Dark Angel *will* pay in a court of law for what she did to my two buddies.' Homily delivered, Finn figured a little bolstering was in order as Kate was obviously suffering from a bad case of battlefield jitters. 'Do you have any idea how much it costs to train a special ops soldier? I'll tell ya – it costs three quarters of a million dollars.' He paused, letting the fact soak in. 'In other words, I know what I'm doing. Besides, they have no idea that we're even here.' 'They' being the Seven, who had their headquarters on the thirty-fifth floor of the Grande Arche. *The penthouse suite directly below them.*

According to Fabius Jutier's calendar, an eleven o'clock board meeting of the Seven Research Foundation had been scheduled. With all of the principal players in attendance, it was Finn's chance to storm the castle gate.

'You're right.' Kate smiled sheepishly. 'Sorry for being such a nervous Nellie.'

'Hey, it's understandable.' Glad they'd got over the hump without incident, Finn sat down beside her.

Granted, it wasn't the most comfortable seat in the house, but he'd seen one too many uniformed police prowling around below deck. Just as worrisome, with the exception of the rooftop, there were video cameras mounted everywhere. If his image was captured and matched to his military photo – enabling the authorities to close in on him – he'd have no choice but to abort the mission. And leave Dixie and Johnny K hanging in limbo. No way in hell was he going to let that happen.

In this man's army, you don't leave your comrades behind.

Leaning against the metal bench, Finn put an arm around Kate's shoulders while he took in the view. While the Grande Arche came in at a respectable height, the marble-clad structure was dwarfed by the towering steel and mirrored glass buildings that surrounded it. The reflected light near blinding, Finn slipped his shades back on.

'I'm curious, Finn . . . why *did* you join the army?'

An innocent enough question but, unbeknownst to Kate, it struck a deep chord.

Seventeen years may have come and gone, but Finn could still vividly recall his treeless South Boston neighbourhood with the ramshackle three-storey terraced houses and chain-link fences, the streets lined with dented aluminium trash cans. *Oppressive as hell.* It became even more oppressive after his brother Mickey joined the McMullen Gang. On more than one occasion, Finn was picked up by Boston's finest, the bad-ass badges mistaking him for his twin brother. That's when Finn decided to get out of South Boston before some rival gang member mistook him for Mickey and pulled the trigger. The US Army offered the perfect means of escape.

'Since I've always been something of an adrenaline junkie, the military was a natural choice,' he told Kate, that as good an answer as any. 'In addition to all of the action, along the way I've picked up an interesting skills set.'

Kate folded her arms over her chest. A challenging tilt to her chin, she said, 'Let me guess? All of these skills have to do with guns, ammo and chasing enemy combatants.'

'Not true. Back in '92 when I first got out of basic training, I was stationed at a refugee camp along the Iraq–Turkey border. That's where I learned how to deliver a baby.'

Almost comically, Kate's mouth fell open. 'Are you kidding me? *You*, the rough, tough, macho commando, delivered a baby?'

'No easy feat given that those camps were like the wild, wild west. Except instead of six-shooters, they carried Kalashnikovs. I was with the army battalion responsible for maintaining order in the camps. Because of the Islamic prohibitions, I wasn't supposed to look this pregnant woman in the eye, let alone peer at her, um –' Finn cleared his throat, no further explanation needed. 'I'd already radioed HQ that I needed a female nurse, doctor, soldier, *anyone* female to come to my assistance.'

'Did anyone arrive?'

'Just as I'm standing there holding this itty-bitty bloody baby in my hands, tears of joy streaming down my face that the kid was even breathing, the nurse finally showed up.' He chortled, able now, years later, to see the humour in it. 'From South Boston to Kurdistan. Of course, I've been all over the world since then.'

'Which no doubt explains why you're so jaded about Paris,' Kate retorted, good-naturedly elbowing him in the ribs.

'If you think I'm unaffected by all this –' he gestured to the Arc de Triomphe L'Étoile, visible in the hazy distance – 'think again. The difference between us is that I refuse to let the romance of the place go to my head. The Seven know that we're in Paris. Trust me, they're just waiting for that split-second when I go all ga-ga because I'm standing in front of some famous Parisian landmark and I drop my guard.'

A dubious expression on her face, Kate shook her head. 'I cannot imagine you going "ga-ga" over anything.'

Oh, you'd be surprised.

Last night, sacked out on a hard floor, he kept dreaming about Kate. Talk about going ga-ga. Hot dreams full of wild, writhing sex, he was finally forced to sneak off to the bathroom to get some relief.

Removing his arm from her shoulders, Finn unzipped his Go Bag and retrieved a bottle of water. 'Here you go.' Unscrewing the cap, he handed it to Kate.

'Thanks.'

He watched as she took several sips, the muscles in her throat rhythmically working with each swallow. Thinking it was a sexy sight, Finn snorted caustically. *Great. Another night of getting in touch with myself.*

'Do you think the Seven Research Foundation is actually going to give you the Dark Angel in exchange for the Montségur Medallion?' Kate asked, returning the bottle to him.

'I won't know until I make the offer. If they accept, the exchange will occur at the place and time of my choosing. Probably as close to the American Embassy as can be arranged. Then, when I have the Dark Angel in my custody, I'll alert Marine Security at the embassy that we're on our way.' And if they didn't accept, he had a back-up plan.

'You do know that if the Seven Research Foundation has the Montségur Medallion, they can use it to find the Grail?'

'Like I care.' He glanced at his watch. *1110*. Time for

Phase One of the mission op to kick off. 'The scheduled meeting started ten minutes ago.' He unclipped his cell phone from his waist. He then removed a small digital voice recorder and earbud microphone from his Go Bag. 'We're wheels up in fifteen seconds. You ready?'

Kate nodded weakly. While not as gung-ho as he would have liked, the tepid response was to be expected. Scrolling through his phonebook, he selected the number he'd earlier programmed for the Seven Research Foundation.

The call was answered on the first ring by a French-speaking female.

'Hey, how ya doin'? This is Finn McGuire calling. I'm trying to get a-hold of the Seven Dwarfs. It's real important that I speak with Dopey. Although if he's not available, you can patch me through to the head dwarf, Ivo Uhlemann.'

'*Un moment, Monsieur McGuire.*'

'So far, so good,' Finn said to Kate in a lowered voice as he inserted the small earbud into his left ear and connected the cable into the jack on the digital recorder. One of his newly purchased toys, the earbud mike would enable him to record both sides of the cell-phone conversation on the digital recorder. The digital recorder would, in turn, date and time stamp the conversation. Absolutely necessary for an evidentiary recording. He knew it wasn't enough to capture the Dark Angel and turn her over to the authorities. He needed proof that the Seven Research Foundation had ordered the hits on Dixie and Johnny K.

As they'd earlier rehearsed, Kate took charge of the digital recorder. She rolled her free hand several times to let him know that she'd started the recording.

'Ah, Sergeant McGuire. *Guten tag.* We were hoping that you would call,' a male voice said in heavily accented English.

'Are you Ivo Uhlemann?'

'I am Doctor Ivo Uhlemann. And may I offer my condolences for the loss of your two comrades?'

'No, you may not,' Finn tersely informed the polite bastard. 'In case you haven't heard, you can't take the pee out of the pool. That said, a few days ago I spoke to one of your compradres, a dude by the name of Fabius Jutier. Unfortunately, the conversation dead-ended on me.'

'I trust this conversation will have a more satisfactory ending,' Uhlemann replied, refusing to comment on Jutier's suicide. 'In exchange for the Montségur Medallion, we've put together an offer that I think you will find most interesting.'

Finn decided to play along. 'Okay. What are you putting on the table?'

'We are offering you a place *at* the table. Yesterday, we were greatly impressed with your skills . . . We believe that you would make an excellent addition to our organization.'

49

Seven Research Foundation Headquarters, Paris

1113 hours

'And will you issue me a Nazi uniform?' Finnegan McGuire taunted. 'Or better yet, can I get one of those cool Black Sun tattoos on my left pec?'

Deeply offended, Ivo Uhlemann glared at the telephone console. Sitting at the head of the brushed-metal conference table, he involuntarily placed his right hand over his heart. In 1940, the head of the SS, Heinrich Himmler, had decreed that each member of the Seven must be tattooed with the Black Sun emblem. At first, all seven men were horrified. However, as the years passed, the tattoo came to symbolize their undying dedication to finding the *Lapis Exillis.* To honour that commitment, their progeny bore the same tattoo.

'The Seven Research Foundation is a consortium of enlightened scholars and scientists,' Ivo replied, curbing his annoyance. 'Given your background, we would like to make you our Chief Security Officer. In addition to the yearly five-million-dollar salary, you will be provided with a furnished two-bedroom flat in the sixth arrondisement and a BMW E60.'

'A Beemer. Nice.'

Taking the truncated reply as a positive sign, Ivo continued. 'If you join our ranks, we will ensure that all murder charges against you are dropped. Your good name and reputation will be restored. Honour will be satisfied.'

'Then you don't know the meaning of that word,' the American retorted snidely. 'I can't think of anything more dishonourable than allowing that bitch, the Dark Angel, to get away with two brutal murders.'

As Ivo considered his reply, he glanced at the other board members seated around the table. Originally comprised of nineteen members, disease, old age and, in the case of Fabius Jutier, an unfortunate suicide, had reduced their number to ten. As the Chairman, he was their designated spokesman.

'We are well aware, Sergeant McGuire, that you expect us to turn over the Dark Angel in exchange for the Montségur Medallion. Unfortunately, that point is non-negotiable.'

'Then there's nothing for us to discuss. I mean, hell, why should I throw in my lot with the group who ordered the murders of Corporal Lamar Dixon and Corporal John Kelleher?'

'Because, in addition to the generous compensation package, we are offering you an opportunity to join an elite foundation that is engaged in history-altering research.'

The sales pitch met with a lengthy silence.

Ivo saw the uneasy glances. They needed Sergeant McGuire's cooperation. *Das Groß Versuch* could not be performed without the requisite component. Which they could not locate without the encoded map engraved on the Montségur Medallion. They'd just laid an enticing trap. To lure their quarry into the open, the American's greed had to trump his distorted sense of honour.

'Okay, Ivo, I gotta be honest . . . your offer is damn tempting,' McGuire said at last. 'I need to think on it a while.'

'How much time do you require?'

'You'll have my answer no later than midnight tonight. In addition to the allotted time, a cease-fire will be in effect while I ponder my decision. If, during the cease-fire, I catch sight of Goldilocks or the bald-headed dude, I *will* destroy the Montségur Medallion. Unless I'm mistaken, gold melts at two thousand and twelve degrees Fahrenheit.'

'Please give me a moment, Sergeant McGuire. I must confer with my colleagues.' Ivo reached across the table and pushed the MUTE button on the console.

There was no mistaking the palpable tension around the conference table as the other nine members stared expectantly at him.

'The matter is now open for discussion,' he announced.

Matilda Zimmerman, former Director of the Linguistics Department at the University of Heidelberg, was the first to speak. 'Would the American actually destroy the medallion?'

'Sergeant McGuire does not strike me as a man who makes idle threats,' Ivo replied. His assessment caused several in the group to nod vigorously. 'However, the offer that we tendered to him is generous to an extreme.'

'What if he doesn't accept our offer?' Otto Fassbinder enquired anxiously. A retired editor-in-chief of the *Journal of the German Geological Society*, his field of expertise was the effect of crystal geodes on telluric energy currents.

'The Americans are the most avaricious people on the

planet. As they themselves are fond of saying, "Every man has his price."' Ivo opened the manila folder that he'd brought to the meeting. 'We are also monitoring Cædmon Aisquith's movements as a back-up contingency.'

'Why don't we just capture the Englishman?' This from Wilhelm Koch, an American who owned a successful maths-based engineering firm in California's Silicon Valley.

'Because there's a slim possibility that he might actually find the *Lapis Exillis*.' Ivo stared contemplatively at the dossier that he'd received yesterday from his contact at the Ministry of Defence. A recently retired MI5 intelligence officer, Aisquith had an academic background in Egyptology and medieval studies. A unique skills set, to say the least, which was the reason why he'd sent one of his best men to the Languedoc to shadow the Englishman. According to the latest update, Aisquith had left Montségur an hour ago.

'I will give you two minutes to further discuss the matter. Then we will put it to a vote.'

Slowly rising to his feet, Ivo suffered an intense burst of pain. He required more analgesic, the time span between injections becoming of increasingly short duration.

Having already decided how he would cast his vote, Ivo walked over to the plate-glass window on the other side of the conference room. From his vantage point, he could see the Grande Arche reflected in the gaudy mirrored office building directly opposite, the open cube being at the western terminus of the Axe Historique. And just as the Grande Arche owed its existence to the Seven Research Foundation, the Axe Historique owed its existence to the mighty Knights Templar.

At the onset of the fourteenth century, the Templars were poised to become the most technologically advanced force in medieval Europe. In addition to their expansive property holdings, their large fleet of ships and their battle-ready army of warrior-monks, the Templars were a financial powerhouse. For those reasons alone, they gave many European monarchs fitful sleep. But one monarch in particular, the French king Philippe le Bel, had more reason than most to fear the Templars. In the summer of 1306, Philippe had begged asylum at the Templars' Paris headquarters during a bout of civil unrest. An impolite guest, Philippe spent his time snooping through the Templars' extensive library. Which is how he discovered the Templars' secret blueprint for the city of Paris. Although he couldn't comprehend the science behind the design, Philippe astutely realized that the Knights Templar possessed ancient knowledge that could be used to conquer the monarchy. Perhaps the whole of Europe.

It left the French king with no choice but to destroy the mighty order of warrior-monks.

To the consternation of later monarchs, Philippe le Bel was not entirely successful. While the Knights Templar were destroyed, their blueprint survived intact, passed down from one secret society to the next. The Rosicrucians, the Freemasons, Cagliostro's Egyptian Rite – just a few of the groups that endeavoured to complete the ley line in the hopes that *they* might be the ones to find the *Lapis Exillis*.

Acutely aware that time was running out, Ivo stared at the reflected cube. In two days' time, Sirius would rise with the sun. Because the Vril force could only be generated during the heliacal rising of Sirius, when the astral energy of that star was at its peak, *das Groß Versuch* could only be performed on that one specific day.

According to his doctors, he didn't have another year to wait until the next heliacal rising.

'We're ready to vote,' Professor Zimmerman announced.

Returning to the conference table, Ivo said, 'All those in favour of granting a temporary cease-fire, please raise your hand.'

Although there was obvious reluctance etched on to two or three faces, all of the board members, including Ivo, raised their right hand.

Decision reached, Ivo pressed the SPEAKER button on the telephone console. 'We agree to your terms, Sergeant McGuire. A cease-fire is in effect until midnight.'

'Smart chess move,' McGuire said brusquely before disconnecting the call.

'Now what?'

Ivo glanced at Professor Zimmerman. 'As Finnegan McGuire adroitly remarked, it is a chess match. Our trap has been laid and I am confident that it will end in checkmate.'

At which point, Sergeant McGuire will lose the game, the Montségur Medallion and his life.

50

The Languedoc

1130 hours

Grunting, Cædmon finagled his way between the two rough-hewn embankments that formed a narrow V, the gneiss stone brightly glittering with embedded crystals.

The undiscovered country . . .

'From whose bourn I intend to bloody well return. Grail in hand,' he puckishly added, still riding euphoria's high crest.

A few moments later he emerged from the rocky slit and entered a boulder-strewn ravine. Coming to a standstill, he beheld the wildflowers that bloomed in haphazard profusion, the vegetation a welcome sight in the otherwise barren landscape. Winded by his two-hour mountain trek, he gracelessly plunked down on a flat-topped boulder. Studying a topographical map, he could see that Mont de la Lune was located at the other end of the ravine. The next port of call, Moon Mountain, was where the hunt would begin in earnest.

Returning the map to his rucksack, he retrieved a water bottle. The tepid liquid did little to satisfy his true thirst, Cædmon entertaining a fantasy that involved big chunks of ice floating in gin with a splash of tonic and a squirt of lemon.

Of late, he frequently viewed the world through green-tinted glasses, green being the colour of a Tanqueray gin bottle.

Muscles tight, he slowly rolled his neck. First one direction. Then the other. Groaning from the ensuing pain, he found his decrepitude both lamentable and laughable.

Must remember to pull the dumb-bells out of the closet. Or take up jogging. Cycling, perhaps.

Unenthused by the thought of an exercise regime, Cædmon glanced around the ravine. For some inexplicable reason, the abundant stores of rock put him in mind of a cemetery laden with marble headstones.

That, in turn, conjured memories of the annual pilgrimage to his mother's grave site. Where, white lilies in hand, he and his father would stand, heads respectfully bowed, Cædmon afraid to be caught looking anywhere but at that speckled grey stone.

• *Helena May Aisquith* •
• *3 May 1938 – 2 February 1967* •
• *'The maid is not dead, but sleepeth.'* •

The fact that his mother died in childbirth meant that his birthday was always a glum affair. Rather than cake and presents, he was made to suffer his father's piteous glare, wet February winds and thinly veiled accusations of matricide.

'*Did you know, boy, that she was named for Helen of Troy? Flame-red hair and eyes of blue. Stole my heart, she did . . . and then she was stolen from me.*' As if Cædmon had plotted her murder from the womb. Mercifully, his deportation to Eton put an end to the yearly visit.

Disgusted that he'd let himself fall prey to those grim memories, he took another swig from the water bottle. *You, Sir Prancelot, are a sorry excuse for a Grail knight.*

But was any man truly up to the challenge?

Wolfram von Eschenbach, the author of the definitive Grail romance *Parzival*, set the bar for would-be knights exceedingly high. In von Eschenbach's perfect medieval world, only those of chaste body and pure heart could seek the Grail. Inebriates and ne'er-do-wells need not apply.

Unwilling to dwell on his appalling lack of knightly credentials, Cædmon instead wondered how much validity there was to the epic tale. According to von Eschenbach, the Knights Templar had become the Grail Guardians. If that was true, it meant that the Templars had deciphered the Montségur Medallion and collected the prize. And, presumably, like the Cathars before them, they straightaway hid the damned thing to keep it from falling into the Inquisitors' covetous hands.

Hopefully, that part of von Eschenbach's account was pure fiction.

Slinging the rucksack over his shoulder, Cædmon rose to his feet and continued on his way. Since the 'twelfth hour' was significant, he didn't want to be late to the tea party.

Twenty minutes into his trek, he caught his first glimpse of Mont de la Lune, a gleaming spire of granite punctuated with green scrub brush. Seen from below, the rugged peak soared heavenward, the pointed summit disappearing into the hazy clutches of a passing cloud. A starkly beautiful and remote juggernaut.

Anticipation mounting, Cædmon hurriedly removed a pair of binoculars from his rucksack.

'Reddis lapis exillis cellis.'

'The Stone of Exile has been returned to the niche.'

While no location had been given in the inscription, he assumed that the 'niche' in question was located on Mont de la Lune. More than likely on the *northern* façade of Moon Mountain, since that was the side of the mountain visible from Montségur.

Beginning his search through the binoculars at the base, he slowly, methodically, worked his way up the rocky face. Examining each nook, each cranny. To his surprise, the northern façade was riddled with small cave openings. At least a dozen of them. Three-quarters of the way up, he discovered a small fissure shaped like a crescent moon, brilliantly illuminated by the noonday sun.

'In the glare of the twelfth hour, the moon shines true.'

'Bloody hell . . . I think I've found it,' he gasped in wonderment.

Lowering the binoculars, he studied the granite cliff. There appeared to be enough protruding rock ledges that he could ascend in a zigzag fashion, making for an arduous but not impossible climb. Since he'd done a bit of rock climbing in his younger days, he was fairly confident that he could reach the crescent-shaped niche.

As he shoved the binoculars into his rucksack, it occurred to him that in many of the medieval Grail poems, it wasn't the treasure discovered in the mist that mattered, but the spiritual journey that led there.

'Sod that.'

Let some other bloke be saved. He was determined to find the Grail.

51

The Seven Research Foundation Headquarters, Paris

1130 hours

'*Eine bloeder Affe!*' Dolf Reinhardt muttered under his breath as he watched the sports video on his laptop computer, outraged that the Hertha Berliner football team had so many Africans in the squad. Disgraceful! They were stupid apes who couldn't even speak proper German!

Disgusted, he slammed the computer closed.

Sitting outside the conference room in a high-backed chair, he sullenly glanced at his watch, wondering how much longer he would have to wait for Herr Doktor's meeting to adjourn. He was hungry and wanted to take his lunch break. He also needed to return to the Oberkampf flat and check on his mother. While tempted to take his leave, he was a good soldier and would wait to be officially dismissed. After yesterday's fuck-up, he wasn't going to do anything that might jeopardize his position.

Well aware that he had failed miserably in his assignment, he feared that he might have lost Herr Doktor's trust; a trust that he'd striven mightily to cultivate over the last eight years.

The fact that he'd not been promoted during those

eight years rankled, his duties rarely extending beyond the washing and waxing of Herr Doktor's sedan, running errands and walking that little furry *scheisse* Wolfgang. On those days when he felt overworked and underappreciated, he would remind himself that his maternal grandfather had also been a chauffeur.

To the greatest man who ever lived, Adolf Hitler.

A member of the Führer's personal staff, his grandfather Josef Krueger not only drove the Führer to rallies, top-level meetings with his generals and front-line inspections, he was responsible for maintaining the Führer's entire automotive fleet. A responsibility that his grandfather undertook with the utmost devotion. Indeed, he considered it a sacred honour to serve the Führer in this capacity.

When Dolf was a young boy, his mother had regaled him with stories about the Führer and how he'd treated her father with the greatest kindness, often bringing snacks for the two of them to share on long car trips. A man of the people, the Führer always insisted on sitting in the front passenger seat. While he refrained from discussing politics on those extended journeys, the Führer would speak at length about their shared interest in automotive mechanics as he plotted their course on a road map.

A trusted aide-de-camp, his grandfather had been in the Berlin bunker in late April 1945, when Adolf Hitler had taken his own life. It had been his grandfather's grim task to secure the hundred and twenty gallons of petrol that was used to cremate the Führer and his new bride, Eva Braun. A dark and dreadful day for the Reich.

In idle moments, Dolf would sometimes fantasize

about driving the Führer's magnificent 770-K Mercedes Benz with the twelve chassis, armour plate and bullet-proof glass. Attired in a black SS jacket, jodhpurs, polished knee boots and peaked visor with silver braid and *totenkampf* emblem, he would cut a dashing figure. As would the Führer and the other dignitaries in the vehicle.

Smiling, Dolf closed his eyes, able to hear the roar of the crowds as they exuberantly chanted *Sieg Heil!* and the repetitive pound of soldiers marching in picture-perfect *stechshritt*, legs swinging in unison, right arms raised in a stiff salute.

'Sleeping on the job, are you?'

Hearing that seductive purr of a voice, Dolf opened his eyes. A vision in a skintight white suit and stiletto high-heels stood over him, a mocking sneer on her painted red lips.

'No doubt you're exhausted from performing your important duties,' Angelika Schwärz continued. Placing her hands on her hips, she glanced at his laptop computer. 'Looking at a little Internet porn, were you?'

Dolf smoothed his sweaty palms against his trouser legs, uncertain what to say. If he denied the charge, it would make him appear unmanly.

'I am waiting for Herr Doktor to issue my orders for the day,' he muttered, purposefully changing the subject.

Angelika made a big to-do of peering around the deserted antechamber located just outside of the conference room. 'Poor Dolfie. The great man seems to have forgotten all about you. Does anyone even know that you're here, sitting all alone in a dark hallway on the most uncomfortable chair in the entire office suite?' Licking her shiny red lips, she chortled nastily. 'Or are you being punished?'

'I've done nothing wrong.'

'What do you call yesterday's fiasco? A circus clown with a water pistol would have had greater success.'

He bit back a crude oath. For eight long years he'd made numerous sacrifices and put in long hours to prove his worth to the Herr Doktor, often forced to leave his mother unattended for extended lengths of time. He did this without complaint in the hope that he would move up the ranks and become a trusted aide. With the greatest fervency, he desired to have the same type of relationship with Herr Doktor Uhlemann that his grandfather had had with the Führer.

And though he had no proof, Dolf suspected that the blonde woman standing before him was the reason why he'd not been promoted.

Frowning, Angelika slowly tilted her head from side to side. 'It doesn't matter from which angle I gaze at you, with that unsightly nose you have a face that only a mother could love.'

'Leave my mother out of this,' he cautioned. Ire mounting, his right hand balled into a fist. Turning his head, he stared at the empty receptionist's desk at the end of the hallway, grateful that no one was witnessing the humiliating exchange.

'And does she love you, little Dolfie?' Angelika jabbed him in the shin with the pointy toe of her high-heeled shoe. 'Look at me when I speak to you, driver.'

Dolf swung his head in her direction. That he had to obey the bitch infuriated him.

'Does your old *mutti* lavish you with attention, smother you with kisses and let you suckle at her breast?' she taunted perversely. 'I think that's your problem, Dolfie. You've sucked at that withered tit for too many years.' Red lips curved in a come-hither smile, Angelika undid the top button of her tailored jacket, exposing her bare breast. 'If you're a good boy, I might let you lick me. Would you like that, Dolfie? Hmm?'

Rabid with lust, he stared at the perfectly shaped white breast, torn between strangling Angelika with his bare hands and falling to his knees. Licking her from one end to the other. Submitting himself to the most beautiful woman he'd ever seen.

Dolf adjusted the computer on his lap, hiding the fact that he had a boner the size of a bratwurst.

Angelika shot him a pitying glance. 'Poor Dolfie. You remind me of the eunuch standing guard at the pasha's –'

Just then, Dolf's stomach growled noisily.

Throwing back her head, Angelika laughed, her disdain causing his erection to instantly deflate.

'You're quite the ladies' man, aren't you? What will you do for an encore? Seduce me with a deafening fart?'

Bitch! Slut! Whore!

Mortified, Dolf glared impotently at the blonde seductress. If he put the arrogant cunt in her place, he'd lose his job. If he touched her breast, he'd lose his job. If he so much as uttered a rude word to the bitch, Herr Doktor Uhlemann would send him packing.

Herr Doktor thought the world of Angelika Schwärz. That's because he didn't know about his Dark Angel's lurid predilections. But Dolf knew. He'd followed her one night when she went to one of the city's Black Metal clubs. Standing in the shadows, he'd watched her have sex with two leather-clad, metal-studded men while bar patrons cheered her on. Herr Doktor had no idea; like every other man, he was under her spell, unable to see that she wasn't a real woman dedicated to hearth and home. Instead, she was a promiscuous she-devil who revelled in emasculating every man she came into contact with. She possessed none of the virtues of her sex but all of the vices.

Angelika's cell phone rang. With an exaggerated sigh, she re-buttoned her jacket before checking the caller ID.

'I have to take this call.' She blew Dolf a kiss. 'Ciao, darling.'

Panting with suppressed rage, Dolf watched Angelika's hips provocatively sway from side to side as she walked down the hallway.

That beautiful blonde bitch will be my undoing.

52

Mont de la Lune, The Languedoc

1242 hours

Mad dogs and Englishmen . . .

Although the dog, to his credit, knew better than to attempt a perilous mountain climb without a safety harness. Cædmon, to his regret, did not, the ascent proving a savage undertaking. Far more dangerous than he'd originally envisioned.

Or perhaps his vision had been clouded by the same obsessive desire that had led more than a few Grail knights to an untimely death.

Shoving that unpleasant thought aside, he hoisted himself upward. The trick was not to think about the fact that he was 'balanced' on a narrow protuberance of granite no more than fifteen inches wide, while his hands clung to a second, equally narrow, protuberance located a metre above his head. Unable to see the crescent-shaped niche from his current position, he reckoned that he had another twenty metres to traverse.

'Shite,' he muttered, unintentionally jabbing his index finger against a sharp-edged stone. Skin punctured, blood oozed down his hand.

He cautiously tiptoed across the granite shelf. Then,

very slowly, he removed his rucksack and turned around. Leaning against the rough-hewn wall, he took a moment's ease. In the far distance, he heard the merry tinkle of sheep bells. In the near distance, an eagle soared in graceful arabesques.

Rumour had it that Jean-Jacques Rousseau, the eighteenth-century philosopher and part-time daredevil, would spend hours perched on this very sort of sheer precipice, from which he'd gleefully toss stones as he imagined them being smashed to smithereens on the rocky gulch below.

Another mad man, Cædmon mused as he rubbed his bloody finger against his trouser leg. It was a warm day and his shirt was soaked through with perspiration. He was half tempted to disrobe and fling the drenched garment over the edge like one of Rousseau's rocks.

Rested, he hefted the rucksack on to his shoulders. Turning towards the granite crag, he continued to climb. Extending. Then pulling. Occasionally clinging. A slow but steady ascent. The sun beat down mercilessly on his head. He ignored it as best he could. A small rock shifted beneath his feet. He scrambled. Found another foothold just as the rock broke free. A deadly projectile hurtling through space.

Cædmon chanced a downward glance.

A mistake.

Seized with an unexpected attack of vertigo, he leaned into the coarse rock, afraid to breathe, move or even blink for that matter. A bird on a wire, wings clipped.

Panic-stricken, he tightened his grip on the rocky knob. A drop of blood plopped on to his face from the punctured finger, rolling down his cheek to his chin. An instant later, it joined the rock at the bottom of the cliff. Ghoulish images flashed across his mind's eye. *Broken bones. Crushed spine. Smashed skull.*

'Any moment now I'm going to plunge to my –'

Stiffen your backbone, man. To quote the American commando, you seek 'the Holy fucking Grail'.

Cædmon gulped a deep breath. Then another. A soft breeze wafted across his cheek. A gentle caress. The irrational fear subsided. Courage shored, he extended his arm. Securing a handhold, he navigated to the next ledge.

Upsy-daisy.

Long minutes later, he reached the crescent-shaped opening. Peering inside, he saw a shallow grotto about seven feet in height, strewn with rocks and boulders. An inauspicious vault for the most sacred relic in all of Christendom.

Undeterred, he heaved his torso into the breach, wiggling his lower body as he scrambled into the narrow cavity. Crouched on his haunches, he opened his rucksack and removed a torch. Flipping it on, he aimed the beam around the cave. Which is when he saw a set of skeletal remains.

I don't believe it . . . it's the bloody Grail Guardian!

Thrilled by the discovery, he rushed forward, stumbling on a loose stone in his haste.

Kneeling beside the bones, he shoved the torch under his arm as he examined several bits of metal that looked to be a crudely fashioned belt buckle. A dried, translucent snake skin was draped over the bloke's clavicle bone; a fragile strip of boot leather clung to his bony foot; and several horn buttons were scattered about. Everything else had long since disintegrated.

Above the skeleton, a Latin phrase had been clumsily scrawled in what appeared to be a manganese pigment. *Ad Augusta Per Angusta.* 'To holy places through narrow spaces.' Beneath the text was a crudely rendered Cathar cross.

An evocative message scribed for the ages. And while it wasn't proof positive, it strongly suggested that these were the mortal remains of one of the four Cathars who escaped the Montségur citadel.

Cædmon perused the area, wondering if a skeletal companion lurked in the near vicinity. As he peered through the crescent opening, the Pyrenees unfolded in the airy distance like a granite accordion. The last image imprinted on the Cathar's dying brain. Although a lonely place to spend eternity, the view was splendid. To die for, an irreverent wag might say.

'All right, old boy, where's the blasted Grail?' he demanded cheekily. He shone the torch into the far reaches of the stone sepulchre, surprised to see that the cave extended deeper into the mountain.

Hope springing, Cædmon ambled through a craggy chasm which, in turn, led to another grotto. *The womb of the Mother.*

At a glance, he could see that there were no bones, no inscriptions and no Grail.

Angered to think that the Knights Templar may have beaten him to the prize, he turned in a slow circle, searching for a stone depository where the relic could have been stashed. His attention was drawn to a massive slab that jutted out from the grotto wall. He walked towards it, the unusual rock formation meriting further investigation.

A Cathar cross adorned the thick block of stone. Intrigued, he peered behind the slab.

'I'll be damned,' he murmured upon discovering that the slab hid a passageway approximately five and a half feet high and twenty inches wide. 'To holy places through narrow spaces.'

Bending his head, Cædmon stepped into the passage.

53

Grande Arche Parking Garage, Paris

1247 hours

'Aren't you the least bit tempted?' Kate asked, still stunned by the staggering amount of money that had been offered to Finn in exchange for the Montségur Medallion.

'Oh, yeah. Like I want to work for the devil. Which, in case you don't know, is called selling your soul.' Leaning against the railing inside the garage stairwell, Finn unabashedly stared. 'You know, the blonde hair is starting to grow on me.'

'You're *absolutely* certain that I won't be recognized?'

Plucking one of the corkscrew curls, Finn pulled it straight before releasing it. The blonde curl bounced into place like a well-oiled spring. 'Don't worry. I've been living with you 24/7 and even I wouldn't recognize you.'

As with all of the other equipment, the wig had been part of yesterday's spending spree. Although she'd complained about donning it on a hot day, the disguise was absolutely necessary for Phase Two of the mission op. There were video surveillance cameras in the underground parking garage at Grande Arche and the blonde wig would ensure that she wasn't identified. They'd both agreed that it was easier to alter her appearance than disguise a six-foot-four-inch male.

'Time to get the mission underway.' Unzipping his Go Bag, Finn removed a black metal object that resembled a hockey puck. 'Let's go over the instructions one more time. Once you locate Uhlemann's Mercedes Benz, crouch beside the rear tyre well and, reaching underneath, place the tracking device so it can't be seen.' He pointed to the small flat disk. 'This is the magnetized side of the device. In order for it to adhere, metal has to touch metal. Any questions?'

'Just one . . . What happens if I get caught?' Suffering from an acute case of the jitters, Kate gnawed on her bottom lip.

'You're not going to get caught,' Finn assured her. 'This operation is a two-second "stow and go". I'm talking stupid simple.'

While the hyperbole was meant to buoy her confidence, Kate worried that she might not be up to the task. She hadn't even left the stairwell and already her heart was pounding and her knees were shaking. A terrified blonde Mata Hari.

'After I install the device, then what?'

'As soon as you attach the device, return to the stairwell on the double-quick. Then we pray to Bob Almighty that Ivo follows the script and goes for a ride.' Finn glanced at the concrete block walls that enclosed the stairwell. 'This place is like a fortress. If I'm gonna abduct the bastard, I need him in the open, away from his stronghold.'

Since Ivo Uhlemann had rendered the Dark Angel 'non-negotiable', Finn intended to up the ante by abducting the head of the Seven Research Foundation. To secure Dr Uhlemann's safe return, the Seven would have to give

Finn custody of the Dark Angel. He'd demanded the cease-fire in order to lull Uhlemann into a false sense of security.

Steadfastly holding her gaze, Finn took hold of Kate's left hand and gently squeezed it. 'Hey, Katie, I know that you're scared. If it wasn't for the security cameras, I'd go out there and install the device. But I'm confident that you can pull this off.'

Faking a brave front, she mustered a smile. 'Roger Wilco, Sergeant McGuire.'

'Um, you're not supposed to say "Roger" and "Wilco" at the same time,' Finn corrected, a teasing glint in his brown eyes.

'Are you sure about that? I'm certain that I've heard people in the movies say "Roger Wilco".'

' "Roger" and "Wilco" mean the same thing. It's one or the other.'

Conceding the point, Kate rolled her eyes. 'I make a lousy commando, don't I?'

'Yeah, 'fraid so,' Finn agreed. Then, one side of his mouth quirking upward, 'But damned cute.'

Kate glanced at their two wedded hands, having long since got over the shock of Finn's missing finger. The first time she'd set eyes on Master Sergeant Finnegan McGuire at the Pentagon, she'd dismissed him as a stereotypical warrior. A Rambo. Only recently had she begun to realize that the fierce façade masked a deeper complexity. Not only was Finn brave, considerate and loyal to a fault, he was sweetly demonstrative.

She kept envisioning a younger version of Finn, tears rolling down his face, holding a newborn infant in his hands. He probably didn't realize it, but she'd found the story deeply moving. Four days ago, she didn't want to know anything about this rough, tough Alpha male. But something had changed. The situation was different now. For some unfathomable reason, she felt emotionally attached. And not just because she was dependent on him to keep her alive.

Given that Finn wasn't her type, she wondered if the heart didn't contrarily follow its own rules.

Finn waved a hand in front of her face. 'Earth to Kate. Let's get this bad boy installed, okay?' Stepping over to the door, he shoved the lock bar, swinging the door wide open. 'Ready?'

'Set, go,' she said in a chipper tone as she stepped through the doorway. Hit with a blast of musty air laced with car oil, she wrinkled her nose.

Hoping she didn't appear as nervous as she felt, Kate headed for the reserved section of the car park. Each car was in a designated spot with the name of a person or corporate entity printed on a placard attached to the concrete wall in front of the vehicle. From the dossier that Cædmon had given to them yesterday, Kate knew that Dr Uhlemann owned a Mercedes Benz S-class sedan with licence plate 610-NGH-75.

Reaching the section reserved for the Seven Research Foundation, Kate spared a quick glance around the deserted parking garage. Not only was the stairwell nearly a hundred feet away, she couldn't even see it from her current position, elevating the fear factor several notches.

A few moments later, catching sight of a graphite-grey Mercedes parked next to the elevator door, Kate ducked behind a large concrete pier. Fingers trembling, she opened her new tote bag. Very carefully, she removed the magnetic-mount vehicle tracking device. Although heavy, it easily fitted into the palm of her very sweaty hand.

Stomach churning, she approached the big four-door Mercedes Benz.

Just then, the elevator bell pinged. *One time*. The signal that the doors would momentarily open. Kate gasped, her hand tightening around the tracking device.

Hurriedly going down on bended knee, she crouched next to the Mercedes' rear tyre well. Placing her left hand on the concrete floor to keep from tipping over, she reached under the tyre well and –

– stuck the tracking device on to the metal underbelly of the vehicle, the powerful magnet holding it in place.

She lurched to her feet just as the elevator doors slid apart.

At least half a dozen people rushed forth. Frozen in place, Kate stood by the Mercedes and watched the mass exodus, the last person to exit the elevator a tall, bald-headed man in a dark suit. A Goliath with a hideously swollen nose.

The gunman from the Jardin du Carrousel!

Head cocked to one side, the brute glared at her as he approached the Mercedes.

Kate stood motionless. Uncertain what to do. She wasn't a courageous Joan of Arc type or a glib-tongued Mata Hari. She was a scared ninny who –

'Fifi! Yoo-hoo!' Bending at the waist, she peered under the grey Mercedes sedan. Never a good actress, she hoped that she resembled a woman who'd just lost her dog. 'Where are you, sweetie?'

A shadow fell over her, the brute standing directly behind her.

'*Qu'est-ce que vous faites?*' the monster rasped, demanding to know what she was doing.

Barely able to draw breath, Kate straightened her spine and slowly turned to face the man who, only the day before, had tried very hard to kill her. Up close, he was truly menacing, with a blotchy face disfigured by an engorged, off-kilter nose, thin lips and a deeply cleft square jaw.

For one horror-filled instant, Kate imagined him wearing a Nazi uniform.

'I'm s-searching for my l-lost d-dog.'

'Vat does it look like?' he asked in a thick German accent.

'It's a little, um –' Her mind went totally blank. 'Oh, yes! A Yorkshire terrier! With long brown hair and a black –' she inanely swished her hand in front of her mouth to indicate a muzzle, the word eluding her.

Eyes narrowing, the monster scrutinized her intently. 'You are an American, aren't you?'

Too late, Kate realized she'd spoken in English rather than French. *Stupid, stupid mistake.*

'Actually, I'm a, um . . . Canadian,' she stammered. 'You know what? I'd better call my husband.' Opening her tote bag, she grabbed the disposable cell phone that Finn had purchased for her.

Without warning, the monster snatched hold of her wrist, preventing her from opening the cell phone. 'You can't make that call.'

Terror-stricken, she glanced at his hand. It was huge.

If he grabbed her by the neck, he could easily crush her windpipe with one mighty squeeze. Barely able to swallow, let alone scream, she frantically glanced from side-to-side; everyone who'd been in the elevator had dispersed, no one in sight. In the near distance, she heard the roar of several car engines.

'W-why not?' Kate warbled, certain that he intended to kill her on the spot.

'Because of the concrete walls, there's no reception in the garage.'

Relieved, she visibly sagged. 'Right. Silly me.'

'Hey, Bridget! Where are you?'

At hearing Finn's loud holler, both she and the bald-headed monster turned their heads in the direction of the stairwell.

'Are you Bridget?' the monster enquired gruffly.

'Oh, yes . . . yes, I am Bridget and that's my husband calling me.' Kate gestured towards the stairwell. 'He's on the, um, other side of the parking lot searching for Fifi.'

The monster let go of her wrist. 'Go. Your husband has summoned you. A woman must always obey her man.'

54

Mont de la Lune, The Languedoc

1415 hours

Down the rabbit hole Sir Prancelot merrily traipsed.

'Although the bastard should have been more wary than merry,' Cædmon grumbled, accidentally bashing the crown of his head against the low-slung stone ceiling. Holding his rucksack in one hand and the torch in the other, he compressed his tall frame in an uncomfortable stoop-shouldered twist, the constrictive corridor designed for a knight of shorter stature.

He'd trekked approximately one hundred and fifty feet when the corridor abruptly switched directions, veering ninety degrees to the left. At which point the passageway gradually sloped downward. When he was a doctoral candidate at Oxford, he'd tramped through catacombs and medieval crypts, but he'd never navigated anything as strangely surreal as this. Whether by design or accident, the passageway put him in mind of a hewn birth canal.

Which, in turn, incited an existential unease, Cædmon's heart beating noticeably faster.

He estimated that he'd traversed another hundred feet when the passageway unexpectedly ended. Bewildered, he awkwardly turned around, aiming his torch in the opposite direction. The golden beam struck an aperture, approximately two feet in diameter, near the ceiling.

Committed to following the trail to its terminus, he peered inside the hole which opened into a long tunnel. Satisfied that the shaft was wide enough for him to engineer through, he shoved his rucksack and torch into the hole. Hefting himself into the chute, he proceeded by slithering centipede-like, pushing with his feet as he dragged his body forward with his hands.

Nearly twenty minutes had lapsed at a maddeningly sluggish pace when Cædmon belatedly realized that there was no room to turn around. If the tunnel didn't expand sufficiently further down the line, he'd have to make a backward egress. A tortuous prospect.

'Although that might be a moot point,' he muttered as the balls of his shoulders scraped against the rough stone, the tunnel suddenly tapering.

Unable to move – either forward or backward – he drew in a ragged breath.

I'm plugged tight as a cork in a bottle.

Biting back a yelp of pain, he pulled his elbows together, squeezing his shoulders towards his chest. Awkwardly contorted, he shimmied through the narrow orifice, relieved when it widened to its former diameter.

In dire need of a drink, he opened his rucksack and retrieved a water bottle. Having begun the day with three full bottles, he was down to his last litre. Gracelessly tipping his head – and banging it against the top of the shaft – he took a measured sip. As he returned the bottle to the rucksack, the beam on his torch flickered twice.

The only warning he had before the light went out, plunging the tunnel into a stultifying darkness.

Unable to see anything, he swiped his hand from side to side, searching for the malfunctioning torch. Snatching hold of it, he pushed the ON switch. When that produced no result, he banged the torch against the palm of his hand.

'Shite!'

Discouraged by the latest setback, he conceded that the venture was proving a mental and physical challenge; the thought of squirming backward, in the dark, was too daunting to contemplate at the moment.

Exhausted, he squirmed on to his back, pulling the rucksack under his head. A makeshift pillow. The phrase 'silent as the grave' took on a whole new meaning as Cædmon folded his arms across his chest and closed his eyes.

I'm interred in a damned stone coffin in a remote mountain. And no one knows that I am even here.

'Not to worry. "The maid is not dead, but sleepeth",' he whispered, envisioning his red-haired mother eternally resting in a satin-lined casket. '"Brightness falls from the air; Queens have died young and fair; Dust hath closed Helen's eye."'

The same dust that closed Juliana Howe's eyes two years ago.

Christ.

Because his mother died in childbirth, grief had never been part of that equation. Which might be why he was so ill-equipped to handle the emotional tumult that erupted in the wake of Juliana's death. It was as though his chest cavity had been pried open, his heart flayed and the organ left to hang in long bloody strips.

In the months that followed, the raw grief mutated into a numbed apathy. An improvement, some might claim. Cædmon wasn't so sure. At least with the former, you knew that you had a heart. Never quite certain with the latter.

So many milestones, so many mistakes, he thought, unable to shut off the memories that flashed in frantic succession: *Holding a white lily at his mother's grave. 'Say a prayer, Cædmon. The poor woman martyred herself to bring you into the world.' No prayers for Juliana. What was the point? And no lilies. Hate lilies. Long-stemmed white roses instead. Damn. Pricked my thumb. And now I've stained my shirt. Jules would be amused. She loved to laugh. Or was that sweet Kate? Such a lovely sight perched in an oriel window seat at Queen's College. 'There wasn't anything quite as beautiful as when the setting sun tinted your centuries-old window a rich shade of tangerine.' Yes, yes, quite true. The sun never sets on the British Empire. Or the Kingdom of Heaven, for that matter. Since 'I cannot bend Heaven, I shall move Hell.' Oh, sod Virgil. Time spent with the devil takes its toll. And now Lucifer wants his bloody stone back!*

Chilled to the bone, Cædmon shivered. A heavy weight suddenly pressed against his chest, as though the granite shaft was cinching around him. In fact, his heart muscle was so painfully constricted, he wondered if he might be on the verge of a full-blown heart attack.

Suppose this is the close of business, eh?

For the last two years he'd heard the rapacious lion panting at his backside. Only a matter of time before the beast caught up with him.

'You had it coming, old boy.'

Did I? Maybe so. In that case, now I lay me down to sleep . . .

. . . forever and a day.

55

Hotel des Saints-Pères, Paris

1936 hours

Horny as hell, Finn stared at the painting of naked nymphs cavorting in a woodland glen.

Although he'd seen similar works of art yesterday at the Louvre, the fact that this painting hung over the hotel bed seemed blatantly erotic. Like an ornately framed striptease. And an expensive one at that, the luxury accommodation costing a jaw-dropping five hundred euros. A far cry from the hundred and thirty euros he'd spent the previous night.

However, this hotel, located on Rue des Saints-Pères, was *directly* across the street from Ivo Uhlemann's eighteenth-century apartment building. Not only that, he'd scored a room with a view; from the expansive window, he could peer right into Uhlemann's study. Which was the reason why he was willing to overlook the price, the painting and the girly décor. As in, pink upholstered armchairs, floral curtains with silk tassels and a delicate antique bureau.

'I'm starving. What's on the menu?' Kate enquired cheerfully as she stepped out of the bathroom. Dressed in a white terrycloth robe, wet hair combed back from her face, she glowed with a womanly sheen. A lot like the woodland nymphs.

Realizing that he still had two plastic shopping bags looped around his wrist, Finn deposited them on the bedside table. Trying his damnedest to ignore the fact that Kate looked good, smelled good and probably tasted good, he unloaded the groceries. 'I bought a loaf of bread at the bakery, a wheel of Camembert at the cheese shop and smoked salmon at some little hole-in-the-wall market around the corner.'

Kate reached for a bottle of water. 'Are those apples?' she asked, pointing to the second shopping bag that was in the process of rolling off the table.

'Apples *and* oranges,' he said, making a grab for the runaway bag. 'I didn't know which you preferred, so I got a coupla each.' Feast laid out, he unsnapped the small leather sheath hooked on the side of his waistband and removed his penknife. Extracting a blade, he sliced the cheese and smoked salmon.

Sidling next to him, Kate tore a hunk of bread from the loaf, the terrycloth robe gaping slightly. Transfixed, Finn stared at the upper curve of her breast.

Jaysus.

Aware that he was acting like a perv at a peep show, he averted his gaze. Uncomfortable as hell, he picked up a slice of salmon and popped into his mouth.

'Delicious, isn't it?'

'Uh-huh,' he grunted inanely around a mouthful of fish.

Loading her meal on to a piece of white butcher-block paper, Kate carried it over to the bed. '*Bon appétit*,' she trilled as she sat cross-legged on the middle of the mattress. Right under the painting of naked nymphs.

Finn nearly choked on his salmon.

Given the close quarters, his attraction to Kate Bauer was to be expected. Hell, that was the reason why women weren't allowed to fight alongside men in combat. Put a man and a woman together in a foxhole, they're going to start thinking about getting it on. And even though he knew sex wasn't a pill that you popped when you were having a bad day, he couldn't stop thinking about the two of them engaged in a good old-fashioned life-affirming fuck.

Uncertain how to deal with his pent-up sexual tension, Finn strode over to the window. Grabbing the Bushnell binoculars off the bureau, he aimed them at the window directly opposite. A grey-haired woman, probably Uhlemann's maid, lackadaisically pushed a vacuum cleaner across the oriental carpet.

'I trust that the coast is clear.'

'Uh-huh,' he grunted again, setting the binoculars back on the bureau.

The foxhole getting smaller by the second, Finn ripped open the Velcro flap on his cargo pants and retrieved his new palm pilot. He'd purchased it yesterday because he needed to log on to a secure website in order to track Uhlemann's vehicle. Using a stylus to navigate through the menus, he pulled up the real-time map and checked the vehicle location.

'What's the status report?' Kate asked as she dabbed at her upper lip with a paper napkin.

'The Benz is still parked at the Grande Arche.'

Hoping that Uhlemann would hurry up and leave his marble fortress, Finn set the palm pilot next to his binoculars. Jaw clamped tight, he leaned against the side of the bureau and moodily stared out of the window. The late-evening sun shone through the glass, casting a golden sheen on to the striped wallpaper.

How the hell am I going to get through the next couple of hours holed up in this damned hotel room?

It'd reached the point where he wanted Kate so badly, he was willing to forego the sex. Just spooning with her, feeling her ass snuggled against his groin, would be pleasure enough. About to implode, he was afraid to go anywhere near the bed. *Push-ups might help.* Although it'd probably take a couple of hundred of 'em to take the edge off.

Hearing Kate wiggle around on the mattress, he ground his teeth.

A few moments later, she appeared at his side. 'I should have gone with Cædmon to the Languedoc,' she said in a snippy tone as she disposed of her rubbish in the waste-basket next to the bureau. 'At least he knows how to have a pleasant conversation.'

'I don't want to converse with you,' Finn growled, hit with a gut-churning burst of jealousy. Grabbing Kate, he yanked her into his arms. 'I want –'

Too revved up to be romantic, he kissed Kate with a bruising intensity. Roughly. Wildly. Sliding a hand down her back, he palmed the curve of her buttock. Fully aroused, he was on the verge of taking her right there against the bureau.

Clutching his shoulders, Kate moaned, whimpered, arched into him.

Jaysus.

Chest heaving, he dragged his mouth away from hers.

'Okay, here's the deal. I'm not real good at courtly love so I'll just be blunt . . . I want you, Kate. All I need from you is a straight-up "yes" or "no" answer.'

Staring him directly in the eye, Kate pulled the tie on her robe. Then, gracefully rolling her shoulders, she let the garment fall to the floor. Completely naked, she took hold of his right hand and placed it on her bare breast.

'Yes.'

56

Oberkampf Neighbourhood, Paris

1942 hours

Stepping out of the bathroom, Dolf Reinhardt glanced at his watch.

Scheisse! He was scheduled to go back on duty in forty-five minutes. Striding over to the wardrobe, he pulled a freshly laundered shirt off the hanger.

A few minutes later, dressed in his chauffeur's uniform, Dolf grabbed the black cap and jammed it on his head. He despised the ridiculous hat, but Herr Doktor Uhlemann insisted that he wear it.

Ready to leave, he quickly strode down the dingy hallway to the second bedroom.

'Hello, *Mutter*.' He wrinkled his nose at the faint scent of dried urine and sour perspiration.

The grey-haired woman who sat at the window didn't acknowledge the greeting. She never did. Diagnosed with advanced Alzheimer's disease, his mother had withdrawn into a non-verbal state. Day in, day out, she sat beside the window staring at the Paris rooftops, a blank, slack-jawed expression on her face. Dolf didn't have the money to put her in a nursing facility and the one time he'd hired a health-care worker, he'd come home and found the aide yelling at his mother. He nearly killed the bitch on the spot.

While he loved his mother with all his heart, a part of him deeply resented that she'd become such a burden. The daily monotony of cleaning her foul bed pans and soiled bed sheets was grinding him down. Of late, he kept wishing that she'd hurry up and die. If she could carry on a minimal conversation, the situation would be easier to withstand. But living with a silent, frail ghost was becoming unbearable. A strange type of hell in which they shared the same space and yet she was unaware of his existence.

In a hurry, he stepped over to the dresser and retrieved a green plastic prescription bottle from the top drawer.

'Time for your medicine,' he told his mother, gently inserting a capsule between her lips. Grabbing the water glass from the nearby table, he finagled the straw into her mouth. 'Take a sip, Mother.'

Never taking her gaze from the window, his mother sucked a bit of water through the straw. Dolf returned the glass to the table then pried open his mother's mouth to make certain that she'd swallowed the sleeping pill. He next checked the restraints on her wrists. To keep her from wandering off, he was forced to strap her into the chair whenever he left the flat.

Bending down, he kissed his mother on the cheek, making a mental note to give her a sponge bath in the morning. 'I'll be back later this evening.'

It was the same one-sided conversation that they had each and every night.

As he turned to leave, Dolf glanced at the framed picture hanging on the wall next to his mother's chair. The faded photograph, published in a 1943 edition of the *Völkische Beobachter* newspaper, was of a six-year-old girl with long blonde braids attired in a traditional dirndl dress. Arms extended, she offered the Führer a slice of freshly baked black bread on an ornately carved wooden platter. Taken during *Walpurgisnacht*, the pagan spring festival when bonfires burned bright to lure witches from their covens, the photograph had captured the hearts and souls of the German people. Enthralled by the sight of their Führer with such a lovely child, households across the Reich framed the photograph and hung it alongside their cherished family portraits.

An overnight celebrity, his mother, Hedwig Krueger, became known to an entire generation as 'the Führer's Little Handmaid'.

Before she lapsed into a demented state of mind, his mother often spoke of that long ago May day, fondly recalling how the Führer, his piercing eyes as blue as the lake waters at Königsee, pinched her cheek and squeezed her shoulder, thanking her profusely for the slice of *schwarzbrot.*

Dolf stared at the photograph for a few more seconds before turning to leave.

When he was a young boy and his mother would tuck him in at night, she used to always tell him that good things come to those who wait.

At thirty-seven years of age, Dolf Reinhardt was tired of waiting.

57

Mont de la Lune, The Languedoc

2159 hours

Catching his first glimpse of the stacked mound of kindling and the dour-faced Dominican priest, Cædmon's heart slammed against his breastbone.

'There's been a mistake!' he fearfully exclaimed. 'I'm not supposed to be here!' 'Here' being an unlit funeral pyre at the foot of Montségur.

The priest smiled humourlessly. 'This is penance for your sins.'

'What sins?' he demanded to know as two soldiers, each garbed in a bright blue surcoat emblazoned with a white fleur-de-lis, roughly grabbed him by the arms and dragged him to the pyre. Grinning, they bound him, hand and foot, to a stake in the middle of the wood stack. Horrified, he stared at the fleur-de-lis. The monarch's royal lily.

'Repent, sinner!' the priest commanded in a booming voice.

'But I did nothing wrong!'

'You were born with the taint of original sin.'

'At least I don't bugger little boys on the sly!' he shot back. 'How many indulgences did that cost, you feckless bastard?'

The Dominican motioned for the fire to be lit. Then, wearing the sneer of the self-righteous, he said calmly, '"Nulla salus extra ecclesium."'

Outside the Church there is no salvation.

Christ.

Almost immediately, the flames set his khaki trousers ablaze. Cædmon screamed, the pain of seared flesh more than he could bear.

'For the love of God! Give me another chance!'

'Am I dead?'

Grappling with the odd sensation of being tethered to his own corpse, Cædmon opened his eyes. To his dismay, he could perceive no difference in the tarry gloom. Even more worrisome, his chest cavity felt empty. Hollowed out. Ready for the Egyptian embalmers to begin the laborious task of mummification.

'Ah . . . still among the living,' he murmured a few seconds later, able to hear his own faint breath. Unwilling to take a chance with the grim reaper hovering so near, he inflated his lungs with a robust, life-affirming gulp.

It came as something of a surprise to realize that he *wanted* to live.

While there had been times over the course of the last two years when he thought death might be a welcome alternative, he now knew that was an illusion born of grief. The same dark illusion that usually induced a burst of frantic regret somewhere between the sixth and fifth floor.

He reached for his water bottle, the side of his hand bumping against the defective torch. A split-second later, the light came on, the narrow confines of the tunnel softly illuminated.

'There *is* a God,' he murmured.

Turning on to his belly, he took a swig of water before

packing the bottle in his rucksack. In the golden beam, he could see that the tunnel took a sharp turn up ahead. Shoving the rucksack and flashlight in front of him, he doggedly squirmed forward. He'd come too far to back out of the venture.

A few minutes later, grunting, he navigated the tight turn, worming his way into a small vestibule. Although there wasn't enough room to stand upright, he was able to squat comfortably. As he inspected the space, he noticed that one of the walls was constructed of densely packed rubble rock. *A false wall!* Lacking excavation tools, he clawed excitedly at the rocks with his bare hands.

Ten minutes of diligent digging exposed a small opening. Cædmon poked his head through the breach.

Un-bloody-believable!

Bowled over, he stared in wonderment at the hidden chamber. Scores of stalactites dripped like icicles while stockier stalagmites rose up from the rock floor. A few had conjoined, giving birth to lone columns, the unexpected juxtaposition of wobbly shapes breathtakingly surreal. Imbedded mica and crystallized rock created a shimmery effect. In a word, it was spectacular. A limestone cathedral hidden in the depths of Mont de la Lune.

The fact that the cavern had been deliberately hidden made him eager to explore. Wriggling his way through the opening, Cædmon stood upright, taking heed not to touch the fragile rock formations.

'"Take my counsel, happy man; act upon it if you can,"' he sang in a deep baritone, testing the acoustics with the silly Gilbert and Sullivan ditty. Enchanted, he listened to the sound of his own voice echoing back at him.

Torch in hand, he turned in a slow pirouette, shedding light on numerous nooks and niches. Any one of which could have concealed a treasure. Near the end of the rotation, his breath caught in his throat.

The cathedral had an altar!

Hurriedly wending his way between the limestone formations, he approached the simple altar comprised of a granite slab supported by two sturdy boulders. However, it wasn't the altar that ensnared his attention; it was the stone ossuary prominently displayed in the middle of the slab. In ancient times, ossuaries were used to store the bones of the dead.

Excitement mounting, he shined the torch on the limestone box. As he did, he lightly grazed his fingers over the elaborately incised sides that depicted the sun, moon and a star. The same symbols that were on the Montségur Medallion. He tucked the torch under his arm. His mind racing wildly at the thought of whose bones might be nestled inside the box, he slowly raised the lid.

'How utterly extraordinary!' he marvelled, astonished to find not a set of desiccated bones, but a golden statuette.

Even more astounding, it was a figurine of the Egyptian goddess Isis. Nearly a foot in length, the idol clutched a small ankh, had a star on her headdress with cow horns and wore a sun orb *menat* necklace. Isis, who ruled the heavens and governed the depths of the earth. Isis, who could create and destroy with equal aplomb. Isis, who lovingly gathered the dismembered pieces of her mutilated husband Osiris so that she could conceive her divine son Horus.

Isis. Whom the ancient Egyptians revered as 'the Mother'.

Cædmon adjusted the torch beam to better examine the figurine. Although the outer layer of gold leaf was remarkably well preserved, enough of it had flaked away for him to see that the idol was actually cast from bronze. Since Egypt was the only civilization in the ancient world to gild bronze, the idol's provenance was indisputable. If he had to make an educated guess, he'd date the figurine to the Ramses Dynasty. Which meant that it was at least three thousand years old.

Un-bloody-believable.

'This shouldn't be here. *You* shouldn't be here,' he whispered to the figurine. Granted, in ancient Egypt the devotees of the Isis mystery cult worshipped in underground sanctuaries; a tribute to the goddess in her guise as the wife of Osiris, Lord of the Dead. But to find an Egyptian divinity in the Languedoc defied conventional history. While a seafaring people, the Egyptians had never ventured into this part of the world. Yet Isis, *somehow*, made the journey.

Which begged the question . . . *Was Isis the beating heart of the Cathar heresy?*

In the third century BC, in the wake of Alexander's conquest of Egypt, the worship of Isis spread like wildfire throughout the Greco-Roman world. The last of the great Mother goddesses, a few centuries later, Isis worship competed with the burgeoning new religion of Christianity. When the Church Fathers embarked on a violent campaign to eradicate their competitors, the Isis cults simply re-branded themselves as Marian cults. A fluid transition given that Isis, often depicted suckling the infant Horus, was the *original* Madonna, sharing many traits with her Christian counterpart.

With that history in mind, it was conceivable that the underground network of goddess worship made its way to the Languedoc. As for the three symbols incised on the Montségur Medallion – the sun, moon and a star – Cædmon now realized that they represented Isis, her husband Osiris and their son Horus. The Egyptian Trinity.

No wonder the Church Fathers were so determined to wipe the peaceful Cathars off the face of the planet. According to the official history, always written by the victors, the Cathars believed in two separate gods. But perhaps there was more to their heretical dualism than the simplistic belief that the forces of good and evil, in the guise of the Light and *Rex Mundi*, were locked in eternal battle, mortal man caught in the crossfire. Perhaps the Cathars' *real* crime was that they worshipped a female Egyptian deity.

Reaching into the ossuary, Cædmon removed the golden statuette.

Spellbound, he stared at the small, perfectly formed goddess. *The Mother.* Suddenly light-headed, he spread his feet wide to steady himself. The limestone sanctuary all but spun around him, stalagmites morphing into an unearthly coterie of female adherents.

'*The maiden phoenix, her ashes new create . . .*'

To his surprise, tears rolled down his face. In that instant, he couldn't distinguish between the sacred and the profane. Reason and desire. The inane and the arcane. What he knew about the Cathars and what he knew about the Egyptians was now jumbled together, separate strands of history that *should not* be tied together.

Yet here was the knotted proof cradled in his hands. A collision of two different cultures bound by the common worship of Isis. Woman primeval. Indeed, the Church Fathers in Rome had been horrified by the role that women played in Cathar society. In the Languedoc, women were not seen as the devil's handmaidens, but as vibrant members of the community who participated equally with men in religious rites and political affairs.

His gaze fell on the miniature ankh that the figurine grasped in her right hand, so blatantly similar to the Cathar cross that had been carved at the cave entrance.

Bloody hell. The clues have been there all along. Staring me right in the face.

The Latin phrase incised on the back of the Montségur Medallion – *Reddis lapis exillis cellis.* The last two letters of each word spelled the phrase 'Isis Isis'!

His curiosity running at full throttle, Cædmon wondered what other elements of the ancient Egyptian religion the Cathars might have incorporated into their religious practice. And what of the *Lapis Exillis*, the Holy Grail? Supposedly it had been 'returned to the niche'. He knew that in the Middle Ages, the 'aumbry' was a niche, typically located to one side of the altar, specially designed to hold sacred vessels.

Replacing the figurine in the stone box, he anxiously shone the torch at the limestone wall behind the altar, which had been sanded smooth. In the angled beam of light, he saw a delicately carved image of a dove in flight. A Christian symbol for the Holy Spirit, the dove was also sacred to Isis. A bird of gentle disposition, it symbolized the ancient maternal instinct. Beneath the incised dove, a large rock had been wedged into a square recess.

Cædmon stepped towards the aumbry. Trembling with anticipation, he pulled the rock out of the recess.

As he caught his first glimpse of the *Lapis Exillis*, his breath hitched in his throat.

'Un-bloody-believable.'

58

Hotel des Saints-Pères, Paris

2250 hours

Slipping on her robe, Kate tiptoed away from the bed.

Finn, sprawled on top of the tangled sheets, still dozed.

Achy all over, and discomfited about the reason for the sore muscles, she snatched an apple from a plastic shopping bag and limped over to the antique bureau. Seating herself in the upholstered Regency-style chair, she stared at the drawn curtains. Thoughts racing, she silently counted the pink peonies that patterned the heavy fabric.

In the last three hours, her relationship with Finn had undergone a major upheaval and she didn't have a clue what would happen next. It was like driving down a winding mountain road, at night, with no headlights. While a collision might not ensue, there would be an aftermath. A repercussion. A consequence that neither had considered during the exuberant free-for-all. They'd shared something profoundly intimate; she couldn't shrug it off and pretend that hadn't happened.

Although, being a man, that might be exactly what Finn would try to do. So be it. She wasn't going to make any demands. Didn't even know what she would demand if she was so inclined, still grappling with her newfound feelings.

Given all that had transpired in the last four days, she wondered if her life would ever again be the same. At some point in time, would she be able to return to Washington and pick up where she'd left off? For the last two years, her few remaining friends had been urging her to make a change. Somehow she didn't think *this* was what any of them had had in mind: being on the run in Paris.

Hearing a drawn breath, Kate turned her head. Finn, attired in a pair of low-slung cargo pants, stood next to the bureau.

'I'm not sorry,' he said without preamble. 'And in the spirit of full disclosure, I'm thinking that was a couple of days overdue.'

Kate forced herself to meet his gaze, to get past the embarrassment of having writhed naked on the bed with him. 'I'm not sorry either.'

'Man, that's a relief.' Grabbing the twin to her chair, Finn pulled it over to the bureau and sat down.

'Although . . . I owe you an apology,' she said haltingly. 'I didn't mean to throw it in your face about Cædmon.'

To her surprise, Finn grinned good-naturedly. 'Glad that you did, actually, seeing as how it got things kick-started between us. And I know you're not the type to purposefully play the jealousy card. I just – um – overreacted. Talk about going ga-ga.'

Kate blushed, well aware that she was guilty of the same crime. On paper, they were an 'odd couple', hailing from different backgrounds, with little in common. But the paper trail wouldn't show the deep-down, inexplicable sense of 'rightness' that she felt with him. Or the intense physical attraction.

Without asking, Finn took the apple out of her hand. Removing his penknife, he pulled out a blade and began to peel it for her.

The next few moments passed in companionable silence.

Extending a hand towards Finn's chest, Kate lightly fingered the silver Celtic cross that he wore around his neck. 'I've always thought that a Celtic cross on a treeless hillside was a hauntingly beautiful sight.'

'The *cheilteach* belonged to my da.' Finn stopped what he was doing, a red apple ribbon dangling from his knife blade. 'Only keepsake I have. He died when I was fifteen years old. The Guinness finally got the better of him.'

'I'm sorry.'

Finn sliced a wedge of peeled apple and offered it to her. 'When we were at the houseboat in Washington, you mentioned that you were divorced.'

She dug her toes into the thick carpet pile, the conversation having just skidded off the runway.

Perturbed, Kate stared at the piece of fruit. She didn't like to think, let alone talk, about her marriage to the soft-spoken, brilliant, boyishly handsome Jeffrey Zeller. A fellow cultural anthropologist, they'd met at a symposium at Johns Hopkins University. On the surface, they were the perfect couple. Behind closed doors, it was a different story entirely.

'My marriage didn't work out. I won't bore you with the details,' she intoned woodenly, head downcast, gaze still focused on the apple wedge.

'Kate, don't take this the wrong way, but . . .' Finn's brow furrowed slightly. 'I noticed that you have a couple of stretch marks on your –'

'That usually happens to a woman who's given birth,' she interjected, beating him to the punchline.

'I know. That's why I brought it up.'

A heaviness, like late-afternoon thunder, hung between them.

Finn gently nudged her forearm. 'Hey, Katie, y'okay?'

Defensively crossing her arms under her breasts, Kate hitched her hips, twisting her upper body away from him. 'No, I am not okay. My infant son died two years ago because his negligent father was busy screwing a twenty-four-year-old graduate student and he couldn't be bothered with checking the baby monitor.' The confession, unplanned and uncensored, slipped from her lips before she could slam on the brakes.

'Christ, Kate. I had no idea.'

'He died from SIDS . . . sudden infant death syndrome. Which means that no one could ever tell me the reason why he –'

Kate closed her eyes, the horrible night replaying in her mind's eye. *White crib. Blue-eyed baby boy. Heart pounding. Limbs shaking. She opened her mouth to scream. Oh, God! There is no God. If there is, I hate him.*

Suddenly dizzy, she grabbed the edge of the bureau. In that same instant, a muscular arm slid around her waist, Finn lifting her out of her chair and on to his lap, protectively tucking her under his wing. His pity more than she could handle, Kate struggled. Finn simply wrapped his arms around her that much tighter.

'Don't let your thoughts go there,' he whispered.

Flattening her hands against his chest, Kate rigidly permitted the embrace.

Surrender, a voice in her head chided. *Just for a few moments. He can't take your pain away. And, not having any children of his own, chances are Finn can't comprehend the depth of your despair. It doesn't matter. He's offering you some much-needed comfort. Take it.*

With a shuddering sigh, she sagged towards him, leaning her head on Finn's shoulder.

In the days and months following her son's death, she'd been like an airborne bird in a slow-motion death spiral. No one knew how to console her. Her parents tried, but Kate refused to accept that her suffering was due to her attachment to the ego, the tenets of Buddhism cold solace to a mother who had just lost her only child. Her husband, Jeffrey, was too busy excusing his complicity in the tragedy. Her friends, many of whom were new parents, began to shy away once they realized that she couldn't bear to be around their children. Although wary, she attended a SIDS support group meeting. She lasted ten minutes. While they meant well, their heartbreaking stories only compounded her own grief.

Propping a curled hand under her chin, Finn coaxed her into looking at him. 'I'm curious. What was your son's name?'

Kate blinked, surprised; very few people ever thought to ask. 'His name was Samuel,' she replied in a strained voice, a husky whisper the best she could manage. 'But from the day he was born, everyone called him Sammy. Had he lived, he'd now be two and a half years old.'

'Samuel . . . that's a nice name.'

'The first year after he died, I'd sometimes wake up in the middle of the night and, for a brief infinitesimal second, I could smell baby powder. I thought I was losing my mind.' Glancing at Finn, she grimaced self-consciously. 'The jury's still out on that one. What I did lose was my interest in just about everything, including my career at Johns Hopkins. Suddenly, I no longer cared about getting tenure. "Publish or perish" –' she shrugged her shoulders – 'it no longer mattered to me.'

'Death has a way of rearranging our priorities.'

'It's true. Jeffrey's adultery became inconsequential. Although it contributed to my leaving academia. Cultural anthropology is a close-knit clan.' She snorted at the pun. 'I certainly didn't want to run into *her*. And I never again wanted to see *him*. That's how I ended up as a subject-matter expert working at the Pentagon.'

'Want me to pay the bastard a visit?'

'Yes. *No*,' she amended a split-second later. She'd long ago closed the book on Jeffrey Zeller.

'I can't imagine the heartache of losing a child. That said, over the years I've lost some really close friends and . . . it takes a long time before you can think about them and maintain any semblance of composure.' As he spoke, Finn absently combed his fingers through her hair. 'When I do remember them, I *never* think about that last day.'

'The fact that Sammy only exists in the past tense is what hurts so much.' She paused, letting the pain wash over her. 'It's why I have such a hard time envisioning the future.'

'You just have to concentrate on the present. If you start living in the now, the future will eventually come into focus.'

She glanced at the Celtic cross. 'I thought you were a Catholic, not a Buddhist.'

'Honestly? I don't know what the hell I am.' Warm lips nuzzled the side of her neck, his left hand sliding from her waist to her hip. 'Happy to be with you, Katie. That's what I am.'

'I'm happy, too, Finn.'

They'd spent the last four days together. Hardly the makings of a lifetime commitment.

But could it be the beginning of one?

To tell the truth, she didn't know. But she was willing to find out, Finn having proved himself a far better man than her ex-husband.

A far better man that most, I'll warrant.

Just then, Finn's palm pilot began to vibrate loudly against the bureau.

'I programmed it to alert me when the Benz left the garage.' Finn picked up the device and scrolled through the menus. A few seconds later, he turned the display screen so that she could see the tracking map. 'Uhlemann's headed this way. Time to do the Hustle.'

59

Mont de la Lune, The Languedoc

2315 hours

I've just found the Lapis Exillis! The Stone in Exile.

The Grail!

Astounded, Cædmon stared at the gold pyramid-shaped object cached inside the limestone aumbry.

'First an Isis idol and now *this*,' he marvelled, flabbergasted that the Grail of legend was actually the Benben stone, one of ancient Egypt's most sacred relics. To have unearthed the artefact in Egypt would have been noteworthy. To find it in the south of France was mind-boggling.

Bending at the waist, he peered more closely, able to see that there were hieroglyphs carved around the base of the stone.

'"*I come from the Earth to meet the star*,"' he translated, the 'star' in question undoubtedly Sirius, the celestial abode of Isis.

Bracing both hands around the pyramidal stone, Cædmon carefully removed it from the niche and placed it on the altar. Roughly the size of a kettle, it was surprisingly heavy, weighing at least seven pounds.

'Yellow, glittering, precious gold.'

But unlike the gilded Isis figurine, the Grail wasn't

fashioned from thinly hammered gold applied to bronze. Instead, the pyramidal stone had actually been *electroplated*! A technology that supposedly didn't exist prior to the year 1800 when Alessandro Volta engineered the first electric cell battery.

And because it was gold-plated, he had no idea what comprised the core substance. Was it a stone? A crystal? A fallen meteorite? Whatever it was, the very fact that it had been electroplated proved that the Egyptians knew how to produce electricity.

What else did they know how to do? he wondered as he stared contemplatively at the Grail, still in a state of confused awe.

My God! It's the bloody Benben stone!

Shrouded in mystery, Egyptologists were divided over the precise meaning of the Benben stone. Some claimed it symbolized the first lump of earth enlivened by the blessed rays of the sun. A few thought it was a perch for the *Bennu* bird, the mythological Phoenix that engendered the creative process. Then there were those who claimed the pyramidal stone symbolized a drop of semen that fell from the god Atum's penis when he masturbated the world into existence. Indeed, the Coffin Texts intimated that the Benben stone had magical powers, although he suspected that the ancient object had more to do with technology than the occult.

A key to unlock scientific knowledge that had been lost eons ago.

Whatever it was, the Benben stone had supposedly been smuggled into Syria in the twelfth century BC during a popular uprising against the Pharaoh Merenptah. Where it promptly disappeared in the desert sands.

Could that be the reason why the Cathars referred to the pyramidal stone as the *Lapis Exillis*, the Stone in Exile? The same appellation used by Wolfram von Eschenbach to describe the Grail.

Overwhelmed with tantalizing questions for which he had few answers, Cædmon lifted the golden stone from the altar and deposited it in his rucksack. Unfortunately, he couldn't take both the Isis idol *and* the Grail. It would be difficult enough worming his back through the tunnel with just the one relic. The Grail was the prize. He could retrieve the Isis figurine at a later date.

As he turned his back on the altar, Cædmon was guiltily put in mind of Prometheus forced to steal fire from the gods. An act for which the mighty Zeus had Prometheus tethered to a rock while an eagle dined on his liver. Day after agonizing day.

Penance for his sins.

60

Rue des Saint-Pères, Paris

0130 hours

'Is the Taser really necessary?'

'As soon as Uhlemann realizes that he's been ambushed, chances are he'll go ape shit,' Finn replied bluntly. 'So, yeah. Absolutely necessary.' Taking Kate by the arm, he ushered her across Rue des Saints-Pères.

At that late hour, there were few motorists on the narrow street and even fewer pedestrians.

'Maybe we should try to contact Cædmon,' Kate suggested in a worried tone of voice. 'What if he found the Grail? Uhlemann might be more amenable to turning over the Dark Angel if –'

'I'm only gonna say this one time, Kate: I'm not going to jeopardize my mission because of a half-baked, half-ass theory concocted by your harebrained buddy.' Finn shot her a meaningful glance, willing her compliance. Not altogether certain that he'd secured it, he checked the palm pilot. 'Looks like the Benz is driving around the block. Which means that we have approximately forty seconds to insert.'

They dodged behind a tall topiary tree, one of a pair that framed the entrance to Ivo Uhlemann's apartment building. Stowing the palm pilot in his Go Bag, Finn removed the Taser. Purchased under the table at a military supply store in Montparnasse, the stun gun was the most powerful weapon in his arsenal.

'What if Doctor Uhlemann's chauffeur is armed?'

'Don't worry,' he said reassuringly, needing Kate to hang tight. 'When Uhlemann's chauffeur walks around the Mercedes to open the rear passenger door, I'll neutralize the bastard before he can draw a weapon. Because of the dark tint on the Mercedes' windows, Uhlemann will most likely be unaware of what's happening.' He reached into his Go Bag and removed a roll of duct tape and a pair of wire cutters. Handing both items to Kate, he said, 'After I zap the driver, you're to cut the wires on the Taser darts.'

Just then, a graphite grey Mercedes sedan pulled up to the kerb. Standing in the shadows, they stared at the faint puffs of diesel fumes emitted from the exhaust pipe of the idling vehicle.

The driver's side door opened. A large man dressed in a black chauffeur's suit got out of the Benz.

Kate gasped.

Well, what do ya know? It's ol' Cue Ball.

'Stay on my six,' Finn whispered as he stepped forward, the Taser tucked out of sight behind his leg.

'Hey, Baldy. How's it hanging?'

On hearing Finn's voice, the chauffer stopped in mid-stride.

Having caught the big bastard off guard, Finn whipped his right arm into a firing position and pulled the trigger. Two darts, each connected to a metal wire, were ejected.

A split-second later, the chauffeur began to convulsively twitch as 50,000 volts of electric current travelled from the stun gun to his chest. A crackling sound accompanied the graceless jive.

The instant that he released the trigger, the other man lurched forward. Like a felled tree in the forest.

Catching the heavy bastard in his arms, Finn propped him against the side of the Mercedes. Kate, wire cutters in hand, snipped the connection. Finn patted him down, smiling as he removed a Heckler & Koch Mark 23 from the other man's waistband.

Shoving the Mark 23 into his Go Bag, he removed a second cartridge and quickly reloaded the Taser. 'Okay, one more fish to fry.'

'Funny,' Kate muttered under her breath as she opened the rear passenger door.

A white-haired man stuck his head through the opening, clearly unaware that he was in any danger. Still holding the goon against the Benz with his left arm, Finn raised his right and pulled the trigger.

A frenetic pulse of electricity arced through the air.

A shocked expression on his face, Uhlemann writhed gracelessly. Completely incapacitated, he fell backward into the Mercedes.

Kate ran around to the other side of the vehicle, opened the rear door and dragged Uhlemann across the leather seat, giving Finn enough room to shove the chauffeur into the Benz.

'Quick! Hand me the tape.'

Roll in hand, Finn ripped off a long piece with his teeth and strapped Uhlemann's hands together. That done, he bound the older man's ankles and finished by slapping a piece of tape over his mouth.

'Time to boogie,' he told Kate, relieved that the operation had gone down without a hitch.

'Aren't you going to truss his hands and feet?' Kate asked, gesturing to the unconscious chauffeur.

'Nope.' Opening the front passenger door, Finn hopped into the Mercedes. 'I plan on cutting the big bastard loose as soon as we get to the next stop.'

Kate, the designated driver, got behind the wheel. Noticing that he'd exchanged the Taser for the HK Mark 23, her eyes opened wide. 'Finn, I don't think you should be brandishing –'

'I know what I'm doing,' he interjected. 'Now, let's hit it.'

Looking none too pleased, Kate pulled away from the kerb and headed down the street, turning right at the corner and driving around the block to Boulevard St Germain. As per the mission op that Finn had earlier devised, they would cross the Seine at Pont de Sully then proceed to Place de la Bastille.

Finn popped the magazine from the pistol. Seeing twelve .45 bullets, a full mag, he smiled. *Beautiful.* He next pulled the slide a fraction, just far enough to glimpse the chambered bonus round. His smile widened. He always liked the heft and feel of a Mark 23, the sidearm carried by most of the Special Forces. It was a good, reliable piece. Of course, the last time he used one, it'd been blown out of his hand by a trigger-happy Syrian.

'I think the chauffeur's coming to,' Kate announced anxiously a few moments later when a huge bald head suddenly appeared in the rear-view mirror.

Twisting at the waist, Finn peered over the back of his seat at the black-suited chauffeur. '*That* is a wicked broken nose,' he remarked smugly as he appraised his handiwork. Like any man, he took pride in a job well done.

Clearly disorientated, the chauffeur turned his head from side to side. At seeing his employer slumped against the seat, his face contorted into an ugly grimace. '*Du verdammter arschficker!* You killed Herr Doktor Uhlemann!'

'The old dude's not dead. Just down for the count.' Ready for a confrontation, Finn aimed the Mark 23 at the goon's forehead. 'Take off your clothes.'

The other man vehemently shook his head. '*Nein!* I vill not!'

'Shuck the monkey suit.' He toggled the gun barrel. A silent threat.

Muttering under his breath, the chauffeur tugged at his garments, flinging each discarded piece into the footwell. Teeth clenched, he divested himself of his last bit of dignity, yanking off his tidy undies.

Finn glanced at the German's chest, wondering if the big bastard sported a Black Sun tattoo. 'Nice jugs,' he snickered. 'Since you don't rate a tattoo, I'm guessing that makes you low man on the totem pole.'

'We've just arrived at Place de la Bastille,' Kate informed him. Both hands gripped on the steering wheel, she navigated the Mercedes to the inside lane of the traffic circle. Following the mission op, she continuously drove around the circle.

'Listen up, Cue Ball. When you get back to the Seven Research Foundation, you're to tell your pals that I want the Dark Angel,' Finn said in a measured tone of voice, thrusting the gun barrel against his broken schnoz. 'And if I don't get her, Doctor Ivo Uhlemann will not be returning. Those are my demands. Here's the number where I can be contacted.' With his left hand, Finn slapped a strip of duct tape on to the naked man's chest, his cell phone number scrawled on it. Knowing that a naked man was a vulnerable man – and that a vulnerable man would not carjack a vehicle and give chase – he jutted his chin at the passenger side door. 'Okay. Time to head out into the wild blue yonder and let your freak flag fly.'

'*Fich dich, arschgesicht!*' the chauffeur hissed, beady eyes narrowed.

'Right back at ya. Now get out of the car, asshole!'

'*Nein!*'

'Hey, grow a pair, will ya? Or I *vill* put a bullet between your eyes.'

Slowing the vehicle to a snail's pace, Kate released the door locks. Several annoyed drivers laid on their horns. All of 'em got an eyeful when, several seconds later, a stark naked man emerged from the back of the Mercedes.

Lowering the window, Finn shot the chauffeur a parting glance. The bastard stood beneath a huge marble pillar situated in the middle of the traffic circle, his hands cupped over his groin. Which was when Finn noticed that there was a statue of a naked man on top of the pillar.

A damned funny sight to behold.

61

Rue de la Roquette, Paris

0213 hours

Nerves frayed, Kate spared a quick glance in the rear-view mirror.

'Don't worry. Uhlemann's still out cold.' An implacable expression on his face, Finn stared straight ahead.

What in God's name was he plotting? The episode at Place de la Bastille had come as a complete surprise to her.

As the Mercedes sped down Rue de la Roquette, Kate tightly grasped the steering wheel. 'Finn . . . I think you should know that . . .' She hesitated, afraid to broach what she knew would prove a touchy subject. 'I'm starting to have second thoughts about all this. Surely you have enough incriminating, if not damning, evidence on the digital voice recorder?' Taking her eyes off the road, she looked over at him. 'Don't you think that's enough?'

Surprisingly calm, as though he'd been expecting the question, Finn said, 'While the conversation that we recorded earlier today at the Grande Arche will probably clear me of the murder charges, it's not enough for the police to arrest Angelika, a.k.a. the Dark Angel. The police are gonna need more than just a first name to make an arrest.'

Full of misgivings, Kate followed up with the obvious: 'What if the Seven Research Foundation refuses to bargain with you? What then?'

'You mean what am I planning to do with the old dude?' When she nodded, Finn shrugged and said, 'Since I'm not in the habit of making idle threats, let's hope it doesn't come to that.'

Kate's breath caught in her throat.

If the Seven Research Foundation failed to comply, she *would* do all in her power to stave off a deadly turn of events. Not just for Dr Uhlemann's sake, but for Finn's as well. She feared that, blinded by his need for vengeance, Finn couldn't foresee the consequence of a violent reckoning. The night that Sammy died, the ambulance driver had had to physically restrain her from plunging a steak knife into her husband's heart. Thank God that he did. While she was no longer a practising Buddhist, she still believed that purposefully taking a life would keep one chained to the wheel of *Samsāra.* Haunted by karmic fallout.

Her feelings for Finn McGuire were too strong to let that happen.

As they drove through a somnolent neighbourhood, neither spoke, each wrapped in their own thoughts. Approaching the terminus of a dead-end street, Kate applied the brakes, bringing the Mercedes to a full stop. Straight ahead was a bright green metal gate in the middle of a tall brick wall surmounted by barbed wire. The back entrance to Cimetière du Père Lachaise. The fabled cemetery, situated on the outskirts of the city, was the final resting place for some of France's most prominent citizens: Molière, Proust, Delacroix, Sarah Bernhardt, Edith Piaf. The list went on and on.

'Do you want me to turn off the engine?'

'Leave it running,' Finn told her. 'Now get out of the car.'

'*What?*' Since this hadn't been part of the plan, the unexpected request bewildered her.

'You heard me, get out. I'll let you know when you can get back in.'

Wondering if he intended to leave her stranded on the outskirts of Paris, Kate yielded without a fight, too stunned to protest. Arms folded over her chest, she stood on the pavement as Finn got behind the wheel of the Mercedes. Where he intended to go was a mystery. Since the cemetery was closed for the night, the entrance gate was locked.

Finn gunned the powerful V-12 engine.

Oh, no! Don't tell me!

Realizing that he intended to drive right through the locked gate, Kate shoved a balled fist to her mouth, muffling a horrified shriek. Breaking into the historic cemetery had not been part of the mission op. But, then again, that business with the naked chauffeur had not been part of the original plan either.

Seconds later, engine roaring, Finn rammed the Mercedes Benz into the iron gate, nearly ripping it from the hinges. No match for German engineering and American resolve.

Opening his car door, Finn waved his arm, signalling for her to get back into the vehicle. Afraid that a local resident might sound the alarm, Kate sprinted towards the Mercedes. If the police showed up, they'd be arrested on the spot.

Fear mounting, she slid into the front seat. Finn offered no explanation and no apology. As he drove down a narrow cobbled lane, she detected a faint smile on his lips. She realized that he had thoroughly enjoyed using the now dented and dinged luxury sedan as a mobile wrecking ball. *Boys and their toys*, she mused disagreeably.

'Now what?' she enquired, dreading the reply.

'Now we find a place to hunker down.'

She raised a dubious brow. 'In a graveyard?'

'You're not scared of ghosts, are you?'

'No. And that's not why I asked,' she muttered under her breath, only now beginning to understand that Finn was operating on a 'need to know' basis, revealing the mission op to her in piecemeal fashion.

Several twists and turns later, he stopped the car and cut the ignition.

Kate glanced at the still-unconscious Uhlemann. 'What are you planning to do with our passenger?'

'Take him with us.'

Getting out of the car, Finn opened the back door and hauled Uhlemann out of the Mercedes. He then hefted the unconscious man over his shoulders fireman-style and strode down the cobbled lane. Banked on both sides by stately mausoleums, it reminded Kate of the visit she'd once made to New Orleans' famed St Louis cemetery.

'"We die only once and for such a long time,"' she read aloud as they passed an elaborately designed crypt, struck by the morbid phrase that had been carved over the doorway. Not exactly the sort of sentiment that one would ever see printed on a Hallmark condolence card. Unnerved, she shivered.

A trio of tabby cats eyed their approach warily, the cemetery home to a motley tribe of feral cats.

'This'll do,' Finn muttered as he stopped in front of a large crypt, the name 'Touzet-Guibert' carved above the lintel. Without warning, he kicked in the metal door. 'Wait out here until I get a couple of light sticks out of my Go Bag.'

Kate silently complied, in no hurry to enter the mausoleum.

A few moments later, Finn motioned her inside. Reluctantly entering, her gaze was drawn to the two light sticks wedged into wall crevices, the makeshift sconces illuminating the crypt with an eerie green glow. The unmoving Ivo Uhlemann was on the floor, propped against a marble wall.

'Have a seat,' Finn said, gesturing to an ornately carved sarcophagus.

Envisioning what was inside that stone coffin, Kate shook her head. 'No, thanks. What's next on the agenda?' she asked, thinking it was time for Finn to divulge the rest of the mission op.

Turning his head, he glanced at Uhlemann. 'Time to wake up Sleeping Beauty.' None too gently, he ripped the piece of duct tape from the older man's mouth. He then slapped Uhlemann once on each cheek.

Dr Uhlemann blinked his eyes. With his perfectly coifed white hair, neatly trimmed beard and expensive, tailored suit, he cut an elegant figure. Hardly Kate's image of a villainous neo-Nazi.

'Where are we?' their captive enquired calmly, remarkably composed.

Removing his penknife from its sheath, Finn squatted in front of Uhlemann and cut the duct tape binding his wrists. 'We're in a mausoleum on the outskirts of town.'

'What an ironic choice given that you intend to kill me.' Dr Uhlemann glanced at the beautifully crafted marble walls. 'My compliments, Sergeant McGuire. Such a lovely setting in which to spend the eternal quietus.'

'Actually, I intend to trade you for the Dark Angel. Your chauffeur – nice fella, by the way – volunteered to deliver the ransom demand to your pals at the Seven Research Foundation.'

The older man slowly moved his hands in a circular motion to restore circulation. 'A futile exercise since the Seven will *never* remand the Dark Angel to your custody,' he replied. Then, smiling enigmatically, he said, 'To save time, may I suggest that you put the gun to my head and pull the trigger?'

62

The Seven Research Foundation, Paris

0215 hours

'*Du bist ein dummkopf!*' Angelika Schwärz railed, furiously pounding on the driver's chest with a balled fist. Standing in the middle of the front lobby, she didn't care who witnessed the dressing down. The big oaf was lucky that she didn't jab a letter opener into his heart and impale him to the wall. 'How could you have bungled this so badly? You couldn't take a piss in the dark without wetting both feet.'

A computer technician who worked down the hall scurried past. Although bug-eyed, and clearly shocked, he knew better than to intervene.

'It's not my fault,' Dolf Reinhardt whined, brow-beaten and pussy-whipped. 'McGuire ambushed us!' Attired in a too-tight trench coat with no buttons and belted with plastic bags that had been twisted and knotted together, he looked like a woebegone tramp. Obviously, he'd scavenged the garment from a rubbish heap.

'Of course he ambushed you. That's because McGuire is a real man with a big swinging dick. Not like your shrivelled little *schwanz*.' Angelika forcefully ripped the piece of grey duct tape off of Reinhardt's chest, causing the driver to squeal like a little girl.

Eyes watering with tears, Reinhardt stared at the floor. Somewhere between losing the Mercedes and the clothes on his back, the big oaf had also lost his manly pride. If ever he had it.

Bunching the strip of tape into a tight ball, Angelika disgustedly tossed it into a nearby waste bin.

The driver wiped a meaty hand over his lip, swiping at a ribbon of snot. 'Aren't you going to call him?'

'Who? McGuire? Only if I need a good fuck.'

'But he said he would kill Herr Doktor Uhlemann if you didn't remand yourself to his custody!' Reinhardt doggedly insisted. 'Do you not care what happens to –'

'I care.' *More than you will ever know, pussy man.*

Still in a murderous rage, Angelika strode over to the computer station at the reception desk and sat down. Like a lost puppy, Reinhardt followed after her.

'What are you doing?'

'I'm locating the Mercedes Benz,' she informed him, quickly typing in a secure password.

'But you have no idea where McGuire is hiding.'

'I will soon know *exactly* where he is hiding. The vehicle is outfitted with a GPS tracking device.'

The buffoon's mouth fell open in a slack-jawed 'O'. 'No one told me.'

Ignoring him, she pulled up the satellite data. *Père Lachaise Cemetery.* With its many monuments and hilly terrain, it was the perfect hideaway. *Clever, McGuire. Very clever.*

Angelika spared the driver a quick glance. 'Of course there's a tracking device on the vehicle. Do you think we would trust you with such an expensive automobile otherwise?'

'Herr Doktor Uhlemann trusts me implicitly.'

'He trusts you to change the oil and clean up after Wolfgang when he shits on the pavement. That is all.'

'But I . . . I am . . . Herr Doktor's aide-de-camp,' the big oaf sputtered, a crestfallen expression on his face.

'You are the village idiot.' Grimacing, she put the back of her hand to her nose. 'And what is that stench? Go and find some disinfectant.' She dismissed the driver with a wave of the same hand.

Contemplating her next move, Angelika pulled up an aerial photograph of Père Lachaise. For several seconds, she stared at the computer screen. Luckily, she had the element of surprise in her favour. That, and a full moon.

She smiled, actually looking forward to the upcoming battle with the American commando.

Soon, McGuire. Very soon.

63

Père Lachaise Cemetery, Paris

0245 hours

Furious, Finn lowered the Mark 23 pistol, shoving it into his waistband. 'You better hope to God that your cohorts at the Seven Research Foundation meet my demand and turn over the Dark Angel.'

'God? That half-mad despot who demands constant ego-stroking?' Uhlemann mocked.

'Yeah, *that* God.'

'Not only are you brash, Sergeant McGuire, but you clearly have no idea what's at stake.'

'So, why don't you fill me in?' he taunted, hoping to pry loose a few answers.

'Very well.' Even in the dim light, Finn could see the calculating gleam in the other man's eyes. 'I take it that you know about the *Lapis Exillis*?'

'You mean the Grail?' Finn sauntered over to the sarcophagus. 'Yeah, big whup.' Pronouncement made, he plunked his ass on the marble lid.

'While Finn may not be interested, I'm admittedly curious,' Kate remarked as she sat down beside him. 'We know that your father was a member of the SS Ahnenerbe and, as I understand it, they were actively hunting for the *Lapis Exillis*.'

'You are, if anything, well informed. Touché.' The derision in the German's voice countermanded the compliment. 'In the 1930s, my father, Friedrich Uhlemann, was teaching theoretical physics at Göttingen University. Something of a rebel, particularly given the anti-Jewish climate of the day, he was using Einstein's Theory of General Relativity to explore the effect of gravity and light on the space–time continuum.'

'That's an interesting research niche,' Kate conceded in a polite tone.

'Heinrich Himmler, the head of the SS, thought the same thing. Greatly impressed, he placed my father in an elite interdisciplinary think tank that came to be known as the Seven.'

'You make it sound like your old man won the Nobel Prize,' Finn harrumphed. 'Hell, he was just a jackbooted SS thug.'

'How dare you! My father was a brilliant scientist!'

'No doubt he was,' Kate readily agreed, quick to smooth the old rooster's feathers. 'I assume that Heinrich Himmler ordered the Seven to find the *Lapis Exillis*.'

Mollified, Uhlemann nodded curtly. 'Although Reichsführer Himmler first ordered them to find out why the Egyptians built the Sacred Axis at Thebes. Determined to solve the ancient riddle, in 1938 the Seven set sail for Egypt.'

'But your father was a theoretical physicist . . .' Kate paused. 'What could he possibly contribute to the project?'

'Really, my dear, you must learn to think outside the

box. When Jean-Claude Jutier, the Seven's resident archaeologist, unearthed a hieroglyphic inscription regarding a sacred stone that emitted a "blue fire", it was my father who astutely realized that the inscription described an exothermic reaction involving a massive energy transfer. Had it not been for my father, the Seven would never have uncovered the Lost Science of ancient Egypt.'

'I take it that the blue fire mentioned in the inscription was the Vril force.'

Uhlemann clapped his hands mockingly. 'My, my, aren't you the clever puss?'

Having hit his bullshit quota, Finn rolled his eyes. 'So where the hell are the mathematical calculations and scientific equations to back up this Lost Science? Did your old man find any of those carved on a temple wall? Wait! I think I know the answer . . .' He paused. Snickered. Then said, 'There aren't any calculations or equations. Ergo, Ivo, there isn't a "Lost Science".'

The old German snorted disdainfully.

'Actually, Finn does raise a valid point.'

'Ah! Time for a history lesson.' Lips twisted in an ugly smile, Uhlemann folded his arms over his chest. 'Did you know that Albert Einstein first conceived his Theory of General Relativity in 1905?'

'Are you sure about that?' Kate's brow wrinkled. 'I could've sworn that Einstein came out with that theory in 1915.'

'1915 is when he first *published* his Theory of General Relativity. But the idea for it was here –' Uhlemann pointed to his white-haired noggin – 'in his head ten years earlier in 1905. The problem was that in order to disseminate this revolutionary scientific theory to the world, Einstein had to first learn tensor calculus.'

'Okay, I'll bite,' Finn said, jumping back into the fray. 'What the hell is tensor calculus?'

When Uhlemann made no reply, Kate said, 'Unlike the calculus that we learned in high school, which deals with change and motion in three-dimensional Euclidian space, tensor calculus deals with the same problems of change and motion, but in a curved space. In his Theory of General Relativity, Einstein stated that matter, or gravity, causes the space–time continuum to actually curve.' As the daughter of an astrophysicist, Kate had a clear advantage in the science department. 'The easiest way to think of it is to imagine a heavy bowling ball, which represents the Sun. If you put the bowling ball on a trampoline, which represents the space–time continuum, then –'

'I get it,' Finn interjected. 'The bowling ball causes the trampoline to warp in the same way that matter creates a curve in the space–time continuum.'

Physics lesson concluded, the German continued the history lesson. 'In order for Einstein to scientifically explain what he had already conceived and perfectly understood in his mind, he had to spend ten years learning the mathematics that would enable him to publish his theory. The ancient Egyptians were no different. They had the science *here*.' Again, Uhlemann pointed to his head.

'And even if they had wanted to write down the equations, higher mathematics didn't exist in ancient Egypt,' Kate pointed out. 'Euclid didn't invent geometry until the third century BC and it wasn't until the tenth century that the Arab polymath Alhazan made the link between algebra and geometry. Which then enabled Newton to invent calculus in the seventeenth century.'

'How ironic that you should mention the great mathematician Alhazan. Did you know that Abu Ali Alhazan was a member of the *Dar ul-Hikmat*, the Egyptian House of Knowledge?'

A bewildered look on her face, Kate shook her head. 'Um, sorry, but I'm unfamiliar with that.'

'Forcing me to retract what I earlier said about you being well informed,' Uhlemann derided, proving, yet again, that he was a mean fuck. 'A prestigious university, the Egyptian House of Knowledge was founded in the eleventh century by the Fatamid Caliphate as a centre for Arabic scholarship. More importantly, it housed a magnificent library with a vast collection of ancient texts. As fate would have it, a disreputable Cairo antiquarian hoping to curry favour with the Nazi high command gave the Seven one of the library's most valuable manuscripts. Although scribed in the tenth century, it was based on ancient Egyptian texts that had been destroyed centuries before. To the Seven's delight, the *Ghayat al-Hakim* proved to be the missing link that they so desperately sought.'

Kate's eyes opened wide. 'Do you mean that the *Ghayat al-Hakim* contained a blueprint for the Sacred Axis at Thebes?'

'My dear, your powers of deduction are truly remarkable.'

'Can the sarcasm and answer the damned question,' Finn impatiently growled, ready to grab the old dude by his scrawny neck and hurl him across the mausoleum.

'In response to Doctor Bauer's very clever query, yes, the *Ghayat al-Hakim*, or "Goal of the Wise", was an instruction manual that detailed how the ancient Egyptians built their Vril Generator at Thebes using the *Lapis Exillis.*'

'Okay. Now how about fast-forwarding to the part where Himmler Meister tries to use the Vril force to build weapons of mass destruction.'

White brows drew together in an annoyed frown. 'The Seven was never involved in weapons research.'

Finn didn't buy that for one instant. 'If your old man wasn't interested in weaponizing the Vril force, what the hell was he planning to do with it, make a big blue campfire?'

'If you must know, my father theorized that the blue light associated with the Vril force could be used to create a closed time-like curve.'

'A CTC!' Like a snapped rubber band, Kate's head instantly whipped in Uhlemann's direction. 'Do you actually mean that the Seven wanted to generate the Vril force so they could *time travel?*'

64

Père Lachaise Cemetery, Paris

0321 hours

'You needn't look so shocked, Doctor Bauer. As you undoubtedly know, the existing laws of physics don't preclude time travel.'

Nonetheless, Kate *was* shocked. Within the physics community, time travel, or a closed time-like curve as it was commonly called, was a hotly debated topic. While many scientists believed it theoretically possible, none of them had successfully created a CTC.

She opened her mouth to reply; Finn beat her to it.

'Hey, Doctor Dufus! Get for real, will ya!'

Unperturbed, Ivo Uhlemann shrugged and said, 'Even the great one, Albert Einstein, claimed that time can be altered.'

'Yeah, I read H. G. Wells' *The Time Machine*, too,' Finn scoffed. 'But unlike some of us in the room, I knew it was a work of fiction.'

'Allow me to draw your attention to the mausoleum's funerary plaque.' Raising his arm, Dr Uhlemann pointed to the French inscription carved above the door. '"For he who can wait, everything comes in time,"' he obligingly translated. 'Rabelais mistakenly assumed that time is not only linear, but that it moves in only one direction. Anyone who accepts that is a victim of out-dated Newtonian physics.'

'And you're being damned disrespectful to the guy who invented calculus. Not to mention gravity.'

'As a theoretical physicist, I have the greatest respect for Sir Isaac. But what was innovative thinking in the seventeenth century has subsequently been proved invalid. While possessed of a great mind, Newton wrongly believed that space and time were not only separate, but absolute, conceptualizing time as an imaginary universal clock set in the heavens. *Tick-tock, tick-tock.* Always fixed. Never changing.' Dr Uhlemann paused before delivering the punchline. 'And, then, along came Einstein.'

'Who proved that gravity wasn't a force, as Newton had described it, but was, instead, the movement of matter in a unified space–time continuum.' The bowling ball on the trampoline from her earlier example. *But what did that have to do with time?*

'Einstein conclusively demonstrated that just as we can move backwards and forwards in space –' Dr Uhlemann moved his index finger, first one way, then the other – 'we can move forwards and backwards in time.'

'Well, Finnegan's Law says that you can *only* move forwards or backwards in time if you reset the clock.'

'Pish-posh!' Dr Uhlemann snorted. 'Do you know why Einstein considered the Theory of General Relativity his greatest achievement?'

'No. And I would have thought that the *Special* Theory of Relativity and $E=mc^2$ would take top honours,' Finn countered, proving that he knew more science than he let on.

'A proud achievement, certainly. But Einstein understood the inherent possibilities that arise when matter curves space. That curving of space is what we call gravity. Since Einstein proved that space and time are a single unified continuum, one can also use gravity to curve time.'

'While that's a scientifically valid argument, you would need an *enormous* amount of matter,' Kate pointed out. 'Only an object as big as a planet can produce enough gravity to bend the space–time continuum.'

'And you wrongly presume that only matter can create gravity. According to Einstein's theory, *light* can also create gravity.'

Suddenly, Kate realized where his argument was headed. 'And since gravity can bend time –'

'– light can also bend time,' Dr Uhlemann finished. His lips curved in a gloating smile. 'Light is how we can move backwards and forwards on the space–time continuum. A beautiful and elegant theory that my father mathematically proved. Moreover, he was convinced that the light shed by the Vril's "blue fire" would produce the necessary torque to bend time.'

'It's an intriguing theory, I'll grant you that. But it can't be tested without . . .' Kate hesitated. Although loathe to broach the topic, she had to know. 'Without some sort of time machine.'

'Who said that we don't have one?' Dr Uhlemann replied smugly.

'Shit! I don't believe that I'm hearing this!'

'Nor do I,' Kate murmured, stunned.

My God! No wonder Ivo Uhlemann is so obsessed with generating the Vril force. If the Seven Research Foundation had a working mechanism, they could theoretically open a tunnel in the space–time continuum.

'My candour is not without motive,' Dr Uhlemann confessed with a shrewd smile. 'My hope is that, intrigued by the theory, you will wish to participate in our great scientific experiment.'

Finn, hands on hips, sneered derisively. 'So we give you the medallion; you find the Grail; and then what? You go back in time and the Nazis win the war? You guys couldn't win the first time around. What makes you think the second time will be the charm?'

'Because with hindsight, one has the gift of perfect vision,' Dr Uhlemann replied, making no attempt to deny that he intended to change the course of a war that nearly destroyed the world. 'The mistakes have been identified and corrections will be made. This time we *will* win.'

Hearing that, Kate's jaw nearly came unhinged.

'Wake up and smell the sauerkraut, Ivo Meister. Having spent half my life as a soldier, I can attest that it takes a whole lot of oil to run a war,' Finn argued, refusing to back down. 'Without oil, your tanks and planes are worthless. That's the reason why Hitler invaded Russia, so he could seize the oil fields in the Caucasus. But the Nazis didn't even get close to the Caucasus. Invading Russia is what doomed the Reich. Correct me if I'm wrong, but I believe that eighty per cent of all German casualties happened as a result of the Russian invasion. That's a lot of dead soldiers. No way can you get around that catastrophe.'

'Oh, but we can,' Dr Uhlemann asserted quietly.

'Okay, I'll play your little time-travel game. Let's suppose that you go back in time and stop the German army from invading Mother Russia. That same army still needs oil.'

Like the cat that swallowed the canary, the other man slyly grinned. 'As I understand it, Sergeant McGuire, the largest oil fields in the world are located in Iraq, Iran and Saudi Arabia.'

'Shit! You wily old bastard!'

'I agree that it was a colossal blunder for the Führer to think he could conquer the Soviet Union. A poorly thought-out strategy, it was driven by an egomaniacal desire to enslave the Slavic race. Hitler thought the Germans had only to kick down the door and the whole Russian house would fall to pieces. A horrendous miscalculation. Instead, we will abide by the 1939 German–Soviet Non-aggression Pact.' As though it were already a done deal, Dr Uhlemann then said blithely, 'Peace with Stalin is a small price to pay for victory.'

'And it's a helluva long way from Berlin to Baghdad. Just how are you planning on getting there?'

'Thanks to Italy's dictator, Benito Mussolini, Greece was under German control. From the Greek Islands, we will invade Istanbul.'

'The Turks are a tough bunch, but compared to the Ruskies, a soft target,' Finn readily admitted. 'Once Turkey falls, I assume that you'll attack Iraq from the north.'

Uhlemann confirmed with a nod. 'At the same time, we will reinforce Field Marshal Rommel's forces in North Africa so that he can invade Saudi Arabia from Egypt.' A triumphant gleam in his watery blue eyes, Dr Uhlemann shoved the figurative blade a little deeper. 'By the end of 1941, we will have secured the entire Middle East. That done, we can turn our attention to India while Japan secures Southeast Asia.'

Noticeably subdued, Finn folded his arms over his chest. 'I gotta admit, had you gone with that plan instead of invading Russia, the Axis of Evil would have conquered almost the entire non-English-speaking world.'

'Before the Americans even entered the war, I might add.'

Horrified by Uhlemann's evil plan, Kate rose to her feet. Wrapping her arms around her waist, she walked over to the porthole. On the other side of the thick glass, charcoal shadows lent an other-worldly air to the dimly lit cemetery, the marble statues like mother-of-pearl ghosts.

'My colleagues and I believe that war is a purifying force for good,' Dr Uhlemann intoned.

'It can be,' Finn conceded. 'It can also inflict unimaginable pain and misery. Just like National Socialism imparted a shitload of pain and misery on the whole of Europe.'

'You say that because you are sadly misinformed about the ideology behind National Socialism.' Ivo held up a blue-veined hand, forestalling Finn's objection. 'The slaughter of the Jews was a heinous crime. And one that will not be repeated. On that, you have my word. We have a mandate bequeathed to us by our fathers. We *are* committed to carrying it out.'

Still peering through the porthole, Kate caught the bright flash of a headlight.

'Someone just drove through the cemetery gate!' she exclaimed, her heart forcefully slamming against her breastbone.

Finn rushed over to the window, shouldering her out of the way.

'We've got movement,' he hissed, reaching for the gun shoved into the small of his back. 'About seventy-five yards northwest of the mausoleum.'

Dr Uhlemann cackled softly. 'Oh, did I not mention that every vehicle in our fleet has a tracking device?'

'You evil old fucker!'

'If you want to leave here alive, you *will* give me the Montségur Medallion.'

A murderous gleam in his eyes, Finn pointed the Mark 23 at Ivo Uhlemann's left temple.

'The only thing I'm giving you is a bullet to the brain.'

65

Mont de la Lune, The Languedoc

0344 hours

Sheep bells jangled in the distance.

Normally a soothing sound, for some reason Cædmon found it jarring. In fact, he found the entire scenario unsettling. The pumpkin moon half hidden in the clouds. The night wind. The intermittent flashes of lightning that preceded the stentorian groans of thunder. And most disturbing of all, the brooding silhouette of Montségur on the northern horizon. *Looming.* Keeping silent vigil as it had for the last eight hundred years.

I feel like a castaway from a damned Brontë novel.

No sooner did that thought cross his mind than Cædmon tripped on a gnarled tree root that had burst free from the imprisoning terrain.

'On second thoughts, maybe a screwball comedy,' he muttered, managing to catch himself in mid-pratfall. Rather than hiking back to Montségur in the dead of night, he probably should have stayed in the mountaintop eyrie. But spurred by his staggering discovery, he was anxious to return to Paris post-haste.

Certain that he heard a branch snap, his ears pricked.

Thinking he might not be alone, he dodged behind a pitted boulder.

Had he been followed to Mont de la Lune?

Or was he simply overreacting to the Gothic shadows?

Unnerved, Cædmon skimmed the torch beam across the ravine. Unable to detect any movement in the blotchy moonlight, he suspected the predator lurked only in his imagination and that what he'd heard had been nothing more than the wind bouncing off the granite crenellations.

He glanced at his wristwatch. Three hours until daybreak. Worried that if he continued the trek the tangled matrix of loose rock and uneven terrain might get the better of him, he scoured the vicinity. The prudent course would be to catch a few hours sleep and hike back to the village of Montségur at first light. He could then collect his hire car, drive to Marseille and catch the northbound train for Paris. No sense wandering the moors like the poor bedevilled Heathcliff.

Espying a cantilevered overhang, Cædmon trudged in that direction, sidestepping a thicket of hawthorn bushes. He tucked the torch into his jacket pocket, freeing his hands so he could climb on to the stone slab.

As good a bed as any, he decided. An alpine meadow would have been better but he didn't relish sleeping with a mob of burly sheep. Slipping his rucksack off his shoulder, he carefully set it down, mindful of the precious cargo nestled in the bottom. Parched, he retrieved his water bottle. *Down to my last quarter litre.* When added to the hunk of stale bread and a wedge of warm cheese wrapped in a tea towel, it made for a meagre supper.

Cædmon raised the water bottle to his lips. As he did,

he heard the crunch of dried underbrush. Before his brain could process the meaning of that telltale sound, a bullet struck the side of his skull.

He spun to the left. Hit with an excruciating burst of pain.

The next bullet slammed into his upper arm. Hurling him up and over the ledge.

He crash-landed in a hawthorn bush, the branches instantly clamping around him, like the sharp maw of a predatory beast.

A torrent of warm blood flowed across his face, blurring his vision. Cædmon could taste it. Ash in the mouth. Certain death.

'Poor Siegfried,' the gunman jeered, standing at the edge of the stone slab. 'The Valkyries await you at the gates of Valhalla.'

With that, the bastard took his leave, the rucksack with the *Lapis Exillis* slung over his shoulder.

Horrified, Cædmon railed against the death sentence. He tried to move, but couldn't, his body shocked into paralysis. Trapped in the void between heaven and hell, the moon and stars whirled overhead in an off-kilter precession. No sun. Only dark of night.

Lying in that thorny nest, his cheek slathered in his own blood, Cædmon could feel the life force leach from him. The branches of the hawthorn rustled violently, the wind squalling through the ravine; a requiem composed by the winged Zephyrus, accompanied by the harsh jangle of distant sheep bells.

Send not to know for whom the bell tolls . . .

66

Père Lachaise Cemetery, Paris

0408 hours

Kate placed a restraining hand on Finn's arm. 'If you kill Doctor Uhlemann, you'll spend the rest of your life in prison. If that happens, you'll never be able to apprehend the Dark Angel.'

Finn glared at the white-haired man huddled on the floor, the muscles in his arm piston tight.

'Please, for my sake,' she whispered. Desperately hoping to get through to him, she was afraid to break eye contact. Worried that if she did, he'd pull the trigger.

'The old bastard knew they'd show up,' Finn rasped. 'He's just been sitting there biding his time. Waiting for 'em to kick down the door.'

'Actually, I've been trying to persuade you to come to your senses,' Dr Uhlemann declared in a noticeably weakened voice. 'Play your cards right and you can become a member of the most elite military force in history. I am offering you a chance to not only save your life, but to improve your lot in life. All you have to do is hand over the Montségur Medallion.'

'Fuck you!'

'If you insist on behaving like a fool, Sergeant McGuire,

you *will* die an inglorious death. On that, you have my word.'

'News flash: I plan on getting out of here alive.' Finn took a menacing step in the older man's direction. 'But I'm gonna need a human shield.'

Kate spared their captive a quick glance. Face drawn, brow beaded with perspiration, Ivo Uhlemann was clearly in a great deal of pain. Although the man was a monster, he was an ailing one. 'We can't take him; he's too frail. Just look at him. He'll only slow us down,' she added, hoping that would sway Finn.

'You just cut a break, you damn Nazi bastard,' Finn muttered under his breath as he unzipped his Go Bag. Retrieving the Taser, he unceremoniously shoved it in Kate's direction. 'If you have to fire it, make sure you're within fifteen feet of the target. Slide the safety back and hold the trigger for at least three seconds. You'll only have the one cartridge so make sure your aim is true. Got it?'

'I understand.' Kate wiped her sweaty hand on her trouser leg before taking the Taser from him. It was the first time in her life that she'd ever held a weapon. It felt like a foreign object. The fact that it looked like a child's toy made her all the more nervous.

Still muttering angrily, Finn slapped a piece of grey duct tape over Dr Uhlemann's mouth before restraining the older man's wrists and ankles. That done, he rejoined Kate at the porthole window.

'On the count of three, we're going to bolt out of this mausoleum, hang a Louie and run like the wind.' Instructions issued, Finn flung open the heavy iron door.

'*Three!*' arrived so suddenly that Kate's legs and feet

involuntarily moved of their own accord, her brain playing catch-up as they charged through the gloom. Because of the glut of burial crypts, monuments, tombstones and funerary statues, it was impossible to 'run'. Instead, they managed a fast trot as they wended their way through the jumble.

'Be careful,' Finn whispered, cinching a hand around her elbow. 'The cobbles are slippery.'

Knowing that an answer wasn't necessary, or even desired, she nodded breathlessly.

They'd gone approximately a hundred yards when Kate started to lag, her shin muscles painfully protesting against the uphill trek. Lungs on fire, she strained to draw breath, her rucksack smacking against her spine with each plodding stride.

Still holding her by the elbow, Finn headed for an enormous marble statue of a seated woman garbed in classical robes. *Morta.* The Roman goddess of death.

Kate wedged herself into the protective crevice between *Morta* and the iron portcullis that marked the entrance to a Roman-style crypt. Legs wobbling, she gratefully slid to her haunches.

Finn dropped on bent knee beside her. 'We'll rest here for a few moments while I figure out how the hell we're gonna elude the bad guys.'

'Not only do we have to contend with the hilly terrain, but it's like a big marble maze,' she huffed.

'That's the least of our worries. The *only* way out of here is through the same gate we entered. All of the other gates are locked until nine o'clock when the cemetery opens to the public.'

'Do you think our assailants are aware of that fact?'

Grim-faced, Finn nodded. 'And I guarantee they've got at least one sentry posted at the open gate.' He shoved his hand into his Go Bag and removed a pair of night-vision goggles. Pivoting on his heel, he raised the goggles to his eyes and peered in the direction of the mausoleum where they'd left Dr Uhlemann. 'I count a total of four unfriendlies.'

Oh, God!

'Damn it!'

'What's the matter?' she asked anxiously.

'One of the uglies is using a walkie-talkie. That means there's more than four of 'em prowling about.' He stuffed the NVGs into his bag.

'Do you think we even have a remote chance of getting out of here alive?'

Several seconds slipped past, the question hanging between them. Unanswered.

Raising a hand to her face, Finn gently brushed aside a hank of flyaway hair that had snagged in the corner of her mouth. 'Ready to move out?'

Kate gamely nodded. 'I'm ready,' she told him, scrambling to her feet. Heart thumping erratically, the brave front was all for show.

Finn set a brisk pace, holding on to her upper arm as they dodged between crypts and monuments. To her right, on the eastern horizon, dark clouds were plastered to the skyline like a well-worn suit.

Several minutes into the trek, Finn thrust a fist into the air, signalling Kate to a halt. He then motioned for her to get behind a chipped marble ledge.

'*On the double quick*,' he mouthed.

Biting back a fearful yelp, she ducked behind the low-slung wall. Finn squatted beside her. The iron gate that they'd earlier driven through was fifty yards away. A sentry paced back and forth in front of it.

Leaning close, Finn placed his mouth against her ear and whispered, 'I'm going to soft-foot up to the guard and take him out.'

'What do you want me to do?' she whispered back at him.

'Stay here while I take care of business. When you hear a high-pitched whistle, that'll be your signal to haul ass through the open gate. There's a subway station about a block to the northwest. Assuming we get out of here undetected, that'll be our next rallying point.'

'Be careful, Finn. And, please, no do-or-die theatrics.'

'Roger that.'

Clutching the Taser to her chest, Kate watched as Finn dashed towards the gate in a crouched zigzag pattern. A few seconds later, he faded into the shadows.

A few seconds after that, a striped tabby cat nimbly jumped on to the ledge in front of her. About to shoo the kitty aside, Kate caught a blur of motion out of the corner of her eye. She automatically turned her head.

Even in the murky light, she instantly recognized the diaphanous blonde halo.

The Dark Angel!

No more than twenty-five feet away.

Hit with a burst of fear, she accidentally dropped the Taser.

Frantically swiping her hand across the dew-dampened

grass, Kate grabbed hold of the plastic weapon. The cat, thinking it a game, batted at her hand with its paw. Bumbling, unable to see what she was doing on account of the frisky feline, she tried to locate the trigger.

Got it!

Wrist shaking, fingers trembling, she took aim and fired.

To her horror, nothing happened.

Realizing that she'd forgotten to deactivate the safety, Kate hurriedly slid the shield cover. A red laser light immediately appeared, frenetically bouncing off a nearby tombstone. She lurched upright. Committed, she re-aimed the Taser and pressed the trigger.

Two thin electric wires blasted through the air . . . before harmlessly dropping to the ground.

'*If you have to fire it, make sure you're within fifteen feet of the target.*'

'Oh, God,' Kate moaned. She'd just made a costly and, more than likely, deadly mistake.

Standing approximately twenty feet away, the blonde-haired woman raised her right arm in Kate's direction. In her hand, she clutched a sinister-looking weapon.

'*Guten tag*, little mouse.'

Kate dropped the Taser, this time on purpose, and raised both hands.

Casually sauntering towards her, the beautiful leather-clad Dark Angel smiled coldly as she aimed the gun directly at Kate's heart.

67

Père Lachaise Cemetery, Paris

0421 hours

A ghost warrior, Finn wended his way through the dark necropolis, purposefully keeping to the charcoal shadows.

Fifty feet from the cemetery entrance, he ducked behind a granite plinth. Knowing that there were more than four enemy gunmen prowling about, he strained his ears, listening, unable to detect any sound save for the innocuous rustle of leaves.

Stuffing the Mark 23 into his waistband, he snatched the night-vision goggles out of his Go Bag.

Fuck. The sentry posted at the gate was packing a Heckler & Koch MP5-K sub-machine gun. German-made *bang-bang* that had thirty rounds of nine mil ammo. When set to 'full automatic', it could blow that many holes in a man in a matter of seconds. Urban warfare at its deadliest.

Stuffing the NVGs back into his Go Bag, Finn wrapped his hand around the grip on the Mark 23 and quietly made his approach, the sentry now forty feet away.

Thirty.

Twenty.

His actions honed from years of training, he flipped on the laser sight. Grateful that his weapon had a sound suppressor, he stilled his breath as he raised his right arm. A red dot instantly appeared on the other man's forehead. Not about to second-guess the morality of the act, Finn squeezed the trigger.

The force of the shot hurled the sentry backward, knocking him off his feet.

In the split-second before he crash landed and his brain permanently shut down, the bastard reflexively pulled the trigger on the MP 5-K, strafing the night sky with nine mil bullets, shattering the silence.

PaPaPaPaPaPaPaPaPaPop

Fuck!

Knowing that the burst of gunfire would draw unfriendlies like buzzards to road kill, Finn spun on his heel and took off running.

For God's sake, Katie, stay put! I'm on my way!

Chest tight, heart thundering, he charged through the labyrinth, dodging statues and headstones.

In his peripheral vision, a dark blur suddenly materialized. Finn turned his head; verified that it was an unfriendly. Raising his right arm, he took aim and fired. The bullet entered the other man's brain via his eye socket. Like a marionette jerked by a puppeteer, the gunman twitched viciously. Then, strings cut, he fell gracelessly to the ground.

No time to gloat, Finn kept running.

A few moments later, he vaulted over the marble ledge.

Where the hell was Kate?

'Katie!' he whispered urgently. 'It's me!'

The only sound he could hear was his own harsh breath. Hit with a hinky feeling, Finn turned full circle. Which is when he spied the black plastic Taser laying on the ground. Still connected to two metal wires. Obviously, Kate had fired it. And missed the target.

Fuck!

Acting purely on impulse, Finn leaped back over the ledge and headed towards the mausoleum where they'd left Ivo Uhlemann. He figured – *hoped* – that Kate was still alive. Had they killed her on the spot, they would have left her corpse behind. A gruesome message. He figured – again, *hoped* – that they'd abducted Kate to force his hand.

Hauling ass, Finn cannonballed down the hill. To hell with stealth. They already knew he was coming.

As he neared the mausoleum, Finn could see that someone had pulled the Mercedes sedan in front of the crypt. The engine idling, twin plumes of smoke wafted out of the tailpipes.

Thank God! There was still time to make the trade.

Needing to collect his thoughts, Finn quickly devised a game plan, well aware that he had to be proactive, not reactive. No question, he'd give Uhlemann what he wanted – the Montségur Medallion – but, in return, he needed an iron-clad guarantee that Kate would be given safe passage out of the cemetery. Like Kate said earlier, he had enough evidence on the digital voice recorder.

Fifteen yards from the mausoleum, Finn stopped in his tracks. Although he had the Mark 23 clutched in his right hand, he held it off to the side. Non-threatening, but still in plain sight. Just in case.

From where he stood, he watched as Ivo Uhlemann, supported by a big dude in a black chauffeur's suit, exited the mausoleum. Given his shuffling gait, the old German looked to be in a lot of pain. Next, Kate and the Dark Angel emerged from the crypt.

Turning her head, Kate caught sight of Finn standing in the middle of the cobblestone lane.

'Finn! It's an am–' Kate was silenced in mid-shout, the Dark Angel viciously shoving a gun muzzle to her head.

Decked out in skintight black leather, the blonde bitch smiled flirtatiously at Finn – just before two men, each armed with a MP5-K sub-machine gun, lunged from the shadows and opened fire.

Weapons set on full auto, they unleashed a torrent of nine mil bullets in Finn's direction.

PaPaPaPaPaPaPaPaPaPop

Shit!

Finn dived behind a mortuary statue. Hitting the ground, he tucked and rolled. In his wake, marble chips flew through the air like wedding confetti, clumps of turf pelting the statue's granite base. An instant later, a leafy tree branch crashed to the ground beside him, severed from its limb by the hail of bullets. The noise was deafening.

Hugging the granite plinth, he peered around the corner. Muzzle flashes flickered like a swarm of fireflies, spent shells arcing through the air. He pulled back. Mark 23 clutched to his chest, he waited. Although he couldn't see, he heard the squeal of tyre rubber as the Mercedes floored it down the cobblestone lane towards the open gate.

Just as Finn hoped would happen, both gunmen ran out of ammo at the same time.

A three-second lull at the most, he seized his chance.

In one smooth, well-practised move, he spun around the corner and dropped to his knee. Grasping his right wrist with his left hand, he sighted the first target and pulled the trigger. The gunman on the left barrelled through the air, a hole blown through his heart. A split-second later, he pivoted, aimed and fired again, taking out the gunman on the right.

Both targets neutralized, he lurched to his feet. The acrid smell of gun smoke permeated the air. In the near distance, he heard the distinctive two-tone bleat of French police sirens. At any moment, the cops would careen through the gate at the end of the cobblestone lane.

Time to beat a hasty retreat.

Galvanized into action, Finn shoved the Mark 23 into his Go Bag before taking off in the complete opposite direction to the cemetery gate. Nerves sizzling, brain synapses firing, adrenaline pumping, his brain and body chemistry quickly adapted to the new situation. Charging uphill, he didn't venture a backward glance. Intent on escaping, he couldn't spare the half-second to look over his shoulder.

He spied a mausoleum situated next to an oak tree, which in turn was rooted next to the eight-foot-high cemetery wall, and headed in that direction. Literally flying by the seat of his pants, Finn leaped on to a sturdy headstone. From there, he lunged on to the roof of the mausoleum. Waking the dead, he charged across the clay-tiled roof to the towering oak tree. An instant later, he was airborne. Grabbing hold of a limb with both hands, he catapulted over the barbed wire strung along the top of the brick wall . . . landing on the hood of a Renault hatchback parked on the other side of the wall.

Mercifully, he caught a break; the Renault wasn't rigged with an anti-theft alarm.

Jumping off the bonnet, Finn sprinted across the street towards an apartment complex, managing to duck behind a large plastic rubbish container just as a police car sped past.

Not about to be caught red-handed with a damned smoking gun, he raised the lid on the rubbish bin and dumped the Mark 23. *Disposing of some very incriminating evidence.*

He then slipped into the shadows and made good his escape.

The easy part done, he now had to figure out how the hell he was going to rescue Kate.

68

Rue de Rivoli, Paris

0448 hours

Finn was dead.

Shell-shocked, Kate huddled against the Mercedes back seat, her cheek pressed to the tempered glass. No one could have survived that deadly barrage. So much sound. So much fury.

It's my fault that Finn's dead. He died trying to save me. Earlier, at the hotel, she'd been too afraid to reveal her true feelings. Now he'd never know.

The heartache more than she could bear, Kate jammed a balled fist to her mouth.

Don't scream!

She could mourn later. Right now, she had to stay focused. *It's what Finn would want me to do.* The two gunmen had undoubtedly retrieved the Montségur Medallion from Finn's bullet-riddled body. Which meant that she was the only person who could stop the Seven Research Foundation from finding the *Lapis Exillis* and using it to perform an unthinkable scientific experiment. One that would *literally* turn back the hands of time.

Kate glanced at the white-haired man seated beside her, Dr Uhlemann in the process of removing a hypodermic needle from the crook of his arm. Withered lips curved in a dreamy smile, he handed the used needle to the blonde-haired woman in the front passenger seat. Angelika, in turn, placed the needle into a plastic case.

Rolling down his shirt sleeve, Dr Uhlemann nonchalantly returned Kate's stare. 'You look like a terrified mourning dove. It's a drug. Nothing more, nothing less. Doctors administer it to patients all the time under the pharmaceutical name diamorphine.' Buttoning the cuff at his wrist, he added, 'I wonder how many of the sick and dying are aware that their doctors have turned them into heroin addicts?'

Angelika affected a horrified expression. 'I'm shocked to learn that you've become a skag junkie.'

Chortling, Dr Uhlemann absently stroked a small salt-and-pepper Schnauzer that was curled on his lap. A moment later, his facial muscles reconfigured into an ill-tempered frown. 'Why isn't Dolf driving? I don't like looking at the back of this man's head.'

'The view from the front isn't much better,' Angelika remarked cruelly. 'As for Dolf, I dismissed him early. Not only did he smell like a shit pile, but he looked like one, too.'

Worried that she might be the only sane person in the vehicle, Kate took a deep, serrated breath. The gunfight, the dog, the needle, the J. S. Bach cello suite softly playing on the sedan's sound system. It was all so surreal. As though she'd just landed in the middle of a Fellini movie with a cast of macabre characters.

Angelika peered over the back of her seat. A quizzical

expression on her face, she said, 'I'm curious, little mouse . . . did you love Finnegan McGuire?'

Refusing to share something so personal with a heartless killer, Kate bowed her head. Eyes welling with tears, she clasped both hands together and placed them squarely in her lap, Angelika's mocking tone the proverbial dagger to the heart.

The little Schnauzer, sensing Kate's distress, whimpered softly.

'Alas, Sergeant McGuire has no one but himself to blame for his demise,' Dr Uhlemann intoned, proving that his blade was just as sharp. 'Like Thor, he arrogantly thought that he was invincible.'

'Only to discover that a hammer is no match for a sub-machine gun,' Angelika jeered. Removing a tube of lipstick from a storage compartment, she flipped down the sun visor and proceeded to apply a coat of crimson red lipstick.

Sickened by their callous remarks, Kate turned her head and stared out of the window. Although it was difficult to see through the tinted glass, she recognized the wrought-iron fence that bordered the Jardins des Tuileries.

The chauffeur slowed for a red light.

'When I was a child, I visited my father while he was stationed in Paris.' Raising his arm, Dr Uhlemann directed Kate's attention to the esplanade on the other side of the fence. 'The SS officers, attired in white shorts and tank tops, would perform their morning calisthenics on that grassy field to your left.'

'Ooh-la-la! How I would have enjoyed seeing *that*,'

Angelika cooed before lifting a folded sheet of paper and blotting her lipstick.

'Parisians, notoriously slothful by nature, would stand at the fence and gawk. What they didn't grasp, and still don't comprehend, is that communal exercise provides the foundation for a vigorous society.'

'Don't you mean a martial society?' Kate counter-punched.

'*Any* society,' Dr Uhlemann retorted, a marked edge to his voice. 'Indolent people are inherently weak. Of body *and* mind.'

Still preening in front of the visor's mirror, Angelika said, 'And since we have no souls, you need not enquire about that.'

The traffic light changed to green.

'Driver, take us to the obelisk. Wolfgang needs to be walked,' Dr Uhlemann ordered, an imperious monarch who couldn't be bothered using a polite tone with one of his subjects.

Wordlessly nodding his head, the nameless chauffeur turned left at the corner. A few moments later, in typical Paris fashion, he pulled the vehicle on to the pavement at Place de la Concorde. At that hour of the day, there was no one lurking to protest the illegal manoeuvre.

The back-seat locks popped up with a loud *click!*

Clipping a leash on to Wolfgang's collar, Dr Uhlemann glanced over at her. 'I insist that you accompany us, Doctor Bauer.'

Intuiting that it was a royal command, Kate dutifully got out of the sedan. Angelika stood at the ready beside the open door. Red lips curled in a smirk, the blonde flipped open her leather jacket, letting Kate glimpse her holstered gun.

'You can't run fast enough, little mouse.'

'As I am well aware,' Kate muttered under her breath. Although the occasional car drove past, there was no cover, Place de la Concorde being an open plaza that encompassed nearly twenty acres. She'd be shot in the back before she could flag down a passing motorist.

Grabbing hold of Kate's elbow, Angelika ushered her over to the wrought-iron fence that surrounded the base of the obelisk. She then took the leash from Dr Uhlemann and proceeded to walk the Schnauzer.

At a loss for words, Kate stared at the 75-foot-high monument. Illuminated by spotlights, the red granite appeared tawny hued. In a city dominated by neo-classical architecture, the ancient Egyptian obelisk was an exotic sight.

'Given that it weighs over two hundred tons, it's amazing to think that it's carved from a single piece of granite,' Dr Uhlemann remarked conversationally. 'In order to transport it from Thebes, a special ship had to be built, an engineering feat. The details of that epic journey are illustrated on the pedestal.' He pointed to the inlaid gold diagrams that decorated the base of the obelisk. 'As you undoubtedly know, the monument is a key element on the Axe Historique.'

Hoping to establish a rapport with Dr Uhlemann – Captivity Tactics 101 – Kate asked the obvious: 'How exactly does the obelisk fit into the Vril equation?'

'At the heliacal rising of Sirius, a tremendous burst of astral energy is released. The obelisk acts as an antenna to transmit and direct that astral energy along the Axe Historique.'

Kate tipped her head back and peered at the gold cap on top of the monument. 'So the obelisk acts like a radio tower?'

'Precisely.'

Just then, Angelika walked towards them, Wolfgang obediently trotting at her heels. 'I love this feeling,' she purred. 'It's incredibly invigorating. Like the time I rode the waves at Big Sur.'

She was right; there was a palpable energy in the air.

'What you're feeling is the discharge of negative ions from the electromagnetically-charged telluric line. The water spewing from the fountains magnifies the effect.' Dr Uhlemann jutted his chin at the two massive water fountains situated approximately fifty yards away.

'I don't care what causes it,' Angelika replied as she flung her long blonde tresses over her shoulder. 'It feels so wonderfully –' A buzzing sound stopped her in midstream. Unclipping the cell phone at her waist, she glanced at the display screen. 'I must take this call.' She handed the dog lead to Dr Uhlemann before stepping away from them.

The call was brief, Angelika returning within moments. Approaching Dr Uhlemann, she placed a hand on his shoulder as she leaned close to whisper something in his ear.

Clearly stunned, he said, 'Are you absolutely certain?'

Angelika nodded. 'He has an eight-hour drive back to Paris. We'll have it by one o'clock this afternoon.'

'Just in time for tomorrow's heliacal rising.' Dr Uhlemann turned towards Kate. 'Our mission in the Languedoc was successful. I've just learned that we retrieved the *Lapis Exillis* from your cohort, Cædmon Aisquith. Twenty-six hours from now we will be able to perform *das Groß Versuch* and generate the Vril force. "O brave new world!"'

Hearing that jubilant exclamation, Kate's heart painfully constricted. 'Is Cædmon still alive?' she asked, barely able to get the words out of her mouth.

'I would certainly hope not,' Dr Uhlemann snapped testily.

Oh, God . . . Finn and Cædmon, both dead.

Afraid that she might collapse, Kate grabbed hold of the wrought-iron fence. Unbidden, one of the Four Reminders that Buddhists chant daily popped into her head. *Death comes without warning, this body will be a corpse.*

'What about me? Are you planning to kill me, as well?'

His blue eyes glazed from the narcotics in his bloodstream, Ivo Uhlemann tipped his head to one side, scrutinizing Kate as if she was some rare specimen.

A long silence ensued.

Then, shrugging carelessly, he said, 'I'm still undecided.'

69

Saint Clotilde Basilica, Paris

0638 hours

Bending over the elaborately carved font, Finn scooped holy water into his cupped hands rather than politely dipping his fingers. Eyes closed, he splashed the cool water on to his face. A bracing wake-up tonic.

Out of habit, one engrained at Catholic school, he silently blessed himself. *In the name of the Father, the Son and the Holy Ghost.* Then, for good measure, he murmured, 'Bless me, Father, for I have sinned.'

Water dripping off his chin, Finn snorted to himself. *Like I'm telling the Big Kahuna something he doesn't already know.*

Not only had he earlier committed four mortal sins, but he'd committed a major screw-up. He should never have left Kate alone in the cemetery. *Christ!* What had he been thinking? He was supposed to have kept Kate safe from harm. To protect her from the big bad wolf. But, instead, he left her alone. Sweet, gentle little Katie. Who was too inexperienced to escape from danger. And too scared to hit the target. Hell, she probably didn't see the Dark Angel approach until it was too late.

Yanking his T-shirt hem up to his face, Finn dried his wet cheeks before he stepped through the double doors that led inside the nave.

Again out of habit, this one engrained by the US military, he scanned the cavernous interior, checking for unfriendlies, and points of egress should he run into any. He could not, under any circumstances, fall into a police dragnet, for the simple reason that he couldn't rescue Kate from a Paris jail cell.

Although the basilica was constructed in the nineteenth century, it had a distinctly Gothic feel to it. Intimidating in the way that only a Catholic church could be. On each flank, dour-faced martyrs were eternally trapped in the long line of stained-glass windows. Sunken-cheeked and hollow-eyed, they were the guardians of the Faith. Ahead of him, prominently displayed above the altar, was a big golden cross with a dying Jesus nailed to it.

Damned if I do, damned if I don't.

Verifying that the only person inside the church was a humpbacked crone plying her fingers to a set of rosary beads, Finn walked towards the apse. He didn't bother bending his head or displaying false piety. He wasn't there to repent, ask for pastoral guidance, or seek absolution. He was there to reconnoitre. To take a much-needed rest and figure out his next move.

Because, so far, the situation had gone belly up and totally fubar. As in 'fucked up beyond all repair'.

And had become more fucked up with each passing hour as he'd hit one dead-end after another. If he'd had a knotted cat-tail whip, he would have flogged the shit out of himself. *Mortification of the flesh.* A time-honoured Catholic tradition practised by those wracked with guilt.

Now, because of his mistake, Kate was at the mercy of –

Don't go there, soldier! a voice inside his head boomed. In order to find and rescue Kate, he had to stay calm. That meant suppressing his emotions. Turning 'em off and shutting 'em down.

Determined to do just that, Finn ducked to the left, parking his ass on a rush-bottomed chair. Unlike the Catholic churches in Boston, there wasn't a pew in sight. Exhausted, he stared at the suspended dust particles, tinted red and blue from the early-morning light that shone through the stained-glass windows. Refusing to give in to the urge to close his eyes and catch a quick catnap, he unclipped his cell phone from his waistband. He'd already called Ivo Uhlemann. Repeatedly. Twice at his apartment and three times at the Seven Research Foundation headquarters. Each time, he'd left the same message. '*The Montségur Medallion is yours in return for Kate Bauer.*'

None of his calls had been returned.

Why the hell wasn't the evil bastard answering the phone?

Surely Uhlemann knew that he had him by the short and curlies. That's why they'd abducted Kate rather than execute her, to force his hand.

Hand broken, Finn was willing to give them what they'd wanted all along, the damned medallion.

So, just answer the fucking phone! Or at least let me find your sorry ass so we can make the trade.

Since the subway had been closed, he'd earlier retrieved Cædmon Aisquith's Vespa, using it to go to the Grande Arche. A wasted effort. The Seven Research Foundation office suite had been locked, all of the lights turned off. Not about to call retreat, he then headed to Rue des Saints-Pères, hoping to catch Uhlemann at home. Although he'd scared the hell out of the live-in maid, she claimed that she hadn't seen or spoken to Herr Doktor Uhlemann in the last twenty-four hours.

Belly up and totally fubar.

For several long moments Finn stared at the cell phone; he had one option left.

Shoving his pride to the wayside, he dialled the number. The call immediately went to Aisquith's voice mail.

'Call me the instant you get this. It's urgent!'

He hit the 'disconnect' button.

'Shit! Why isn't anyone answering their damned phone?'

On hearing the muttered expletive, the old bag on the other side of the aisle momentarily stopped reciting the rosary and glared at him. Finn mumbled an apology.

Where did they take Kate? I have *to find her!*

Gut churning, he took a deep breath, able to smell incense and candle wax. Along with the unmistakeable stench of his own fear. Out of options, Finn grabbed the chair in front of him and dropped to the stone floor.

On his knees, he clasped his hands to his chest . . . and prayed his ass off.

Part IV

'There was a thing called the Grail, which surpasses all earthly perfection' – Wolfram von Eschenbach, *Parzival*

70

Paris

1932 hours

Cædmon Aisquith slowly made his way down Rue de la Bûcherie. Jaw clamped. Teeth clenched. By dint of sheer will.

A battered warrior come home from the wars, he owed his life to a wizened old shepherd. Barely conscious, trapped in a hawthorn bush, Cædmon had used the torch in his pocket to flash a distress signal on to the granite cliffs of Mont de la Lune. Three short light beams. Three long. Three short. Over and over. *My soul is beyond salvation, but for God's sake, save our ship.* Before it sinks into the oblivion of chill death. Tending to his flock in the nearby mountain meadow, Pascal Broussard had seen the SOS.

'*O what can ail thee, knight-at-arms, alone and palely loitering?*'

For starters, a hole in his upper right arm and a shallow furrow along his outer skull. Both courtesy of an unknown assassin who hit the target but missed the mark.

Utterly demoralized by what had happened in the Languedoc, Cædmon had no idea who had ambushed him on that dark stretch of rocky terrain. He presumed it was someone in the employ of the Seven Research Foundation. Without question, *La belle dame sans merci* was merrily laughing at his plight. *He had actually found the Grail.* But, like Parzival after his first visit to the Grail Castle, he'd been tossed on his arse, the castle having vanished into thin air.

Cædmon glanced at the wadded bandage under his shirt-sleeve, relieved to see that there was no blood seepage. The sutures were holding. Forced to operate in primitive conditions, the shepherd had removed the bullet from his triceps brachii with a pair of needle-nosed pliers, the man actually annoyed that Cædmon ordered him to first sterilize the pliers in boiling water. As well as the needle used to suture his flesh together. For an old man with gnarled, arthritic hands, Pascal sewed a surprisingly neat stitch.

He was lucky to be alive. The first bullet had grazed his skull, leaving a superficial gully above his left ear. The second bullet had lodged in his arm muscle, missing the arteries and veins that siphoned blood to and from his heart. A blessing, Pascal claimed. More jaded, Cædmon knew better. After he'd tended to his wounds, the shepherd gave Cædmon the only painkiller he had – a half-full bottle of Pastis. Although he loathed aniseed, Cædmon gratefully accepted the gift. Polished it off, in fact, during the three-hour train ride to Paris.

A gruelling journey, made worse by the vile tasting liquor, he slept fitfully on the train. Twice he awoke, panic-stricken, frantically patting the seat, searching for his rucksack, worried that someone had pinched the Grail while he slept. And then he remembered that an assassin *had* stolen the Grail. Both times, in a Pastis-induced haze, Cædmon wondered if he'd actually found the blasted relic. Or had it all been a figment of his wild imagination?

On seeing the bookshop sign – emblazoned with the naive Fool about to embark on his grand adventure – Cædmon wearily sighed. Head throbbing, he gingerly touched the bandage wrapped around his skull. It felt like an iron band. One that tightened with each footfall.

Just a few more steps.

He pulled a key ring from his jacket pocket. A storm-damaged man-of-war about to sail into safe harbour.

Inserting the key in the lock, he opened the door. The hinges noisily squealed. He grunted, hit with an incendiary burst of pain that radiated from his arm to his skull. As he stepped across the threshold, Cædmon was greeted by a miasma of dust motes lazily floating in the slanted light. He waited a few seconds, giving his eyes a chance to adjust to the dimly lit shop before he walked over to the wall-mounted key pad. His shuffling gait was that of a much older man.

Squinting, he peered at the digital display.

Shite!

The security alarm had been deactivated, two loose wires protruding from the device!

Hackles instantly raised, he spun on his heel. He then proceeded to scrutinize each dark shadow.

Everything seemed in order.

On high alert, he cautiously made his way to the closed door at the rear of the shop that led to his flat. Holding his breath, he reached for the doorknob. Uncertain what he would find on the other side, he flung the door wide open.

'What the bloody hell do you think you're doing?' he bellowed crossly.

'What does it look like I'm doing?' Finnegan McGuire retorted. 'I'm catching some Zs.' Stretched out full-length on the tufted leather sofa, the commando propped his head on a beefy arm.

The tension left Cædmon's body in one fell swoop, replaced with a jaw-grinding pain. He walked over to the sofa.

'Nice place you got here,' McGuire quipped as he rose to his feet. 'I was almost tempted to pull out the feather duster and plug in the vacuum cleaner.'

'Sod you.' *With bells on.*

Glancing down, Cædmon noticed a plastic shopping bag on top of the cluttered coffee table. Although the flat was an untidy wreck, books stacked on the floor, newspapers lying about, the bag was unfamiliar to him. Eyes narrowed, he examined its contents. A bottle of bleach. Toilet paper. A bag of sugar. A ball of string. Loose wine corks. And a green metal box of Twinings tea. All-in-all, a strange assortment of sundry items.

Damn the man. He'd made himself right at home.

Still sneering, McGuire tossed a key in his direction; Cædmon caught it in his left hand.

'I returned your Vespa. It's parked out back.'

Without missing a beat, Cædmon tossed the key right back at him. 'Then rev up and fuck off.'

'I'm not going anywhere until you give me the Grail.'

'Small problem with that, old boy –' grimacing, he lowered himself into his upholstered club chair – 'I don't have the blasted Grail.'

'But you did find it, right?'

Wondering at the bastard's interest, Cædmon nodded

warily. 'However, soon after I uncovered the Grail, an armed thug arrived on the scene. Unless I'm greatly mistaken, the Seven Research Foundation is now in possession of the ancient relic.'

'Ah, shit!' A look of abject desperation flashed across the commando's unshaven face. 'Uhlemann abducted Kate.'

'Good God!'

Stunned, Cædmon slumped ingloriously in the chair.

Neither of them spoke, the only sound the incessant ticking of the wall clock.

'Is she still alive?' he finally asked, emotionally steeling himself for the reply.

'Yeah, I think so. If they wanted her dead, they would've killed her at the cemetery.' Then, with the fierce vigour of the Spartan three hundred, McGuire said, 'I *will* find her!'

'Any idea where the Seven might be holding her?'

'Well, I know where they're *not* holding her. Their headquarters at Grande Arche is deserted and no one is home at Uhlemann's Paris apartment.'

Cædmon ran possible scenarios through his head. His sweet *Rosa Mundi*, in the monster's clutch. *What a bloody nightmare!*

'If we're to find her, I need you to brief me in full detail. Leave nothing out. No stone unturned, understood?'

McGuire nodded his agreement. 'I'll hurl every rock I've got. But I'll tell ya right now, you're not gonna like what you're about to hear.'

I already don't like it.

How could it possibly get any worse?

71

Seven Research Laboratory

1945 hours

Quid pro quo. This for that.

The only reason Kate was still alive.

Earlier, at Père Lachaise cemetery, she'd stopped Finn from killing Dr Uhlemann. In return, Dr Uhlemann had commuted her sentence. At least for the time being.

She glanced at the clock mounted on the wall. Ten hours and forty-five minutes until the heliacal rising of Sirius. Still plenty of time for him to rescind the stay of execution.

Although not a lot of time to stop a mad man from changing world history.

Nearly fourteen hours ago, she'd been brought to the Seven Research Foundation's laboratory. She had no idea where the facility was located other than the fact that it was somewhere in Paris; when they left the Obelisk at Place de la Concorde, she'd been blindfolded. Upon arriving, she was ushered to a small annex adjacent to a library. The room was comfortable enough with a sofa, a writing desk and a flat-screen television. While she had access to the library, she was forbidden from leaving her two-room prison. The intimidating bald-headed chauffeur, who currently had guard duty, ensured her cooperation.

Needing to stretch her legs, Kate picked up her dinner tray. Not a big Beaufort cheese fan, she'd forced herself to eat four bites of the sandwich and drink the carton of orange juice. If for no other reason than to maintain her strength.

Tray in hand, she stepped into the library. In the middle of the book-lined room there was a table with two upholstered chairs. Dolf, hunched over a laptop computer, sat at the table.

Kate assumed an amiable expression. No easy feat given that, three days ago, the sullen-faced chauffeur had tried very hard to kill her. In the last hour, they'd not spoken ten words to one another.

'Hello, Dolf. The sandwich was delicious,' she said with forced civility. She knew that in an abduction scenario, it was vitally important for the prisoner to make a human connection to her captor. As difficult and distasteful as that might be.

Dolf simply grunted, not even bothering to glance up from his computer. With his battered, grotesque nose and enormous build, he put her in mind of a latter-day Quasimodo. A disheartened Esmeralda, she deposited her dinner tray on the table and returned to the annex.

Plopping down on the sofa, she stared morosely at the clock on the wall.

How apropos.

We look at a clock, we count the minutes and we foolishly think that we understand the concept of Time. It follows a linear progression. A straight line from yesterday to today to tomorrow. But Dr Uhlemann and his research team had figured out how to alter time so that, rather than being linear, the two ends of the line connect, forming a closed loop. A circle of time rather than a straight line. And that loop would enable them to travel *back* through time.

The fact that Dr Uhlemann had the *Lapis Exillis* and would now be able to generate the Vril force was worrisome. However, it was what he intended to do with the Vril force that was truly terrifying. How many millions of lives would be affected if he could actually change the outcome of the Second World War? What would become of Europe? The Middle East? Africa? Even America? The mere thought of Hitler's brutal regime rising from the ashes incited a dread terror. Even now, six decades after the war's end, the Third Reich was the monster that could not be killed – the reason why a swastika was still a chilling sight.

'Doctor Bauer?'

Hearing her name spoken, Kate glanced up, surprised to see Dr Uhlemann standing in the doorway. She didn't know who scared her more: the monstrous chauffeur or the malevolent scientist.

'Excuse me. I was lost in thought,' she mumbled.

'Plotting your escape, were you?'

'Um, actually, I was trying to figure out how . . . how you can use light to bend the space–time continuum,' she said haltingly, hoping to engage him in a civil conversation for the same reason she'd earlier tried to converse with his minion.

'You have an inquisitive mind. That's what I most admire about you. My daughter, alas, has no interest in science.'

'I didn't know that you had a – oh!' Kate's eyes opened

wide, startled by the belated realization. 'Angelika is your daughter, isn't she?'

'Conceived in a moment of rash passion with a woman I barely knew. Paris can have that effect on a man.' Lips twisted in an ugly sneer, he cackled. An instant later, his expression sobered. 'Would you like me to give you a tour of the laboratory?'

'Oh, yes . . . Thank you.' Surprised by the unexpected offer, she scrambled to her feet.

Smoothing a hand over her unkempt hair, Kate followed Dr Uhlemann into the library. Although she didn't have a clue how she could stop the Vril force from being generated, she needed to gather as much intelligence as possible. Find out everything she could about the laboratory. Then maybe she could devise a plan of action.

'Dolf, go home and see to your mother,' Dr Uhlemann ordered with a wave of the hand. 'I won't require your services until six o'clock tomorrow morning.'

'Yes, Herr Doktor Uhlemann.' The chauffeur respectfully bowed his head before taking his leave.

Playing the gentleman, Dr Uhlemann politely held the door open for Kate. Equally polite, she thanked him as she stepped across the threshold. Just outside the door was a walkway that overlooked a magnificent three-storey atrium, the library located on the third floor. Although there were no windows, banks of frosted glass created the impression of a light-filled space. With the exception of an armed guard standing sentry at the end of the walkway, the atrium was deserted.

Dr Uhlemann escorted her to an unmarked door. He then brushed his right index finger against his lab coat before placing it on a scanner affixed to the door-frame.

A few seconds later, the bolt on the biometric security system popped open. Again, Dr Uhlemann politely gestured for Kate to precede him through the doorway. Admittedly intrigued, she quickly surveyed the laboratory.

'Sterile' and 'industrial' were the first two words that came to mind. And while most of the apparatus set out on stainless-steel work stations was unfamiliar to her – instrumentation panels and high-tech gadgets galore – Kate ascertained that Dr Uhlemann ran a state-of-the-art facility. In the middle of the lab was a large glass enclosure. Inside the enclosure were four matte-black columns inset with mirrors. The columns were of equal length, approximately six feet high. Evenly spaced three feet apart, they formed a square.

'Is this the laboratory where the Vril force will be generated?' she enquired.

'No. *Das Groß Versuch* will take place in a specially designed chamber. If you behave yourself, I might be persuaded to show it to you.'

Kate made no comment, unsure why he was even taking her on *this* tour. She suspected that it might have something to do with his immense ego. It wasn't enough to gloat about having the *Lapis Exillis.* Dr Uhlemann wanted to rub her face in it.

As if to prove that very point, Dr Uhlemann, triumphantly smiling, gestured to the glass enclosure. 'What you see contained within this hermetically sealed structure is our CTC device.'

CTC. A physics acronym for 'closed time-like curve'.

'And these are my father's mathematical calculations that prove the gravitational effects of light.' Dr Uhlemann next directed her attention to an indecipherable equation that filled two entire chalkboards. 'Embedded in that elegant equation is the secret to exploring the boundaries of time.'

72

L'Equinoxe Bookstore

2015 hours

'Time-travelling Nazis! It's a plot straight out of a penny dreadful!'

Leaning back in his club chair, Cædmon stared, slack-jawed; McGuire's update was mind-boggling.

'If the Nazis had invaded the oil-rich Middle East instead of the Soviet Union, it would have been damned dreadful,' the commando declared, his voice raw with emotion. 'Ivo Uhlemann has had more than sixty years to devise a winning strategy. Trust me. If they go with the new, improved plan, Germany *will* win the Second World War.'

'Assuming the Seven Research Foundation can actually perform their fantastical experiment.'

Seated opposite him on the tufted leather sofa, McGuire reached for the chipped teapot on the Edwardian table. As he spoke, he refilled both their cups. 'Uhlemann is convinced that Einstein's Theory of General Relativity is the key to time travel. While he didn't go into specifics, evidently it can be done using gravity and the blue light emitted from the Vril force. Once he opens his tunnel in the space–time continuum, he's gonna party like it's 1941.'

Cædmon ran a hand over his unshaven jaw. The Universe, for all its marvels, was an intrinsically dangerous place. He'd never doubted that the Vril force could be generated; but it was what the Seven Research Foundation intended to do with it that staggered him.

Still grappling with the idea of time travel, he raised the teacup to his lips. Grimacing, he took a few sips of McGuire's potent Irish brew. Were it not for the fact that he needed to keep his wits about him, he would have opted for a G&T. The headache powder that he'd mixed earlier was doing little to dull the throbbing pain radiating from his skull down his cervical vertebrae to his right arm.

McGuire snatched the carton of milk and poured a dollop into his teacup. 'If I don't take out these bastards, we're talking doomsday scenario.'

'If *we* don't take out these bastards,' Cædmon stated matter-of-factly, having thrown in his lot with Finnegan McGuire the instant he learned Kate had been abducted. He glanced at his wristwatch. 'The heliacal rising of Sirius will take place in ten hours and thirteen minutes. At six thirty sharp. While rescuing Kate is a priority, we must also prevent Doctor Uhlemann from creating the Vril force. From what you've told me, it's the linchpin in his time-travel experiment.'

'That isn't a helluva lot of time. Particularly since we don't know where their hidey-hole is located.'

'I assume that Dr Uhlemann has a laboratory somewhere in Paris.'

'Makes sense.'

'As with any laboratory, it would require electricity to operate.' Leaning towards the coffee table, Cædmon unthinkingly reached for his laptop computer with both hands, his right triceps painfully protesting the rash move. He bit back a groan. 'I'm going to contact my old group leader at Five and have him pull the utility records for the Seven Research Foundation.'

One dark brow quizzically raised, the commando was clearly surprised. 'Your guy can do that?'

Pulling up his email account, Cædmon quickly typed a missive. 'In the grand scheme, it's a rather low-level request for MI5. Information is to spooks what bullets are to commandos.'

'Indispensable ammunition.'

'Precisely. Hopefully, our digital shot across the bow will hit a target.' He hit the 'send' button.

'Better blow it out of the water or we're fucked.'

Cædmon made no comment. He and the commando were tentatively dancing around the ring, pugilists sizing up the opponent. Except they were no longer opponents. They were now, for better or worse, mismatched allies. Soldier and spy. Each had a strength and expertise that the other lacked. As long as they acknowledged that, their unlikely partnership should hold.

Shrugging off his fatigue, Cædmon set the laptop on the coffee table. 'Knowledge is all about the connections between seemingly disparate elements. Once you make those connections, knowledge becomes a powerful tool. That said, is there anything else which Doctor Uhlemann disclosed that you haven't told me?'

Scowling, as though annoyed by the request, McGuire said, 'Don't know if it's important, but he mentioned that the original Seven came into possession of an ancient

Egyptian manuscript that contains step-by-step instructions for generating the Vril force.'

'How fascinating.'

'Yeah, I was real enthralled,' McGuire deadpanned. 'I think he called it the *Ghayat al-Hakim*.'

'The *Ghayat al-Hakim* . . . Yes! That makes perfect sense.' The pieces starting to fall into place, Cædmon got up and walked over to the floor-to-ceiling bookcase that lined the back wall of the 'drawing room'. Dragging the wheeled library ladder to the middle case, he gingerly climbed several rungs to reach a book on the top shelf.

As he walked back to his club chair, he blew a puff of dust from the gilded edge of the leather-bound volume.

'This is a corrupted version of the *Ghayat al-Hakim*,' he said, retaking his seat. 'Entitled *Picatrix*, it's a fifteenth-century Hermetic grimoire that was translated into Latin by the Florentine scholar Marcilio Ficino for his patron Lorenzo de Medici.'

'Does the Latin version mention anything about the Vril force?' McGuire asked, cutting to the chase.

'Not specifically. As I said, it's a corrupted version of the Arabic original. Nonetheless, encoded within the text's magical incantations are instructions for manipulating astral energy.' Cædmon idly flipped through several pages, momentarily distracted by a lavish illustration of a knight, astride a griffin, a sword in one hand and an enemy's head in the other. 'I'm going out on a limb here, but I suspect that, like the Seven, the Knights Templar also had a copy of the original *Ghayat al-Hakim*. It would explain how the Templars devised their blueprint for the Axe Historique in Paris.'

'According to Uhlemann, a shady Cairo bookseller gave a copy of the original Arabic text to the Nazis,' McGuire informed him. 'How the hell did the Templars get their copy of the *Ghayat al-Hakim*?'

'When the Knights Templar were arrested en masse in 1307, the Grand Inquisitor accused the Templars of being in league with the agents of Islam.'

'A charge that will land you on a waterboard in Guantanamo these days.'

'And on the rack in the fourteenth century,' Cædmon countered, the torture tactics of the Dominicans far more brutal than those used by the CIA. 'Unlike most of the charges brought against the order, this one actually had merit. During their tenure in the Holy Land, the Knights Templar did maintain a secret affiliation with Rashid ad-Din Sinan. Better known by his *guerre de nom*, the Old Man in the Mountain, Rashid led a group of Syrian warriors called the Assassins.'

'Those were the dudes who smoked hash before they went into battle, right?'

Cædmon nodded. 'The hashish induced a psychoactive response, the effects of which turned the Assassins into raving berserkers on the battlefield. Invincible warriors who knew no fear.'

'You mean warriors who scared the crap out of the enemy,' the commando affirmed with earthy aplomb.

'Which mightily impressed the Knights Templar. Although they hailed from different religions and different cultures, the Templars and the Assassins were nearly identical in one regard: both belonged to a brotherhood of warriors who believed that dying bravely in battle was the only means of achieving glory in heaven. As such, they immediately recognized one another as kindred spirits.'

'I'm a soldier so, yeah, I get it. The Templars wouldn't have had much in common with dandified European knights trying to impress their lady loves at a jousting match,' McGuire sagely observed. 'But they'd be on the same wavelength with the *fedayeen*.'

'*Those who redeem themselves by sacrificing themselves*,' Cædmon reflected, having always thought that the *fedayeen*, a.k.a. the Assassins, were a class of warriors unto themselves.

'During the Crusades, the Templars and the Assassins maintained this covert relationship, beheading and disembowelling one another on the field of battle, but embracing one another as blood brothers behind closed doors. That clandestine relationship continued after the Europeans lost control of the Holy Land. Which leads me to one other shared commonality.' Cædmon paused, certain that his next remarks would elicit a sceptical jeer from the commando. 'Both the Templars and the Assassins were deeply involved in acquiring esoteric and arcane knowledge. Although the Old Man in the Mountain maintained his base of operations in Syria, he was a subject of the Fatamid Caliphate who –'

'Built the House of Knowledge in Egypt,' McGuire interjected, much to Cædmon's surprise. 'Uhlemann mentioned it when we were at the cemetery. The *Dar ul-Hikmat*, or House of Knowledge, was an academic centre of learning with a renowned library.'

'You're quite right,' Cædmon murmured, impressed with the commando's flawless recall. 'The House of Knowledge was also the repository for ancient Egyptian esoteric texts that had been smuggled out of Alexandria before the Christian horde destroyed *that* Great Library. As I've already mentioned, I suspect the Old Man in the Mountain, who would have had access to the House of Knowledge, bequeathed a copy of the original Arabic manuscript to the Knights Templar.'

'Which is how the Templars got a hold of the instruction manual for building ley lines and generating the Vril force.'

Cædmon nodded. 'While the Templars had the knowledge, they didn't have the essential component, the pyramidal Grail stone. Had they located the ancient relic and used it to generate the Vril force, in the words of the famed occultist Eliphas Lévi, the Knights Templar would have attained "the secret of human omnipotence".'

'Incoming,' McGuire said abruptly, canting his chin at the laptop computer as it emitted an electronic chirp.

'Right.'

Using his left hand, Cædmon pulled the computer on to his lap. The incoming email was from Trent Saunders, his old group leader at Five. He quickly opened the attachment and scanned the utility records for the Seven Research Foundation. As he'd hoped, there were two separate accounts: one for the Seven's headquarters in the penthouse office suite at the Grande Arche and a second electric bill.

'It seems that their laboratory is located at the Grande Arche.'

'Fuck!' McGuire pounded on the sofa cushion with a balled fist. 'You mean that's where they've been hiding out? I went there three times and nobody was home.'

'You went to the penthouse suite three times. According to the billing records, the Seven Research Foundation has a laboratory in the *basement* of the Grande Arche. Most people are unaware that there's an extensive complex beneath the building.'

'The Seven would've had to obtain construction permits to build their lab,' McGuire stated, quickly stowing his anger. 'Can you get me the architectural plans and the schematics for the mechanicals? I need to know where the power lines, air-conditioning and heating vents, and water pipes are located.'

'Consider it done.' Cædmon quickly typed an email reply to Trent Saunders and hit the 'send' button.

'Before we move to the next phase of this operation, I just want to make sure that we're on the same page.' Eyes narrowed, McGuire stared at him. Cædmon had the distinct impression that the other man was taking his measure. 'The Seven Research Foundation is a clear and present danger. Is that your take on the situation?'

'No need to worry; we're singing from the same page of the hymnal.'

The other man smirked. 'Glad to have you in the choir. And before you even ask, no, we can't go to the authorities. Since I'm a fugitive, this has to remain a two-man duet.'

Cædmon let the addendum pass, McGuire having uncannily pre-empted him.

'How do you propose we combat the danger?' he asked instead, deferring to McGuire's expertise as a Special Forces commando.

'To win the battle, you have to go on the offensive.

Now that we've got a fix on their location, we can charge the barricade.' Getting up from the sofa, McGuire walked over and retrieved his plastic shopping bag. 'Earlier today I bought a few supplies. I always say, "No need for calculus when simple math will do".' He hefted a bag of sugar in one hand and a bottle of bleach in the other. 'Sucrose plus potassium chlorate equals *Kaboom!*'

Cædmon smiled humourlessly.

'*Götterdämmerung* . . . bloody brilliant.'

73

Seven Research Laboratory

2015 hours

'My father's equation is a stunning scientific achievement,' Dr Uhlemann continued, standing beside the chalkboard. 'Unfortunately, he will never receive the credit and acclaim due him.'

Staring at the lengthy equation, Kate winced. For theoretical physicists, advanced mathematics was their window on to the world. For everyone else, her included, those elaborate, seemingly never-ending series of numerals, letters and symbols were like seeing 'through a glass, darkly'.

'This is a particularly elegant calculation,' Dr Uhlemann remarked, using a piece of white chalk to underline a section of the equation. 'Since your father is an astrophysicist, I assume that you've heard of frame dragging.'

The last comment caught Kate by surprise. Studying the equation with renewed interest, she nodded. 'In fact, my father's research involves the frame-dragging effect of black holes.'

'Then you undoubtedly know that frame-dragging occurs when a rotating body, such as a planet or a black hole, drags the space–time continuum around itself.'

'When I was a child, my father described it as swirling a

bowling ball in a tub full of caramel, the bowling ball being the rotating body and the caramel, the space–time continuum.' A silly but effective visual description.

'That stirring up of space–time was first described by Einstein in his Theory of General Relativity. Amazingly, Einstein correctly predicted the effect eighty years before it was actually observed on X-ray astronomy satellites.' Dr Uhlemann waved a blue-veined hand in the air. 'But I digress. To get back on point: when frame-dragging occurs, if the twisting of space is strong enough, it will also twist time, producing a closed time-like curve.'

'And once you have a CTC, you can travel backward in time.' A split-second later, befuddled, Kate shook her head. 'But that's specific to black holes. How are you going to create a frame-dragging effect in a laboratory setting?'

Still holding the piece of chalk, Dr Uhlemann vigorously tapped the underlined equation. '*This* is the part of the equation where my father proved that a rotating beam of light could create the same frame-dragging gravitational effect as a rotating body. Using my father's equations, our research team designed a tower of continuously rotating light beams, one stacked on top of another.'

Kate glanced at the hermetically sealed glass enclosure. 'I'm having a really difficult time envisioning how *that* is going to turn into a rotating light tower which will then created a frame-dragging effect.'

Stepping away from the chalkboard, Dr Uhlemann walked over to a nearby computer console. A monster in the guise of an old-world gentleman, he held the back of an office chair, motioning for her to sit down. As she did,

Kate recalled that Adolf Hitler reputedly had perfect Viennese manners.

'Engineering a working prototype took years of research and development. At first, we thought optic fibres could be used to build a rotating light tower, but that proved a futile endeavour. We even briefly considered photonic crystals.' As he spoke, Dr Uhlemann pecked on the keyboard, typing in what appeared to be a coded password. 'We finally settled on a system of stacked lasers.' Finished typing, he spun around in his chair and gestured to the four rectilinear columns set in the middle of the enclosure. 'The prototype that you see before you was constructed using red laser lights. Each of the four columns is lined with twenty-five hundred diode lasers. Are you familiar with laser technology?'

Nodding, Kate said, 'Most people are unaware that the word "laser" is actually an acronym for "light amplification by stimulated emission of radiation".'

'And what differentiates laser light from normal light –' Dr Uhlemann picked up a pen-like laser from the computer console and flipped it on – 'is that a laser projects a thin beam.' He emphasized the point by shining the red beam of light around the laboratory. 'A coherent beam of thin light is the key to creating the light tower. Allow me to demonstrate.'

With an air of heightened drama, he hit the 'enter' key. Instantly, ten thousand red laser lights switched on, swirling within the confines of the four black columns at a dizzying speed. It immediately put Kate in mind of a spectacular light show at a big-name rock concert. The only thing missing was the smoke machine and blaring guitar.

'*Une tour de la lumière*, as the French would say. Beautiful, isn't it?' Like a proud father, Dr Uhlemann stared at the six-foot-high blur of radiant red light.

'Wow,' Kate marvelled, grudgingly impressed. Shielding her eyes with her hand, she said, 'Since light normally travels in a straight line, how did you get all of those laser lights to continuously swirl in the same direction?'

'The mirrors embedded on the columns cause the light to swirl in a circular pattern. What you can't see is that the rotating beams create a gravitational field which will produce a frame-dragging effect. The area inside the tower of light is where space is being twisted. Once we have a strong enough light energy, the twisted space will create a closed time-like curve. When that happens, any particle placed in the gravitational field will be dragged along the closed-time loop.' Dr Uhlemann spoke with barely restrained emotion, his voice rising and falling, a verbal pendulum that increased momentum with each impassioned swing.

Getting up from his chair, Dr Uhlemann walked over to the enclosure. Pointing to the light tower, he said, 'This CTC device was built with laser light. Once we have generated the Vril force, we will use the Vril to create what we call a vaser light.'

'I assume that you'll then reconfigure the CTC device, replacing the lasers with ten thousand vaser lights.'

The red light reflected eerily off Dr Uhlemann's face, bathing him in a demonic glow. 'Those ten thousand vasers will give us a coherent rotating swirl of high-frequency Vril light.'

Still shielding her eyes, Kate glanced at the enclosure.

‘Why can’t you just use laser lights to operate the CTC device?’

‘For the simple reason that a laser doesn’t have a high enough frequency to twist the space–time continuum,’ Dr Uhlemann informed her. ‘I’m sure you’re aware that Einstein won his Nobel Prize not for his Theory of General Relativity but for his work with the photoelectric effect.’

‘In which he proved that the higher the frequency of light, the greater maximum kinetic energy produced.’

‘Exactly so. When we replace the lasers with our specially designed vaser lights, the rotating light tower will have sufficient energy and torque to twist space. When the frame-dragging effect is strong enough, it will not only twist space, but it will create a closed time-like curve in the space–time continuum.’

‘But how are you going to send a human being through your closed-time loop?’ Having been a Trekker when she was a teenager, Kate envisioned the transporter chamber from the *Star Trek* television series.

‘At this stage in the research, it would be impossible to transport a human through the CTC device.’

Hearing that, Kate did a double-take at the red swirling lights. Bewildered, she asked the obvious: ‘Then what’s the point of all this?’

‘While it’s not possible at this stage to transport a human being, it is entirely possible to transmit information.’

‘So you’re – *what?* – going to send an email or fax through a closed time-like curve?’

‘Don’t be flip, my dear. It’s unbecoming,’ Dr Uhlemann snapped churlishly as he stepped over to the computer console and retook his seat. ‘Although we’ll be able to transmit information, we can't utilize any technology that didn't exist in the year 1940. Because of that constraint, we're going to send radio signals through the closed-time loop. Which is why it's more appropriate to refer to this –' he gestured to the swirling red tower of light – 'as a communication machine rather than a time machine.'

While her grasp of physics lacked his breadth, Kate understood enough to see the flaw in Dr Uhlemann's design. 'In order to transmit information *backward* into time, someone would have had to have built a communication machine in the past that can receive your transmission. Otherwise, you have nothing to send your information *to*.'

Dr Uhlemann smiled knowingly, as though he'd been anticipating her objection. 'In December of 1940, my father designed and activated a receiver apparatus for that very purpose. The information we transmit through our CTC device *will be* received by the original Seven in 1940 on their receiver.'

'Jeez, talk about thinking ahead,' Kate murmured. Gnawing on her lower lip, she tried to come at the problem from a different angle. 'But wouldn't your father's receiver have to be turned on and running *right now* in the twenty-first century?' When Dr Uhlemann confirmed this with a nod, she then said, 'If he turned on the receiver in 1940 and left it running, the battery to operate it would have drained decades ago. Rendering it useless.'

'As I've told you before, Doctor Bauer, you need to start thinking outside the box.' Insult delivered, he folded his arms over his chest. 'Do you happen to know how the first telegraph wires were powered in the mid-nineteenth century?'

Actually, she did know the answer, Cædmon having mentioned it a few days earlier when they were at the Louvre. 'An earth battery using telluric currents was utilized.' No sooner were the words out of her mouth than the realization hit, like a broad-handed slap to the face. 'The Seven manufactured an earth battery for their receiver, didn't they?'

'Ensuring that it will *never* run out of power. A simple, but ingenious, solution.' Dr Uhlemann chuckled conceitedly, well aware that he was holding four aces in his hand. 'The original Seven knew that it would be years, decades even, before a working CTC device could be designed and constructed. They had to find a means to keep a receiver fully charged and operational in perpetuity. Caching the receiver in the catacombs beneath Paris, they were able to directly tap into underground telluric currents.'

Kate glanced at the mathematical equation on the chalkboard. The 'T's had been crossed decades ago by the original Seven. All that remained was for their children to dot the 'I's.

'Will you be able to have two-way radio communication with the original Seven?'

'Alas, no. While our fathers will be able to receive our transmission, they won't be able to reply. Nonetheless, they are anxiously awaiting the transmission.' Blue eyes excitedly gleaming, he gestured to the glass enclosure. '*This* is our dream about to come to fruition. Knowing that our fathers are poised and ready to act, we have already put together a comprehensive information packet.'

Information. The ultimate weapon of mass destruction. *Scientia potentia est.*

'Knowledge is power' as Cædmon used to always say.

Soon, Dr Uhlemann and the Seven Research Foundation would be able to transmit to their fathers the ultimate war plan that would secure victory for the Third Reich.

The few bites of her dinner that she'd managed to eat began to congeal in her stomach.

Earlier, she'd wondered how Dr Uhlemann would use light to create a closed time-like curve. Now she knew.

She also now knew what was meant by the phrase 'evil genius'.

74

Oberkampf Neighbourhood, Paris

0500 hours

Dolf Reinhardt ran the carbon steel blade across his head, carefully shaving the blond stubble from his scalp.

It was important that he look his best today. For today he aimed to impress. He didn't know *what* was planned to occur later this morning; he wasn't privy to the closed-door meetings at the Seven Research Foundation. But he knew something momentous was in the works. He'd eavesdropped on enough conversations to ascertain that it had to do with the Third Reich. Perhaps Herr Doktor had plans to launch a new National Socialist Party to oust the immigrants from Germany. Whatever it was, Dolf instinctively knew that he would soon be able to prove his worth.

He stepped closer to the cracked mirror above the bathroom sink, making one last pass with the cut-throat blade. Tilting his head from side to side, he inspected his handiwork. Unable to detect any stubble, he rinsed the blade clean. He then swabbed his head with a soapy cloth, washing away the residue from his peppermint-scented shaving oil. Removing the bath towel knotted at his waist, he used it to dry his head.

'*Scheisse*,' he muttered angrily, accidentally bashing his swollen nose.

Flinging the damp towel into the corner, he strode naked out of the bathroom.

He'd not realized until yesterday that his mother had been the one holding him back all these years. Because of her, he was like a horse tethered to a post. A thoroughbred stallion full of *sturm und drang*. Not the pliant plough horse that everyone made him out to be.

'*Go home and see to your mother, Dolf.*'

Herr Doktor Uhlemann, knowing that Dolf's primary responsibility was to his aged mother, had been unwilling to promote him. Instead he'd kept him hobbled these last eight years behind the wheel of the Mercedes Benz. He didn't hold it against Herr Doktor. His vision clear, Dolf now understood. He'd finally figured out that Herr Doktor Uhlemann had been unwilling to give him additional responsibility, fearing his professional duties would always come in a distant second.

Today, Herr Doktor would learn that he could *always* depend on Dolf.

Opening the wardrobe, he removed a velvet-covered box from the top shelf. He pried the lid open, the hinge softly creaking. Inside, nestled on a bed of white satin, was a gleaming disc on a green grosgrain ribbon. His European Junior Boxing gold medal. Dolf slipped his shaved head through the ribbon, adjusting the medal so that it rested squarely in the middle of his chest. It proved that he was a champion. That he could hold his own in any ring.

In a hurry, he hastily donned the clean clothes that he'd

laid out on the bed. Before slipping into his black suit jacket, he brushed it with a piece of tape to remove any stray pieces of lint.

Finished dressing, he left his bedroom and made his way down the dimly lit hall to his mother's room. Opening the door, he smiled broadly as he stepped across the threshold. The bedside lamp illuminated the room in a golden glow. Dolf always left the light turned on at night, worried that his mother might be afraid of the dark.

'*Guten morgen, mutter*!'

The cheerful greeting met with a slack-jawed stare. Dolf took the blank stare in his stride as he walked over to the metal hospital bed and gave his mother a kiss on the cheek. Before putting her to bed, he'd changed the sheets and tidied the room in preparation. He wanted everything to be perfect.

With a tender hand, he smoothed her bunched nightdress so that it modestly draped her withered body. He then unpinned the coiled braids at the top of his mother's head and arranged one thick grey braid on each side of her face. There was a time, when Dolf had been a very small boy, that his mother had been vibrant of body and mind. But those days were long gone.

Humming softly, he secured her wrists and ankles to the metal bed railing with leather straps. Noticing that her toenails needed to be clipped, he glanced at his wristwatch. *Scheisse.* Too late now. There wasn't enough time to hunt for the nail clippers.

Refusing to get riled over the small blunder, he walked across to the bureau and opened the top drawer, removing a green plastic medicine bottle. Reaching under a folded towel, he also retrieved an ornately carved oak bread plate. As he did, Dolf glanced at the framed photograph hanging on the wall of his six-year-old mother offering the Führer a slice of freshly baked *schwarzbrot*. He'd always been immensely proud of the fact that he was named after the Führer. Proud of his family's close connection to that great and good man who had been a saviour to Germany.

Pleased that he'd remembered the plate, Dolf carried it over to the bed and set it on top of his mother's chest. In the centre of the oak plate was a carved *Sonnenrad Hakenkreutz*. A German sun wheel. Although he couldn't be certain, he thought he saw a glimmer of recognition in his mother's faded blue eyes.

As he did each morning before he left for work, Dolf gently inserted a sleeping pill between her lips, holding up her head so she could swallow it without gagging. Then he inserted another. And another . . . until the bottle was completely empty.

'"Cattle die, kinsmen die. The self must also die; I know one thing which never dies: the reputation of each dead man,"' he quietly recited. It was his mother's favourite line from the *Hávamál*, the collection of old Norse poems. 'Do not fear, *mutter*. You will always be "the Führer's little handmaid".'

He stuffed the green plastic bottle in his pocket before turning out the light. Now there were no more encumbrances to hold him back.

Today, Adolf Reinhardt was finally a free man.

75

Grande Arche, Paris

0528 hours

'You seem oddly calm for a man who might soon be the guest of honour at his own funeral,' Cædmon remarked as he and McGuire made their way on foot across the deserted esplanade in front of the Grande Arche. At that somnolent hour, the skyscrapers of La Defense business district had an otherworldly aspect. A forest of steel and glass silhouetted against a slate-grey sky.

'Got over my fear of death years ago.' The commando carefully adjusted the canvas rucksack slung across his chest. Inside his Go Bag were six homemade pipe bombs packed in wadded cotton fabric. 'Being a soldier, I know *how* I'll die. I just don't know the when of it. Only Bob Almighty knows that.'

'And, how may I ask –'

'Hail of bullets, buddy boy. Hail of bullets.'

Taken aback by McGuire's exuberance, and that he considered his violent demise a *fait accompli*, Cædmon said quietly, 'You shall be missed when you're gone.'

'Gee, didn't know you cared that much.'

'I was thinking of Kate.'

The other man's expression instantly sobered. 'Yeah,

I can't seem to get her off my mind. I hope to hell she's all right.'

As do I.

While they were going into the breach armed with six pipe bombs and one Ruger P89 semi-automatic pistol, a pitiful arsenal by any standard, Kate was utterly defenceless.

Unnerved by the eerie silence, Cædmon looked over his left shoulder. The pedestrian esplanade, a concrete meadow in the midst of the steel forest, afforded him an unobstructed view to the east of the Arc de Triomphe L'Étoile. Though he couldn't see beyond the famous monument, he knew that it was exactly seven kilometres in distance from the first arch on the Axe Historique, the Arc de Triomphe du Carrousel, to the Grande Arche. *Seven*. One of the most sacred of all numbers, it symbolized the totality of the Universe, the Heavens conjoined to the Earth. Astral energy fused to telluric energy. How ironic that Ivo Uhlemann's despicable group was named 'The Seven'.

Put in mind of an initiate making his way to the holy shrine, he stared at the gleaming white cube. An impressive sight in broad daylight, the Grande Arche was utterly stunning at night, the alabaster marble gleaming with an ethereal lustre. He'd once read that the Cathedral of Notre-Dame would fit *perfectly* inside the cube's open space.

Was that merely a coincidence or was it a profound and purposeful design element?

Cædmon suspected the latter, the cathedral having been built over the top of an ancient temple dedicated to Isis, the Egyptian Queen of the Heavens – the reason why the city had originally been called 'Parisis'. In point of fact, the Axe Historique was the Axis of Isis, the massive ley line perfectly aligned to the heliacal rising of her sacred star Sirius. A star that would appear in sixty minutes after an absence of seventy days. *Seven plus zero equals seven.*

As Cædmon glanced at the high-rises that flanked the esplanade, he wondered if any of the thousands of Parisians who worked in those office buildings knew that the centrepiece of La Defense, the Grande Arche, was a *porte cosmique*. A star gate built to harness astral energy.

Though spectacularly modern in execution, the Grande Arche was ancient wisdom articulated in marble and granite. That wisdom had been safeguarded through the centuries by a succession of secret societies: the Knights Templar, the Rosicrucians, the Nine Sisters Lodge, the Egyptian Rite, to name just a few. Deemed heretical, one and all, by the Church Fathers, those underground societies had been the Guardians of the Lost Science. Each group had gleaned a different piece of the puzzle. None of them possessed all of the knowledge. Or the requisite component, the *Lapis Exillis*, which would have enabled them to generate the Vril force.

Until the Seven Research Foundation retrieved all of the puzzle pieces and put them in order.

A dedicated group of educated zealots – a secret society in the guise of an academic think tank – the Seven Research Foundation intended to exploit the Lost Science. An unknown force of nature, the Vril was derived from fused energies. It had been the power behind the Egyptian civilization. For all he knew, it was the very power that ultimately destroyed that same empire. Since the Vril force was created through the manipulation of astral and telluric energies, if there was the *slightest* miscalculation, he feared catastrophe would ensue.

Given that it had been more than three thousand years since the Vril force had last been generated, the possibility of error was great.

Well aware that the clock ticked loudly, neither he nor McGuire said a word as they ascended the steps which led to the Grande Arche veranda. Each of them knew what had to be done. Earlier in the evening as they'd prepared the pipe bombs – a laborious endeavour that had taken hours to complete – they'd gone over the mission op in excruciating detail. Their plan was two-pronged: he would find and rescue Kate; McGuire would set and ignite the six pipe bombs.

Reaching the fifty-fourth, and final, step, they hurriedly slipped into the shadows. Moored on the far side of the veranda were the glass elevators used to whisk tourists to the rooftop observation deck. Canopied directly above them was the white canvas 'cloud' that spanned the open-ended courtyard. *Le Nuage*. Cædmon had always thought it more closely resembled a hovering white moth than a floating cirrus cloud. An eyesore from any angle, it had been installed to reduce the wind shear. He peered at the esplanade below. From his elevated position, it was akin to standing at a window that opened on to the world.

As outlined in the mission op, they veered away from the bank of revolving glass doors that led to the north and south lobbies, both of which were manned by a night-duty guard. Instead, they proceeded to a single glass door that was out of the guards' line of sight. Head bowed so he couldn't be easily identified on the security camera, McGuire quickly punched an eight-digit code into a keypad affixed to the door jamb. An instant later, the door buzzed open. Because the Grande Arche was a potential terrorist target, all of the building's security codes were kept on file with the Ministry of Interior, the government office responsible for national security. Calling in an old favour with a computer engineer at Thames House, Cædmon had acquired the necessary codes.

Hopefully the guard stationed at the video monitors would pay them short shrift. Not only did they use an authorized security code, they'd come through a designated after-hours entryway. Just a pair of overworked office cogs getting an early start.

'Well done,' he whispered, relieved at the ease with which they'd entered the building.

'Unlike you, I'm not gonna wrench my arm out its socket to pat myself on the back. Do that and somebody will shoot you in the back for sure,' McGuire muttered. He glanced at his wristwatch. 'We've only got fifty-two minutes until sunrise.'

'Right.'

Properly chastened, Cædmon followed the commando down the dim corridor. A long-forgotten line popped into his head: 'From battle and murder, and from sudden death.'

He hoped to God that it wasn't a grisly premonition.

76

Seven Research Facility

0528 hours

Ivo Uhlemann carefully set the phonograph needle on to the vinyl disk.

His choice of music admittedly ironic, he walked over to the rosewood bureau as the opening strains of Wagner's *Götterdämmerung* reverberated throughout his private study. He'd always considered the 1966 recording by the Berlin Philharmonic the classic rendition of the operatic cycle.

The irony, of course, was that the fall of the Third Reich had been Germany's great *Götterdämmerung*. Not Brünnhilde's immolation. What happened in April of 1945 was the *true* 'Twilight of the gods'.

Wracked with pain, Ivo gingerly opened the bureau's top drawer and removed a wooden box with a carved sun wheel on the lid. An authentic Ahnenerbe-commissioned chest, he'd paid an exorbitant price for it at a private auction. It'd always angered him, as it did his father, that Himmler and his cronies misappropriated the *Sonnenrad Hakenkreutz* symbol, foolishly believing that the swirling energy that radiated from the Black Sun, Sirius, would somehow magically transform them into avatars. *Fools! All of them!* They could not comprehend that Sirius was simply a key to unlock the door of space and time.

Ivo lifted the lid and removed his drug paraphernalia. As he did so, he glanced dismissively at the Iron Cross in the bottom of the box. He'd been awarded the medal on 20 April 1945 by Adolf Hitler in the bomb-blasted Chancellery Garden. To this day, he could still envision in his mind's eye the tottering Führer who, his brain addled, destroyed by the cancer of occultism, would lead the glorious Reich into fiery defeat.

It could have been different. Had men of greater intelligence been making the decisions. But the occult wing of the German high command had been trapped in a hall of mirrors which, ironically, they had created. For them, indeed, for the whole of Germany, there was no escape from the madness.

Soon that would all change. Soon the Reich would be created anew.

Stepping over to his upholstered chaise longue, Ivo carefully sat down, every movement inciting an agonized riot. At the end of the elongated chair, Wolfgang slept peacefully, curled in a furry ball.

A few moments later, as the pain-numbing heroin coursed through his veins, he reclined on the chaise longue. While science and mathematics spoke to the mind, art, literature and music spoke to the soul of mankind. A universal language that could inspire greatness. Overcome by the rich orchestral tones, he closed his eyes and dreamed the sweetest of dreams.

Of a different world. A different childhood. One in

which he didn't have to join the Hitler Jugend because there would be no need for children to do the work of men. To martyr themselves for their fathers. *How very sweet.* And in this different, *better* world, his father would come home each evening after teaching at the university, greeted with a warm kiss from his wife Berthe and big hug from his son Ivo. The smell of *Aprikosenkuchen* baking in the oven would swirl around the three of them like a heavenly apricot cloud. *Sweeter, yet.* And, later, freed from the onerous burden of fulfilling his father's dream, Ivo wouldn't have had to become a physicist. He could follow his own passions and inclinations. Perhaps become an art historian. *Yes, very sweet indeed.*

'Is there anything that I can get for you?'

On hearing Angelika's voice, Ivo opened his eyes. Breathtakingly lovely, she stood in the doorway, a concerned look on her face.

His beautiful dark angel.

When Angelika was just a small child, she had begun to exhibit vicious tendencies, deriving pleasure from the pain of others. First insects. Then small animals. Then other children. Since her mother had abandoned her, Ivo had full responsibility for raising the child. Faced with a thorny dilemma – to institutionalize Angelika or to keep her with him, he settled for the latter. Which meant that he had to find a way to channel her homicidal urges. To teach Angelika how to kill judiciously. While he was not always successful, he'd done the best he could.

Blut und Ehre. Blood and honour. And family. The holy trinity.

'I am fine. Thank you for checking.' Patting the Schnauzer's head one last time, he smiled wistfully and said, 'Take Wolfgang with you, please. You know what must be done.'

Ivo watched as the docile little beast obediently trotted after the beautiful Angel of Death.

Although he had every confidence that *das Groß Versuch* would be successful, there was always the possibility of a calamitous error. That was the reason why the board members of the Seven Research Foundation would observe the proceedings via CCTV from the safety of an off-site location. Because of his terminal illness, his death a certainty, Ivo was the only one among them who would be physically present for the Vril generation. On the off-chance that something went wrong during *das Groß Versuch*, he had every confidence that the board members would continue their fathers' work. Committed, they would discover what went wrong and make the necessary adjustments so that, next year on the heliacal rising, they could attempt the experiment again. But, this year, the honour was his alone.

Staring at the ceiling, Ivo imagined himself as the *Rückenfigur*, that solitary figure in a Caspar David Friedrich painting, always seen from behind, gaze set on the horizon.

He closed his eyes, the moment too sublime for words.

Dein Reich koimme. Thy kingdom come. On earth as it is in heaven. The fate of the Reich linked to one particular star in the heavenly firmament.

Very soon now.

77

0538 hours

Having committed the Grande Arche building plan to memory, McGuire promptly headed for a door located thirty feet away from the exterior entry. The placard read '*escalier*'. Beneath that was the international zigzag symbol for 'stairs'. The commando wordlessly opened the door and entered the stairwell, Cædmon following right behind him.

They went down four flights of steps, descending into the bowels of the building. Exiting the stairwell, they traversed another dimly lit corridor lined with office suites, left and right. All of the doors were closed; each had a security keypad above the door knob. A uniformly designed rabbit warren. Although the chance of running into someone at that hour was remote, Cædmon nonetheless slid his right hand under his jacket. Ignoring the burst of pain in his upper arm, he grasped the Ruger's gun handle, suddenly wishing they'd had more time to prepare for the mission.

McGuire came to a halt in front of a closed door with a polished bronze plaque engraved 'SEVEN RESEARCH FOUNDATION'. The shiny surface reflected their joint image. He keyed in a security code, the door unlocking with a soft *click!*

Pulling a military-style torch from his Go Bag, the

commando smirked and said in a hushed voice, 'Come on, Jonah. Time to gut the whale.'

As he stepped across the threshold, Cædmon, worried they might have tripped a silent alarm, slid the Ruger P89 pistol from its holster and thumbed the safety lever to the 'off' position.

Nerves jangling, he scrutinized the shadowy antechamber, searching for a surveillance device. Relieved when he didn't see any, he released a pent-up breath.

'Nice joint,' McGuire said as he shined the torch around the room.

Boasting a sleekly modern design, the reception lounge was a notch above the typical office suite. Behind the curved reception desk, cascading water sluiced over a floor-to-ceiling copper panel. Off to the side, four leather chairs were grouped around a square-topped table on which there was an abstract marble sculpture and a few glossy magazines artfully arranged. A large Dufy canvas hung on the wall. A cheery Fauvist seascape, it was an unexpected splash of colour in an otherwise monochromatic setting.

The commando elbowed him. 'According to the architectural plan, there's supposed to be a door leading to the laboratory. Where the hell is it?'

'My guess is behind the waterfall. At least that's where a door *should* be located.'

The designated point man, McGuire strode towards the water feature and peered behind the sturdy copper frame. Nodding his head, he disappeared behind the panel.

Gun tightly gripped in his hand, Cædmon stepped around the faux wall. McGuire, the torch protruding from his mouth, stood in front of an intimidating black door with a security keypad inlaid above the knob. Unlike the door on the other side of the office, this was a bullet- and fire-resistant, galvanized steel entry.

Shining his torch at the numeric pad, McGuire keyed in the third, and last, hacked security code.

The lock softly popped. Removing the torch from his mouth, the commando pushed down on the polished steel handle and eased the door open a few scant inches. Just far enough for him to peep through the crack and scan the environs beyond.

'Coast is clear,' he whispered, swinging the door open and making his exit.

Ruger at the ready, Cædmon stepped cautiously into the research facility, the steel door automatically closing behind him. He glanced about, stunned.

It was as though he'd just entered another world.

Designed as a spacious three-storey atrium, the lofty space very cleverly fooled one into thinking that it was an airy, light-filled courtyard when, in fact, it was a subterranean bunker. An ethereal one, at that, with abundant white marble, polished chrome and alternating banks of clear and frosted glass. The illusion was further enhanced by potted Areca palm trees and towering rubber plants.

Directly across from them, the centre of the mezzanine resembled a collegiate study hall. There were seven identical tables each outfitted with flat-screen computer monitors and ergonomic roller chairs. On the far side of the mezzanine there was a capsule-like lift. From the architectural blueprints, Cædmon knew that there was an enclosed stairwell in the atrium's northwest quadrant.

Grim-faced, McGuire ducked into the shadows cast by

a rectangular pillar, Cædmon following in his wake. Like a medieval cloister, columns were set every eight feet around the perimeter of the mezzanine supporting the promenade above.

'Forty-six minutes and counting,' McGuire informed him in a lowered voice. 'Time to say "ta ta" and go our separate ways.' His objective was to locate the maintenance room below the mezzanine where the mechanical systems were housed.

While he did that, Cædmon would search for Kate.

'Good luck, McGuire.'

'Yeah . . . same to you, Aisquith.' One side of the commando's mouth quirked upward. 'If things don't go according to plan, I'll meet you at the pearly gates.'

Not the least bit amused, Cædmon said, 'Heaven or hell, dead is dead. Ask any corpse.'

78

Seven Research Facility

0538 hours

Angelika dumped the knotted heavy-duty plastic bag into the rubbish bin. 'Bye-bye, doggie.'

Finished with the chore, she walked over to the lavatory mirror and checked her make-up. Puckering her lips, she decided that another coat of lipstick was in order. She reached for the lacquered tube – *crimson red* – her favourite shade.

'Better,' she murmured, pleased with the effect, the slash of crimson the only colour on her pale face. That and her cornflower blue eyes. Today she wore her hair pulled back in a tight chignon, a severe style that accentuated her pale skin.

Make-up applied, she reached for the HK semi-automatic holstered on her thigh. She quickly rechecked her weapon, having cleaned and oiled it before taking care of Wolfgang. Satisfied that everything was in working order, she slid the pistol back into the holster.

While she might look like a woman, she thought like a man. Fought and killed like one, too. *That* was her strength. Her power. It always had been. Ever since that first time when she'd persuaded another little girl to walk out on to the thin ice in the middle of the lake. When the silly child fell through the ice, Angelika had stood on the shoreline, thrilled, as she watched the frantic struggle take place. Only to feel keenly disappointed when the little girl disappeared beneath the ice, having succumbed too quickly. She decided then and there that killing from afar was no fun. It was always better when you could see the tears well in their eyes and hear their voices crack as they begged and pleaded.

In high spirits, Angelika turned off the light in the lavatory and stepped into the hall. She peered over the railing that overlooked the mezzanine below. The atrium was deserted, not a soul in sight. All of the researchers had been dismissed two days ago, informed that the facility would be temporarily closed while new carpet was installed. A few minutes ago, as a stop-gap measure, she'd gone into the security computer system and changed the code for the facility entry.

Needing to issue a few last orders, she headed for the library. To her vexation, the little mouse was still alive. For some inexplicable reason her father had not yet given the kill order for the Bauer woman and seemed reluctant to do so. Earlier in the day she'd come very close to shoving the little mouse over the railing, but had been thwarted when an armed sentry showed up for guard duty.

Rankled by the recollection, Angelika entered the library. Dolf Reinhardt sat at one end of the table, watching football on his laptop, and Axel Weber, an ex-military gun-for-hire, sat at the other end, expertly shuffling a deck of cards. She glanced at her watch; the chauffeur had clocked-in twenty minutes early. No doubt trying to make up for his colossal fuck-ups. *I'd like to shove him over the railing.* What a useless excuse for a man.

Ignoring the bald-headed oaf, she turned her attention to Weber. 'You are to report to the *Groß Versuch* viewing room for guard duty.'

Impudently smiling, Weber ran his thumbs over the edge of the deck before cutting the stack. 'As you can see, Angelika, I'm still on my break. Another five minutes and *then* I will do your bidding.'

'You will do my bidding *now*.'

Weber put the deck aside and folded his arms over his chest. The chauffeur looked up nervously; then just as quickly tucked his chin into his chest and stared intently at his laptop. *Hear no evil. See no evil.*

'My break is over in five minutes,' Weber reiterated. 'Time for one last cigarette.'

'You don't smoke.'

'I have five minutes to learn the habit.' He eyed Angelika, a lewd gleam in his eyes. 'Would you like to light my cigarette?'

Angelika reached for the HK semi-automatic, sliding it from her thigh holster. 'I'd be happy to oblige you.' She aimed the gun at his crotch.

Not the least bit intimidated, Axel chortled. 'Warm and creamy on the inside but, oh, so cold on the outside.'

'I was going to let you kill the little mouse, but I don't think you're man enough to do it,' she taunted.

'But you are, aren't you, sweetheart?' The macho bastard leaned back in his chair. 'I only kill when I get paid to do so. If I don't get paid, I don't pull the trigger . . . unless somebody makes the mistake of waylaying me in the dark.'

Angelika returned the pistol to its holster. 'I wouldn't dream of it,' she purred, already plotting the ambush. She glanced at the oaf. 'Dolfie, go and ask the little mouse what she wants for breakfast.'

Orders issued, Angelika turned around and walked towards the door. *Very slowly.* Letting them both get an eyeful.

Her strength. Her power.

79

0544 hours

The two men headed in opposite directions, their plan to divide and conquer.

Although Cædmon would settle for finding Kate, retrieving the Grail and getting out alive.

While McGuire surreptitiously made his way to the stairwell, Cædmon navigated a different route, crabbing along the mezzanine's colonnaded walkway. Since they had no idea where Kate was being held, his job was to systematically open each closed door on the mezzanine level. A total of eight doors. After checking each and every room, he would then ascend to the second level and repeat the process. If that proved fruitless, he would search the third floor. Again, proceeding room by room until he found her.

He glanced at the upper levels of the atrium, counting half a dozen frosted glass walls that incandescently glowed – two on the second floor and four on the third – indicating that the lights had been turned on in those rooms. That implied that there were bodies afoot. No doubt preparing for the astral event soon to take place. However many troops were on hand, it was a sure bet that he and McGuire were outnumbered.

Approaching the first closed door, Cædmon reached

into his jacket pocket and removed a small torch. He clicked it on and stuck the slender rod between his pursed lips, freeing his left hand to open the door. At a glance he could see that he had just entered the employee lounge. Like the rest of the facility, it was starkly modern, what one might expect to see in an upscale bistro. He backed out of the lounge and proceeded to the next door.

Three minutes later, having opened all eight doors on the mezzanine level and verified that all eight rooms were vacant, he headed for the stairwell at the end of the walkway. He'd taken no more than three steps when the lift unexpectedly began to glide upward.

Cædmon hurriedly concealed himself behind a concrete pillar. A few moments later, he heard a high-pitched chime. Whoever had summoned the lift descended to the mezzanine.

He furtively peered around the corner . . . just in time to see an armed man – a semi-automatic pistol holstered at his waist – exit the lift. One of Uhlemann's foot soldiers, he had a mean street look about him. Clearly someone who could comport himself in a firefight or a fist fight. Oblivious to the fact that he was being watched, the armed man strode towards the stairwell. Opening the door, he disappeared from sight.

Where the bloody hell was he going?

Since the armed thug had just come from the third floor, completely bypassing the second, Cædmon surmised that he was headed to the maintenance level, one storey below. Finnegan McGuire's current location.

Baffled by the unexpected turn of events, Cædmon slid the Ruger into its holster. Unclipping a phone from his waistband, he quickly typed a text message to McGuire and hit the 'send' button. Warning issued, he stepped away from the pillar.

Only to hurriedly retreat when the lift unexpectedly returned to the third floor. Presumably to pick up another passenger.

Shite! The research facility was fast turning into Victoria Station.

Holding the pistol in a two-handed grip, Cædmon waited. The skin on the back of his neck prickled. For a fleeting instant it felt as though the earth turned faster on its axis.

The chime pinged again. A few seconds later, like a theatre curtain, the lift doors slid open, a Goliath of a man emerging on to the stage.

The bald-headed brute from the Arc de Triomphe du Carrousel!

Plastering himself to the pillar, he watched the black-suited Myrmidon stride across the mezzanine to the employee lounge. The instant the bald brute disappeared into the break room, Cædmon hastily made his way to the stairwell.

Circumspect, he opened the door and assessed the dim interior. When no malevolent shape emerged from the shadows, he stepped inside. He then stealthily climbed the steps, hugging the outer wall so that he could better view the shaft above.

Reaching the second floor, Cædmon paused, wondering if he should deviate from the mission op.

Decision made, he continued to the third floor.

80

0545 hours

Cracking the door on the stairwell, Finn scanned the shadowy hallway. Not a soul in sight.

Dumb bastards.

The reason why there weren't any sentries posted in the laboratory was because the Seven didn't think that he and Aisquith had a snowball's chance of breaching the security system. Big mistake, underestimating the enemy. It will always come back to haunt you.

Making like a ghost warrior, Finn hoofed down the hall. According to the architectural blueprint, the maintenance engineering room was located sixty feet from the stairwell, entry on the right. His mission was straightforward: destroy the laboratory's infrastructure and functional capability without compromising the structural integrity of the building above. With his training in explosives, Finn was confident that he could demolish the mechanical system without bringing down the house.

In theory, it would be similar to what happened in '93 when the car bomb went off in the basement of the World Trade Center. The blast did a helluva lot of damage underground, but didn't disturb a thing top side. Which, in retrospect, proved a bad thing, inciting the terrorists to change tactics. Terrorists, like Uhlemann and his Nazi fuckers, were a primeval force of evil.

Arriving at the maintenance engineering room, Finn opened the door and peered inside the dark recess. No unfriendlies. *I love it when the op goes according to plan.*

He stepped across the threshold, closed the door and turned on the light switch. His ocular nerve was instantly blasted with a blinding burst of light. It felt like he'd just gone snow blind.

'I don't care if fluorescent lights are more energy efficient,' he muttered. 'There ought to be a law against 'em.'

Still squinting, he scoped out the room. Basic concrete block construction with a poured cement floor. Everything, including the walls, was painted a blah shade of grey, khaki or black. Strictly utilitarian. Unlike the slick Euro design of the research facility. Upstairs, downstairs. World of difference.

At a glance, Finn could see that the room housed a state-of-the-art system with an array of pipes, ducts, tubes, coils, conduit boxes, boilers and compressors. Building anatomy no different to human anatomy, these were the internal organs that made the pretty office space upstairs functional. The heart, bladder, liver and kidneys.

He walked over to a large industrial panel box bolted into the wall. Opening the metal door, he smiled at seeing the configured cables, connectors and signal modules. *Sweet.* It was the building automation system. An integrated assembly that controlled the electric, heating and air-conditioning. The joint's cerebral cortex.

The six homemade pipe bombs would more than do the trick.

I got a feeling this is going to be a clean job instead of a suicide mission, Finn thought with a measure of relief as he removed the towelling-wrapped bundle from his Go Bag.

'God, I hope so.'

There were things that he needed to tell Kate. *Should* have told her back at the hotel. But didn't. Probably because he didn't have a lot of experience with the man–woman thing. At least, not the emotional part of it. The physical part, oh yeah. Put a blush to your face.

Walking over to a nearby work bench, he removed his supplies from the Go Bag. He felt a strange tightening in his gut. He didn't know if he loved Kate Bauer. Hell, he barely knew her. But she was different from any other woman he'd ever known. Serene, smart, sexy. And incredibly fragile. He had no idea whether she'd be interested in a man like him. For the long haul, that is. Find out soon enough. Hopefully.

Not there to sightsee, Finn rummaged through his Go Bag, retrieving a plastic zip-lock bag that contained two lighters. One he stuck into his T-shirt breast pocket; the second one – the emergency back-up lighter – he stuffed into his boot. That done, he surveyed the room, determining where to set the pipe bombs to achieve maximum effect. The plan was to set the six bombs then wait until he had confirmation from Aisquith that Kate had been safely removed from the premises before he detonated. The gasoline-soaked fuses would ensure a slow burn and that, in turn, should give him enough lag time to clear out. Wouldn't want to get his ass blown to Kingdom Come.

Logistics figured out, he very carefully picked up two pipe bombs. Ready to rock and roll.

As if on cue, his phone softly vibrated against his waist.

Finn set the bombs back on the table and checked the LCD screen. Incoming from Aisquith. He assumed the Brit was letting him know that he'd found Kate. He flipped the phone open.

Fuck!

Message read, Finn flipped the clam phone shut and clipped it on his waistband. According to Aisquith, there was an armed unfriendly headed in his direction.

He re-wrapped the six pipe bombs in the towel, taking care even as he hurriedly cleared the work table. He did not want it carved on his tombstone that he was a dumb-fuck bomb maker who died from bad dumb luck.

No sooner had he slipped the bundled pipe bombs into his Go Bag and unsheathed his KA-BAR knife than he heard footsteps just outside the door.

He ducked behind a rotund hot-water boiler, stashing his Go Bag in the corner.

The doorknob turned. Finn stilled his breath. Completely hidden out of sight, he had the advantage. And the beauty of an edged weapon? It would not run out of bullets or jam on him. If you knew how to hit the sweet spot, a knife could be just as lethal as a loaded gun.

The door swung open. Finn peered between the boiler and a set of copper pipes. A big bruiser with a solid build entered the room. He had the confident stride of a man who had some serious military training. Uhlemann's muscle, obviously.

Luckily, the bruiser didn't seem the least bit perturbed that the overhead lights were turned on. Finn's gaze honed in on the holstered Sig Sauer P6.

Finn wanted that gun in the worst awful way.

Quickly he ran through his options: attacking and using the KA-BAR in a close-quarter situation, slicing or punching a hole in a major artery; tossing the KA-BAR at the dude's heart; or tossing the knife at his backside, then disarming him from behind.

Settling on the last option, he soft-footed away from the boiler, keeping to the shadows. The bruiser was headed for the trio of big aluminium condensers on the other side of the room. Finn took aim and hurled the KA-BAR knife.

The bruiser, seeing the blur of motion reflected in the shiny aluminium, lurched out of the way at the last possible instant, the KA-BAR puncturing a hole in the condenser instead of the bruiser.

Possessed with quick reflexes, the other man spun on his heel as he reached for the P6.

Fuck!

81

0550 hours

Acting on a hunch, Cædmon silently trod the third-floor promenade that overlooked the mezzanine. Like a guilty thief with the goods in his pocket, he clung to the shadows. Off-script, he headed for the nearest room that had visible light shining through the frosted glass. Something was *here*, on the third floor. He could feel it in his blood.

The same blood that coursed through his heart muscle in dizzying contractions. The same blood painfully thumping against the gauze bandage wrapped around his skull.

Where are you, Kate?

He prayed that he'd find her sooner rather than later, his energy flagging. The tension wrought by the situation, his recent injuries and the lack of sleep, it was all starting to wear on his pitiful reserves, the initial burst of adrenaline having run its course.

Christ! Bugger the horse. My kingdom for a wee sip of gin.

Kicking that thought to the kerb, he trudged forward, walking, breathing, *everything* now noticeably laboured.

Ruger in hand, he approached the illuminated room. Grasping the doorknob with his left hand, he pushed the door open a few inches and furtively peered inside. On the other side of the threshold was a snuggery lined with floor-to-ceiling bookcases. All of them jam-packed with leather-bound volumes. For a crazed half-second, he thought he'd been transported to a parallel universe, albeit a tidier universe than the one at L'Equinoxe.

Cædmon cautiously stepped into the library, closing the door behind him. Like every other room he'd investigated, it was eerily vacant, although he sensed it had recently been occupied – there was a small stack of books and an open laptop computer on the centre table. He walked over and perused the pile. *Nazi Mysticism. The Secret of Luxor. Parzival. The Monuments of Paris.* An eclectic assortment, to be sure. And, in one way or another, all related to the Grail and the Axe Historique. He next examined the laptop computer, the screen frozen on an image from a football match. *Curiouser and curiouser.*

Espying a narrow passageway between two bookcases, Cædmon padded over to it. Holding his gun in front of him, he peeked around the corner. Although the lights were low, he could see that it was a small study. His gaze zoomed over to the boxy sofa set against the far wall. There was a huddled body, backside turned to him, curled on the cushions. Shoulders visibly shaking, the occupant was clearly sobbing.

Kate!

Clicking off the safety, he shoved the Ruger into its holster before rushing over to the sofa. Without turning her head, Kate raised a hand and limply waved it in the direction of the library.

'You can set the tray on the table,' she warbled in a tear-weakened voice.

Cædmon went down on bent knee beside the sofa and

gently touched her shoulder. 'It's me, Kate. I've come to rescue you.'

'You can't rescue me,' she said between doleful sobs. 'You're dead. Both of you.'

'I fear those rumours have been greatly exaggerated. While I might be mistaken for a corpse, I'm still among the living. As is McGuire.'

Kate rolled over. 'I don't believe it! Cædmon!' Clearly stunned to see him, she grabbed his face between her two hands. 'You're alive!' Then, a sense of urgency about her, she said, 'You have to leave! Now! Before –'

The look of dread fear that immediately marred Kate's face was the only warning that Cædmon had before a dark shadow fell over the two of them.

There was someone behind him!

Still on bent knee, he straight away reached for the Ruger. Just as his hand grazed the stippled grip, the unseen intruder grabbed his right wrist, snatching his hand away from the gun. Imprisoning his wrist in a bone-crunching grasp, the assailant pulled tight, cinching Cædmon's arm around his own neck. Jamming his chin into the crook of his elbow.

Cædmon bellowed in agony as several sutures instantly popped open.

The brute forcefully jerked on his wrist, spinning him in a semi-circle. Cædmon reflexively swung his left arm; a wild scything slash that connected with a leg muscle. Before he could retract his arm to take another swing, a giant fist smashed into his left temple. Hammer on anvil.

The ferocity of the blow hurled Cædmon to one side. The brute hauled him up by his manacled wrist. With his free hand, the attacker yanked the Ruger out of the holster before shoving Cædmon to the floor.

'That vas too easy,' the brute snarled in a thick accent.

Immobilized with molten pain, Cædmon spat out a mouthful of yellow bile. Dazed, his vision suddenly gone blurry, he struggled to bring the attacker into focus. It took several seconds before the scene crystallized. It took several additional seconds before he realized that he was one bullet from death, the bald-headed Myrmidon pressing the gun muzzle against the same temple he'd just tenderized with his fist.

Enraged that his life was about to end in such humiliating fashion, Cædmon impotently glared at the bald-headed gunman. He didn't have the strength to stagger to his feet, much less rebuff another blow. Callously smiling, the brute's right thumb flicked the safety into the 'off' position. *Any second now.*

'You can't shoot him!' Kate exclaimed frantically, scrambling off the sofa. 'Cædmon Aisquith has valuable information pertaining to the *Lapis Exillis* that Doctor Uhlemann will be *very* interested to hear.'

Frowning, the Myrmidon retracted the muzzle several inches, his confusion plainly evident. In that instant, Cædmon intuited that the big German could not juggle more than one ball.

'It's imperative that Doctor Uhlemann be briefed about the *second* stone before the heliacal rising occurs,' Kate continued, pressing the brute.

Cædmon tossed another ball into the ring. 'You heard the lady. I have important information to convey to your employer. Pull the trigger at your own peril.'

Relenting, the browbeaten Myrmidon jabbed the gun in Cædmon's direction. 'Get up, *wichser*! I will take you to see Herr Doktor Uhlemann.'

Realizing that he'd just been granted a temporary reprieve, Cædmon heaved with his left arm, clumsily shoving himself off the floor. Kate rushed to his side. Wrapping both arms around his chest, she assisted him to his feet.

'When you meet Doctor Uhlemann, be sure to emphasize the catastrophe that will ensue without the second stone,' Kate told him. 'Earlier, he showed me the Vril Generator and I could see that –'

'Shut up! Both of you!' the brute roughly ordered. 'Now get moving!'

Unable to stand up straight, Cædmon took a wobbly step, further disgracing himself. Leaning close, Kate placed a stabilizing arm around his waist. Then, risking the brute's ire, she whispered under her breath, '*Scientia potentia est.*'

Cædmon stared beseechingly at her.

Knowledge might be power, but he didn't know a damned thing about a second stone.

82

0548 hours

Realizing that Finn was unarmed, the gunman stared quizzically. Sig Sauer clenched in his right hand, he then grinned. A big jolly smile that conveyed a simple, straightforward message. *Ho, ho, ho! I'm about to blow your head clean off your shoulders. But first I'm going to toy with you.*

'I understand that Hell is a nice place to visit this time of year,' Mr Smiley Face goaded in a jovial *biergarten* accent, dispensing the first toy from his goody bag.

The gig up, Finn shrugged resignedly. 'Heaven or Hell, dead is dead.' And damn Cædmon Aisquith for mentioning it.

Just then, one of the overhead fluorescent bulbs crackled loudly, the sound accompanied by an erratic flicker. The gunman reflexively glanced up. Finn seized his chance and dodged behind the boiler, swerving out of the line of fire just as the big bruiser pulled the trigger.

The bullet slammed into the stainless-steel boiler, instantly creating a spigot of scalding hot water.

'*Gottverdammt!*'

Finn quickly unbuckled his belt. 'Take another step, Herr Fucker, and I'll pull the trigger,' he blustered, hoping to buy a few extra seconds.

A cocky bastard, the bruiser didn't dive for cover. He

knew damn well that phantom guns fire make-believe bullets. Still wearing his doofy-ass grin, the German sauntered towards the boiler.

'If you had a gun, we would not be having this conversation. You would have shot me dead the moment I walked through the door.' The German was now directly opposite Finn on the other side of the rotund tank.

With a quick tug, Finn yanked his belt through the loops. He then wrapped the leather strap around his right hand, buckle dangling. Flail at the ready, he waited until the German was a few inches from the torrent of hot water that spewed from the tank.

You're gonna wish to God I had shot you, Finn thought maliciously . . . just before he whipped the belt around the corner with two hundred and twenty pounds of torque, smashing the metal buckle into the German's face. The force of the assault knocked the gunman's head into the metal tank. Scalding his left cheek with 170°F water. Forty-two degrees shy of a fast boil. *Shock and awe, baby. Shock and awe.*

The German howled in pain. Dazed, he staggered and fired two wild shots.

Finn immediately reeled in his belt. Surging forward, he crisply whipped it again, this time parallel to the ground. Hard and fast. The heavy buckle hammered into the German's hand, knocking the Sig Sauer loose.

The gun clattered to the concrete floor, discharging a bullet. The German immediately came at him with a roundhouse high kick. Finn swivelled nimbly. Dropping the belt, he snatched hold of the bruiser's raised boot with both hands and jerked upward as hard as he could, pulling the big German completely off balance. Literally sweeping him off his feet.

Upended, the bruiser's head hit the concrete floor with a dull thud, his skull cracking on impact. Like a watermelon hitting the pavement.

Finn stared dispassionately at the dead German. *Well, that sure as hell wiped the grin off Herr Fucker's face.*

'Well done, Finnegan. You have, once again, proved yourself the better man.'

Hearing that sultry French accent, Finn's jaw tightened. Although he figured it was a futile gesture, he raised both hands in the air and slowly turned around.

The Dark Angel – decked out in curve-hugging black leather pants, skintight black tank top and fingerless black leather gloves – leaned casually against a circuit box. She held a Heckler & Koch semi-automatic in her right hand. No surprise that it was pointed directly at Finn. *Game over. Fade to black.*

Not about to antagonize her, Finn kept silent. There was no doubt in his mind that the bitch would shoot to kill. And given that she was one sick bitch, she'd probably keep on firing long after he was dead.

Hips swaying provocatively, she strolled towards him. Smiling, she nudged the muzzle of the semi-automatic against his lower lip.

'Suck very hard on that and maybe I won't pull the trigger.'

Finn glared. The bitch wanted to emasculate him before she turned his grey matter into slurry.

Summoning all the false bravado he could muster, Finn looked her right in the eye and said, 'You've got two choices, Angelika . . . kill me or take me to your leader.'

83

0610 hours

'Oh, my God!' Kate gasped. 'He's dead!'

Cædmon glanced at the corpse sprawled on the floor of the maintenance engineering room, a lake of blood pooled at his head.

'I daresay the bloke had it coming,' he remarked, unmoved at seeing the slain foot soldier.

The bald-headed Myrmidon prodded him in the back with the gun muzzle. 'Shut up, *wichser*, and keep moving. Herr Doktor Uhlemann is expecting us in the viewing chamber.'

Trooping past a trio of aluminium condensers, Cædmon saw a knife hilt protruding from one of them. A battle had clearly taken place between Finn McGuire and the dead man. He hoped to God that the commando had escaped with his life. And would very soon come to their rescue.

To his astonishment, a steel door was hidden behind the condensers. Since the entryway had not been included on the architectural blueprints that he'd obtained for the facility, he assumed that it led to a secret 'viewing chamber'. A security keypad was attached to the doorframe.

The Myrmidon hesitated, then stepped over and keyed in a numeric code. '*Scheisse*,' he muttered under his breath when the door remained locked. He tried again, actually sighing with relief when the lock popped open. Holding the door ajar, he motioned impatiently for Cædmon and Kate to enter.

As he stepped across the threshold, Cædmon immediately saw that there would be no rescue. The vanquished Finnegan McGuire was seated against the far wall. Standing beside him, a leather-clad Valkyrie had a semi-automatic pressed to his left temple. Wearing a white lab coat, Dr Ivo Uhlemann stood a few feet from the pair.

A small room, the viewing chamber was no bigger than a home theatre with a glass partition in lieu of a movie screen. On the other side of the glass was the Vril Generator, housed in a pyramid-shaped bunker. The centrepiece of the device was the Grail, configured in some sort of crystal array. A second door led to the bunker. Like the steel door they'd just come through, it had a security keypad on the doorframe.

Still clutching the Ruger, the faithful Myrmidon slunk over to his master, insinuating himself between Dr Uhlemann and the blonde Valkyrie.

'Oh, Finn . . . I'm so happy to see you!' Kate rushed towards McGuire, only to draw up short when the Valkyrie took aim at her with the semi-automatic.

'Sorry I couldn't come through for you, Katie.' The commando's apology was punctuated with a rueful half-smile. Turning slightly, he jutted his head in Cædmon's direction. 'Hey, buddy. Glad to see that you're still alive. The Death Star is due to appear in eighteen minutes. So you better grab yourself a front-row seat.'

Cædmon sensed that embedded within McGuire's swagger was a covert message. *But what?*

He surreptitiously glanced around the viewing chamber. There was a clock above the glass partition, a chalkboard affixed to one wall, a video camera set on a tripod and three empty viewing chairs lined up in front of the glass partition. '*Grab yourself a front row seat.*' Perhaps McGuire thought Cædmon could use one of the wood-backed chairs as a weapon.

Right.

He deliberately touched the blood-soaked bandage on his head as he turned to Dr Uhlemann and said, 'May I have leave to sit down? Before I fall down,' he added, hoping he appeared sufficiently pathetic.

'By all means.' The request was granted with a regal wave of the hand.

Playing the nursemaid, Kate solicitously helped Cædmon to his seat. In truth, he *was* a bloodied weakling, having yet to recover from the earlier thrashing. The painful crown that insistently pressed against his bashed head had become damned near excruciating.

Although not as excruciating as a bullet to the brain.

No time to waste, Cædmon quickly sized up the enemy. *Crisply knotted silk tie. Perfectly tailored trousers. Tasselled leather loathers.* All-in-all, a revealing book cover. Conservative, yet eloquent, the wardrobe indicated that Ivo Uhlemann was a man with a taste for the finer things. Cædmon suspected that the German was also something of an aesthete, a lover of all that was beautiful and perfect. As 'Herr Doktor' defined those two terms, of course, his arrogance plain to see. Paired with that conceit was a keen intelligence. Unlike the gauche Myrmidon who couldn't juggle two balls at once, the elder German was a spatial thinker. A theoretical physicist who could problem solve in multiple dimensions.

He'll prove a damned difficult nut to crack, Cædmon acknowledged dispiritedly.

As for the blonde Valkyrie, he didn't intend to turn his back on her any time soon.

'I am delighted that the three of you will witness *das Groß Versuch*,' Dr Uhlemann announced with an air of mocking conviviality.

Since cadavers can't speak, Cædmon assumed that the witnesses would be summarily shot at the conclusion of the 'Great Experiment'. The gloating victor, Dr Uhlemann wanted first to lord his hard-earned triumph over them. And it had been hard-earned, years in the making as he understood it.

Acutely aware of the ticking clock, Cædmon examined the Vril Generator.

Noticing the direction of his gaze, Dr Uhlemann said, 'The design for the generator was extrapolated from a careful reading of the *Ghayat al-Hakim*. Crystal matrixes are part of the Lost Science.' He removed a laser pen from his pocket and aimed the red beam at the Vril Generator. 'As you can see, the nucleus of the design is the *Lapis Exillis*, which is bracketed, top and bottom, by a tubular quartz crystal. The ancients were well aware that these crystals can hold a high-frequency electric charge.'

'That's what modern-day scientists refer to as piezoelectricity,' Kate remarked as she sat down beside Cædmon. Turning her head ever so slightly, she shot him a pointed glance.

Earlier, when they were in the library, she had tried to tell him something about 'two stones'.

But there was only the one Grail.

Christ! What in bloody hell is she trying to communicate to me?

He needed more intelligence. And he needed to be damned quick about gathering it.

'Doctor Uhlemann, how exactly does the crystal matrix work?' he enquired, hoping to pry loose a useful nugget.

'Astral energy is directed into the quartz crystal suspended from the pyramid's apex. Conversely, the crystal on the floor acts as a magnet to attract telluric energy from deep within the earth,' the German informed him in a professorial tone. 'The two quartz crystals simultaneously funnel their respective energies into the *Lapis Exillis* which then generates the Vril force. All in all, a simple but efficient means of energy production.'

'Fascinating.' Cædmon then asked the question that had been plaguing him since he'd first found the Grail stone hidden inside the Isis Sanctuary. 'Do you have any idea what's beneath the gold plating?'

'According to our scan, it's a layered configuration, a lapis lazuli stone embedded in the centre. We have yet to determine the material used in the insulating second layer.'

'Blue, of course, is the colour ascribed to Isis, Queen of the Heavens. Prized by the Egyptians for its unique hue, the stone was used as a protective talisman, a lapis lazuli scarab often buried with the dead to guard them in the afterlife.'

Kate gently nudged him with her elbow. 'And, like the quartz crystal, lapis lazuli has a high resonance frequency.'

Cædmon took the nudge as a silent caution to keep the conversation grounded in the scientific and not veer off on to the esoteric realm.

Right.

Taking his cues from Kate, he made a quick course correction. 'As I recall from a long-ago physics lesson, high resonance frequency has to do with the stone's accumulated vibrational energy.' He glanced at the clock mounted on the wall. Eleven minutes left. *How can I possibly stop the Vril generation from taking place in the few minutes remaining?*

Jaw clamped tight, Cædmon refocused his attention on the Grail.

Think, man, think.

'Doctor Uhlemann, I'm curious about the relationship between the Vril Generator and the monuments on the Axe Historique,' Kate ventured politely. 'Specifically, I'm wondering how the Louvre Pyramid figures into the equation.'

Hearing this, Cædmon whipped his head in Kate's direction. The 'second stone'. Of course! That was it!

Kate, you're brilliant.

He gave her an answering nudge, signalling that, while late to the game, he now understood.

'As you know, each monument on the Axe Historique has a purpose. The obelisk functions as a radio tower, drawing down the astral energy from Sirius, and the three arches channel the earth's telluric energy. The glass pyramid serves as a counterbalance to the pyramidal *Lapis Exillis.*' With his laser light pen, Dr Uhlemann pointed to the Grail. 'Perfect symmetry.'

'I concur. However . . .' Cædmon paused, ensuring that he had the other man's full attention before he dropped the bombshell. 'That is precisely why your Vril Generator is a flawed design.'

The elder German's eyes narrowed dangerously, like Zeus about to hurl a lightning bolt.

'Anyone who's been to the Cour Napoléon knows that there are *two* notable pyramids on the eastern end of the Axe Historique,' Cædmon continued, bracing himself for a full-out Titanomachy. 'The famous upright glass pyramid and *La Pyramide Inversée*, the inverted pyramid.'

'Which is only visible *below* ground,' Kate emphasized. 'In fact, most people strolling in the courtyard are unaware of its existence.'

'The Pyramid Inversée is the unseen twin. As above, so below. *That*, old boy, is perfect symmetry. Not this asymmetrical configuration that you've patched together,' Cædmon derided. Then, going for the jugular, he said, 'The Vril Generator is not going to work . . . you're missing the *second* pyramidal stone.'

84

0621 hours

Yes! Two stones! Message sent and received.

Sagging against her chair, Kate released a pent-up breath.

'Furthermore, I strongly urge you to immediately deconstruct the Vril Generator. And do hurry.' Cædmon jutted his chin at the clock hanging on the wall. 'You have only nine minutes to avert disaster.'

'I refuse to countenance this preposterous claim!'

Kate anxiously glanced between the two men. She'd spent hours poring over books in the upstairs library, trying to find the fatal flaw in Dr Uhlemann's design concept. Since he was a man of science, they had to sway his mind. Not his heart. If he even possessed one of those.

'The blueprint on the Axe Historique is clear: *Two* pyramidal stones are required on each end of the axis.' Undaunted, Cædmon put his left hand on her shoulder and said, 'Kate, would you do the honours and sketch the correct design for Doctor Uhlemann?' His face drained of colour, Cædmon drew her attention to the small puddle of blood on the floor next to his chair, his right jacket sleeve stained a deep burgundy. 'Afraid that I'm not up to the task.'

Biting back a commiserating whimper, Kate got up from her chair and walked over to the chalkboard.

As she limned the geometric configuration, she had to stop several times and take a stabilizing breath. It was a desperate gamble, trying to persuade a mad scientist to adopt the sane course of action. *But what else could they do?* They had no guns. No reinforcements. And no contingency plan should they fail. They *had* to prove that the generator was imperfectly configured. There was no other way to stop Ivo Uhlemann from changing the course of history.

In truth, she didn't know if the generator design was actually flawed. They just had to convince Dr Uhlemann of that fact. Worried she might not be persuasive enough, she would leave it to Cædmon to explain the drawing.

Craning her neck, Kate peered at the clock. *Seven minutes.* And counting.

Finished, she placed the piece of white chalk on the metal ledge beneath the board. *Please, please, please!* she silently begged of any god who would listen, *Make this work.*

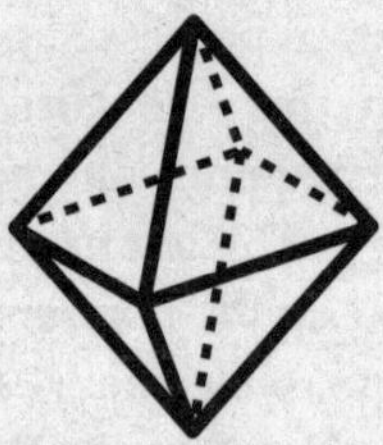

'Two pyramidal stones placed in this configuration form an octahedron, a Platonic solid comprised of eight equilateral triangles, four of which meet at each vertex,' Cædmon iterated, getting right to the gist. 'An octahedron would allow for each quartz crystal terminator point to transmit directly into the apex of a pyramidal stone. Point to point. It's counter-intuitive. Your design is clearly defective. What you have here –' raising his left arm, Cædmon pointed to the Grail on the other side of the glass partition – 'is *half* of an octahedron.'

'Which makes it half-ass in my book,' Finn sneered, having been noticeably quiet.

'The Vril Generator *must* be reconfigured,' Cædmon insisted doggedly. 'This is a flawed design that could have catastrophic consequences. My guess is a massive explosion due to the energy build-up.'

Clearly unmoved by Cædmon's argument, Dr Uhlemann tersely shook his head. 'The only way to determine if the Vril Generator works is to proceed with the experiment.'

'In addition to white marble, the Grande Arche building was constructed with vast quantities of granite rock. Granite, as you undoubtedly know, is a transmission stone. It's also slightly radioactive. Moreover, the Axe Historique is built over limestone bedrock which creates a natural water aquifer.'

Realizing where Cædmon was headed, Kate said, 'And when water moves through limestone, it produces an electric charge.'

'The Earth's electromagnetic field is most powerful just before dawn,' Cædmon stated, elaborating on her point. 'Since the Axe Historique has never been used to fuse astral and telluric energies to create the Vril force, you could well be playing with a fire that you won't be able to control. This is a technology that has not been used since the days of the pharaohs. Have you considered the possibility that there might be a deadly reason why?'

'Your question lacks merit and has no bearing on *das Groß Versuch*,' Dr Uhlemann bristled.

Kate clasped her hands to her chest. 'I implore you, Doctor Uhlemann. Any other scientist would cancel the experiment rather than court disaster.'

'I will not postpone *das Groß Versuch*.'

'Even if you destroy half of Paris in the process?'

Dr Uhlemann shot Cædmon a withering glance. 'The only thing that we intend to destroy are the dark forces of German history.'

'And here all along I thought *you guys* were the dark force of German history,' Finn deadpanned. 'I get all of you goose-stepping rat bastards mixed up.'

The older German blanched at the crude insult.

Snarling, Angelika shoved her gun muzzle against Finn's temple. 'I would be happy to show you the difference.'

'Do you mind if I take a rain check? The show's about to begin and I'm really looking forward to seeing what all the hoopla's about. There's only a few things in this world that make me go ga-ga.' Point made, Finn purposefully looked over at Kate. And smiled wistfully.

Oh, Finn . . . You brash, beautiful man.

Feeling the sting of tears, Kate glanced anxiously at the clock. *Six minutes until the heliacal rising of Sirius.* If the Vril Generator *didn't* work, something disastrous could happen. But, on the other hand, if it *did* work, they could all end up living in a fascist regime ruled by an ego-maniacal mad man. Both prospects incited a dread fear.

'You're dealing with cosmic forces that no one fully

comprehends,' Cædmon asserted. 'There's a very real possibility that a catastrophic event will occur.'

Expressionless, Ivo Uhlemann shrugged. 'According to my oncologist, I'm not long for this world. Death, like the speed of light, is one of the few unchanging constants in the Universe. That said, we constructed the Vril Generator according to the instructions in the *Ghayat al-Hakim*. It *will* work.'

'While I haven't read the Arabic original, I have read *Picatrix*, the Latin translation,' Cædmon counterpunched, refusing to surrender the field. 'It's a magical grimoire composed in metaphoric and symbolic language that can easily be misinterpreted. In my experience, when one dives into the occult, the waters turn very murky very quickly.'

'I am a scientist, not an occultist!'

'Anyone familiar with the history of the Nazi movement knows that the occult strain ran deep in its ranks. I find it hard to believe that you would stray far from those beliefs.'

'How dare you!' Dr Uhlemann physically recoiled, as though he'd just been splashed with acid. 'The occultists are no different to those addicted to the crutch of organized religion. They should all be led to the nearest funeral pyre.'

'As I recall, your Führer once claimed that "A new age of magic interpretation of the world is coming".'

'Pure poppycock!' Dr Uhlemann exclaimed angrily. 'They ruined our perfect society. The one that we worked so hard to achieve. For them, *everything* had a mystical implication. Even the initials SS had a magical meaning.'

'The word "*Schutzstaffel*" means special staff.' Cædmon's

brows drew together in a questioning pucker. 'What in God's name is magical about that?'

'Absolutely nothing. However, those two initials also stand for "*schwarz sonne*".'

'Ah! Of course. The Black Sun,' Cædmon translated. 'Also known as Sirius. Which, coincidentally, is due to rise at any moment.'

The irony of the addendum was lost on Dr Uhlemann.

'They worshipped their Black Sun like a coven of superstitious pagans. There were officers in the SS who thought they could win the war with Ouija boards and Runic magic. Outright quackery is what it was. How educated men could fall victim to such outlandish delusions is truly astonishing.'

'Not so astonishing given that many in the Nazi high command dabbled in the dark arts.' With only four minutes left, Cædmon was still grounded, still steady at the helm.

'They did more than dabble. They were brainwashed devotees, Hitler their prophet and Himmler their high priest,' Dr Uhlemann said accusingly. 'In the end, their minds had become unhinged, corrupted by occult lunacies. Is there any wonder that we lost the war?'

'Most historians would agree that their occultism proved a fatal *idée fixe*.'

Dr Uhlemann concurred with a vigorous nod. 'That is the reason why our fathers *will* rid the German high command of this dangerous occult element. Once that is done, the way will be paved to immediately begin the military campaign in the Middle East.'

'But, as you said, Hitler himself was a member of this

esoteric coven.' Cædmon frowned, clearly perplexed. 'How are you going to persuade him that science is superior to magic?'

'We have no intention of persuading him . . . we intend to assassinate Adolf Hitler.'

Hearing that, Kate's eyes opened wide. The moment, indeed, the entire situation, had just turned unbelievably surreal.

'Or, rather, my father and his colleagues in the Seven will have the honour of committing the regicide,' Dr Uhlemann clarified.

If Cædmon was surprised by the announcement, he hid it well. 'There were many attempts on Hitler's life, most of them plotted by members of the Nazi Party. How can you be so sure that your attempt will succeed?'

'To use an oft-repeated cliché, hindsight is twenty-twenty vision,' Dr Uhlemann informed him. 'We know that the Führer and the occult members of his inner circle will all be in attendance at the 1940 *Schutzstaffel* Christmas party. The festivities will be held at the Löwenbräu Keller in Munich. We have put together a detailed assassination plan which we will transmit to our fathers via our CTC device. Trust me . . . no one will leave the Löwenbräu Keller alive.'

'Damned diabolical,' Cædmon muttered. 'Part of me actually hopes that you succeed.'

Dolf Reinhardt suddenly stepped forward. Eyes glistening with unshed tears, he shook with a barely restrained emotion.

'Nein! Nein! Nein!'

85

0628 hours

'Obviously, someone forgot to send Cue Ball the "Kill Hitler" memo,' Finn muttered under his breath.

'What is happening here?' the chauffeur bellowed. 'Has everyone lost their mind?'

'If you cannot control yourself, Dolf, you will have to leave the room,' Uhlemann threatened in a patronizing tone, speaking to the big goon as though he were a six-year-old child. 'It's obvious that you're confused.'

'I want you to answer my question, Herr Doktor! *What is happening here!?*' Wide-eyed, Dolf clutched the Ruger P89 to his chest; his very own nine-mil teddy bear.

Finn glanced at the clock. *Fuck*. Two minutes until sunrise. Aisquith was convinced the design flaw in the Vril Generator would cause an explosion due to an energy build-up. Add to that the six pipe bombs stashed next door in the maintenance engineering room and they'd all be blown to Sirius and back.

Determined to go down fighting, Finn swung his head in Aisquith's direction, silently signalling to the Brit that he had a plan. He then looked over at the bewildered bald dude.

'Not only are you confused, but you are definitely out of the loop,' Finn told the chauffeur, hoping to stoke him into shutting down the show. A lame duck, if he so much as lifted his ass off the chair, Angelika would put a bullet right between his eyes. 'Here's the simplified version. The star Sirius is due to appear in the dawn sky in two minutes. When that happens, your boss is gonna use the astral energy from the star to generate the Vril force. That's a kind of fused energy that emits a blue light. Uhlemann needs that blue light to open a hole in the space–time continuum so he can travel back to the year 1940 and kill Adolf Hitler.'

'Is this true, Herr Doktor?' The chauffeur's expression of disbelief was almost comical.

Clearly outraged by the insurrection, Uhlemann shot his subordinate a glacial stare, refusing to answer.

'It's true, Dolf,' Kate volunteered, her features stamped with abject fear. 'Doctor Uhlemann showed me the time machine.'

To say that Dolf was crestfallen would be putting it mildly; tears were running down his cheeks and snot was dripping from his nose.

'My mother was the Führer's little handmaid,' the big slobbering bastard rasped in a hoarse voice. 'My grandfather was his chauffeur.'

'Hitler's chauffeur? No shit. I'm impressed,' Finn lied. 'I'm guessing he was in the SS, right?'

Wiping a ribbon of snot with the back of his hand, the other man nodded. 'He was an officer in the Reich Security Service.'

Realizing that was the perfect segue, Finn, winging it all the way, said, 'So it's a given that he would have driven the Führer to the Christmas party in 1940. The two of them probably sang a couple of rounds of "Silent Night" on the way to the big shindig. Once they get there, your grandfather will be having a good time, drinking a little eggnog, then *Kaboom*! Silent night. *Auf wiedersehen.* You heard Uhlemann; no one is gonna leave the Löwenbräu Keller alive. Helluva way to go.'

The realization that his own grandfather would be killed in the planned massacre suddenly dawned in Dolf's watery eyes. In that instant, he went from confused lapdog to snarling Rottweiler. Teeth clenched, he aimed the Ruger P89 at his master's head. 'How could you destroy my family like this? I sacrificed *everything* for you.'

Proving that he was an old-school Prussian, Uhlemann glared at his rabid dog. Unbowed and unafraid.

'Hah! What did you sacrifice?' Angelika jeered. 'A few dinners with your old *mutti*?'

'Leave my mother out of this!'

'This is sheer idiocy. Give me the gun.' A leather-clad dominatrix, Angelika stomped her booted foot imperiously on the floor. '*Now!*'

'*Nein!*' Dolf abruptly changed targets, Ruger now aimed directly at Angelika's head. 'Shut up, bitch! You're always telling me what to do!'

Well, well, well . . . Sounds like the two winged monkeys have some wicked bad history. Finn just hoped he didn't get caught in their crossfire.

Changing tactics, Angelika's sneer instantly morphed into a smile. A come-hither invite that oozed sex like a volcano oozing molten lava. 'I can make all of your dreams come true, Dolf. You know the kind of dreams I'm talking about . . . those naughty dreams that you have in the middle of the night.' Her gaze slowly travelled down Cue Ball's chest to his crotch.

Teary eyes narrowed furiously. 'Slut!'

'If you want me to be.' Still smiling, and still holding the HK semi to Finn's head, Angelika held out her left hand and wiggled her fingers. 'Dolfie, give me the gun. If you don't, I will tell your *mutti* that you were a very bad boy.'

'I told you not to mention my mother!' Last Rites administered, 'Dolfie' pulled the trigger.

Before the blonde bitch even hit the deck, Finn cannonballed out of his chair and hurled himself at the bald-headed gunman . . . who now had his weapon trained on Ivo Uhlemann.

In a fast *wham-bam* move, Finn, attacking from behind, cinched his left hand around Dolf's thick neck. With his right, he knocked the gun loose. Two pounds of stainless steel thudded on to the concrete floor, the impact causing a round to discharge. Galvanized, Finn secured his right hand on the other side of the big man's neck. And squeezed like hell.

Pumped up on adrenaline, the goon thrashed violently, clawing Finn's wrists with his huge boxer-size paws. Locked in a ferocious embrace, the two of them slammed against the concrete wall.

'It's six thirty!' Kate screamed. 'You have to stop the experiment!'

Hearing that, Finn spared a quick glance. Kate was yanking on Ivo Uhlemann's arm, while Aisquith was frantically trying to open the door that led to the Vril Generator.

'Yes! Yes! It's happening!' Uhlemann shouted jubilantly.

Out of the corner of his eye, Finn saw a luminous blue haze surrounding the Grail.

Shit!

Jaw clenched tight, Finn squeezed for all he was worth on the chauffeur's thick, muscle-roped neck . . . *But it was like squeezing a damned tree trunk.*

86

0630 hours

Standing in front of the steel door that led to the Vril Generator, Cædmon turned his head and peered through the plate-glass window.

A blue phosphorescent corona had completely enveloped the Grail.

Christ! The energy fusion has already begun!

Having tried all three of the hacked security codes – with no luck – Cædmon rushed over to Dr Uhlemann.

'There's no time to waste! Give me the security code to bypass the lock!'

Ignoring his shouted demand, the German scientist pressed both palms to the glass partition as he gazed through the glass. 'Soon! Soon! Soon!' he chanted, his rheumy eyes gleaming with excitement. Obsessed with his creation, he was oblivious to the danger.

Kate, standing on the other side of Dr Uhlemann, urgently tugged on his arm. 'You have to stop the experiment!'

A loud crackling sound reverberated from the other side of the glass as blue sparks began to fly frenetically off the stone. The crackling was near-deafening, Cædmon afraid that his eardrums were about to burst. A jagged blue streak arced through the air, the stench of ozone filling the chamber, the ambient temperature rapidly escalating.

Cædmon could feel his body vibrate painfully, as though his internal organs were being agitated from within.

'The generator *must* be shut down this instant!' he hollered.

'No!'

Cædmon spun on his heel and grabbed a wooden-backed chair. Biting back an agonized bellow of pain, he slammed it against the glass partition.

A wasted effort, the safety glass too thick to penetrate.

Just then, the energy fusion produced myriad streamers, each branching out from the Grail into hundreds of thin blue filaments that streaked ominously in every direction.

'For Christ's sake!' Cædmon yelled, barely audible over the shrill cacophony. 'Give me the code, you bloody contemptible –'

Bang! Bang! Bang!

Three gun shots were fired in quick succession, the glass partition immediately shattering.

A split-second later, a ragged blue bolt of current ripped free from the Grail and struck Ivo Uhlemann square in the chest. The force of the blow hurtled him ten feet through the air, the German careening into the concrete block wall at the back of the room.

Cædmon heaved the chair through the open partition – dislodging the Grail from the crystal matrix.

In an instant, all went eerily silent.

'It's over,' he murmured, his shoulders slumping in relief. 'The experiment has been stopped.'

He turned his head. McGuire stood over the dead Myrmidon, the Ruger clutched in his hand. Gracelessly sprawled on the floor, the bald brute's neck was bent at an unnatural angle. Grim-faced, the commando charged towards the video camera that was set on a nearby tripod. Grabbing the camera with his free hand, he flung it against the concrete wall, the device smashing on impact.

'Uhlemann's buddies were watching the proceedings on a live video feed,' he said by way of explanation. 'So we better hustle before they send in the reinforcements.'

'My God . . . I feel like I just came through a war zone,' Kate gasped, a shell-shocked expression on her face.

Indeed, the floor was littered with bodies.

Cædmon glanced dispassionately at the crumpled figure of Ivo Uhlemann.

'Jaysus,' McGuire softly swore as he examined the body. 'Not only did the Vril force blow a gaping hole clean through him, but it carbonized the skin around the wound.' Stepping away from the dead German, he shook his head in disgust. 'Although I gotta tell you, I don't have an ounce to spare for any of 'em.'

'Nor I,' Cædmon seconded.

'Me, three,' Kate whispered.

McGuire checked his watch. 'We still need to stick to the game plan and destroy the Vril Generator. And we don't have a whole helluva lot of time to do it.'

'I'll climb through the partition and retrieve the Grail,' Cædmon informed him.

The commando clamped a hand on his left shoulder, stopping him in mid-stride. 'No way are we taking that stone with us,' he bluntly informed Cædmon, a determined look in his eyes. 'I don't want to be running this same op again next year. If the Grail does what everyone claims it can do, every military in the world will be vying for it. Hell, look what it did Ivo Meister.'

'I'll make certain that it's safeguarded.'

'You're good, buddy, but you're just one man. Trust me. You won't be able to safeguard that damned thing once the Powers-That-Be catch wind of it. The gold will melt in the explosion.'

Rendering the Grail worthless.

Cædmon turned and stared at the legendary stone gleaming on the concrete floor. *Beckoning.* Parzival's *Lapis Exillis.* The same stone sought by the Knights Templar.

And the scientists of the Third Reich.

Knowing that McGuire spoke the truth, Cædmon nodded his head in resignation. 'Right. Let's destroy the chamber and get the bloody hell out of here.'

'You also have to destroy the CTC device,' Kate informed them.

In unison, both he and McGuire swung their heads in her direction.

'*What?*' they jointly exclaimed.

'It's the working prototype for the Seven's time machine. Doctor Uhlemann showed it to me. While I'm not a scientist, I'm fairly certain that it *will* work!'

'Provided you have the Vril force to power it.' Cædmon nodded at the crystal matrix. 'Which will be impossible to create without a functioning generator.'

'The crystal matrix is just one way to generate the Vril force,' Kate countered. 'What if there are multiple ways to create it?'

Cædmon turned to the commando. 'She has a valid point.'

'Okay,' McGuire said, persuaded. 'I've got enough pipe bombs to destroy both the Vril Generator and this CTC device. Where's the time machine located?'

'Upstairs on the third floor. The laboratory is two doors down from the library.'

'Gotcha.'

Kate's brows suddenly knitted together. 'But you're not going to be able to get into the lab.'

'Why not!?' Both Cædmon and McGuire again exclaimed in unison.

'The door to the laboratory is secured with a biometric device. It requires a fingerprint scan to unlock the door. And Doctor Uhlemann is no longer –'

'Which finger?' the commando interjected.

'Right index.'

'Then I'd better retrieve my KA-BAR knife.' Without a backward glance, McGuire charged over to the door that led to the maintenance engineering room, propping it open with a chair.

Belatedly realizing what the commando intended to do, Kate's eyes opened wide, a horrified expression on her face. 'Oh, my God! We can't let him –'

'I can assure you that Doctor Uhlemann won't feel a thing.' *Moreover, the bastard has it coming.*

A few moments later, McGuire returned to the viewing chamber, his Go Bag slung over his shoulder and a business-like knife gripped in his right hand. 'This is the plan: I'll toss three bombs through the partition then run upstairs to the third floor. I'll wait to enter the lab until the two of you are clear and free of the mezzanine.'

Kate placed a hand on McGuire's chest. 'Finn, please be –'

'Don't worry, Katie. I'll be just fine,' he said reassuringly. 'I'm doing what I was put on this earth to do. Improvise, utilize, then haul ass.' His lips curved in a cocky grin. 'It's what I do best.'

'Second best,' Kate whispered. Going up on her tiptoes, she lovingly kissed him full on the lips.

Wrapping an arm around her waist, McGuire pulled her close. Suddenly feeling like an unwanted intruder, Cædmon discreetly turned his head.

'Aisquith's a stand-up guy. He'll get you out of here,' McGuire said a few moments later.

Her grey-blue eyes glistening with unshed tears, Kate rushed out of the viewing chamber. Just as Cædmon was about to follow her, McGuire grabbed hold of his left arm, preventing him from leaving.

'You get her out of here safely or you die trying.'

Cædmon put a hand on the other man's shoulder. 'You have my word.'

'If I don't make it out alive, I want you to take care of Kate,' McGuire told him in a gruff, emotion-laden voice. 'And if you don't, I will seriously haunt your ass.'

'Consider it done.'

McGuire smiled, visibly relieved. 'Good. Now get the hell out of here. I got work to do.'

87

Cædmon yanked open the door at the top of the steps, motioning for Kate to precede him.

'Ladies first,' he said, his lips twisted in a semblance of a smile.

Kate wasn't fooled for a minute – he was in a tremendous amount of pain. The bandage on his head was completely saturated with blood and his right jacket sleeve had a large bloody splotch. She had no idea how Cædmon had come by his wounds, but it was obvious that he needed immediate medical attention.

Free and clear of the stairwell, the two of them sprinted across the low-lit mezzanine. Two shadows charging through the penumbra.

Heart pounding, Kate pushed herself to keep up with Cædmon's long-legged stride. Although the temperature inside the atrium was downright frigid, she was heated from the exertion. Stress, combined with lack of food and sleep, was sapping what little energy she had left. To prevent herself from stumbling, she focused on keeping her arms and legs coordinated.

Worried that Finn might run into trouble, she spared a quick glance over her shoulder. She hoped to God that Dr Uhlemann's associates didn't send armed reinforcements to ambush him. She didn't know a lot about pipe bombs other than the fact that they were incredibly volatile and dangerous to handle. If he got caught in a firefight, it might trigger an unintended explosion.

As if to prove that very point, a loud blast suddenly thundered in the level below them, Kate feeling the reverberations in her spinal column. A few seconds later, a second bomb detonated. And then a third.

'Excellent!' Cædmon exclaimed. 'McGuire has ignited the first three bombs.'

A few moments later, they arrived at the exit door, both of them slightly out of breath.

'Bloody hell! Who puts a security lock on both sides of the door?' Cædmon gestured to the numeric pad affixed to the right side of the door jamb. 'Luckily, I have the access code.'

He keyed in a six-digit number.

'Damn . . . I must have mis-keyed.' He tried again, slower this time.

When nothing happened, Kate asked the obvious question. 'Why isn't the door unlocking?'

'I have no idea. Not to fear.' Cædmon absently patted her arm. 'I have two other codes. I'm sure one of them will work.'

Despite his assurance, she literally crossed her fingers as she watched him carefully key in a second numeric code.

Six attempts later, Cædmon turned to her and delivered the bad news. 'It would appear that we're locked in.'

Kate gasped. Swayed. Saw spots in front of her eyes.

They were trapped inside the facility!

88

Like he was a launched ballistic missile, Finn charged out of the third-floor stairwell, hung a Louie, and ran towards the library.

'*The laboratory is two doors down from the library.*'

'Two Doors Down' – one of his favourite Dolly Parton songs.

Finn smiled, everything going according to plan. Soon it would all be over. And when he'd completed the mission, he planned on sweeping little Katie right off her feet.

His smile widened. He wasn't supposed to let his emotions flare during a mission. But what the hell? This was his last op. Once he cleared himself of the murder charges, he was going to put in for a transfer to Fort Bragg. Get himself a cushy position as a Delta Force training instructor. And while he didn't want to get ahead of himself, he was feeling pretty confident that Kate would sign up for the move.

Arriving at the second door, Finn peered at the mezzanine below – Aisquith and Kate were already at the exit, about to make good their escape. *Perfect.*

Ripping open the flap on his cargo pants, he removed Uhlemann's severed index finger, using the hem of his T-shirt to wipe off the excess blood. That done, he placed the fleshy tip on to the biometric reader.

A white light flared. An instant later, the bolt on the door popped open.

'In like Finn,' he chortled, riding a little happy high. He flung the butchered finger aside and opened the door. 'I love it when the op goes without a hitch.'

Stepping across the threshold, he hit the light switch. A row of fluorescent bulbs washed the laboratory in antiseptic bright light.

'There it is, the Flux Capacitor.' But unlike the DeLorean time machine from the *Back to the Future* movie, this was the real deal. Not some contrived Hollywood invention.

He strode over to the glass enclosure. *The remaining pipe bombs will definitely do the trick.*

In a big-ass hurry, Finn went down on bent knee in front of the enclosure. He then carefully removed the last three bombs from his Go Bag and lined them up directly in front of the heavy-duty glass. Retrieving the cigarette lighter from his breast pocket, he quickly lit all three fuses.

Okay, boys and girls. 'It's home from work we go.'

Lurching to his feet, he rushed over to the door . . . Only to draw up short an instant later.

Seeing the metal security panel attached to the side of the doorframe, Finn's heart skidded. *Full stop.* Little Katie forgot to mention that there was a biometric security lock on *both* sides of the laboratory door, Uhlemann's severed finger now on the *other* side of the locked door.

Ah, shit.

89

Refusing to surrender, Cædmon glared at the numeric keypad, the locked door an unforeseen wrinkle in the plan.

'If we can't exit the facility, Finn won't be able to get out either,' Kate anxiously informed him. Visibly shaking, her concern had already leapfrogged from moderate to acute.

'Not to worry. I'll call for help.' Cædmon removed his cell phone from his jacket pocket and flipped it open, relieved that Uhlemann's bald-headed minion had lacked the foresight to confiscate it.

Damn!

Bewildered, he showed Kate the dark screen. 'It's completely dead. I don't understand . . . the battery was fully charged.'

'I'm guessing the Vril force emitted an electromagnetic pulse that somehow disabled it.'

He shoved the phone back in his pocket. 'Do you recall seeing a fire alarm anywhere in the research facility? If so, I could trigger it, alerting the guards in the lobby.'

Kate's brow furrowed. 'No, I . . .' She shook her head dejectedly. 'I'm sorry, Cædmon, but I can't –'

'It's not your fault.' He hesitated, worried that if he shouted for help, an armed interloper might answer the summons.

Bugger it.

Cupping his hands to his mouth, Cædmon stepped away from the door and bellowed, 'McGuire! Where are you? We need your assistance!'

Ears still ringing from the first three bomb blasts, he cocked his head to one side and listened attentively.

Not so much as a pin. Damn.

He walked back to the exit door. 'Doctor Uhlemann's postmortem revenge, I daresay. Not only are we in the stocks, but we're unable to communicate with the outside world. Only one thing left to do.' Although his right arm ached and his head throbbed ferociously, Cædmon forcefully beat on the steel door with his balled fist in the hope that someone might be on the other side.

The painful shock waves that pounded his body in the aftermath were for naught. No one replied.

'Wait!' Wide-eyed, Kate clutched his forearm. 'Didn't Dolf key in a security code to gain entry to the viewing chamber?'

Cædmon replayed the scene in his mind's eye. 'He did, but I didn't take note of the code.'

'Um . . . let me think a minute . . .' Closing her eyes, Kate raised her right hand. She then took several deep breaths before her fingers moved across an imaginary keypad. An instant later, her eyes popped open. 'Three, eight, two, five, six, three. Try it.'

He hurriedly keyed in the code.

Hearing the lock click open, Cædmon sagged against the door jamb. Although he wasn't a church-going man, he offered up a grateful prayer.

'What a relief,' Kate murmured. 'We need to wait here until –'

Just then, a blast detonated on the upper level of the atrium. The force of the explosion blew out an entire bank of frosted glass, strafing the mezzanine with thousands of white shards. A deadly snowfall. A second later, the next blast detonated, hurling a section of railing through the air.

'Finn! Where are you?!' Kate screamed over the third and final bomb blast.

90

Washington, DC

Two weeks later

The waiter placed an iced coffee in front of Kate. She promptly reached for the ceramic sugar bowl. He then set a glass of tonic water, *sans* the gin, in front of Cædmon, prompting him to grit his teeth. Mindful that gin had rendered him an unfeeling brute, he was now determined to retain what few shreds of humanity he still had left. The going wasn't easy. Case in point.

Res ipsa loquitur. The damned thing speaks for itself, in a blaringly loud voice.

'I'm glad that, in the end, you and Finn managed to overcome your differences,' Kate remarked as she stirred a teaspoon of sugar into her glass, ice cubes tinkling merrily.

Assuming a solemn air, Cædmon placed his right hand over his heart. 'As the Buddha so wisely extolled: "Holding on to anger is like grasping a hot coal with the intent of throwing it at someone else; you are the one who gets burned." '

Her brow puckered. 'Did you have to mention the Buddha?'

Reaching across the table, Cædmon gently patted her hand. 'Give it time, Kate. Yours is a forgiving religion.'

'Other than the fact that everyone is speaking English, it almost feels like we're sitting at an outdoor Paris café,' she effused, effectively changing the subject.

Cædmon glanced at the Georgetown cityscape, the quaint eighteenth-century brick architecture more reminiscent of London than Beaux Arts Paris. Kate, no doubt, referred to the weather; a typical August evening, it was hot, humid and oppressively muggy, the air so thick it was palpable. A week ago when they had left Paris, the city had been in the midst of a fiendish heat wave.

'I can't thank you enough, Cædmon, for helping me get everything settled. I had no idea that there would be so much paperwork to fill out, what with the insurance forms for what used to be my house, police reports and a slew of security statements.' Shaking her head, Kate amiably chuckled. 'I'm thinking of changing my middle name to "Affidavit".'

'I was happy to assist.'

'All the same, treating you to a glass of tonic water seems small recompense.'

'More than I deserve.'

Particularly since he'd damned near got her killed at the Seven Research Facility. No surprise that after the bomb blasts they'd immediately been apprehended, the explosions bringing the official sector out in force. Debriefed *ad nauseam*, they'd finally been exonerated of any wrongdoing, with security agencies on both sides of the Channel relieved that Dr Uhlemann's 'Great Experiment' had been disrupted. Although those same security agencies were none too pleased that the CTC device had been destroyed, quick to recognize that it was the sort of game-changing technology that could easily alter the balance of power.

Thank God it had been destroyed. Cædmon didn't trust his own government with that kind of technology, let alone a foreign rival.

In exchange for the blanket annulment, they were forced to sign a confidentiality agreement, a draconian contract which secured their vow to never mention, write about, whisper, or mutter in their sleep *anything* to do with the Seven Research Foundation, the Vril force, or what took place in that underground bunker beneath the Grande Arche.

As fate would cruelly have it, the Grail had been obliterated in the pipe bomb explosion. For the best, Cædmon grudgingly conceded, the reality far more dangerous and deadly than the innocent prize that Parzival sought. The mass of men could not comprehend the breadth of the Grail's power, while the few who did were hell-bent on using it to advance their own twisted ambitions.

Because of that, the Grail would forever remain that most elusive of relics.

'So, what's next on your agenda?'

'Er, if you must know, I intend to further investigate the Cathar sanctuary at Mont de la Lune,' he confessed diffidently, worried that Kate might think him bonkers. Or that he was biting off more than he could reasonably chew. 'There's a mystery there that I'm keen to solve. Perhaps I can shed some light on what has always been a dark page in medieval history.' The confidentiality agreement didn't cover the time that he spent in the Languedoc. Since the 'powers that be' had failed to enquire, he had accordingly failed to volunteer the details of his trip. *How fortuitous.*

'I can't wait to read the book.' Kate moved her right hand theatrically through the air, disclosing an imaginary book title. 'You can call it *Isis Revealed*.'

'Such high expectations. I might crumble under the strain.'

'You're a stronger man than that.'

'We shall see,' he quietly replied, still navigating the shoals.

Just then a bloke blithely strolled past their table in a pair of rudely tight trousers. Emblazoned on the front of his T-shirt was a single word, boldly printed all in capital letters: HUNG.

'Talk about being boastful.'

Raising his glass of tonic water, Cædmon chortled good-naturedly. 'At least give the fellow credit for using the correct verb tense.'

'While I love Washington, there are some things that I'm not going to miss.' Kate rolled her eyes at the retreating braggart. '*That* was one of them.'

'Just letting his freak flag fly, as your commando is wont to say. Ah! Unless I'm mistaken, this is him now come late to the party.' Cædmon nodded at the yellow cab that had pulled up to the nearby kerb.

The back door opened and Finnegan McGuire got out of the taxi. Mercifully, he'd survived the explosion at the research facility, managing to take cover behind a brawny 3000-pound mainframe computer before the pipe bombs detonated. While he'd been bashed up quite a bit, suffering several cracked ribs, deep lacerations and a nasty concussion, he'd lived to tell the tale. He'd also had the foresight to record enough of the tale on to a digital voice recorder. Though it'd taken nearly a week for CID, the French National Police and INTERPOL agents to verify the evidence, he was eventually cleared of the murder charges.

'Ask the driver to wait please!' Cædmon called out. Bending over, he retrieved his piece of carry-on luggage, slipping the leather strap on to his shoulder.

'I wish you'd booked a later flight. There's still time to call and cancel,' Kate added, smiling winsomely.

'Needs must.' He wasn't about to admit that he felt like a third wheel. Overcome with an unexpected burst of nostalgia, he grabbed her by the shoulders, warmly kissing her on each cheek. 'Goodbye, Kate. You're in good hands now.'

Farewells always awkward, he left it at that. Hitching the luggage strap a bit higher on his shoulder, he walked towards the waiting taxi, meeting the commando midway.

'Come on, buddy. Why don't you stay another day?' McGuire entreated, placing a congenial hand on his shoulder. 'There's a great pizza joint –'

'Thank you, but I really must catch my flight.' Then, with a self-deprecating snort, he said, 'My Grail quest has finally come to an end.'

'If it's any consolation, Cædmon, you made a believer out of me.'

'High praise, indeed, coming from such a diehard sceptic. Good luck, Finn.' Cædmon extended his right hand in a heartfelt show of friendship. 'And pity the poor lads who have you as a drill instructor.'

'Yeah, I'm looking forward to becoming the most hated man at Fort Bragg,' the commando retorted with his trademark smirk.

'But loved by the one person who matters.' Cædmon glanced pointedly at Kate, who stood waiting by the bistro table. Two weeks ago, he had mistakenly thought them strange bedfellows. He knew better now.

Ducking his head, Cædmon slid into the back seat of the taxi. 'Ronald Reagan National Airport, please.'

As the cab pulled away from the kerb, he peered out of the window, casting his gaze towards the western horizon. The sun's fiery last light had softened into a burgundy blush, making for a breathtakingly beautiful sight. He stared, awestruck.

''Tis not too late to seek a new world.'

Smiling at the thought, he folded his arms across his chest.

Eat. Sleep. Live to fight another day. But it was the moments that took one's breath away that made it all worth while.

And the fact that it did, gave him hope.

Acknowledgements

The author would like to thank Jeanne Chitty and Peter Scheer for assisting with the book illustrations.